BET]

ALYSSIA KIRKHART

*Jennifer —
Thank you! I sincerely hope you enjoy the book that started it all. Keep reading & dream big. ♡
— Alyssia*

Jennifer -

Thank you! I truly hope you enjoy the book. Started reading it yet? Dream big. ♥

Jyl

BETROTHED

Copyright © 2012 by Alyssia Kirkhart

This book is a work of fiction. The names, characters, places, and incidents are products of the writer's imagination or have been used fictitiously and are not to be construed as real. Any resemblance to persons, living or dead, actual events, locales or organizations is entirely coincidental.

All rights reserved. No part of this book may be reproduced, scanned, or distributed in any manner whatsoever without written permission from the author except in the case of brief quotation embodied in critical articles and reviews.

For those who raised me, educated me, and believed when I didn't. This one's for you.

ONE

Dublin

"Who do you suppose that is?"

"Who?"

"This rider," Sara said, "charging up Father's driveway. One would imagine a raging herd of jungle pygmies were on his heels." She was standing at her bedroom window, trying not to swear every time she felt her ribs contract beneath her new pink silk corset.

Sara Ballivar, only daughter to the last duke in Ireland, loathed corsets. *Every proper lady wears one*, her maid had declared, *especially the ladies of the London beau monde.*

But Sara didn't care about London ladies. She was an Irish. Every other poor soul in the world only wished they had been born so lucky.

Mrs. Lana Brennan, housekeeper to His Grace the Duke of Kilkenny and, admittedly, the closest soul Sara had to a mother, pushed aside the white sheers. "I say, my lady." Her eyes formed into mere slits. "That's a soldier, that is."

Sara felt her brow pucker. "A soldier?"

"Aye. Can't very well miss that redcoat, now, can you?"

"No," Sara said dubiously. "I suppose not. But why would a British soldier be in Dublin this time of year? The festivals won't begin for another four months."

"Business with your father, I presume."

Just then, the rider came to a skidding halt. Gravel flew in all directions, landing in the grass, the flowerbeds. He dismounted quickly and hurried up the short flight of stone steps, an envelope grasped tightly in his white gloved hand.

Lana thrust a palm to her breast. "Bless my soul! Mr. Bell is sure to have an apoplexy when he sees rocks in his delphiniums! Why, it will take hours to pick them all out!" Fisting her grey woolen skirts, she made for the door. "We'll just see about this. The duke will not be pleased."

The door slammed, and Sara sighed.

The duke will not be pleased. Oh, she'd heard that one on more occasions than she cared to remember. Mostly in reference to her and the uncanny ability she possessed of falling short of the duke's expectations.

Well. She couldn't stand about like a complete ninny.

A brief stop in front of her cheval mirror and Sara picked up the hem of her new mauve muslin, heading for the stairs. Her mind raced. Had something happened? And if so, what? Since the end of the Napoleonic wars, she and her father had lived a quiet, peaceful life at Northwood, their palatial country manor in Dublin. Certainly, after all these years, he wasn't being called back to England?

Sara's heart thundered in her ears, and as her feet hit the lower landing, her gaze falling upon her father and the British officer, a sickening bubble of nervousness claimed her insides.

One of her father's trembling hands held a letter, while the other lay clamped over his mouth. Something was terribly wrong.

"Your Grace," the officer intoned. "The Duke of Tethersal has asked I return, post-haste, with your response." He fidgeted with his white gloves, while her father reread the letter.

The hand he had covering his mouth fell, lifeless, at his side.

"Father?" Sara whispered, and his blue eyes flashed up at her.

"Sara." He outstretched an open hand, which she took without hesitation.

He bid the officer wait in the foyer, and proceeded to pull her past the watchful stares of guards and servants--the same people who had been her family since forever--and into his study.

"Father, what's happened?"

"Sara, sit down."

Obediently, she chose the smaller of the two ornate chairs positioned in front of her father's desk.

He paced for an eternity, the letter clutched tightly in his hand. With every step he took, her eyes followed, and the uneasiness in the pit of her stomach grew stronger and stronger.

"You are frightening me, Father," she said, because eventually he had to stop. Either that or wear a hole in the already-threadbare Aubusson rug beneath their feet.

The pacing ceased. "Forgive me, Sara." He dragged a hand through his hair.

"For what?"

He took in a shuddering breath. "The Duke of Tethersal is ill."

Sara frowned. Her father and the Duke of Tethersal--Phillip, she dimly remembered--had a close friendship. But years of peace had all but severed the amiable bridge between them. Now they only spoke through letters, and even those had dwindled to one every several months or so.

"I am sorry, Father," she murmured, meaning it. "But why should His Grace's ailments require my forgiveness?"

Another lengthy sigh. "Do you remember when you were young, I told you of a contract the duke and I arranged? Directly after the war, it was."

"Aye, I do." She didn't want to remember. But how could she let something as consequential as being betrothed to fully escape her memory? She'd suppressed the truth for so long it no longer seemed real.

"He has asked that I honor our arrangement, and send you directly to London. Apparently, he doesn't believe he'll survive to …" His throat worked with emotion.

Sara couldn't find the will to console him. No matter how much the news of Tethersal's illness had stricken him to utter speechlessness.

She was betrothed.

Betrothed. The word sounded medieval and grim in a world where arranged marriages had been long since forgotten. The only person she knew who had been fixed with an arranged marriage had thrown herself from a bridge last winter. Ten days passed before her frozen body was found. And her estranged husband, who happened to be an English viscount, remarried within a fortnight, heedless to proper mourning customs.

Now, Sara stood to share the same fate.

Frozen. Forgotten. Unhappy. Unloved.

She did the only thing she could think to do. Ignoring her father's tears, she dashed for the stables, bridled her horse, and galloped bareback to the Dublin shoreline.

Minutes passed.

Hours.

Centuries.

Yet, she remained. Debating on whether to take her chances and keep running. To where, she hadn't the slightest inclination. The fishermen were still out at sea, but not one of them would willingly gamble the life of Kilkenny's daughter to aid in her escape. No matter how much she paid them.

Sara wrapped her arms around her waist, hugged herself against the icy breeze wafting in from the Irish Sea.

She loved Ireland. Neither could she imagine a place more exciting nor a finer land on which to settle. From one rolling hill and over to the next, from Dublin shore to the mighty cliffs of Moher, the land was beautiful and green, rich and prosperous.

How could she possibly be expected to leave all this behind? And without knowing where she was going? What to expect once she got there?

"M'lady?"

Sara closed her eyes.

"Are you well?"

Never a moment's peace.

"M'lady?"

"Yes, Lana," Sara said wearily. "And I know-"

"Saints preserve us, child, we've been looking all over for you, we have!" Lana, whose naturally round hazel eyes had rounded even further as she stood there panting with fright, slapped a hand to her heaving breast. "You've put the entire household in a fright! And your father in such distress as he is. What were you thinking?"

"I wasn't."

"Clearly! Your father is in pieces." She shook a slim finger at Sara. "And don't think for one minute you won't apologize for your actions, young lady. His Grace has suffered and sacrificed on your account for far too long."

"Yes, yes. I know." Irritated, Sara brushed past Lana to untie her mare. "And I'll speak to my father." In one swift jump, she was straddling her horse's back, and Lana, old-fashioned woman she was, glared up at her in blatant disapproval.

"Proper ladies ride side saddle," she said, one hand resting on the generous curve of her hip. The other shook a rather commanding finger. "I know you are well learned in horseback techniques, m'lady – God bless His Grace's soul – but your father still raised you to be a lady."

Sara smiled. Nodded curtly. "Side saddles hurt my arse."

Lana sputtered. "Such language! You'll be quick to mind your manners once you're in London," she said, adding as Sara galloped away, "The wife of the heir of Tethersal will not be so eagerly received if obscenities are sprouting from her mouth!"

*** *** ***

For the next two days, Sara managed to steer clear of her father. She was too upset for conversation; more than ever after she'd watched Lana and two other servants pack nearly all her belongings.

"You shall require party dresses as well," said Lana.

Sara glared at her, incredulous. "Whatever for? This is hardly an occasion for celebration."

"They are in the middle of the season in England, my dear." Lana tilted her head a fraction as she folded each of Sara's stockings into perfect little squares. "In fact, I hear the Duke of Tethersal hosts the finest parties of all. You'll be wanting to look your best when presented as Lord Carrington's intended."

Sara complied with a sigh and chose several of her best dresses, each of which had a matching set of slippers, gloves and even undergarments.

They weren't meant to be worn at English balls. She'd had them made for parties in her own country, where she and her friends, people she had known her whole life, laughed, shared in the latest gossip, and spent hours dancing in the arms of some of Ireland's most handsome young men. She knew no one in England. Didn't want to.

And she definitely did not want an engagement to a complete stranger.

What would he expect? As his betrothed, would he anticipate certain ... liberties? She'd been kissed before. Twice. And although neither of those instances could be considered exactly passionate, they belonged to her all the same.

One had even earned her a marriage proposal, which her father had adamantly refused, forbidding her to engage in any further late night strolls with would-be suitors.

"You are promised to another, Sara," he'd explained after turning down the offer from Sir Dunmore's eldest son.

Patrick Cavanaugh--or *Cav*, as most called him--had left the manor that day red-faced in his embarrassment, surely never to speak to her again for the humiliation of being denied her hand.

"At least until you are well past eighteen," her father had gone on. "There will be no more false illusions on your part to these lads who can't help but pour out all their attentions on you, Sara. You're the most beautiful girl in Ireland. At least do right by allowing them to find another. Someone who is not already spoken for."

There had been no point in arguing.

Even now, she knew there was no use in starting a quarrel. The duke had little tolerance for the desperate pleadings of a headstrong young woman. Even those of his own daughter.

Her father's word, calm and collected though he spoke it, was always final.

Lana sent for several footmen to carry Sara's belongings downstairs and to the awaiting coach, while Sara took one last look at the room she'd occupied since she was but a small child.

Everything dear to her had been packed. The small cameo frame which held her mother's photograph, the tattered doll that had been her favorite, and the musical ballerina trinket box containing her mother's jewelry.

All that remained of her previous life was a four-poster bed, matched draperies, and the paintings of the Irish countryside she'd cherished since childhood.

And she'd never see it again.

"Come, Sara," Lana urged. "Your father awaits belowstairs." She hesitated. "He's sending me with you."

Sara snorted. "Doubtless to ensure I don't run away." She shouldered past Lana for the stairs.

But the maid caught her by the arm. "My lady," she murmured as Sara whirled around.

Worry, and something which looked a bit like disappointment, tautened Lana's features. "Please do not make this any harder on your father than it already is. No, listen to me, I beseech you." She drew a languid breath. "His Grace doesn't wish to send you away any more than you want to go, my lady, but this is irreversible. And if there is one thing His Grace stands by more than anything, it is his word. He will not dishonor the Duke of Tethersal by breaching a contract."

"Even if it means my unhappiness." Sara jerked her arm free.

The duke, her father, was chatting with the driver when Sara approached. He regarded her evenly for a moment, took inventory of her appearance, watched in mild amusement as she threaded her fingers into her new calfskin gloves.

She arched an eyebrow.

He mirrored it, and, evidently satisfied, continued with his conversation.

Sara heaved a sigh and turned away, cursing herself for not fleeing two days ago when she had the chance. She could've surely made it to Galway by now, begged for Dunmore's protection, and persuaded Cav to elope with her. Her father would have had no choice then but to decline Tethersal's request. Even if it did cost him his pride.

Contract or no contract, he wouldn't dare take her away from her husband, regardless that he'd already denied the man her hand.

He was handsome, Patrick Cavanaugh was. With his dark-gold hair, fine, slightly pointed features and eyes so green they appeared as shards of emerald glass, he stood the epitome of what any young woman would want in a husband.

Sara was no different from the masses. She knew a marriage to Cav would be agreeable. Perhaps more than agreeable. Maybe she could've even fallen in love with him.

Now this.

Now she was being handed over to a stranger. A stranger who was doubtless arrogant, self-righteous, and prude. No one in their right mind could expect any less of a man bred into English aristocracy. Heartless, haughty prigs, all of them. Overfed, overzealous, and long overdue of a good chastising from a priest, too.

Preferably an Irish one.

This Englishman would be no different.

He probably wasn't even handsome.

"Your thoughts are distant, *a thaisce*," her father said, breaking through her reverie.

"My thoughts are always distant," she replied. Her lips began to quiver, eyes welled with tears. Without thought, she flung herself into her father's arms. "Oh, Papa. Please don't make me go. Please."

"Sara," he whispered, stroking her hair. "Do not fight me. You won't win. Not this time."

"I don't even know him." Her tears threatened to ruin her father's fine velvet coat, but she didn't care. "How can you cast me away so easily? And to strangers?"

"Hardly strangers. True, you've never met them, but very dear to me is the Tethersal family. And I'd trust the duke with my own life, as I trust him with yours. He's raised an honorable son, one worthy of you. I wouldn't honor the agreement otherwise."

"But why send me so quickly? Certainly we have plenty of time?"

"Out of love for you." He pulled back, looked at her directly. The pad of his thumb brushed across her cheek. "Tethersal and I are giving you and Justin, Lord Carrington, the opportunity to become better acquainted before the agreement is fully honored."

He molded both his hands to her face. "But mark my words," he said, and the graveness in his tone was so acute she trembled. "I leave it in your hands to make the best of the situation. Because in the end, you will marry Lord Carrington."

She wanted to scream. She wanted to beg. She wanted to turn and run, fast as she could. Only none of those options would change or remedy the situation.

"Now, *a thaisce*, get into the coach," he said, and Sara's lips tightened.

She would not scream. She would not beg. Run? No.

"A ship waits at Dublin shore to ferry us to Liverpool."

Albeit reluctant, Sara nodded, and allowed her father to lead her to the coach. "How far to England?" she asked as Lana reached out a hand to aid her.

"Not far. Less than a day." Climbing inside, the duke took the seat next to Lana, murmuring, "Mrs. Brennan," when she immediately shifted to make room for him. "As always, I'm obliged to your thoughtfulness."

Lana blushed furiously. "Of course, Your Grace."

Grinning, he settled back against the crushed velvet squabs, folded his hands over his stomach, and closed his eyes.

Perfectly relaxed, as always, Sara thought, wishing she had the strength to do the same.

She turned her head and gazed pensively out of the small window. Farewells had gone unsaid, as farewells often do. But if she'd had the chance, she would have done. She would've kissed the dressmaker, thanked the milliner, and tossed a shilling to the baker for all the sweetmeats he'd given her over the years, free of charge. Hugged all the servants and, of course, the footmen, stable hands and gardeners.

She would've given Patrick Cavanaugh a right proper goodbye, too; kissed him as he'd never been kissed before, though she hadn't a clue how one goes about so promiscuous a thing. Molly O'Shannon said it had something to do with touching tongues and exchanging saliva and bumping noses or some such, the details escaped her. But certainly she and Cav would've discovered an easier method, as he was quite intelligent and always thinking up new ways to improve upon this and that.

But she hadn't been allowed that chance.

And so, as the carriage picked up speed, and her family's estate passed in a rapid blur, Sara said her goodbyes by way of the old tradition. She sang them. And soon her father joined in, though his eyes were still closed, and Lana, too, though she wasn't very good at it. But together they sang of the land, of Ireland. Of tall towers, reels danced under summer sunsets, and the haunting sound of the western shore. And to Sara's mind that was good enough.

It had to be.

TWO

Liverpool

"It is half past eight."

Sebastian, Marquess Beaufort, cracked a smile, tucked away his pocket watch. Steadied his anxious stallion. "She's right on time." His blond brows drew taut. "You seem nervous, Justin. Surely you're not worried about a young chit from Dublin?"

Justin, Marquess Carrington, chuckled at the easy jeer, the tension in his limbs impairing his will to defend his less-than-perfect reputation. He smoothed a gloved thumb over the grip of his reins, flicked a piece of dried mud from the supple leather.

It was true enough. He shouldn't be worried. This ... *girl*, his betrothed, would be no different than the dozens upon dozens of other women he'd encountered over the past couple of seasons back home. By all accounts, she would be worse. One, she was far too young. *Eighteen*, his father had told him. Two, she was an Irish. Together, those faults should have been enough to put a scowl on his face and throw worry to the wind.

But he *was* worried. Why? Had to be the sheer mysteriousness of a marriage to someone he'd never even met. Well, at least he couldn't recall ever having met her. Then again, he'd had plenty of first encounters with young women, whether in passing or at a ball or soiree. Hell, he'd even met a couple at Sunday meeting. Though he was certain the debauchery following services went far beyond being considered holy.

She'll be no different, he'd told himself over and over. Like every other woman: easily seduced, easily controlled. A marriage of convenience. For status. For title.

For honoring a ridiculous contract made between Father and a man he doesn't even speak to anymore, over a few glasses of God-only-knows-what in the wake of England's victory over France.

Life won't be any different than it is now.

"She's probably not even pretty," Sebastian mused aloud when Justin didn't answer. "Irish women usually aren't, you know. At least, nothing worthy of poetry."

Justin looked ahead at the docking ship and gave his horse's neck a good pat. "I've yet to find any woman worthy of such," he said, and Sebastian laughed. "But you are undoubtedly right about this one, my friend. She's probably too thin."

"Or too fat." Sebastian's frosty blue eyes flickered in the moonlight. "With crooked teeth and a witch's nose."

"Or a witch's mole."

"Ha!" Sebastian clapped a hand over his taut stomach, covered by layers of linen and broadcloth. "You may have lost your nerve this evening, old chap, but you certainly haven't lost your sense of humor."

With a slight tilt of his head, Justin regarded his friend from under the brim of his slouch hat. "I have not lost my nerve," he stated firmly, and the smile slowly fell from Sebastian's face. "This entire situation reeks awkward, as I'm certain you can understand. So, if my mannerisms fall short of my usual self, I'll kindly ask they be overlooked."

Sebastian nodded, curtly.

"Now, being she is most likely a fat witch with a crooked set of teeth and a hooked nose," Justin continued, and Sebastian's mouth curled back into a smile, "it shall be all the easier to politely set her aside."

"And keep your mistress."

Justin grinned, the fleeting thought of Milly passing through his mind, and his body, like a wave of intrinsic heat.

As soon as they returned to London, and his betrothed was promptly deposited at his family's Mayfair estate, he would take his leave for a few days, perhaps even a week or two, and steal to the old bachelor house or, perhaps, the country estate in Dover.

After a healthy stint of animalistic sex with Millicent St. Clair, a wealthy widow ten years his senior, perhaps he'd be ready to face the bitterness of having to marry the damned Irish halfwit his father had bound him to when he was but twelve years old--too young to regard the opposite sex as anything but repulsive.

But he couldn't spare another thought on that now. There would be time aplenty in which he could bury himself between Milly's thighs, but not tonight. Tonight was about honoring his father's wishes.

He loved the old man. Sometimes to a fault.

"My lord." A footman appeared at the shoulder of Justin's mount. "They've arrived."

Breathing deeply through his nostrils, Justin upturned his gaze to the night sky and made an attempt, once again, to align his thoughts. The moon was full, accompanied by a canopy of brilliant stars in a clear night sky, and the wafting breeze from the sea stirred the air around him. If he didn't know better, for pleasing aromas of any kind were uncommon this close to the shoreline, he would have sworn he'd caught the faintest scent of flora.

Impossible, of course. Perhaps he was merely eager to get home. His mother did have the most exquisitely aromatic gardens.

"Ready the coach," Sebastian told the footman, and the man bowed and stepped away, snapping for the help of the coachman. "Justin, are you well? You look a trifle pale."

"I'm fine." Justin glanced down at his horse's mane, so black it appeared blue in the moonlight. "Dismount and let us greet our guests, shall we?"

Sebastian nodded, and the two of them masterfully swept in unison to the ground.

"Remember," Sebastian said quietly, as he and Justin walked side by side toward the docks, "she'll not be anything you haven't handled before." He chuckled before adding, "Good God, Justin. She might be easier, if you understand my meaning. I'd wager the men she's accustomed to in Ireland, if she's even been offered by any, cannot possibly hold a candle. You have a hard enough time keeping beautiful women at bay."

"Your flattery is riveting, Sebastian," Justin said, glancing at his friend askew. "That is, however, untrue and highly unlikely. She probably doesn't want this marriage any more than I do."

He looked forward again, only this time four distinct figures-- two men, two women--came into view. His footmen rushed ahead, greeting them with swooping bows, which were countered with curt nods and well-practiced curtsies.

He felt Sebastian's fingers tugging at his coat sleeve. "Neither is fat."

"I have eyes," Justin ground out slowly, quietly.

He narrowed his gaze, discovering one of the men, the one giving instructions to the dockhands, was unmistakably a servant.

While the other, dressed in a coat of brocade superfine and buff breeches, was likely Kilkenny himself.

The taller, curvier of the two women fell behind, and wagged her finger at a dockhand who had dropped a piece of luggage. The smaller, daintier one linked her hand inside the duke's arm and leaned into him, whispered something in his inclined ear.

The duke smiled and patted her gloved hand.

This must be her.

He couldn't see her face; she wore a wide brimmed bonnet and a plain muslin gown, both of which appeared black in the night. Though, as he looked closer, the moonlight hinted they could have been a dark shade of blue.

As she approached, she kept her face averted. Justin repressed a grin. Indeed, the bonnet and gown were blue. *Union Jack blue*, if he had to make a comparison. A mighty appealing contrast to the expanse of pale skin glowing like raw innocence in the moonlight.

Intrigued, Justin allowed his male eyes a downward trail, an indulgence in the hint of soft cleavage peaking from a bed of lace fringe. It was then he noticed the subtle shimmer of black curls falling over one creamy shoulder.

Suddenly, Milly's locks of goldenrod seemed dull and lifeless.

"My, my, Lord Carrington." Kilkenny smiled, the small lines at his eyes creasing. "It's been a long time."

Justin removed his hat, mirrored the duke's bow. "Your Grace," he murmured. "I assure you, the honor is all mine. My father speaks of you often."

"Your father is a good man." Kilkenny's brow sketched a frown. "How is he?"

"Better, actually," said Justin. He attempted to steal another glance at the young lady attached to the duke's arm, but to no avail. She remained statuesque, her face down-turned just enough he still could not see her fully. Was she embarrassed to show herself?

Ridiculous. That any woman would grow suddenly shy to the point of not wanting to show her face in his presence? Almost every woman he'd encountered, whether dreadfully ugly or even moderately agreeable, had been eager to prove herself to him, to win his attentions.

He'd never had this effect on a woman before now.

Strange, that.

"That is indeed good news," Kilkenny returned in kind. His gaze shifted to Sebastian. "I do not recall having ever met your friend."

Perturbed by the lady's shyness, Justin's speech remained taut. "Forgive me, Your Grace, may I present Sebastian Rochford, Marquess of Beaufort, and a close friend of mine?" He paused as Sebastian bowed, with a touch of over-exertion as was merely his nature, and then added, "He agreed to accompany me in escorting Lady Ballivar to London."

At this, the lady's head lifted, and Justin, who prided himself in his ability to maintain perfect reserved composure in even the gravest of situations, felt his breath catch hard in his throat.

In an instant, awareness spread through his body like a thief in the night. His limbs stiffened, froze. Their gazes tangled. A pair of rich brown eyes, the color of expensive whisky, assessed him carefully. As though he was on display, not her.

His hands started shaking.

She was lovely. Divine. More than divine. "Beautiful," he murmured aloud.

The duke cleared his throat. "My daughter, Lady Sara Ballivar."

The lady, Sara, curtsied, her gaze leaving Justin's for but a fleeting moment before returning again.

Letting out a shaky breath, Justin managed a short nod. "My lady." The greeting exited a trifle huskier than he'd anticipated. He barely noticed Sebastian had turned away, his broad shoulders shaking with laughter.

Those whisky eyes shifted, and the tiny space between her perfect winged brows knitted as she regarded Sebastian's behavior.

"I trust your journey was satisfactory," Justin continued in a quick attempt to regain her attention. Her eyes were mesmerizing, her long dark lashes framing their demureness like a veil he itched to unsheathe.

"Yes, my lord."

Her accent was beautiful. The kind of ancient, refined Brogue so pitifully rare among Irishmen these days.

"I'm pleased to hear it," he said, unable to refrain from smiling as she bit her lower lip. My, but she did have the most delicious looking mouth. To the duke, he said, "I've taken the liberty of securing the inn for tonight, Your Grace."

"Splendid." Kilkenny murmured something to his daughter, and she nodded compliantly, retrieving her hand from the crook of his arm and taking a step forward.

She eyed Justin warily. "Help me to the coach, my lord?"

She proffered her hand, and Justin took it, raised it to his lips in a gesture that, while uniform in expected formalities, sent a scorching wave of pure lust through his loins.

She smelled of lavender, sweet yet refined.

He couldn't deny the thought of what it would be like, exploring her perfumed body with his hands, his mouth. He wanted to kiss the hills of her cheeks, flushed the most innocent shade of pink. Kiss the mounds of supple cleavage straining against her gown with every breath she took. Kiss those lush, rosebud lips until they cried his name.

And he'd only touched her hand. Her *gloved* hand.

Sweet Mary and Joseph. This was not going at all as he'd expected. She was not what he'd expected.

Struggling to maintain what little poise he had left, Justin stiffened his back, tucked her hand into the crook of his arm, and led her to the awaiting black lacquered coach.

Sebastian, who still had a grin of amusement playing at the corners of his mouth, swung an open-palmed hand in a grand gesture as the footman opened the door and unfolded the steps.

Justin nearly cursed aloud. He'd hear it later, the look of shock on his face upon discovering the chit was far from hideous. Sebastian never missed the chance for a good laugh, especially at Justin's expense.

Sara climbed into the coach, her hand sliding from Justin's as she settled onto the plush velvet seat. Justin braced a hand on either side of the door, leaned in, and flashed his most charming smile.

She regarded him through widened eyes.

"There is a foot warmer just there." He pointed to a pottery container on the floor. Anticipating cooler weather, he'd had it filled with boiling water before reaching the coastline. "And a blanket, if you should get cold. It's not far to the inn from here."

"Thank you." Whispered so softly that, had his eyes not been focused on her mouth, he mightn't have heard.

"Thank you," he repeated absently. "That is, you're most welcome. Shall I ride with you?"

She shook her head. A lock of dark curls fell over her shoulder, brushed the exposed skin below her neck.

"That won't be necessary, my lord." Folding her hands in her lap, she turned her gaze straight ahead and stared blindly into the green velvet upholstery across the way.

So, she was choosing to ignore him. Not that he could blame her. If the circumstances were awkward for him, he could only imagine how difficult they were for her. She was young and, by the look of her, quite virginal. If asked, he'd almost stake his life she hadn't even been kissed, much less experienced any sort of intimacy with a man.

Two matters he could remedy easily enough.

Justin returned to the duke and suggested he ride with his daughter in the warmth of the coach. That he, along with Lord Beaufort, would follow on horseback.

The duke wasn't pleased. In fact, he appeared to be quite vexed, snapping his fingers at his footman and the other woman--Sara's maid perhaps?--to follow him.

Both shot him a strange look, as if he weren't always so brash, but willfully obeyed, the maid climbing into the coach and the footman seating himself beside the driver.

Raised voices came from inside as the vehicle lurched forward, its candlelit lanterns flickering wildly in the wind.

Justin heaved a sigh, swept up into his saddle, and urged his horse forward.

"Bloody hell," said Sebastian, riding alongside Justin. "She's beautiful. No, by all accounts, she's ..."

"Striking," Justin murmured without thinking.

To his surprise, Sebastian did not utter another word. He'd expected to hear the obvious; that the look on his face had been priceless, as he was sure it had been.

He'd never seen anything like her. She was small in stature, yet the boldness in her eyes hinted she had more courage in that petite body than Hercules. Not to mention the Irish were notorious for their brazen nature, though he'd never seen one quite so lovely.

And God help him, was she lovely.

He'd never been one for poetry, had hated studying the stuff more than listening to his mother's attempts at playing the pianoforte. But at that moment, riding closely behind the coach that carried his bride-to-be, he thought about every bloody love poem he'd heard. Wordsworth. Byron. Bloody Shelley.

"Well, I will say one thing." Sebastian paused. "Wait. No, two things. You are officially the luckiest man I know, and ..." His wintry eyes sparkled with mirth. "She's all yours."

A curious smile grew upon Justin's lips as he contemplated Sebastian's statement. "Yes," he said as they neared the inn, a small establishment owned by one of the oldest families in Liverpool. "Yes, she is."

THREE

"Of all the ... self-righteous ..."

Sara stopped pacing, closed her eyes.

Taking a deep breath, she stomped a boot heel on the wooden floor, curled her hands into fists, and through gritted teeth screeched, "*Díomasach!*"

Lana gasped.

Sara paid no heed. Screaming the old language always took a little more off the edge than using plain English. Be that as it may, she was beginning to believe even Gaelic could not possibly, nor accurately, describe this man.

Her betrothed.

God, but that word made her cringe.

Ever shrewd, Lana made a little *tut* sound, and continued spreading Sara's night garments on the bed. "Arrogant, my lady? He did not speak but a few sentences to you, none of which could be considered arrogant. On the contrary, I thought his attentiveness was quite charming."

"Charming?" Sara removed her wide-brimmed hat. Tossed it on the bed, along with her shawl. She pulled at the fingers of her gloves, tugging jerkily at each inch of precious lace until, losing all fortitude, she used her teeth.

"Well. He wasn't disagreeable," Lana offered, cringing as she observed Sara's patience, or lack thereof, at its worst. She reached out a hand, withdrew it. Reached again. "Oh, my lady, please let me help you with those. They'll--"

Sara's eyes rounded as the ring finger of her right glove ripped between her teeth.

"Tear." Lana's shoulders slumped, as Sara handed over the damaged glove. She carefully thumbed over the dainty lace finger. "I think I can repair it."

"Don't bother, Lana." Sara squared her shoulders. "I am not staying."

"But we've come all this way, my lady, you cannot choose now to flee. The ship will not agree to ferry you back to Dublin. Not when they've already been instructed by His Grace that if anyone should see you attempting to run, they are to promptly retrieve and return."

Sara drew a sharp breath. "He did not!"

"Aye. He did."

Defeated, Sara lowered herself to the chair at the small vanity in her room at the inn. She sat up straight. She would not cry. She *wouldn't*.

But it was useless.

Her lashes lowered, and droplets of tears spilled onto anger-flushed cheeks.

And then she asked herself the same question she'd pondered while still in Dublin, when she was still in the security of her homeland.

How could her father do this to her?

"You might as well make the best of things, child," said Lana, and Sara sank her face into her hands. "Because this is not a game. You are betrothed, have been nearly all your life. And His Grace will not debase himself, Tethersal, and, more importantly, the Crown, by dishonoring an agreement."

She paused, her faint laugh filling the fire-warmed room. "If you don't mind my saying so, Lord Carrington is quite handsome."

Sara peeled her hands from her face, regarding Lana through tear-soaked lashes. "I do mind you saying so." Standing, she brushed the smooth fabric of her dark blue gown. "And that is well beyond the point of this ludicrousness."

Lana's eyes widened hopefully. "Ah, you do find him handsome?"

"I didn't say …" Sara impatiently swallowed her response, thinking it better to end the conversation. Lifting her chin, she turned and made for the inviting warmth of the stone fireplace.

Lana did not further pursue the subject, but continued setting out the items Sara would need for the night and the next morning.

Of course she found him handsome. What woman wouldn't? He was tall but not too tall; she imagined her eyes would align exactly at the jut of his strong chin.

If she were ever that close to him.

He was thick, his shoulders broad beneath the fabric of his tweed riding coat. Well-defined thighs under fashionable buff breeches. His skin held a bronzed hue, and Sara fleetingly wondered why the son of a duke should be so tanned. Most noblemen were dreadfully pale. Some even powdered their skin, though why any man would desire to appear so feminine was beyond Sara's comprehension.

But Lord Carrington was anything but feminine.

On the contrary, he was perhaps the most masculine creature she'd ever encountered. Everything about him was inarguably male, from his build to his mannerism. And that roguish, mischievous smile that belonged more on the face of a renowned rake than an heir to a ducal seat. She could still see him smiling at her from the doorway of the carriage, his teeth gleaming white in his sun-kissed face.

And his lips. Those immodestly full lips …

Sara started as a knock came to the door, followed by the easy drawl of a rich male baritone. "Lady Ballivar? May I have a word?"

Her gaze snapped to Lana, and she shook her head hastily, even as Lana scurried across the room for the door, the skirts of her gray dress rustling like crepe paper.

The door opened, and there, leaning lazily against the frame, stood Lord Carrington. He'd removed the hat which reminded her of the leather oilskin hats the horsemen wore in South Ireland, revealing a head of mussed, shiny dark hair, a lock of which fell carelessly over his forehead. His shirt lay undone at the collar.

Sara swallowed as her eyes involuntarily slid from his face to the tanned, smooth skin of his neck.

All at once, the sight of him caused an unfamiliar weakness to gather in her knees, a pleasurable shiver in her innermost parts. As if she'd just indulged in too much wine and dancing. Strange, yet stimulating.

Most unwelcome given the present situation.

Lana curtsied respectfully. "My lord."

"Good evening." He flashed an easy grin. "Forgive me. I didn't catch your name earlier. Miss …?"

"Mrs. Brennan."

"Intrigued. I trust you'll be accompanying Lady Ballivar to London?" His voice was like a web of fine silk, both alluring and captivating. In spite of his brawny appearance, there was no denying this man had come from a long line of aristocrats.

"Yes, my lord." Lana turned a cheek-popping smile on Sara, her eyes rounded with so much gaiety Sara felt certain she'd let out a squeal at any moment.

Irritated, Sara forced herself to look his lordship square in the face. "I was just about to prepare for bed, sir."

One of his dark brows lifted inquiringly. Heat infused her cheeks as he pressed his lips together, the hint of a devilish smirk tugging at one corner.

"So," she continued, "whatever brought you to my door tonight, I'll kindly ask that you please make it quick."

Lord Carrington pushed away from the mottled door frame and strode inside. The air in the room swelled and stirred. Sara felt the nerves in her body ignite, a trickle of intimate tingles developing in places she couldn't understand.

"I came to ask if I could interest you in some supper." His eyes were dark brown, almost black, veiled by a set of long--*too long to be wasted on a man*--dark lashes. "And perhaps a bath?"

For reasons she could not explain, the very sound of the word *bath* coming from him made her blush. As if the innocent word had suddenly accumulated some sort of wild intimacy.

"I ... that would be nice, my lord," she managed. "However, I should like to dine in my room. Alone, if it is all the same to you."

The shadow of a frown flashed across his lips, and for a second she felt ashamed for not agreeing to have a meal with him. No matter. She couldn't take it back now, and how dare he make her feel ashamed? Wasn't as if she owed him anything.

"As you wish." Sweeping a short bow, he turned for the door.

Sara closed her eyes, breathed an inward sigh of relief for having successfully evaded his company. Bad enough she'd be engaged in an entire journey with him upon the dawning of the next day, indisputably having to rely on him for more than just meals and baths. She was entitled to her privacy for at least one night.

He paused at the opening of the door and turned his head slightly. "I'll have your supper sent up in a few minutes, as well as some hot water for your bath. Good evening."

"Good--" Sara began, but he left quickly, the thunder in his stride bouncing off walls as he retreated down the hall.

"I think," Lana said, easing the door shut, "that he might have wanted you to dine with him, my lady."

"Then he should have said so." Sara returned to the warmth of the fire. "I'm not interested in playing mind games with him, or anyone else for that matter. Especially not him. Furthermore, I don't like the way he looks at me. It's as if … as if …"

"He finds you attractive, perhaps?"

Sara felt the heat in her cheeks rising again. "I don't know what it is." No man had ever stirred such odd feelings inside her. They were as foreign as her surroundings. Pleasant, yet strange. "It just makes me uncomfortable. That's all."

"Mmm," came Lana's vague response. "I see."

*** *** ***

Justin slowed his steps as he reached one of the few parlors hailed at the inn. From inside, he could make out the familiar sound of Sebastian's voice as well as the deep, heavy Brogue belonging to the Duke of Kilkenny. Both broke into laughter. Knowing Sebastian, it was most likely over a glass of fine whisky, and the conversation had gone from steam engines to gambling to whores in less than ten minutes.

For a moment, Justin waited outside the cracked door, attempting with all he had to collect his wits.

He could still see her, smell her. That wonderful, mild scent of lavender which made him feel as though he'd entered a meadow in spring. Bereft of her hat, he'd had the luxury of seeing her properly. Lovely eyes, cheeks, and lips. Hair so fine and so dark it appeared wet, the silken strands were that shiny. Her body was small, yet softly curved. As though the sculptor had seen fit to maintain an essence of innocence without denying the assets of a woman.

Assets which fully peaked a man's desires.

And heaven help him, his were definitely peaked. But he couldn't very well carry out the rest of the evening like this. Pining over beauty like some reckless schoolboy with no couth or sense. For pity's sake, hadn't he any pride?

Praying male conversation would somehow put him to rights, Justin stepped inside the parlor. "Your Grace. Lord Beaufort." He left the door three quarters of the way closed, as he had found it. Habit of living with a meticulous duchess.

"Ahh, Justin." Sebastian raised his half-empty glass. "We were just discussing the railway industry up north. Booming, it is. Father has been meeting with Pease and Stephenson for a few months now. There's no stopping the old man from slapping the Worcester name on those steam engines, you know."

"Yes, how well I do." Justin sank into the leather armchair across from the duke.

"Whisky, Lord Carrington?" The duke started to pour another glass of the amber liquor.

Justin waived a dismissive hand. "No, thank you. I don't drink."

The duke looked surprised.

Sebastian chuckled. "Never has, Your Grace," he said, and drank a generous swill from his own snifter. "Can't hardly convince him to have a glass of wine with dinner either. What was it you said, Justin? It's too inebriating?" He leaned back in his chair.

Justin cut his eyes in Sebastian's direction. "Something like that," he muttered, and Sebastian lifted his glass in salute. He turned to the duke. "I don't welcome anything that clouds my ability to reason."

The duke's face was kind, and surprisingly young, warmed by one of those smiles some men wore as a seal. "Admirable, Lord-- may I call you Justin? Wonderful. But I have to wonder then, and by all means, forgive me for being so forward, if you've ever been in love." His grin widened. "Nothing could possibly be more inebriating than dousing the entirety of one's being upon the women he loves."

The observation *was* forward, to say the least. "Love is something for which I haven't had much time, Your Grace," Justin answered politely. "My involvement in other matters has left but only a small portion of my freedom, most of which consists of when I sleep at night. I've also had to handle my father's duties more frequently as of late."

The duke frowned. "Yes. Please, tell me about your father's condition. The letter I received from your mother, while most welcome, was rather vague in elaborating on his illness."

Justin raked a hand through his hair and leaned forward, forearms on his knees. "It's some form of wasting disease. At least, that is what all the physicians tell us. Apparently he's been living with it for years, but only recently has it become noticeable."

The crease in the duke's brow deepened. "Noticeable?"

"Night sweats, fever, coughing, blood. At first the doctors thought it was consumption, but he's lived with it for so long that ... well, we're all aware of how consumption works."

The duke nodded. "He is bed ridden, I presume?"

"At times, yes. Then again, he has his good days. Where he can rise and sit down to eat with the family. He likes sitting outside, mostly. In the sun."

"And your mother? Your sister? How are they?"

"Mother is in constant distress. Rarely leaves Father's side. Takes nearly all her meals with him. Refuses to leave him alone for more than a few minutes at a time."

His mother had become so fragile in the past few months, waiting on his father hand and foot, only allowing a small amount of assistance from the hired help. That the duchess loved his father so unconditionally, with her whole heart, had always been an enigma to Justin. His father was a kind man, but years of being in the king's service and the hierarchy of England had taken its toll on the family. Justin, his sister, and the duchess had been forced early on to face the reality that having a normal life was a luxury even they could not afford.

"My sister, Lady Anna," he continued, as Sebastian stood to refill his glass, "is ... well ... she's Anna. There's no possible way to describe her, really. She's not like any lady in the peerage, always the talk of the *ton*, and I have genuine reason to believe that's exactly how she likes it."

This elicited a hearty chuckle from the duke. "She was always a bit on the capricious side," he agreed. "Like your mother. How old is she now? Nineteen?"

"Twenty. Though I assure you, her mannerisms are nothing short of a woman with much broader experience. She's always ahead of fashion, sometimes scandalously so, much to my mother's protests."

He glanced at Sebastian, who shifted in his seat, resting the ankle of one leg on the knee of the other. Restless, that one. Couldn't sit still to save his life.

"All in the good name of being the only daughter of the most influential peer in England, she insists," Justin finished.

"Naturally," the duke commented. "I'm afraid young women are drawn to fashion the way moths are to a flame. They cannot help it." He paused reflectively and rubbed his chin. "Of course," he continued, and swallowed the last bit of his cognac, "that is what I keep telling myself."

"Your daughter enjoys fashion, does she?" said Sebastian. "She and Lady Anna should get on well."

"My daughter enjoys fashion as much as the next woman her age, Lord Beaufort, but I assure you, like Lady Anna, she is quite unpredictable. I've never seen a girl so adamant in refusing to ride side saddle or insisting, and frequently proving, she can play a game of Rounders better than any of my male servants."

Justin smiled. "A sportsman, eh?" He was surprised, yet altogether unsurprised. Amusing, it was, that he had been right in his earlier assumption. She was a spitfire, his intended.

"Sportsman, statesman. She's even been known to sing a note or two. And she's a fine dancer, I must say. Much better than I ever was. And she's fluent in the old language." A husky chuckle rumbled in his chest. "Don't ever make her angry. You'll never get her to stop cursing you in Gaelic."

His eyes shifted, the humor vanishing as he stared unseeingly past Justin's shoulder. "Just like her mother."

Justin felt his lips quirk. The duke's expression softened, his eyes clouding as if he'd slipped into an open-eyed slumber. He missed his wife; that much was obvious.

"Well, then," Justin murmured, "I shall look forward to ..." His breath caught, lodged in his throat. Through the crack in the door, a pair of whisky-brown eyes peered inside. Blinked. Widened.

Vanished.

"Ah, beg pardon, but ..." Justin came to his feet. "I think I am in need of some fresh air."

"By all means." Sebastian twiddled his elegant fingers. "I would come along, but as you can see I'm a bit ... *inebriated*." He flashed a crooked smile, and Justin shook his head, knowing

Sebastian would be hard pressed to make it out of that chair tonight.

"Your Grace." Justin bowed to the duke, who was on the verge of sleep himself, his eyes falling heavier and heavier by the second.

"Lord"--the duke yawned--"Carrington."

The hallway was empty when Justin stepped outside the parlor, this time shutting the door behind him. He knew it was her. There was no mistaking those eyes. Moreover, the way they stared at him in the most accusing way. As if it was his fault all this was happening.

"Sir?" Justin stopped the innkeeper, who was making his nightly rounds. "Have you seen Lady Ballivar within the past few minutes? Dark hair, small in stature." He leveled a hand to illustrate her height.

The innkeeper grinned. "Ye finally marryin' the lass, are ye? A bonnie lass she is, tha' one. Jes' saw 'er runnin' back fer 'er room." He pointed a crooked finger toward the stairs, the same ones from which Justin had stormed no more than half an hour ago.

*** *** ***

Sara succeeded in making it past the stairs, taking the last step so fast she nearly tumbled over her own feet. They were too small, and their smallness was even more disagreeable when she was barefoot and running. She'd been struck out on one too many occasions because of it. And now she stood to face the one person she'd so desperately tried to stay away from tonight.

All because she had small feet.

Blast, if she could just make it to the sanctuary of her room, she could stop worrying. She was breathing entirely too hard, her heart pounding against her ribs like a caged animal. A threatening combination in need of finding a happy median if she had any intention on keeping the contents of her half-empty stomach.

She couldn't bring herself to eat tonight, although the grilled fish and seasoned potatoes did look quite delectable, which Lana confirmed after Sara had insisted she eat instead. She was still much too nervous. Especially after he'd barged in as he had, striding toward her like a lion on the hunt while her stomach did somersaults like a circus monkey. And then he'd left, and just like that, she'd lost her wits *and* her appetite.

A con-artist, that's what he was. No other logical explanation existed for how her body had reacted to his nearness.

She'd bathed quickly, washed her hair, brushed her teeth, and prayed the warm water would somehow dull her senses enough to get him out of her brain. Where he had no business being in the first place.

But to her discomfort and utter chagrin, she could think of nothing but him. And the way the word *bath* had dripped like warm syrup from his lips. Which, she noticed, were perfectly shaped, the lower protruding only slightly further from the upper.

The fact she was imagining his lips made her even angrier.

Afterward, she'd lain in bed for an eternity, waiting for her maid to stop stirring in the next room. Once all noise had ceased, she'd made for the hallway. Disregarding her scarcely clad appearance of wearing only her white night rail, she'd hurried as fast as her small, bare feet could carry her to find her father.

And, once again, beg him to reconsider. She was fully prepared to get down on her knees and sob if she had to.

Of course, who should she find with him but Lord Carrington and that other person--Lord Beaufort was he?--who found her so amusing. What gentleman would make such an open display of laughter over a lady that he should have to turn his back in attempt to stifle it? An English one, *that's* who. They were all the same. Mindless, arrogant idiots who thought of nothing and no one but themselves.

Her anger had worked itself into such a boiling point she'd almost mustered the courage to barge through the door, invade their male conversation, when he'd seen her. Just like that, just as he had earlier in her room, he'd caused her to lose her nerve.

All that mattered now was making it back to her room and shutting the door. Locking it was probably a good idea as well. What would he do? Break it down?

Sara froze at the sound of boot-clad feet drawing near. Two more doors and she'd make it to her room. Two more.

She gasped aloud, her arm snatched in the vice of a strong hand. Warmth shot through the fabric of her thin gown and straight to her skin, her bones.

"We need to talk." His mouth hovered mere inches above her ear. He coerced her, gently, into the room, then slammed the door behind them.

He released her, whirling about only to turn the key before his eyes locked with hers. Instinctively, she started backing away, even as he advanced, his long legs covering more distance in three strides than hers could in ten.

"Why were you eavesdropping?" His head inclined. That lock of dark hair fell over his forehead again, where he must have brushed it back earlier. His eyes roved over her, assessed and scrutinized. All at once she felt inexplicably vulnerable.

Naked.

"You look as if you were already in bed. Yet, you got up." His eyes narrowed. "Why?"

"I wasn't eavesdropping," she lied. "I only wanted to speak with my father."

One of his dark brows arched. "Truly? And what, pray, could possibly be so pressing you couldn't wait until morning to speak to your father?"

She lifted her chin, peeved by his arrogance. "That is none of your business."

A ragged gasp escaped her as her back hit the wall between the vanity and the bed. Had she been shying away from him?

Panic swept through her, prickled the tiny hairs at the back of her neck.

He drew nearer, braced one of his large, bronzed hands on the wall beside her head. She dared not close her eyes, though the heat of him, the air of his calm authority, made her want to do just that. He smelled of horses and sweat. And something which reminded her of the Tibetan incense sold at the perfumer's in Dublin.

Exotic and foreign.

Mouth-wateringly male.

"Let's get one thing straight, my lady." His pupils were dilated, making it even harder to distinguish the dark irises. "We are betrothed. And as your intended, I am compelled to remind you that your business *is* my business."

Sara felt her stomach coil into a knot. Her knees threatened to give way. He had her cornered, which by all reasons of sanity should've frightened her enough to duck under his arm and run as fast as she could in the other direction.

But she didn't *want* to move, and that small epiphany was something she couldn't understand, especially since his apparent motive was making her realize just how much bigger he was than she, how much stronger.

As if she didn't know already.

"Furthermore," he continued, and Sara took a sharp breath as he tucked a lock of damp hair behind her ear. Roughened fingertips brushed against her temple. "I will not stand for this wall you seem to be determined in wedging between us. The objective of having you sent prematurely to London was not for us to be apart, but to learn one another, which shall prove impossible if you are insistent upon keeping your distance from me."

"I know," she heard herself say, though as nervous as she was, she couldn't be sure she had said anything at all. His gaze falling to her parted lips was her first clue.

His response was her second.

"Then why the evasiveness? I'm not going to hurt you, Sara. I think you might find my company enjoyable if you'd allow it. I've even been known to be funny every now and again, though if you spend very much time in the company of Lord Beaufort, you might find his humor far exceeds mine." The corner of his mouth kicked up a little at the self-deprecating comment.

"I find Lord Beaufort appalling, Lord Carrington."

His dark brows snapped together. "I agree. He can be rather incorrigible, but then again, you've yet to spend enough time in his presence to make that discovery. At least not accurately. So, I must ask, why is it you find him so unappealing?"

"He was laughing at me," she pointed out, and instead of looking appalled, he adopted a sort of whimsical smile.

And then, since he obviously couldn't make light enough of her comment with merely a smile, he bowed his head and released a fit of gentle laughter. He almost seemed ... Well. *Boyish.*

"Ah, my lady," he said, still fighting laughter. "Trust me. Lord Beaufort was not laughing at you."

His fingers came to her face, and Sara jerked in reaction, paralyzed, only whether with fear or curiosity, she did not know. Downward, his fingers slid, his head tilting as his dark eyes followed the unhurried action.

Sara's breath ratcheted higher. Higher still. Her breast heaved beneath her night rail. Part of her wanted to take his hand and hold it there in effort to keep her heart from bursting through. Or perhaps it was merely the want she suddenly had for him to touch her.

"You are very beautiful," he muttered.

Sara's lips parted, the rapidity of her breaths coming so painfully hard she felt near faint.

She'd been told she was beautiful. In fact, she'd heard that sentiment so many times now she had begun to brush it aside as nothing. Her eyes had driven men to poetry, the sensuous shape of her mouth to sonnets recited on bended knee. Lesser women may have found it all rather flattering, but not Sara. Her father had once called her beauty ancient. The kind mentioned in stories of old: fairy-like and extremely dangerous to the hearts of those who would dare risk their sanity by pursuing her.

Yet somehow the way Justin said those simple words was completely different.

As if it was a problem, not a compliment.

His thumb brushed over her bottom lip, and Sara closed her eyes as she felt a responsive moan welling in her throat.

Sweet heavens. He was going to kiss her. She could feel her face reddening at the thought, her body aching now with a want she'd never felt before, the realization that she actually wanted him to kiss her hitting her like a slap to the face.

But his hand withdrew, and her eyes opened, searching his for something she couldn't comprehend. An explanation perhaps? Did he not find her kissable?

He pushed off the wall and backed away, deliberately preserving the distance between them.

Sara couldn't speak, couldn't move for that matter, and as he executed a stiff bow, she felt a whim of ridiculousness rush over her.

"Good evening, my lady." He strode for the door. "We depart for London shortly after dawn."

The door shut quietly in his stead, and Sara, tired and confused as she was, slid to the floor in a heap of white linen.

One thing was for certain. This was not going at all as she'd anticipated.

FOUR

By the grace of God, and with a little help from Lana, Sara managed to make it downstairs the next morning before everyone-- even the duke, who was, in Sara's opinion, the world's earliest riser. He was usually awake, dressed and reading the morning papers before most people had given thought to opening their eyes. Because of him, Lana had trained herself to rise at least half an hour before the first sounding of the cock's crow.

Heaven forbid the duke should be without a cup of chocolate while reading his morning paper.

Sara, on the other hand, had always been a late sleeper. With her language, philosophy, history and arithmetic studies, and her riding lessons, lasting until nearly half past noon every day, she barely had enough time to change and make it to the playing field for a game of Rounders before afternoon tea. A tiresome schedule such as hers required extra sleep.

Until now, however, her daily habits hadn't included spending time with a gentleman. And Lord Carrington had made it perfectly clear last night that spending time together was exactly what he intended to do.

Sara touched her fingers to her face. Never had she imagined the hands of a nobleman as anything but effeminately smooth. But his were, albeit slightly, rough. As if he'd wielded an axe with those hands, or perhaps a shovel. They were work hands.

"It is good to see you smiling this morning, my lady."

Sara fingers immediately stole from her face.

Lana smiled. "You look refreshed. And my goodness, that yellow dress does fit nicely. Radiant as sunshine. I daresay his lordship will be enchanted."

Warmth rose in Sara's cheeks. "Thank you, Lana." She paused. "Any sight of my betrothed this morning?"

"Aye, my lady. I just passed him having words with Lord Beaufort. Seems as though your father has already departed for Ireland." Lana shrugged; Sara's jaw fell open. "Eager to return home, he was."

She reached for Sara's hand, gave it a cheerful pat. "But not to worry, my lady. He will return to London for your wedding. Now, how about a spot of breakfast?"

"My father's not coming?" Even as she asked, the words sickened her. All she had left in the world was an overprotective maid and a fiancé she barely knew.

This simply would not do.

"My lady, where are you ...?"

Sara picked up the skirts of her dress, layers of butter-yellow muslin trimmed in white lace, and headed for the rooms, determined to find Lord Carrington and give him a piece of her mind. She didn't know why her father had left without so much as a fare-thee-well, but she was nonetheless convinced her betrothed had put that calloused hand of his in it somehow.

She could hear the sweeping of Lana's slippers scurrying over the wooden floor behind her, the sound of her frantic voice, which always became high-pitched when she was mad or upset.

"My lady! Don't interrupt the gentlemen's conversation! It is un-ladylike! Your father would not be pleased! Oh, *a leanbh na páirte*, why do you insist on being so difficult?"

Piece by piece, the coiffure Lana had concocted atop Sara's head tumbled from its neatly fastened pins, finally falling in a mass of cascading silk as Sara rounded the corner leading to the staircase and hit something broad and hard head-on.

"Good Lord." A pair of strong hands caught her by the elbows. "Are you running away already?"

Lord Carrington.

Perfect.

She regarded him narrowly. "You sent my father away,"

The husky whimsicalness of Lord Beaufort's laughter pierced through the ensuing silence. "See you outside, my lord," he murmured, patting Carrington on the back. Then: "My dear Mrs. Brennan." He proffered his arm to Lana. "Would you be so kind? I'm in dire need of some feminine company, you see, and I highly suspect yours would be most gratifying."

His silvery-blue eyes shimmered with friendly mirth as he countered the shocked look on Lana's face with, "For conversational purposes only, of course."

Lana slipped her hand into the crook of his arm, glancing worriedly at Sara from over her shoulder as he led her down the hall.

Reminded she was now very much alone with her betrothed, Sara swallowed and turned her gaze slowly upward. One of his dark brows lifted. She could try and pull herself free, but ... Oh, it was no use. Clearly he had no intention of turning her loose.

"Why did you send my father away?"

"Your father sent himself away, Kitten."

Sara's jaw fell open. "Don't call me ..." Berating him for pet names hardly seemed relevant at the moment. "Why? Why would he leave so abruptly?"

"He thought perhaps you might try to talk him into taking you back to Ireland." He paused. "I think he might have been right. But not to worry. I promised I would take good care of you, and that you would write once we reached London."

"As if hauling me to London could stop me from running away if I wanted to."

Something triggered then, and Sara instantly wished she had never made such a provoking statement.

Anger sweltered in the depths of his dark eyes. His clutch on her arms tightened, and his jaw, defined like the craftsmanship of a fine artist, set as hard as stone.

"You, my lady," he said, "will not run."

He pulled her then, coaxed her along several feet through the dark corridor and into an empty parlor. Moodily he ignored her gasping protests, but kept a firm hold on her even as she struggled to pry herself free.

"Let me go!" she pleaded, as he kicked the door closed.

He didn't seem to hear, and Sara fought with all she had to keep from crying as he pressed her back against a book-cased wall. Letting go of her arms, he anchored her with his body and caught both her wrists, one in each hand, and pinned them on either side of her head.

Any illusion she might have had to claw or hit him vanished. She couldn't cry out for her father, as he was on his way back to Ireland, and she certainly couldn't yell for her maid. Lana was likely too busy allowing Lord Beaufort to amuse her right out of her stockings, the traitorous woman.

She was at his mercy.

God help her.

He smelled differently this morning. Like shaving balm, soap. Perhaps aftershave. His hair was damp, his face smooth. A torrent of emotions flashed in his eyes. Emotions she couldn't name, couldn't place. Never had she seen eyes so dark and indecipherable. It was like trying to find one's way through a labyrinth at night, surrounded by nothing but high yew walls and air black as pitch.

Sara, desperate to calm her racing nerves, finally looked away. She focused on the book beneath her right wrist.

The History of Tom Jones, a Foundling, by Henry Fielding, Esq.

"H-have you read many n-novels, my lord?" His breath fanned across her face. He smelled incredible. "Mr. Fielding's portrayal of Tom and S-Sophia is quite lovely considering …"

"I'm not interested in discussing literature with you, Sara," he said, even as she continued mumbling on about virtue, choosing one's path by right action, anything to take her mind off being alone with him.

"Then what, pray, shall we talk about?" Her pulse raced, driven by the heat of his hands, wrapped tightly around her wrists.

"I'm not interested in talking, either."

Sara tightened her closed eyes, frightened he would see through any sort of façade should she risk looking at him. Not that she had enough courage to put on one, mind.

"Look at me, please." The thick bands of his fingers loosened. Gently, he used his thumbs to stroke the pulse thrumming in her wrists. "Sara?"

She gulped audibly, and blushed because of it. She must've looked like a prized idiot standing there beneath him, trembling like some skittish forest creature. At that point, she couldn't be sure what he'd see should she obey.

"Have it your way, then." The words whispered across her skin, and before she could think of something clever to say in effort to distract him, her wrists were freed, her face was enveloped by his warm hands, and her mouth was taken.

Sensation swirled and tormented. Lapped at her thighs, her belly, her breasts, and in places she dared not name. His lips were insistent, teasing and withdrawing. Repeating the process in a way which excited and frustrated.

What few kisses she'd shared with Cav had been sweet and gentle, but this ...

This wasn't at all comparable.

She never dreamed it could be this wonderful. A tantalizing dance of impatient yet tender caresses that robbed her of all care, all thought. And as Justin's tongue traced the seam of her lips, a wave of heat spread through her body like wildfire through a parched forest.

Breathlessly, she opened her mouth, and in the next instant, felt his tongue sweep inside, tasting her with newfound desire. Her hands, which up until now had been suspended in midair, were slowly, timidly easing themselves around his neck.

The gesture seemed to excite him. The muscles at the back of his neck tensed, the smooth skin beneath her fingertips grew hotter.

And then the kiss deepened.

His large hand coasted down the length of her spine, the other cradling her head, and in one easy motion, he brought their bodies together. Flush.

Weakened, Sara strained against him. His body was solid, his scent intoxicating. And there was something else. Something pressing uncomfortably hard against her abdomen.

Struggling to shift her body in some way to alleviate the strange pressure, she rose tiptoe.

He moaned into her mouth. The hand he had resting idly at her back pressed harder, bringing her even closer, until nary an inch was left between their bodies.

That was the precise moment she realized ... Oh, but it was all so embarrassing, this awareness of him, and her own body's reaction. To her utter chagrin, her innocent attempts at accommodating to comfort had aligned their bodies in such a way the hard protrusion of his masculinity was positioned perfectly should he desire to...

Saints and sinners, she'd aroused him.

There was no other explanation, shameful though it was. But she couldn't very well help noticing, could she?

Discomfited, Sara tore her lips from his, and shoved, hard as she could, against his chest. It was as solid as steel. "Please," she murmured, gasping for air. "Don't."

"Don't?" He sought her mouth again.

Sara turned her head, and his lips brushed across her cheek; attempted to toss her head back, out of his reach, but he caught at the hollow beneath her jaw. Gooseflesh spread all over her skin.

She felt him smile against her neck.

"Innocent darling." He kissed the pulse throbbing wildly in her throat.

Another gentle kiss. Another just beneath the lobe of her ear. Sara grasped two handfuls of his wool coat, struggling to maintain equilibrium.

"I love the way you smell." He sucked an earlobe between his teeth, worried it gently. "The way you taste. So sweet." His lips were restless, skimming the sensitive line of her jaw to her cheek and again to her mouth. He kissed her softly, angelically, his lips barely brushing hers.

Then, he let go.

Sara braced herself against the bookcase, for as drugged as she felt at the moment, collapsing was not an option. She refused to give him the satisfaction.

However, she suspected by the heat in her cheeks, he already knew.

"Don't tell me you've never been kissed, Lady Ballivar." He was attempting, she thought, to sound lighthearted in spite of the desire in his eyes. "After all, you are ... what? Eighteen?"

Inwardly relieved the effect of the kiss hadn't been one-sided, Sara stood taller. She smoothed the wrinkles of her dress with a quick brush of her hands. "Yes."

Gathering her bearings, she ignored the look of arrogant satisfaction on his face. "And on the contrary, Lord Carrington, I have been kissed before."

"Not like that, you haven't."

Sara opened her mouth in retort, discovered she had none, and closed it again.

He moved closer, stunned her when he took her hand and brought it to his lips. "It's nothing to be ashamed of," he murmured against her bare skin. She'd forgotten gloves this morning. Lana would have a conniption. "In fact, I do think I prefer it."

Sara watched as he unhurriedly dragged his lips across her knuckles. "If there is any honor in you, if you call yourself a gentleman, you will promise never to do that again without my permission."

His eyes met hers. A wry smile curved his lips. "I don't call myself anything, my lady. So, I cannot promise you that." He tucked her hand into the crook of his arm and squared his shoulders. "But I can promise you this: the next time I kiss you, you won't say *don't*."

*** *** ***

Justin had never been one to find any sort of appeal in young, virginal girls. In fact, and by all accounts, he tried his damndest to steer clear of them. They were clingy in the worst sense, too innocent, much too eager to land a husband, and, worst of all, they had no ability whatsoever to distinguish love from lust. Smiling at one could earn a man an innocent giggle behind a fan, which was harmless enough until he asked the young lady to dance. And then he'd better hope the dance was a quadrille and not a waltz, because waltzes only made them giggle harder.

But when a man was holding a lady that close to his body, giggles were easy to ignore.

So easy, in fact, he might ask her to accompany him into the garden. Where he'd make the biggest mistake of his life and kiss her. Instantly, she'd be in love with him, declare they were soulmates, meant to be together. All a box of ridiculous fantasies virgins carried around in their virginal heads.

But Lady St. Clair didn't have that problem. She never gave any false illusion she was in love with him, nor did she want anything more out of their relationship than the pleasure he gave her. Justin was well aware he wasn't her first lover, naturally, as she was a widow. He was sure he wouldn't be her last, either; she had too great a sexual appetite to stay with one man forever. And where marriage was inevitable for him, the bonds of matrimony held no interest for her.

But he was more than certain he had been her exclusive for the past several months, during which he'd never gone a full week without visiting her bed, and he was on the verge of two now. In truth, he should have been running back to London with the eagerness of a racehorse, every gallop bringing him closer to Milly and the welcoming warmth of her naked body entangled with his.

He wasn't eager.

If anything, he was dreading the return and reality he would eventually have to face his mistress.

Dread facing Milly? How could he?

Ah, but one look over his shoulder at the black lacquered coach bouncing behind said it all.

He was stricken with his betrothed. Whether with lust or mere curiosity, he could not decide. Her body was heaven, and it fit perfectly to his much taller, broader form. Sweet Lord, her lips. He imagined the richest confection didn't taste anywhere near as decadent. If he were any other kind of man, he could have easily hiked up her skirts and taken her right there against the bookcase. Shown her what it could be like between them, if she would allow it.

What was he thinking? No man in his right mind felt this kind of emotion toward his intended. And he wasn't delusional enough to think she would mean anything more to him in marriage than a mere means of bearing his heirs.

But all at once, in less than a day, Lady Ballivar had given him the idea that he could have a meaningful marriage, like his father. One that, in time, could develop into deep-found affection.

If there was such a thing.

"You know what I was just thinking about?"

Ah, Sebastian. He never could stand for riding without some sort of conversation, even if it was pointless.

"Am I to guess?" Justin forced himself to look away from the carriage. He regarded Sebastian evenly. "Or are you going to enlighten me?"

Sebastian smiled crookedly, still groggy from last night's whisky-laced conversation with the duke. "When I thought I was helplessly in love with Jane Foster." Sebastian gazed ahead, reflectively. "She had me smitten like a fool willing to spend his last pence on a stick of licorice. Do you remember that?"

Briefly taken back by the odd analogy, Justin waited a few seconds to answer. "Of course I remember. That's the day I met you, half-drunk, half-terrified that her ape-of-a-brother was about to beat your head in with his father's hammer."

Sebastian shrugged. "It wasn't the best idea I ever had, fooling around with the blacksmith's daughter." He cast an aside glance at Justin, squinting against the sunlight. "In fact, there was only one other occasion I felt that way. About a woman, I mean."

"Mmm. Well, you were only twelve, Sebastian. Hardly a reasonable age to determine whether or not one is in love."

"I was mature for twelve."

"You're not mature now."

Sebastian gave the accusation thought. "I'm working on it."

"Indeed," Justin muttered. "You never did thank me for saving your skin that day, you know. I could've just left you to the ape-boy. He looked a might determined when he found you--us--at the confectioner's."

A roll of laughter peeled from Sebastian's throat. "The look on his face when he saw your fist coming."

"You're welcome," said Justin, as Sebastian sighed and shook his head. "So, tell me, is it so memorable, how close you came to being pummeled on the streets of London?"

"Memorable," Sebastian repeated, and then matter-of-factly added, "Of course it was. We've been virtually inseparable ever since. But that's not why I was thinking about Jane Foster."

"I won't pull it out of you, Sebastian. You know how I hate evasiveness."

"The expression I wore then," Sebastian quipped, "before the incident with her brother, and you damn near leveling him in one blow. I was smitten. Not a thought went through my mind, however utterly depraved my mind was--is, that didn't consist of her in some way."

He cocked an eyebrow at Justin. "And you, my friend, have the expression."

"What in the devil is that supposed to mean?"

"Oh, come now, old chap. You don't expect me to believe the two of you were playing a game of whist whilst alone in the library for fifteen minutes? Something happened that has you in deep thought. Too deep considering in less than two hours, we'll be back in London. And you'll be free to visit Lady St. Clair."

Justin's brow pulled with uncertainty.

"Or perhaps it is your mistress who has so acutely invaded your thoughts."

Justin did not respond, but listened to the *squeak-squeak-squeak* of his father's new carriage, the pounding hooves of the four fresh horses they'd acquired less than an hour ago in Warwick.

When they'd stopped to rest and gather a few supplies, he'd gone to the inn near the river and purchased a basketful of sandwiches, shortbread cakes, and a bottle of wine, figuring everyone, including his intended, would be famished. He'd offered her a sandwich made of smoked meat and thin-sliced cheese, which she'd promptly refused, assuring him she wasn't hungry.

And then she'd asked him to leave her be. That she was tired and wanted to be alone, though her idea of alone apparently included the company of Mrs. Brennan, who rarely let the lady out of her sight.

Had it been left up to him, Justin would've sent the maid back to Ireland. Then he could properly court Sara, despite her obvious disinterest in being courted. Or held. Or kissed.

Ah, but she had kissed him back. There was no way she could've responded the way she had without feeling some sort of desire for him. He could still feel her cool hands on his neck, that glorious body molding against his, not knowing whether she should pull away or press harder. He could still taste her, smell her, and he could very well imagine tasting more of her.

All of her.

Uncomfortable, he shifted in his saddle, and urged his horse into a steady canter, deciding his first order of business once they arrived in London would be to pay a visit to Millicent St. Clair.

FIVE

Sara blinked as a ray of gleaming sunlight moved across the thin skin of her closed eyelid, awakening her from an uncomfortable nap. While the Tethersal carriage was inarguably exquisite--the finest with its velvet upholstery, polished wood, and fox hunting motif painted upon the ceiling--it was still bumpy in travel. She'd rested her head on the wall, right next to the window, and stared out into the open scenery.

She'd thought on all the trips taken in her father's carriage. He'd never hesitated in letting her lean against him. Sometimes he would recite a poem. Sometimes one of Shakespeare's shorter sonnets, as they were her favorite. At other times they'd ride in companionable silence, with only the sound of her father's breathing and the gentle rise and fall of his chest to induce her into a dreamless sleep.

Fine polished wood was beautiful, but not nearly as comfortable as the warmth of a loving father.

Aside from her unpleasant sleep, and one game of solitaire with Lana, Sara had spent the majority of her time thinking of Lord Carrington. The kiss they'd shared in the library at the inn. As inexperienced as she was in the seductive arts, Sara was no fool. She knew perfectly well what she'd done to him. To *both* of them.

It wasn't supposed to happen this way, she reminded herself. He wasn't supposed to be handsome or charming, and he most certainly wasn't supposed to kiss her.

But he was handsome. Devastatingly so. And he could probably charm the wings off a bluebird if he tried.

Charming wings off avionic creatures aside, Sara had to admit she'd never seen a man with such strong features. His chest rivaled that of the broadest cathedral doors, and his arms felt banded in impenetrable steel. With his impeccable appearance and more than demanding presence, Sara imagined he could enter a room, not utter a single word, and every head would automatically turn in his direction.

It was his blue-blooded breeding that made him this way, she knew, but he was far from being the model nobleman. In truth, his well-honed physicality reminded her more of a day laborer's than that of a peer.

Sara placed a hand over her belly, wishing she would have eaten the sandwich he'd offered earlier. She just couldn't bear to look at him, much less talk to him, which would have been inevitable had she accepted the food.

"You should have eaten, my lady," Lana said tentatively.

Sara focused on the land outside. "Didn't want to."

Acres upon acres of flowing orchards, some newly planted, some towering in maturity, led into a wide open space of rolling parkland. Ironic she'd thought Ireland to be the greenest land she'd ever seen. And it was; the grass surrounding Northwood was so green it appeared blue in the sunlight.

But this was a close second.

The coach lurched forward, circled round a grand stone fountain that stood in the midst of a well-kept courtyard. Sara's heart raced with anticipation. As soon as the horses came to a halt, footmen rushed from all directions, one opening the door while another unfolded the steps. While yet three more began untying the luggage.

"My lady." Outside, an immaculately dressed servant proffered his hand. "Welcome to Mayfair House."

Sara smiled, nodded curtly, and slipped her gloved hand inside his. "Thank you," she said, and stepped down. A soft breeze whirled around her, filled her senses with the aromatic combination of soil and spring flowers. She moved around the coach, and, looking up, beheld the vast structure that was to be her new home.

Designed in the popular Palladian style, Mayfair House was an extraordinary work of architecture. A set of stone steps, surrounded on either side by neat yew hedges, swept into a wide white-columned portico. Towering Venetian windows crowned the upper floor, each with its own stone-railed balcony, and Sara immediately hoped one of them would be hers. She could easily picture herself perched outside, away from the noise and clamor that came with a house of this proportion, enjoying a good book or a cup of tea, perhaps both.

"Lady Ballivar." Eerie that his voice had already become familiar. "I trust your ride was satisfactory. No precarious bumps or anything?"

She looked up at him, and automatically tucked her hand inside his crooked arm. "No," she said, and apparently a little too quickly.

"You were uncomfortable." Concern laced his tone. "You should have told me. I could have gotten you a blanket or perhaps a pillow."

"Really, my lord." She gave his bicep a gentle squeeze, amazed by the swell of muscle beneath. Their gazes held. Sara swallowed. "I am quite well."

He nodded, and led her toward the house, Lord Beaufort running ahead by several paces. She wondered what it must have been like for the two of them, these close companions, growing up together in the heart of British society. Clearly they had been friends since childhood, as there was no other explanation to Lord Carrington's association with such an unrefined character as Lord Beaufort. She imagined they'd gotten themselves into all sorts of boyish mischief as children, and more than likely still did from time to time.

If not all the time.

Heavens. What if Carrington was as vulgar as his friend and was only pretending to be a well-mannered gentleman? He obviously had a bit of a lewd streak. Otherwise, he wouldn't have kissed her without first asking permission, as most gentlemen would have.

Oh, for the love of--she was already thinking about the kiss again. All of a sudden, she became aware of his nearness, the skirts of her dress brushing against his leg as they ascended the steps, the bulge of his arm grazing the side of her breast. Surreal, it was, being with him like this.

A tall, thin-faced butler greeted them at the entrance, bending over a lean waist as they approached. "My lord." He took Lord Carrington's hat and gloves. "We are most grateful for your safe return." His small eyes turned to Sara, the corners of his non-existent lips upturning slightly. "And what a delight it is to have you here at Mayfair House, Lady Ballivar. May I take your bonnet?"

Sara tugged at the satin ribbon tied beneath her chin and removed her bonnet, fully aware of Lord Carrington's watchful gaze. Never had removing a simple head covering seemed so intimate a gesture. The warmth of his breath tickled her skin where the tiny hairs framed her temple. Like a fish out of water, her stomach flip-flopped under the weight of his stare.

Insane. That's what this was. Completely, *flip-floppity* insane.

She handed her bonnet to the butler, and addressed her betrothed. "Your home is lovely, my lord." And it really was. The ceilings in the foyer alone had to be at least thirty feet high, if not higher. Grecian tile, polished to a high shine, covered the floor.

"It's been in my family for generations." He pointed to a statue of a robed woman, positioned upon a square pedestal in a corner at the end of the foyer. In one of her intricately detailed hands was a pitcher, and in the other, a cup. "Hebe," he said, "Goddess of Youth. She was given to my father by an Italian general, after the war."

"She's beautiful," Sara exclaimed.

"Her husband, Hercules." He pointed to the corner opposite the Greek statue, where a stalwart sculpture of a man stood, a knotted club gripped tightly in his white marble hand.

Justin's head lowered, his mouth mere millimeters from her cheek. "Hebe was a gift to him from the goddess Hera, a beacon to his immortality."

Reactively Sara turned her face toward him, the sudden closeness of their lips causing her breath to catch. Her eyes rolled upward, and Justin quirked a smile, as if knowing her inner thoughts--thoughts of kissing him again, of feeling the weight of his body pressed against hers.

"You seem nervous," he quietly observed. "Don't be."

"I'm not."

"Justin!"

Both their heads shot to attention, and Lord Carrington grinned, releasing Sara's hand from his arm as two women, one running ahead of the other, approached, wide smiles spread across their faces.

"Anna." He embraced the younger of the two. "You look well."

"Brother," she murmured as he smoothed a hand over her head of shiny blond curls. "I'm so pleased you're back." She lowered her voice; her deep blue eyes peered at Sara from over his shoulder. "Father's been asking for you."

A frown creased his forehead. "Is he all right? He isn't …?"

"No." She pulled back to look at him properly. "He just had a restless night. Night sweats, bad dreams. Nothing out of the ordinary. At least not for Father. He just wanted to see you, I think."

"And Lady Ballivar," the elder woman added, turning her attention to Sara. She smiled.

This had to be the duchess.

Sara took her extended hand without hesitation, dropped into a respectful curtsy. "Your Grace."

"Forgive me, Mother," said Lord Carrington, garnering a warm smile from the duchess. "May I present Lady Sara Ballivar of Dublin?" And as the duchess nodded: "Lady Ballivar, this is my mother, Elizabeth, Duchess of Tethersal."

"Very pleased to meet you, Your Grace." Sara curtsied again for good measure. "Your home is beautiful."

"How very kind," the duchess replied. She made a small gesture to the blond beauty beside her. "My daughter, Lady Anna."

"Pleased to finally meet you," said Anna. "I was beginning to believe you were but a myth."

"Honestly Anna," the duchess tenderly chided. "Lady Ballivar has only just arrived, and already you are making her uncomfortable. You'll have to forgive my daughter. Improper comments do tend to slip on occasion."

Lord Beaufort gave a snort of laughter as he approached the circle. "Come now, Your Grace. On occasion, you say?" His eyes flickered to Anna, who did not appear the least bit amused by his banter. "I would venture to say Lady Anna slips at least one reprehensible comment into every conversation."

"An accusation such as that coming from a renowned rake? Who would soon see a lady ruined rather than right his wrong?" Lord Beaufort's smile faded, and Anna beamed her satisfaction. "Don't make me laugh."

Sara blinked, astonished. Where had that come from?

"Enough, Anna," Lord Carrington bit off.

At that moment, if Anna's eyes could have shot daggers, Sara guessed they would have.

The duchess grew silent, eyes weary. Perhaps she'd been through so much heartache for so long the will to maintain order in her own household had vanished. Apparently Lord Carrington had borne that chore for a while, or he wouldn't have been so quick to correct Anna's brashness.

Regardless of whether or not Lord Beaufort had started it, which he had.

"Justin, I can very well handle my own," Lord Beaufort began, but Lord Carrington was apparently far from finished.

"Lately, your mouth has backed you into more corners than I care to admit," he told Anna. "But it stops now. You have no business meddling in anyone else's affairs but your own, and while I've been lenient on you in the past, I'll not hesitate in denying you the right to attend the remainder of the Season if you cannot control your tongue."

At this, Anna's jaw set hard. Her eyes welled, and Sara thought she heard the soft, sharp catching of Lord Beaufort's breath. He was stone faced, she noticed, his silvery-blue eyes glued to Anna, who quickly swabbed her tears with the pad of her thumb.

"Justin," the duchess murmured. "Why don't you show Lady Ballivar to her chambers? I'll wager she'd fancy a change of clothes after such a long journey. Lord Beaufort, won't you join us for dinner?"

Beaufort hesitated. "No, Your Grace." Another pause. "I'm afraid I have pressing matters elsewhere. I will, however, see you all at the party this weekend."

He bowed before the duchess, gave Lord Carrington, who muttered a low apology, a quick pat on the shoulder, and without looking back, took his leave.

Stunned by the odd display, Sara stole a surreptitious glance at Lady Anna, who had decisively turned her back to her brother and taken a sudden interest in a landscape painting.

"My apologies, Lady Ballivar," said the duchess. "The air in this house has been rather tense as of late, what with the worsening of the duke's health." She tilted her head, her kind eyes wrinkling at the sides as she smiled.

She was a beautiful woman, the duchess. She must have been striking in her youth. "He very much wanted to greet you himself upon your arrival, but ..." Her words faded, her gaze drifted downward.

"Not at all, Your Grace," Sara assured. "I look forward to meeting His Grace, the duke, when he is able."

Lord Carrington cleared his throat. "Shall we, then?" He offered his arm. "I believe my sister's maid has already shown Mrs. Brennan to her room belowstairs. Yours is on the second floor."

"Thank you, my lord." Nodding respectfully to the duchess, Sara allowed him to lead her from the room.

The faint whispers of a mother to a daughter carried through the air as Sara ascended the stairs, one hand neatly tucked in her betrothed's arm, while the other rested lightly on the white wood railing.

Several elaborately framed paintings, most of the past Dukes of Tethersal, adorned the walls leading to the upper living quarters. At the top of the staircase, a large gilt-framed portrait portrayed a younger Phillip, the sixth and current duke, in his Royal Navy uniform. Sara recognized it immediately. Her father had one of himself, almost identical, hanging above the mantle in the drawing room at Northwood.

"This was commissioned during the war," she said as they reached the last curvature of the stairs.

"Yes," he confirmed, stopping. "Lady Percy painted it in '15. A notable landscape artist, she is, but she made an exception for my father and the Duke of--well, your father. They're very good friends, you see, my father and Lady Percy. She may even be at the party this weekend."

"Speaking of which, my lord."

"Justin." His aside glance made the tiny hairs at the back of her neck stand on end. "Please, call me Justin. Formalities are most exasperating when one is in the comfort of one's own home, in the company of family. Don't you think?"

"But we are not family, my lord."

"Justin."

"Justin," she said softly.

"Not yet," he murmured, leading her along a hallway of rooms. "Now, you were saying?"

"I was?" What had she been saying? Somehow, in the midst of losing formalities, for which she was most grateful, she had forgotten her original question. "Oh, *óinseach*. I cannot seem to …"

He chuckled. "What was that?"

"I cannot recall what it was I meant to ask."

"You said something in a different language."

"Oh!" She bit her lower lip. "It's embarrassing, really." She lowered her voice to a whisper. "I called myself an idiot."

He laughed gently. "Is that what that was? Well, then I shall endeavor to be cautious, Sara. I'm certain I shan't care to be called a … what was it? *Óinseach*?"

Sara fought the urge to laugh at his brutal massacre of the word. "On the contrary, my lord--er, Justin, forgive me--you would be an *amadán*." And then she did laugh.

He seemed rather amused himself. "I'm afraid my language skills are limited to common English and Latin. Spanish, and of course, French."

Of course. "You have an advantage." He showed her into a large room, decorated in matching linens of cream and dusty rose. "I do not know French."

Against one wall stood an exquisite Louis XV vanity made of highly polished dark wood, with a large oval mirror and a cushioned, cream upholstered chair. Beside it, a full length mirror, framed in an etching of twining roses, reflected Sara's awestruck expression. There was also wash basin, also in the popular French style, and a roll-top secretary with quill and stationery.

A smile worked its way across Sara's lips as she noticed the window, framed in yards of rose-colored curtains with cream lace that pooled at the bottom. Through the Venetian arch, she observed she had, indeed, been given a room with a balcony.

Splendid.

"If there is anything you require, anything at all, you needn't hesitate to ring for it." He motioned to the bell pull by the door.

"Thank you." She shifted her gaze to the huge four-poster bed, canopied in cream chiffon. It was luscious, covered in fluffy throw pillows and a thick, downy quilt that promised comfort. She'd almost forgotten how tired she truly was, how cluttered her thoughts had been for the duration of the journey to London.

"You are tired."

Sara whirled about, faced him.

He was so very handsome, her intended. Truly, she'd never met a man who could put on such tranquil airs, when clearly an untamed vitality lay crouched beneath the hard exterior.

He smiled at her, and suddenly being tired no longer mattered. She was in a room. With him. Alone. *Again.* And not just any room. A *bed*chamber, with a bed clearly made for two, not one.

Complicated was one word that came to mind as she stood there, unable to speak.

His eyes shifted to the bed, and back to her. He took a moderate step forward. "We'll share this room once we're married."

Sara thought her cheeks couldn't flame any deeper. "Surely we shall have separate bed chambers, my lord?"

One dark brow winged upward.

"Proper gentlemen do not wish to share a room with their wives."

"A proper husband would do no less than share a room with his wife," he said, moving closer.

Sara stayed grounded. She'd already behaved like a frightened rabbit in his presence. She wasn't about to let it happen again. "You suggest the execution of your husbandly rights as a frequent happening, my lord."

"Justin." His eyes were like deep pools of murky water, darkening by the second.

"Justin."

"Not a suggestion, Sara, a promise. I plan to bed you whenever I desire, and, allow me to assure you, it will be frequent."

Sara's lips parted. Her face burned. Such lewd words, and spilt so easily! They'd known each other all of twenty-four hours and already he'd made clear where she stood as his betrothed, what his intentions were once they were married.

Right down to their marriage bed.

Sara wasn't completely ignorant on matters of intimacy, or those acts which occurred between a husband and a wife behind closed doors. She'd read plenty and had overheard a few of the local Irish debutants discussing what it was like doing *that* with their husbands.

But not one of those noblewomen was married to a man like Justin. Their husbands were older, over-indulgent Irishmen who enjoyed their whisky and cigars, as well as the beds of their experienced mistresses, and spent more time gloating about property and politics than showing any sort of concern with their wives. Which was just as well when one had married a man merely for his title.

Lord, but this society was atrociously fickle.

In light of those truths of young women marrying older noblemen, Sara had concluded intercourse to be but a dutiful act one must endure in order to produce heirs and keep a content husband.

But Justin, Lord Carrington, was no older nobleman. And Sara wondered what it would be like to be--to welcome him in her bed. If he--if he made love to her. If that's even what men like him did, how could she be certain? He was as gruff as a day laborer, yet refined and devilish as the Devil himself. How could one possibly distinguish between the two when considering such intimacies?

Justin crooked a finger beneath her chin. "I've shocked you."

"A little," she confessed.

"My parents have shared a bed their entire marriage," he explained. "I intend to do the same. Granted, our circumstances are a trifle different."

"We are not in love."

The side of his mouth kicked up a little. "A maudlin sentiment, Kitten."

Her lips formed a thin line at the pet name he'd given her.

"But that's not what I meant. Their closeness has made for a fine dukedom, one that has made the tenants of this land prosperous and content. Their respective desires need but be whispered to either the duke or the duchess, and it is done. My parents work well together, you see. It is a companionship, a union I have every intention of carrying on once the seat is mine."

A true marriage of convenience, Sara thought. Not at all what she had wanted for herself.

Not at all what she imagined a marriage to Patrick Cavanaugh would have been.

If Cav had desired to share her bed, it would have been out of love, not companionship, and most certainly not just because they *worked well* together. He would have taken care of her, loved her. Their eyes would have caught across crowded rooms. He would've held her hand on long walks, adjusted her shawl when the air turned cold, and neither of those *maudlin* sentiments would have been out of duty.

"I am tired, my lord." Plus, thoughts of Cav and Lord Carrington did not mingle so well, one with the other. "I think I should like to lie down for a spell."

He made a gravelly sound in his throat. "Yes, perhaps you should."

As he turned for the door, Sara remembered her inquiry from earlier. "The party," she said, and he came to a halt. "What is the occasion?"

He looked surprised. "Why, to announce our engagement, of course."

SIX

The next morning, Sara found herself sitting quietly at the breakfast table, eating a bowl of eggs and cream, and listening intently as Anna and the duchess chattered about some of the latest fashions to arrive in London.

She had slept well, surprisingly, for all the gloriousness of the room she'd been given at Mayfair House, she'd only half expected to get a good night's rest. But she'd awoken late (Liverpool had been a rare exception), allowed Lana to help her bathe, and together they'd pinned up the mass of long, dark hair that fell to her waist.

Back home, Sara might have picked an ordinary day dress for breakfast. One that could stand a stain or two should she decide to go for a ride or join the servants for a game of Rounders in the pasture.

But not today.

She was in England now, and to be married at that, and so she'd chosen a pale blue muslin gown with white lace trimming, to which she had a lovely matching pelisse. And though she'd rolled her eyes a few times at Lana, for her constant insistence on modesty, she'd allowed for a sheer white fichu to be tucked around the dress's low scoop neckline.

Apparently Sara wasn't the only one who had gotten a decent night's sleep. Anna was in a much better mood this morning. Smiling, laughing. Her blue eyes, the bluest Sara had seen save for her father's, danced as she leaned toward the duchess, absorbed in their latest subject of taffeta versus satin.

"Taffeta is much too stiff," Anna suggested, taking a sip of hot chocolate. "Mmm, and"--she straightened her index finger as if making a vital point--"it makes for a sweaty night of dancing."

"A constraining one as well," the duchess put in, and Anna nodded vigorously. "Although satin does fray easily, should it be stitched incorrectly."

"Ah, but mother, it is so very beautiful." Anna batted her long, darkened lashes, and turned to Sara. "What do you think, Lady Ballivar? Taffeta or satin?"

Sara favored neither, though she did remember having tried on a taffeta gown at the dressmaker's in Dublin.

"Indeed, taffeta is stiff," she said, remembering the way the non-giving material had felt against her skin. Anna smiled. "I myself find muslin suits best."

"Only because you've never worn silk," said Anna. "Or have you?"

"Certainly not." Sara recalled the wide selection of intimate nightgowns the dress shop had for sale, most of which were made of silk.

All of which were designed to enthrall a man's desire.

Anna giggled. "My, Lady Ballivar. I do believe you are blushing. Daring negligees are not the only article of clothing made of silk, you know."

The duchess set her fork down. "Anna," she gently warned, even as Anna crinkled her nose with glee. "Not at the table, please. For that matter, not in civilized conversation altogether."

Though certain the traitorous heat in her face did more than add a bit of color, Sara couldn't help but find Anna positively intriguing. Her hair was the hue of sunshine, her creamy complexion smooth and unblemished, eyes an odd shade of deep, azure blue. And her smile dazzled, just like her mother's.

Just like Justin's.

Bewildering, it was, that a girl as beautiful as Lady Anna should still be unwed. In Ireland, she would have already been bombarded with marriage proposals, each one better than the last.

Anna traced a fingertip over the flowery designs on the tablecloth. "So, do we all know what we're wearing to the party?"

"I think you should wear your light green gown, Anna." The duchess laid a stilling hand atop her daughter's wrist. "That color looks heavenly on you."

Anna's eyes flickered to Sara. "And you, Lady Ballivar?"

"I'm not quite certain," Sara answered truthfully. "I'm afraid I haven't had the time to go through the dresses I brought with me."

"Oh, you could wear one of mine!" Anna said. "I think we are about the same size, don't you, Mother?"

"Hmm." The duchess tilted her head a fraction. "Perhaps the pale blue or the pink one. Or maybe …"

"What kind of hen party is this?" a low voice demanded from the doorway.

The duchess beamed. Anna became preoccupied with the tablecloth once again.

Sara's lips parted, unwillingly.

It was Lord Carrington. That is, Justin. Even in her head his name had a poetic palatability. He stood lopsided in the doorway, fingering the brim of his hat as though he were the resident crofter, waiting to give the duchess his daily report.

His gaze drifted toward her. "Lady Ballivar's just arrived, and already the two of you have drawn her into some sort of female alliance."

"Carrington," the duchess said, standing. "Good morning." Her gaze shifted over his attire: buff breeches, tall boots, tweed jacket with no waistcoat but a gleaming white shirt underneath. "I see you've been riding. Have you eaten?"

"Yes, Mother. Thank you." He strode toward them, lanky strides that covered the distance from door to table in but a few steps. His gaze focused on Sara. "You slept well, I trust?" And, as she nodded her assent: "And the breakfast?" He gestured to the sidebar behind them, filled with a variety of ham, fish, cheeses, eggs and bread. "All good?"

"Delicious," Sara whispered, and instantly clamped her eyes shut for the ridiculous, flippant way that word sounded when spoken in his presence. Really, could she sound any more breathless? "It was fine, my lord." She opened her eyes, her heart screaming inside her chest. "Thank you."

"Perhaps Lady Ballivar would enjoy a morning stroll," the duchess suggested. "The air outside is agreeable, I gather, and if she enjoys horses as much as her father…" Her gaze slipped to Sara, who nodded vigorously. "Then, I think a showing of the stables might be an order."

Justin offered his open palm to Sara. "Would you enjoy that, my lady?"

"Yes, of course." Gracefully as possible given her knees had peculiarly weakened, Sara stood from her chair. "Your Grace. Lady Anna. Have a pleasant morning. And thank you for the intriguing conversation. I found it immensely enjoyable."

"The pleasure was all ours, Lady Ballivar," the duchess responded in kind.

*** *** ***

As the duchess had guessed, the air outside was more than agreeable. Paradise, really. Warm, calm, breezy. The sporadic twitters of songbirds floated like prose through the air, mingled with the smell of wildflowers and something even more welcoming: the good earth.

"Are you cold?" Justin said as Sara buttoned her pelisse.

"Not at all." She reached up to her head. "Oh." Not only had she forgotten gloves, but: "My bonnet. I left it inside."

He reached for her hand, encased it in the warmth of his much larger one. "Leave it." He grinned down at her. "I rather like your hair. Bonnetless, I mean."

He placed her hand on his arm, covering it with his own. "So, tell me, Lady Ballivar…" They began a slow walk down the steps and into the courtyard. "What do you think of our side of Mayfair?"

"I fear I haven't seen enough to make an accurate assumption."

"An easy enough problem to remedy. There are plenty of amiable activities in the city, if you can withstand the fog. There is the opera, of course, and the theater. Plenty of shops, dressmakers and the like, but I am afraid my sister would be the better companion should you choose to indulge in a shopping expedition."

Sara laughed.

"I'm a bit of a lousy cohort when it comes to picking out dresses for a lady," he confessed. "The last time, and final one I might add, that I accompanied my sister and the duchess to the dressmaker ended in Anna throwing a shoe at me, hitting me directly in the head, and screaming for me to leave."

"Goodness!" Sara said on a gasp. "How old were you?"

"Hmm. Thirteen or so, I believe. Old enough to know that if I intended on keeping clear of flying shoes, it would be wise of me to forego any further shopping trips with my mother and sister. Indeed, the whelp it left for a week afterwards solidified that decision." He rubbed his forehead, grinned down at her with that boyish smile of his. The one he must have reserved especially for times like these, walking alone with a lady, enjoying fine air and light conversation.

Sara mirrored the gesture in spite of herself; she'd spent the first half of her bath this morning contemplating an escape plan. Only every idea she'd entertained ended in Father sending her packing right back to England.

She wasn't the greatest escape artist.

"When you smile," he said, "you have a little dimple." He touched a fingertip to her left cheek. "Just there. Ah, and now you are blushing. Forgive me."

Unable to hold back a retort, Sara reached up and thumped the brim of his hat. "Why do you wear this?"

His eyes rolled upward. "My hat?"

Sara nodded.

"It is just a hat."

"It's a silly hat."

He took off the silly hat. "It's just a hat."

"It makes you look like ... like one of our horsemen from the South."

His hair rippled in the gentle breeze, thick locks of dark brown with faint strips of gold here and there. Apparently he spent a vast amount of time in the sun.

He put the hat back on, and instead of doing the proper thing of returning her hand to his arm, threaded his fingers with hers and held her hand, palm to palm, skin to skin.

Oh, most improper! She could hear Lana's chiding little voice as clearly as though she were directly behind her. *No bonnet, no gloves! Your father will not be pleased!*

But she couldn't let go. This felt too good, too wonderful to let go now.

"South Ireland is quite lovely, I hear," he said. "The hat shades my eyes when it's sunny and my head when it's raining. I only wear it while riding. Well, mostly."

"You ride in the rain?"

"You don't?"

"Well, I ..." This was her chance to act offended by the insinuation that she, the properly raised daughter of the Duke of Kilkenny, would even entertain the idea of riding in the rain. Let alone ride in any other manner but side saddle, and only for very short periods of time at that.

Proper young ladies rode in carriages, not on the backs of sweaty beasts.

But she had this ridiculous notion that anything short of honesty with him would make her feel worse than having the most terrible of physical ailments.

And so, with a little tip-tilt of her chin, she said, "Yes, I do. In fact, I like taking long rides, even in the rain, and not side-saddle either. I despise riding side-saddle. A terrible invention, that uncomfortable piece of equipment."

"Terrible." The corners of his mouth twitched.

"Why, on one such occasion, when I was much younger, I set off before dawn and did not return until well past supper."

"Positively scandalous."

"And Lana--that is, Mrs. Brennan--made the excuse that I'd spent the entire day with nuns from the convent, handing out food to the poor. I do not think my father very much believed it, though."

"A little hellion, aren't you?"

Sara stared up at him through narrowed eyes. "Are you making fun of me, Lord Carrington?"

"Not at all." Humor lit his eyes. "On the contrary, my dear, I find you to be a breath of fresh air in contrast to our stuffy English ladies."

"Your sister doesn't seem stuffy."

His smile wavered. "My sister is a woman in a league all her own. One moment I am convinced she is the very modicum of decorum, a marvel to all who would seek to find a lady who is both elegant and poised. Other moments, I could wring her neck for being so ... so ..." He couldn't seem to find the right word.

"She doesn't much like Lord Beaufort," Sara suggested.

Justin shook his head.

"Do you mind my asking why?"

"Long story. The shortened version is that Sebastian was courting the daughter of an earl, who so happened to be one of Anna's dearest friends. He had just asked for her hand in marriage, which she had readily accepted, when she became with child. She confided this information to my sister, my sister told Sebastian, and Sebastian broke off the engagement. We never saw the girl again. Last I hear, she left for the Continent."

"Why, that is awful! No wonder your sister is upset."

"Yes, but Sebastian claims the babe wasn't his. And Anna swears her friend would have never lied to her. As you witnessed yesterday, Sebastian can't so much as toss a friendly jeer at Anna without her blowing the situation out of proportion. If anyone can find a way to get under my sister's skin, it is Lord Beaufort. In fact, the ongoing joke amongst the *ton* is that where Anna and Sebastian are, there is sure to be a fight before the evening concludes."

"That cannot be true." Not from the way Sebastian had concernedly looked on at Anna while Justin chastised her. "There must be some occasions where they are civil to each other."

He scooped up a small rock, joggled it in his palm. Threw it into one of the paddocks. "I'd give them an hour, two at the most, before one or the other finds something to argue about at our engagement party."

They were nearing the stables, a great structure made of wood and stone with gigantic double-doors. Sara could already smell it; that gentle, earthy aroma of horses and hay and fine leather.

"An hour or two, you say?" she asked, and he nodded.

"Possibly less."

"With due respect, my lord, I think you are wrong."

Clearly he hadn't expected that. "Oh, you do, do you?"

He led her inside the doorway, into the freshly raked hall, where red painted stall doors lined either side. A few pairs of large, expressive eyes peeked through the iron bars. "I am surprised you make that assumption so readily, given you know neither very well."

"Yes, but given the magnitude of the occasion, which, I might add, is completely unnecessary since I am certain everyone already knows of our marriage contract, that Lady Anna and Lord Beaufort will put propriety ahead of personal squabbles, and play nicely."

He mulled that over for a few seconds. "I think I should like to make a wager on your presumption," he said, coming to halt in the middle of the hallway.

"A what?"

"A bet, Lady Ballivar. You have made a bet before, have you not?"

Sara stared up at him for a moment. "Well, yes, but ..." Propriety, assertiveness. Where was Lana when she needed her? Sara had little to no sense of either without Lana's constant reminders of who she was, and why she couldn't act like a simpleton. At least not when it mattered. "A lady does not engage in making wagers with gentlemen, my lord."

Lana would be proud.

But that wasn't good enough. "Do not tell me you have gone soft, Lady Ballivar. Your father said you play Rounders with the servants. You expect me to believe you've never made a wager with one or two of the young men in the duke's service?"

She gasped. "You go too far, Lord Carrington."

"Have I?" he said, adding with a smile, "And it's Justin."

"I am not making a bet with you. Especially over something so trifling and silly."

"My dear, when Sebastian and my sister engage in a tiff, it is none-too-trifling. And anything but silly. In fact, the last time it happened, my sister left a permanent hand print on Sebastian's face." At her shocked reaction, he said, "You needn't act surprised. My sister's a spitfire, if ever I did see one."

"Your sister is a respectable lady."

"She's a respectable spitfire."

"Lady," Sara insisted.

"Yes, lady," he conceded. "So, are you certain about the bet? It might prove for a very fascinating evening as opposed to the anticipated awkwardness of all this…" He waved his hand about nimbly. "Betrothal twaddle."

"Twaddle?" she repeated. "I am not too familiar with that word, but if you do mean nonsense or perhaps inconvenience, then I shall be quick to agree with you. This is all, indeed, twaddle-ish."

His sun-kissed brow pulled into a frown. "You really do disagree with our engagement."

"I would not call it an engagement, my lord. That term implies I was properly asked to marry you, proposed to by all accounts, which I was not. I do believe the correct word is indeed *betrothed*, lest we forget why I am truly here."

*** *** ***

For all his intelligence and ability to throw witticism wherever needed, Justin found himself at a complete loss for words.

She was right. They weren't engaged. And if he could bet on whether she'd agree if he did properly ask for her hand, he'd place it all on a decisive *no* coming from that prim little mouth of hers. She felt as if she didn't belong here, he knew, and it amazed him how much that realization rankled.

She was walking along the stalls now, tiptoeing at each one to look inside, and Justin, mistress-less man he soon would be, found himself unable to tear his eyes away from her. Though a few years shy of filling out into the lushness of a woman's body, her delicate curves were more than enough to stir his desire. Every rise to her tiptoes required a little bend-over to peer into the stall, and when she did, ah, but her simple gown clung in all the right places.

He wanted to smooth his hands over those curves, spin her in his arms. Crush his mouth upon hers as he'd done before. When she'd innocently told him, "*Don't.*"

The most wonderful idea came to mind.

"What if, my lady," he said, and almost caught his breath as she wheeled around. God, she was beautiful. "What if we were to make our little bet? What would you ask of me were you to win?"

She blinked at him, all long lashes and striking brown eyes. "I would ask for you to petition His Majesty for a breach of our marriage contract. And that I be returned to Ireland, to my home."

So, she had been thinking about it, although he hadn't expected such a bold request. She had spirit, his betrothed. "That is impossible."

Her lips tightened. What had she expected him to say? Had she thought he'd agree to something so preposterous?

"I knew you wouldn't agree." She whipped her head back around. "There is nothing else I want from you. Nothing you could give me could make up for ..." But she broke off, stared silently into the stall.

Slowly he approached her, though he dared not lay a hand on her. He wasn't in the mood to be slapped. "May I make a suggestion, then? And of course, it would only be to your agreement."

She turned around, glared up at him. "Why is this so important?"

"I'm just trying to lighten the situation."

"Well, you're not doing a very good job."

He curled his fingers around an iron bar beside her head. "You're not making this very easy on me, Sara. I'm trying my best to bridge this gap between us, this vague knowledge we have of each other for which neither of us can be blamed. But I cannot work alone. You must be more cooperative."

She pursed her lips, and his eyes immediately fell to them.

Ah, bloody hell. He wanted to kiss her again.

"What did you have in mind?"

"If you win," he began, willing himself to look back into her eyes, which wasn't any better considering he wanted to kiss those, too. "If you win, then I won't lay another hand on you until we are married."

"You were going to do that anyway," she accused.

"I never said that."

"Yes, you did."

"No, I distinctly said the next time I kissed you, you wouldn't tell me to stop." And just like that, his eyes were on her lips again.

Why, oh why had he made her such an offer? He had surely condemned himself, unable to touch her for the next several months before they were properly wed. Having to see her every single day, while his hands itched and his body ached? Torment.

"All right," she said, and he couldn't rightly say whether that was a good thing. "And if you win? If Lord Beaufort and Lady Anna stick to their normal behavior and have an argument in front of everyone, what then?"

"Then I want a night with you--nay, a full day and night with you."

The slap should've been coming at any moment, followed by an outrage of colorful words, telling him what an outlandish rakehell he was. That he should have never even entertained the idea of her agreeing to so vulgar a proposition.

But she didn't do either of those things.

She raised her chin a little, and said, "You would take my virtue before we were properly wed?"

"I did not say anything about taking your virtue," he murmured. "Think more of me than that, please. I merely want you all to myself for a day."

"And a night."

He nodded, surprised by how nervous he'd become.

She looked down, her dark lashes caressing the hills of rosy cheeks. "If I win, you shall not lay a hand on me," she said, and as he said '*yes,*' she added, "unless I choose it."

It was his turn to be shocked.

There were two things he saw as she gazed up at him, neither of which exactly helped his current situation of trying to keep his hands off her. **One:** She was as innocent as a newborn foal. She'd never been aroused, nor had she felt the warmth of a man's hands or the bliss of being cradled against a male body, intimately. **Two:** She didn't seem the least bit repulsed by him.

And those two things, together, made one perfect number **Three:** He'd be the only one ever to touch her. Hold her. Make love to her until she cried his name. His body would be imprinted on hers for the rest of her life. And his.

The thought made him want to claim her now, take what was rightfully owed him. But she would never trust him, and that he couldn't live with.

Bloody hell.

He stood to be in quite the pickle if she won this little bet he'd concocted. Unless...

He could seduce her. If she was willing to add that bit about being allowed to make the first move, then she was not entirely impervious to being seduced.

"All right, Lady Ballivar," he said. "Shall we shake on it? After all, that is what men would do."

"By all means, if that is what men would do." She stuck out her hand, and he took it, gave it a gentle squeeze that promised more than the confirmation of a mere bet. "We have a deal, Lord Carrington."

"Justin."

She smiled a little wider. "Justin."

SEVEN

Sebastian, Lord Beaufort, wasn't the most comely of English gentlemen. By all accounts, he was the epitome of what society had deemed a bona fide rake, had been since the blooms of adolescence, maybe earlier. He'd earned himself a hell of a reputation, consisting mostly of the seduction of women (young, old, middle-aged, made no difference) and the occasional scandal that traveled faster than a streak of lightning through the inner circle.

That is, the gossip channels of the *ton*. Last he heard he'd been spotted with a Russian heiress, who he'd managed to ruin within a fortnight of their introduction. He almost hated that tittle-tattle wasn't true.

The heiress had sounded rather intriguing.

If not for the good graces of his mother, and of course, the Tethersal family who, with the exception of Anna, treated him as if he were one of their own, he would have long since been banned from the social events of the peerage. His scruples, or lack thereof, had gotten him into more trouble than a penniless kid in a candy store.

He was a gentleman with no principles, a scoundrel with impeccable manners, and every woman to whom he'd ever been introduced, and more than likely some he hadn't, had wanted him in some way or fashion, whether she admitted it or not.

Unprincipled scoundrel that he was, however, Sebastian found himself taken completely by surprise when his dearest companion, his *complice dans le crime* as he'd labeled him, stopped by for a social call with a bit of interesting news.

"You did what?" He leaned forward, glass of whisky in hand.

"I made a bet with her," Justin said for the second time. "Nothing you haven't done yourself, Sebastian. So you can damn well wipe that shocked expression from your face."

Sebastian stiffened his features. Indeed, they were a little overly-expressive at times, an inherent trait from his mother, who in her heyday had arguably been the most beautiful woman in London.

"So, let me see if I've understood correctly. You made a bet with Lady Ballivar that your sister and I will argue at your engagement party this Saturday. Is that it?"

"Well, yes, but she believes the two of you will behave for propriety's sake."

"Propriety's sake," Sebastian echoed. "Honestly, Justin, your sister knows no propriety when in the same room with me."

One of Justin's dark brows shot up. "I could say the same for you."

"She always starts it. Don't look at me like that! It's a fact, and you know it. She damn well hates me."

"She doesn't hate you," Justin offered, though he didn't sound very convincing. "She strongly dislikes you."

Sebastian passed his friend a sardonic glare. "That's hate if ever I did hear the word defined." He took a generous swill of liquor, and set the empty glass on a side table. "So, you want me to get into a squabble with Anna. On purpose."

Justin raked a hand through his dark, thick, quite ordinary hair, while Sebastian rolled his eyes, wishing he had been as blessed. Blond and aggravatingly curly, his was a combination women both loved and hated. For while it was striking to the eye, as golden as a guinea coin, it was the devil to maintain. His valet, who had been with him since Sebastian was a mere lad of five, threatened at least once a day to shave it off.

"Not exactly," came Justin's reply. "I do not wish to be unfair."

"Then, why tell me?"

Justin's head sank into his hands. "I have no idea."

"Forgive me, but I find it oddly offensive that the two of you made a bet at my expense. Especially when said bet clearly perceives me to be an arse with an uncontrollable urge to chastise young ladies in public."

"I was only trying to lighten the situation," Justin said, and Sebastian lifted an eyebrow. "It's not as if Mother's soiree is going to be easy. It's awkward enough being betrothed to someone I don't know without my mother's insistence on announcing it to the free world."

"Ah, but you do want to know her, don't you?"

"Of course, Sebastian. The woman is to be my wife for pity's sake."

"Don't pretend as if you don't know what I meant by that observation. You're attracted to her, and that's something you didn't expect, is it?"

Oh, he was digging deep now. He could tell by the look of pure agitation on Justin's face he'd hit a nerve. Possibly two. He'd spent the past ten years learning what made this brusque friend of his tick, and with the right query, or merely an accurate remark, he could almost guarantee Justin's confession of anything.

"Well?" he said when Justin didn't answer.

"Yes, I'm attracted to her, but what sane man wouldn't be?"

"I must admit," Sebastian said, "she's an extraordinary beauty. But why go to this kind of extreme? Surely you can't be that desperate, resorting to childish antics for the sheer purpose of acquainting yourself with a lady."

Justin eyed him carefully. "She's not just any lady."

"Better. She's your betrothed. What could possibly be easier? I daresay Lady St. Clair's affections were harder to obtain than those of an innocent Irish lass."

"Milly pursued me," Justin reminded him, and Sebastian nodded, remembering all too well how Lady St. Clair had spent nearly every ball and soiree chasing after Justin until he finally gave in. "Besides, Sara is entirely different. She's inexperienced. I don't think she's ever been courted."

"Lucky you."

"And courting a woman isn't exactly my forte."

At this, Sebastian let out a guttural laugh. "The deuce! I can name at least ten--no, fifteen women who have spent an entire evening fanning themselves in a corner because you threw a glance in their direction. Trust me, you're better with women than any man I know." He paused. "Except for, of course, myself."

The corner of Justin's mouth lifted slightly. "And the only exception to that is Anna. You really must practice some self-control around her, Sebastian. While your innocent banter may be humorous to the rest of us, to her it's interminable."

"Only because Lady Alwin filled her head with lies." He closed his eyes, the memory of the one woman he'd almost married entering his mind like an unwelcome houseguest.

As if the action could somehow squeeze her from his thoughts, he curled his hand into a fist, clenched hard. "God, she was poison.

It was foolish of me, proposing to her when I already knew how many men had asked and been rejected. But she craved attention, that one, and far be it for me to have denied her what she wanted."

"She was Anna's friend," Justin murmured. "You remember the night they met at Almack's?"

Lord, did he? Sebastian had waited two hours for his turn to come up on Anna's dance card--a waltz it would've been, damnit all to hell--and who should she meet somewhere in between? The devil's incarnate, Lady Alwin. Needless to say, he'd been forced to forfeit their waltz and find someone else, someone far less agreeable.

The memory still burned.

"I believe they spent the entire evening chattering in a corner somewhere," Justin went on. "Mother was furious. But…" He lifted one shoulder in a careless shrug. "They were inseparable since then. Helene was Anna's dearest companion."

"Helene was no one's companion," Sebastian said darkly. "Anna only thought she had a close friend, when in fact Helene took every opportunity in coddling herself with tasteless gossip at Anna's expense. I cannot account for the times I chided her over the jealousy she had for your sister. But in the end, would Anna listen to me?" He huffed an airless chuckle. "Not likely. She believed that mindless pantaloon-chaser over me."

"She'll get over it someday," Justin offered in consolation, but Sebastian knew better.

To his mind, if Anna still believed he'd impregnated the chit, all to abandon her for his complete lack of decency, then she'd spend the rest of her days reminding him of just that. Of what a lowlife scoundrel he really was. In most instances, she'd be right.

But not this one.

"I don't know," he said. "I can't talk about that subject anymore. I'd rather discuss what you plan on doing if Anna and I wow the duchess's guests by behaving ourselves this weekend."

A *humph* whirred in Justin's throat. "The odds are magnanimously against you. Anna's been in rare form lately."

"Anna's always in rare form," Sebastian said thoughtfully. "I'm beginning to think she seeks me out on purpose, looking to pick a fight over anything that tickles her fancy."

"Perhaps it is the other way around," Justin suggested, and Sebastian gave a snort of laughter.

"Not hardly." He tapered his gaze. "No offense, but Anna's not exactly my type."

"Too feisty?"

"Too innocent."

"Yes, well, for all that she is feisty and loud-spoken, she is indeed innocent." Justin paused, staring unseeingly ahead as Sebastian wracked his brain, trying against all odds to read his thoughts. It was almost as if they weren't talking about Lady Anna anymore.

But Justin's focus restored too quickly. "I suppose I should return." He stood, Sebastian standing with him. "Father's desk is covered in paperwork. God only knows what will happen once …" He broke off, and Sebastian didn't have to ask what he'd meant to say.

"How is he?"

The Duke of Tethersal had been like a second father to Sebastian, offering encouragement and advice when Sebastian's own father had pronounced him worthless. To know the duke was sick, that he probably wouldn't live to see another Christmas, pained Sebastian more than he chose to show.

"The same," Justin replied.

"Tell him I asked about him?"

Justin laid a hand on Sebastian's shoulder. "Of course I will. But you must pay him a visit yourself sometime. He's frail, yes, but his spirit remains, and I know he misses seeing you."

Sebastian nodded. "Perhaps I shall arrive Friday evening. Stay the night, spend the day, attend the duchess's party." He smiled ruefully. "Pick a fight with Anna."

A half-smile curved Justin's wide-set mouth. "There's always a fight to be picked with Anna."

"Indubitably," Sebastian agreed.

*** *** ***

"Oh my, but the green does look lovely, what do you think Tippy?"

Sara blinked at Anna's maid, who, despite having both arms full of discarded dresses, scarves, and trimmings, managed to stop and give Sara a good once-over.

"Lovely," she said, and stooped to pick up a bit of lace she'd missed.

Sara smiled.

But Anna was frowning. "Lovely as in, it will do, or lovely as in, we should try another style? Another color, perhaps? Tippy, you know I require more detail!"

The maid sighed, face red and sweating. She plopped the mass of material on Anna's four-poster bed. "Lovely as in, this is the twelfth dress Lady Ballivar has tried on, and I think we'd do better to just choose one and be happy with it." She paused and offered a deliberately short curtsy. "My lady."

Lana smothered a giggle, and Sara, flattered as she was to be playing dress up with a lady whose wardrobe likely rivaled that of King George himself, couldn't have agreed more. Her skin stung from being pricked with straight pins, her feet ached, and her ribs felt close to cracking against the new style of corset Anna had insisted she try.

Whale bone was not meant for this sort of restraint, Sara decided, though a plumper or taller woman might've strongly disagreed. Seeing as she was neither, the corset would have to go.

"I do think this one is my favorite," Sara said, and Anna eyed her carefully. "Really!" She looked down at herself, smoothed her hands over the layers of sheer muslin. "It's lovely."

"Perhaps a bit more lace at the neckline," Anna said, and Lana, pin cushion in hand, took that as her cue to step forward.

"No!"

Lana came to a halt, along with Tippy, who had a handful of white lace ready to be tucked and pinned into the bodice of the mint green gown.

Anna's eyes rounded.

"That is ..." Sara held a hand to her chest. No more pins were going there. "I believe the dress is perfect as it is. Less is more, is it not?"

A slow grin grew upon Anna's dollish face. "I think we are going to become great friends, Lady Ballivar."

Sara felt her limbs relax, and she had to smother the sigh of relief lingering in her throat. Her ribcage could thank her later.

"Fashion is most enjoyable when one has a companion with whom one can share it."

Sara, vowing to give her feet a good soaking before bed, stepped down from the little stool she'd been perched upon for the past two hours and allowed Lana to begin unbuttoning her dress. "The corset too," she whispered, and Lana nodded her understanding. Her hands worked quickly to unlace the dreadful thing, and Sara, feeling her lungs contract, let out a slow, reprieving exhale.

"Thank you, Lana," she murmured. "You were saying, Lady Anna? About having a companion with whom to share fashion? Surely you have a great many ladies eager to assist you in that arena."

"I did, once. But that was over a year ago, and she's moved to France, or so I've heard." Anna frowned, as if a sudden, dreadful memory had come to mind. "She hasn't even written me. Not one letter, and I was her best friend."

"I'm sorry." It was all Sara could think to say. "Had you known each other terribly long?"

"A year, perhaps," said Anna, "but we were close, she and I. Ah, but she was a slave to fashion, Lady Alwin. The most exquisitely dressed lady you can imagine."

"What happened to her?"

"Lord Beaufort." A muscle ticked in Anna's jaw. "Insipid scandal follows him wherever he goes. They were engaged, you see, he and Lady Alwin. But she became ... Well. In the end, he cast her out with no more remorse than he would the silk cravat tied 'round his neck."

"Lady Alwin was ..." Sara paused, choosing her words carefully. She knew this story, or at least Justin's version of it, though she was certain Anna's would prove to be very different. "With child?" she finished, and Anna gave a short nod.

Lana helped Sara step in to a muslin day gown the color of damask rose, and quietly expressed her disagreement when Sara refused another corset.

"It is not proper in this country, my lady," Lana whispered, making quick work of buttoning Sara's dress. "If Lord Carrington should want to see you this afternoon …"

"Lord Carrington is visiting Lord Beaufort," Sara said tentatively. "Do not be such a prig, Lana, honestly. My breasts cannot possibly take any more incessant pushing today."

"Prudence, my lady," said Lana, far under her breath as possible.

"Perhaps it was not his child at all," Sara offered.

My goodness, had she just championed Lord Beaufort? Never mind the look of irreparable shock on Anna's face, nor the second gasp she'd managed to pull from Lana, but had she actually just admitted her disbelief in Anna's side of this--what was it she had called it? *Insipid scandal*?

"It was," Anna stated firmly. "Wanton woman she was, for I daresay any woman finds grave difficulty in resisting the charms of a man like Sebastian, a liar she was not."

"Forgive me," Sara found herself saying, although she wasn't sure why. There was never any proof in scandals such as this.

But no good could possibly come out of arguing with the sister of her betrothed, so in an attempt to change the subject: "Speaking of being intended, have you a gentleman of your own?"

This elicited a burst of bubbly laughter, followed by a, "Of course not! I mean, obviously I have had quite a few offers--some memorable, some not--but no gentleman has come even close to meeting my standards."

"Standards? What sorts of standards? Ah, you mean he must be handsome."

"Naturally," Anna said. "Although, I think I could settle for a man with only a moderate amount of handsomeness if he were intelligent and witty, kind without any of those quirky habits that kind men possess. And let's see ... oh yes! He must, without a doubt, have an exquisite learnedness in poetry."

She fluttered her slender fingers in the air. "And none of that boring old prose every gentleman recites to a lady these days. Oh no, I want original material. The kind that makes me--"she pressed the back of her hand to her brow "--weak in the knees."

Sara giggled, and Anna joined in, wrinkling her nose as she seemed to do when something had amused her to laughter. "Seems as if you seek the perfect man, which I am afraid does not exist. At least, not in my experience."

Anna responded with a shrug. "As well he may not, but I shall not lose hope all the same." She cast a curious glance at Sara from under her lashes. "In your experience, you say? As in, you've been proposed to before?"

Sara hesitated. "I ... no, I ..." Palms suddenly sweaty, she smoothed her hands over her gown and looked to Lana, who had stopped in aiding Anna's maid with the discarded dresses and was now staring at Sara, wide-eyed and visibly nervous.

Slowly, surreptitiously, Lana shook her head.

But Anna was quicker. "Come now, Lady Ballivar--may I call you Sara? Splendid. There must have been at least one gentleman, one man who tickled your fancy. Surely you haven't spent the hours pining for my brother. I admit he is quite a catch, but to spend one's life yearning for him?"

"A catch, am I?" Justin's deep baritone breeched through their conversation. One of his large hands came to his chest. "Why Anna, I never knew you thought so highly of me."

Anna's eyes narrowed to her doorway. "Don't you knock?"

"The door was half-open." He strode inside, his gaze falling on Sara. The room shrunk around him, he was so tall.

Sara licked her lips. Blushed.

He swept a bow. "Lady Ballivar."

Sara managed a curtsy. How much had he heard? Did he suspect her? Did it even matter now? They were to be married, after all. Past suitors or none.

Still, if he had overheard Anna's inclination that a man had once--oh, but the word was ridiculously improper--*tickled* her fancy, he might be drawing the wrong conclusion.

Amazing, it was, and a bit disconcerting, that she didn't want him to draw the wrong conclusion. Why should she care?

His eyes slid in humble regard to Lana and Tippy, who, upon recovering from the initial shock of his presence, had continued in the task of hanging Anna's dresses. "I see the two of you have been playing dress-up this afternoon. All in anticipation of the party, I gather?"

"Yes, obviously, Justin," Anna said, not bothering to hide her irritation. "And in future, if my door is half-open as you say it was,

I insist you knock anyway. Brother or no, it is unacceptable for you to show any less respect to me as a lady."

He bowed again. "Forgive me, dear sister, for intruding upon your privacy. But I only came to see if Lady Ballivar could spare a few moments of her time."

Anna raised her chin indignantly. "Actually we were in the middle of--"

"--finishing," Sara quickly put in.

Anna shot her a look of surprise.

*** *** ***

Sara caught her lower lip between her teeth.

Justin smiled, fascinated. No one ever put his sister on hold. In fact, most women would have given their right hand to spend time with Anna like this, gleaning in her sense of style. But not his betrothed. Nay, his duchess-to-be.

Ah, but he did like the sound of that.

His duchess-to-be favored him a warm smile. "I have several moments to spare, my lord. Shall we take a walk? Evening has not yet fallen."

"Indeed." He proffered his arm. "Perhaps you'd like to see the rose garden?"

Nodding and slipping her hand into the crook of his elbow, Sara turned to Anna. "I had a wonderful time this afternoon, Anna. Truly, I do look forward to wearing the dress we chose."

Despite her clear aggravation, Anna smiled. "As did I, Sara, and you must promise that we shall ready ourselves for the party together."

"Most assuredly." Sara allowed Justin to extract her from the room. "Did you enjoy your day with Lord Beaufort?"

Not half as much as I'm enjoying this right now. "I did, thank you, and you? Was my sister's company appalling or acceptable? You can tell me, you know. I promise I can keep a secret."

Her mouth twisted a little. "Actually, I do enjoy your sister's company. She's a free spirit, and that's admirable considering the restraint with which most women conduct themselves." She sighed delicately. "I am a bit tired. Heavens, but Anna does have so many dresses! Why, I'd venture to assume she hasn't worn any of them twice."

"Not often."

"And they are all lovely. Just lovely. How fortunate that we are almost exactly the same size, she and I."

"That is indeed fortunate, but if you are in need of dresses, I should like to take you to the dressmaker's in London."

Her eyes glimmered in a way that made him feel all willy-nilly inside. As if he could spend the rest of his days offering her anything she wanted, if only to have her smile at him like that.

"How kind of you, my lord," she murmured. "I do believe I would like a few new additions to my wardrobe. A gown or two from London should add a colorful contrast to the ones I have from Dublin."

"That, they would," he agreed. "I shall make the arrangements as soon as possible."

A sprightly grin tipped the side of her mouth. "I thought you despised going to the dressmaker's."

He smothered the urge to laugh. "Are you planning on throwing shoes at me if I accompany you?"

"Probably not. That is, if you are in good behavior."

"And if I am disagreeable?" he challenged as they strolled the narrow walkway that wound through his mother's voluminous rose garden.

Dainty nose upturned, eyes regarding him mischievously from the side, tone hinting nothing short of sheer conviction, she said, "Then I shall throw shoes at you."

Smothering amusement was entirely futile at that point. Justin laughed with a lightheartedness he'd not experienced in months. Years, maybe. Father had been terribly sick, and dukedom was too serious a matter to spare even a moment's worth of joy, let alone allowing oneself to indulge in the gaiety of laughter.

But laugh, he did, until wiping an escaped tear from his eye, he heard a frightful gasp elicit sharply from Sara's throat.

"You're hurt!" She grabbed for his hand. "Cut! What happened?"

It took a moment to register what the sudden fit of distress was all about, although admittedly, it was quite nice having his duchess-to-be fussing over him like a bantam hen. But as he looked down at his hand, which was being traced and stroked by none other than her delicate little fingers, he noticed he was indeed cut.

"I don't know," he answered truthfully, discomfited by the deliberate slowness in which she was stroking the wound with the very tip of her finger.

A breeze carrying the mild scent of rain wafted past them, rustled the ringlets falling from her hairpins, mixed the air with lavender and vanilla.

"It appears, Lord Carrington, you have come in contact with a thorn bush of some sort, perhaps a vine." The words echoed in a concerned whisper as she used her thumb to swab away a droplet of blood.

Justin swallowed. And before he even knew what he was about ...

"The cut is clean, which means that--"

His mouth drifted over hers, capturing her gasp of surprise. Her lips were warm, feathery light, and not at all unwelcome. In fact, he could probably deepen the kiss and she'd--wait, what was he thinking? She didn't want this. That, she'd made perfectly clear.

"Apologies," he said, pulling his lips from hers.

Something lingered between them, or was it just his imagination? *Bollocks.* Nothing was aligning in his mind. Wouldn't for the way she was staring up at him now, all round eyes and parted lips. She was probably thinking about slapping him, not that he didn't deserve it. He had promised her, after all.

But then a cool hand slid round his neck. In the next instant, those warm lips were pressed against his. *Again.*

Pleasure spurred through his loins, burned through his chest and down his legs. She was small, yet extraordinarily curvy in her smallness, and that discovery was reiterated a hundred times over when those small curves molded timidly, but oh-so-finely, to his body.

He pressed his hands to her back, brought her closer against the natural curve of his own body, and she answered him, tightening her slender arms around his neck. She was kissing him fully now, wanting more than a woman her age knew how to give, and the annoying voice in the inner recesses of his mind told him to hold back. To take it slow. To stop, lest she accuse him afterwards of taking advantage.

But she was his, he reasoned. His betrothed, his duchess-to-be. She belonged to him: red lips swollen with his kisses, small curves, ample breasts crushed against his own chest.

Mine, he thought. *Mine. Mine. Mine.*

Ah, to hell with it.

Giving no more thought to reverence, he took possession of her lips with a ruthlessness becoming no less than that of a wild man. She opened her mouth, likely to protest his sudden whim of ferocity, but he couldn't help himself. Instinct had already taken over, thrown propriety to a strong east wind--perhaps a west one, he thought dimly--and with sheer boldness, his tongue swept inside her mouth.

She trembled against him, clearly not knowing what to do, or how to respond. Her arms were still tightly wound about his neck, but whether from mutual desire or fear on her part, he could not tell. No one had kissed her like this. No one had taught Sara how fine kissing between a man and a woman can be, how utterly stimulating, and he was glad of it.

"Justin," she whispered into his mouth.

Ah, but the way she said his name. That beautiful, musical, brogue drawl that made his heart beat a rapid tattoo.

"Yes, Kitten?" He slowed down. Brushed his lips lightly over hers. "You want me to stop?"

She nodded, but kissed him again. If they didn't stop soon, he was liable to carry her to that stone bench over there beneath his mother's peach tree.

Then he'd surely get slapped, beaten, kicked.

Have shoes thrown at him.

He broke the kiss, could've sworn he heard a tiny protesting moan flutter in the back of her throat. His betrothed liked kissing. There was no mistaking the color in her cheeks, that rose-stained hue he'd seen only in watercolors. And by God, if her lips weren't the most beautiful shade of crimson. He'd bet his entire fortune the ripest pomegranate wasn't nearly so lovely.

He touched a finger to those lips. She stared up at him, eyes bright as a summer's day, gleaming like sunlight against rain clouds gathering in the sky.

"We should head back." He retrieved his finger. Touching her was intoxicating. "Rain's coming."

EIGHT

"How does it look?"

The duchess paused. "Too much lace," she declared, and Anna sighed. "You do not want too much up there, darling. You are still unwed, after all."

"If I am to meet a husband, I seriously doubt it will be at my brother's engagement party, Mother. Besides." Anna gazed pensively into the full mirror, cocked her head to the side. "I think the lace adds a nice touch. Father will be pleased. That my bosom is covered, I mean."

"Your father would that you never married, Anna, and that is not pragmatic."

She met her mother's gaze through the glass. "Then my pragmatism matches my father's. The lace stays."

Lips pinched into a thin line, the duchess stepped forward, seized the lace fichu, and, in one swift movement, yanked it free.

Anna slapped a hand over her high white breasts. "Mother!"

The duchess arched a fine brow. "The lace goes. Now, finish quickly, Anna." She moved to the window, her heavy blue satin skirts rustling. "My entire list of guests have almost all arrived, and yet you dilly-dally."

Willing herself to remain calm, Anna inhaled and began fussing with the neckline of her pale pink silk gown. "Did you invite the Duke and Duchess of Leeds?" she asked conversationally, tucking a stray thread at her shoulder.

"Naturally," the duchess said. "And the Earl and Countess of Kensington, the Duke and Duchess of Worcester and their son--"

"Sebastian?" Anna said on a gasp.

The duchess turned halfway. "Did you think I wouldn't invite him? He is your brother's closest friend, Anna, and you know how your father feels about him, as do I. Besides, you can put away your childish antics with Lord Beaufort for one night at the expense of your brother's happiness."

"His happiness?" Anna snorted. "Mother, he's been betrothed to a stranger since he was ... what? Ten?"

The duchess folded her hands in front of her. "Twelve."

"Yes. And while I like Sara, I most certainly won't delude myself by believing she and my brother are a love match."

She paused to fluff the short sleeves of her dress. "I often wonder how much champagne father and Kilkenny had that night. Betrothing two perfect strangers. Positively medieval, if you ask me."

"Medieval, maybe." The duchess crossed the room, brushed a piece of lint from the back of Anna's bodice. "Your brother does seem to like her, though," she murmured. "And she, him. It is a start, at least."

"I suppose. At least they'll have half a chance tonight without the cankerous nuisance that is Millicent St. Clair."

The duchess did not respond.

Anna whirled on her. "Please tell me you did not invite Milly."

The duchess raised her chin. "Lady St. Clair," she said. "And yes, I did invite her."

"Justin's mistress? What about Sara? She doesn't--" Anna pressed a hand to her brow. "Oh, this is going to be a catastrophe. Perfect, Mother. You've managed to add *creator-of-disaster* to your repertoire."

The duchess's lips thinned. "Foremost, you will not speak to me that way. Furthermore, Lady Ballivar need never know of your brother's indiscretions with Lady St. Clair. Besides, I do believe Justin has a mind to end the affair. He's well aware unfaithfulness will not be tolerated in this household."

"You think Lady St. Clair gives a fig about what is and isn't tolerated in this household?"

"It matters not," the duchess replied. "The duke has stated he will no longer abide her, and his word is enough for me, as it should be for you."

"I have always respected Father's opinion," Anna said automatically.

"Good. Then it should come as no surprise that it was your father's idea to invite Lady St. Clair. He feels that by seeing the truth, the reality if you will, of your brother's engagement to another woman, then the problem, the *cankerous nuisance that is Millicent St. Clair*, as you so interestingly put it, shall fix itself."

"One could hope."

"Then we shall dare to hope, my dear." She continued to run her hands over Anna's skirts. "I, too, have grown weary of her. She doesn't belong here, and she doesn't love your brother."

"She loves his youth and vitality."

"Two characteristics which will make him a fine duke," the duchess said, then softly, regrettably added, "and all too soon, I fear."

Anna placed a hand on her mother's slender shoulder. "Mother, do not trouble yourself with these thoughts tonight." She put on a wistful smile, one which never failed to make her mother smile, too. "Tonight is about Justin and the woman he is to marry, and we must, for his sake, be on our best behavior. Just for tonight, we mustn't worry ourselves with Father's frail condition."

The duchess looped her arm inside Anna's. "Too right you are, dear heart. Now, be a darling and accompany me downstairs. The musicians have begun, and I am certain I've just heard a contredanse calling your name."

"Now *that* sounds delightful." Anna grabbed a light scarf, and proceeded with her mother to the party downstairs. But not before contritely adding, "I still don't understand why you had to invite her."

*** *** ***

Meanwhile, Justin waited in the ballroom, wondering that very same thing.

He stood near the orchestra, flanked by his father, who was managing his strength surprisingly well tonight, and Sebastian, who was filling them in on his father's progress with the steam engines up North. Sebastian was droning on about Duke Worcester's current project of connecting some small town to some equally small town when Justin caught sight of her.

Prim as she ever was, blond hair twisted tightly atop her head, white gown revealing an overflowing, voluptuous bosom that would give any man the urge to howl like a damned wolf, Lady St. Clair had managed to comfortably wedge herself between two gentlemen. Both of whom were fawning over her as if she were a French delicacy.

Her gloved fingers were wrapped around the stem of a champagne flute, which was already half-empty. Soon she'd coo for one of the idiots to fetch another. And another. And another. Until she was inebriated into a fit of giggles and fluttering lashes. After which she'd whisper shameless endearments into their ears and proceed to allow one or both of them to escort her from the room.

He knew this woman too well. What in God's name had his mother been thinking to invite her? This was his engagement party, was it not?

"Carrington, are you listening to me?"

"Yes, Beaufort," Justin murmured. "You were telling me about the new railroad in Durham."

"Middlesbrough," Sebastian said.

"Sounds like a sizeable project." The Duke of Tethersal, having been silent for the past several minutes, gave Sebastian a healthy pat on the back.

"Indeed, Your Grace," said Sebastian. "In fact, my father confided just this morning that it will take twice as long, if not longer, to complete. Workers are scarce, you see, and we've had to nearly double our wage offer in order to obtain the number needed to finish the job. Damnable thieves, all of them. No one wants to work these days."

Justin snorted. "Come now, Beaufort. You've never worked a day in your life, let alone acquired a position in which you can accurately judge a person by what they will and will not accept as amicable pay. I daresay you've never tied your own cravat."

"I most certainly have!" Sebastian laid a hand on his flawless neck cloth. "Besides, why do something yourself when you pay servants to do it for you?"

"And if you didn't have your servants?" Justin turned out an open palm. "What then?"

Sebastian hesitated. "Well, I hadn't given it much thought. In any case, that has nothing to do with our plans for Middlesbrough. Unless of course we plan to teach the railroad crew how to properly tie a cravat."

The duke chuckled, eyes alighting as he regarded Sebastian with gentle amusement. Where Justin was serious and determined, Sebastian was lighthearted and indecisive. Which, by the laws of nature, should have kept them at odds, rather than in brotherly company, as they were. But the duke loved them, each for his own unique qualities.

"Who else is in on it?" asked Justin, attempting to keep interest, though he found the effort rather difficult for two reasons: he wholly disliked discussing railroads and steam engines, and he still wasn't certain why his mother had invited Milly.

"Gage Kinsey, for one," Sebastian said. "And Sir Dunmore of Galway. In fact, his son is due to arrive tomorrow, and just in time for Mother's house party, so we can--good heavens, Carrington, have you retained anything I've said? Anything at all?"

"No, he is too occupied wondering why Millicent St. Clair was invited tonight," the duke said.

Justin's stomach plummeted. But seeing as there was no use in arguing, for the duke was as sharp as--nay, *sharper* than--any two-edged sword, he said, "Indeed, Father. Why was she invited? Or does Mother keep her guest list all to herself now?"

"Hmm. Lady St. Clair receives an invitation to a party ..." Sebastian rubbed his chin. "But not just any party, a Mayfair House party, where doubtless she shall rub elbows with Lord Carrington--ah, that is you, my lord--although she hasn't the slightest inclination said party is in honor of that esteemed lord's recent engagement to a one Lady Ballivar of Dublin."

His eyes rolled to meet those of an amused Duke of Tethersal. "Am I getting warm, Your Grace?"

The duke's lips twitched. "That would be the general idea, my dear boy. You are quite correct."

"Allow me to see if I've understood correctly," said Justin. "Mother invited Milly, yet she knows nothing of the occasion?" And at his father's nod, "Wouldn't it have been better if I had spoken to Milly first, rather than have her humiliated?"

"Humiliated?" the duke repeated, and Sebastian's expression soured. "Why in seven hells would you be worried for the humiliation of your mistress? On the contrary, Carrington, I would think your concerns would be more for Lady Ballivar, as she knows nothing of Lady St. Clair."

"This has nothing to do with her, Father."

"It has everything to do with her!" The duke's face flushed crimson. "And the trouble that woman could cause should you allow it."

Now Justin was equally angry. "Well, I will not allow *that woman* to be humiliated. I've vowed to end the relationship, and I intend on keeping my word, but I owe Milly this much, to at least tell her myself. Before she hears it from someone else."

"If she hasn't already," Sebastian put in, but Justin was already making his way across the room.

*** *** ***

"Sara!"

Sara turned and smiled as Justin's sister approached. "Lady Anna." She leaned forward as Anna took her hands and pressed a fleeting kiss to her cheek. "I was worried you wouldn't make it."

"Costume complications. Apparently the duchess believes I should be dressing to catch a husband," she said, looking around. "As if I could find anything worthwhile amongst these snooty aristocrats."

Sara looked around, too. "Oh, I don't know. There seems to be plenty of handsome, available-looking men present. Surely not all of them are snooty aristocrats?"

"Trust me." Anna's eyes stopped on a particular spot across the room. "They all are."

Sara followed her gaze, swallowed a gasp.

She was looking at Sebastian.

"Lord Beaufort?" she said, but Anna did not answer. "Your family seems to think rather highly of him. In fact, I believe the duchess received an invitation from his mother just this morning."

"The Duchess of Worcester's annual house party." Anna sighed. "She throws but one party every year. One highly private, highly indulgent gathering, as she likes to call it, and invites only her closest friends." She shrugged, still carefully eyeing Sebastian, who appeared to be in deep conversation with Anna's father. "Mother won't go, but it is expected of me and Justin."

Remembering what Justin had said about Anna's and Sebastian's inability to maintain decorum when forced into close proximity, Sara said, "Will that not put a strain on the duchess's party? Having her son and yourself in such ... tight quarters?"

Anna let out a peal of laughter. "Quite the opposite, Lady Ballivar. Worcester Hall is grand, you see. Lord Beaufort and I will have no trouble in avoiding each other's company. Besides …" She shifted her gaze again to Sebastian. "The men engage in manly things during the day--hunting, fishing, sporting--while we women sit around talking and having tea."

Boring and even more boring. By the look on Anna's face, she didn't seem too enthused either.

"Lord Carrington," Sara said, "what sport does he fancy?"

"My brother is one of those men who excels at everything. Cricket, fencing, fox hunting, fly-fishing. But archery is his forte. There's not a gentleman in England who can out-shoot him."

"Ah." So he was a master of sporting, her betrothed. Not that she would've thought differently, well built as he was. "Archery takes a strong arm and a steady hand."

Anna's brow shot upward. "Noticed my brother's arms and hands, have you?"

"No, that's not it at all, I …"

"Oh, come now, Lady Ballivar. My brother vexes me to no-end at times, but even I can admit he is adequately handsome."

Sara couldn't respond. In truth, she had noticed his hands and his arms and his thighs and really more parts than she was willing to admit to herself, much less out loud. Modesty said she shouldn't look upon her future husband in this manner, but then how could she help it?

"In any case," Anna continued as Sara scanned the room, "our two week stay at Her Grace's humble abode will begin tomorrow. Tippy and your Mrs. Brennan are almost certainly packing our things as we speak." She paused. "Lady Ballivar? Who are you--ah, have you not encountered the other guest of honor this evening? Let's see."

Face after face, Sara searched through the duchess's guests, some of whom were socializing, some of whom were dancing to the current quadrille being played by the orchestra. The Duchess of Tethersal acknowledged her with a nod from across the room, as did the duke, with a raise of his champagne glass.

"Ah. There." Anna pointed to a pair of French doors. "But it appears as though he is currently detained."

Sara narrowed her eyes. "Who is that to whom he speaks?"

The blond woman before him tossed her head back in laughter, one of her gloved hands resting lightly on Justin's chest while the other clung to a glass of champagne. Her breasts, plump, voluptuous things, strained against the tight bodice of her white gown.

Anna inhaled dramatically. "*That* is Lady St. Clair, the Dowager Countess of Middleton."

"He appears to know her," Sara murmured, attempting to get a closer look. The blond tilted her head to the side, her sumptuous mouth forming a childish pout. "Is she a friend of the family?"

"Absolutely not."

"An enemy?"

"To me, she is. To everyone who isn't Justin or Sebastian, she is."

Sara wanted to ask why she'd been invited if no one liked her, save Justin and Sebastian, the latter being no surprise. But then something strange happened. Justin grabbed the lady by the arm, opened one of the doors, and proceeded to usher her from the room, slamming the door behind him.

"Oh dear," Anna muttered. "Detainment turned sour, I daresay."

"What do you suppose?" Sara stood tiptoe in effort to see over a particularly large man's head.

"Hopefully ushering her off the property." Anna pointed across the crowd. "Those doors lead to a small courtyard which houses the duchess's bird bath, and beyond that is an exit. I would not put it past Justin to--Sara where are you going?"

"I shan't be long," Sara said from over her shoulder, headed for the French doors.

"Not a good idea!" she heard Anna call, but she was already weaving her way through the crowd.

*** *** ***

"I'll ask you one more time to leave," Justin said. The ferocity in his voice surprised him. He'd never spoken harshly to Milly. Never had to. But she wasn't exactly being cooperative either.

Milly thrust out her small chin. "And if I don't?"

"Then you'll leave me no choice but to escort you off this property. By force, if necessary."

She laughed. "My lord, why do you not find this as funny as I? You're engaged, not imprisoned. Yet you act as if the whole world had turned to fodder because your father suddenly decided to honor your betrothal. To, I might add, a scant of a girl whose only solid attribute is that she is the daughter of Ireland's last decent noblemen."

"This is no act, Milly. I meant what I said."

"You intend on ending our affair," she said, repeating what he'd told her inside. After he'd informed her that she was in attendance of his engagement party, not another one of his mother's soirees.

She hadn't responded immediately, though he could see in her eyes she was shocked. Shocked, appalled, a bit angry perhaps. All of which she'd replaced with a few giggles and waves of her hand, as was her way when backed into a corner. He'd mentioned his betrothal only once during their affair, and she'd shrugged it off as if he'd told her the circus had come to town.

Why he expected this time to be any different, he couldn't say.

He traced a finger along the rim of the bird bath, centered in the midst of the small courtyard. "I will not be unfaithful," he said. "So, yes, the affair must come to an end."

"And what if I don't want it to end?"

Unbelievable, the nerve of this woman. "I don't see how you have a choice in the matter." He added just enough mockery in his tone to make her eyes widen. "You knew this couldn't last forever, yet you fight for it. Even as I've informed you of my engagement and no longer require your services."

Her lips pinched, nostrils flared. She drew closer, coming to stand just before him. "You expect that girl in there"--she stabbed a finger toward the closed French doors--"to replace what only I can give you? Are you so dense, my lord, you would think a mere child could attend to a man's needs--and God only knows how very demanding yours are--as well as a woman of experience?"

"My needs," he said, "will be satisfied by my wife, or no one." He favored her an amused half-smile. "Why is that so incomprehensible for you?"

"Because no man does that. Not any normal man, anyway. It's absurd. It's ridiculous, unheard of. It's ..."

"The choice I have made," he said. "And it is not as if you cannot find another protector, Milly. There are a dozen or more innocent souls just inside who would give their right hand to make you a kept woman."

"Spare me your charity."

"I do not offer charity. On the contrary, I am attempting to paint a bigger picture here, for all you seem hell-bent on looking past it."

"I'm not looking past anything, Carrington. I see what this is."

He paused. "Oh, you do, do you?"

"Quite." She splayed a hand on his chest, just over his heart. A devious smile lurked around one corner of her mouth. "'Tis all right, really. You do know I love playing these sorts of games. Especially with you."

"Milly," Justin warned. "Don't."

"Oh, what shall we call this one?" She tapped a finger to her mouth, turned her painted green eyes up toward the night sky. "Something clever."

"How about, 'I'm engaged, our affair is over, and you shall to take your leave with dignity?'"

"How about," she said, ignoring him, "'you're a nobleman, trapped in an unsightly marriage, and I'm the toast of the *ton*, desired by all men, but most of all by you, who find the urge to bed me most irresistible because you hate your wife.'"

"Enough, Milly."

"'On a whim of sheer--oh, what shall we call it? Ah yes! Animalistic instinct! You approach me, grab my arm, haul me to your bedroom ...'"

"I said, enough, Milly!" He grabbed her by both arms, just below where her short sleeves ended and her long, white gloves began.

What happened next was a blur.

Defiantly, Milly had tiptoed and pushed her lips against his. Adding to that defiance, he'd allowed her to do it. His hands were still curled around her upper arms, but they weren't trying to thwart her. Yet, he couldn't bring himself to hold her. She felt foreign, yet all too familiar.

Old habits die hard.

Suddenly, a sharp gasp pierced through the darkness, followed by a small cry coming from the direction of the doors, which led back to the party in honor of him and his ...

Betrothed.

Sara.

She stood just outside the door, eyes wide in her pretty face, hand resting on her heaving breast, looking ever the innocent, as he stood there motionless. Motionless with his ex-mistress beneath him, his hands on her arms, lips wet with her kisses.

Bloody hell.

"Sara." Her name caught in his throat, followed by an exhale that if spoken might've said, *It's not what it looks like*. But for whatever reason he couldn't get past saying her name.

Guilt washed over him, and he shoved Milly backward, causing her to bump into the bird bath with a shriek. He stalked toward Sara, but she shook her head, backing away with every step he took. Her lips trembled, the hand she had at her breast shook, and she was beautiful.

How could he have let this happen?

"Sara, don't." He quickened his steps as she quickened hers. "Sara!"

She jerked open a French door, and rushed inside.

And, damn him, he followed. A cacophony of strings, wind instruments, laughter and raised voices assaulted his ears. He looked left and right. Left again. Scanned the room to no avail, because she was nowhere in sight.

She might've left entirely, he reasoned. Ran straight for her room where she could lock the door and fling herself on her bed. Cry until exhaustion sank in. Because that's what innocent young girls do in situations such as these, right?

But not Sara.

She was standing on one side of the dancing area, looking onto the other side. Sheer terror spread across her soft features.

Instinctively, Justin followed her gaze, all to find the reasons for her apparent state of shock.

Sebastian and Anna. Fighting like a couple of Tories over nonconformists or divine rights or some such nonsense. Sebastian with his hands balled into fists at his sides, Anna with hers flailing about. As if she couldn't possibly express herself without the use of her hands, at least not where Sebastian was concerned. Thank goodness, no one could hear them above the frivolity.

Sara turned, and her fiery gaze held Justin's for but a second before she picked up her skirts and stormed from the party, leaving nearly the entire lot of his mother's guests staring after her.

"Christ," he muttered. He'd made a fowl mess out of things and in record time. She'd been in England for all of a week and already she hated him. Could he blame her? Hell, he half hated himself right now.

To crown the whole, she'd lost their bet.

He frowned at the sight of his sister and Sebastian. No one was making any effort to stop them, naturally, as no one ever did. Their bickering at social events had become more of an interlude now than a shock factor, it was so common.

Forcing himself to suppress the ordeal with Sara, Justin made for the side opposite, murmuring his apologies when he bumped into several guests engaged in the current contra.

He hadn't danced with Sara tonight, which was neither here nor there, considering he'd managed to win her hatred within seconds. But he would've liked to have tried a contra. Perhaps even a waltz, if she favored being that close to him. Closeness hadn't seemed disagreeable a few days ago, when they'd kissed in the rose garden.

When she'd molded into him like clay on a pottery wheel.

But, alas, that was before he'd allowed Milly to kiss him.

He was such an idiot.

"Brother!" Anna said, as Justin approached. "I am so pleased you're here. Would you be so kind as to inform your friend--" here, she cut her eyes at Sebastian, lip curled with disgust "--or whatever he is, that he has no right to tell me what I can and cannot wear in my own home?"

Sebastian's pale blue eyes narrowed into mere slits. "I shall tell you whatever I damn well please." He gestured to her bodice. "That neckline is too low for a girl your age."

"I am no girl!"

"Enough!" Justin said, and Anna's mouth clamped shut. "Out of here, into the rose parlor." He pointed in that direction. "Now."

Sebastian didn't waste a moment's time. Muttering beneath his breath, he pushed his way through the crowd, not bothering with so much as a sideways glance when the Justin's father attempted to get his attention.

The duke cast an exasperated scowl in Justin's direction. Beside him, the duchess fanned herself briskly, as though at any moment she might faint.

Anna's face was red. "I will not stand here and be humiliated like I'm naught but a--"

"Now," Justin reiterated.

"Fine." Anna spun around, wended her way through the crowd, pink satin rustling with every step she took.

Exhausted, Justin dragged in a deep breath, and started after her, finding it dejectedly fascinating how he'd acquired the hatred of three women all in one night.

Surely, this had to be a record.

NINE

Sara stared out the window of her bedroom for all of thirty seconds before she decided to go onto the balcony. The night was cool. The reflection of the full moonlight bounced off the water in the fountain below, tinting the flowers in the surrounding area blue.

Several of the duchess's guests meandered through the grounds, champagne flutes in hand, talking of how splendid the party was, how agreeable the music and hors d'oeuvres were, and how marvelous it was for the future Duke of Tethersal to have found a wife.

Sara cringed. All of it was a lie. The future Duke of Tethersal hadn't found a wife. He'd found a broodmare to bear his children. Nay, she'd been given to him. Freely. A polished present, wrapped in bows and fine paper, she'd been sent to England, and handed over to a man who would rather be with his mistress than her. And it meant nothing to him.

She meant nothing to him.

If she'd been thinking rationally at the time, she never would've allowed him to kiss her. Never would have permitted him to hold her hand, for what good it had done.

Now he was kissing someone else, whoever she was. Big breasted blond trollop, that's who. Probably had the wit of a dung beetle, silly as she looked, fawning over him with all the squalidness of a ... of a ...

Well. Something really disgusting.

Become acquainted with one another, honestly. If he intended on kissing other women while he was ... *whatever* it was he was doing. Courting her, or so it seemed. If he'd already planned on having indulgences with other women, why bother with all that drivel of a united dukedom, or companionship, or however he'd put it?

A load of humbuggery, the lot of it, and so was he, the wretched man.

"My lady?" Ah, Lana. She couldn't have kept to herself for long. "Oh, *a ghrá mo chroí*, there you are!"

If Lana knew Sara had been imagining dung beetles and noblewomen within the same chain of thought, and in reference one to the other, her endearments might have been replaced with one or two choice curse words.

"Yes, Lana." Sara turned around. "I am here."

"Why are you not downstairs?"

How could one put something like this without sounding entirely insane? Having a mistress was an understood practice among English gentlemen, was it not? Of course it was. That didn't change the fact that he'd lied.

"It's complicated," Sara finally said, though really it wasn't. He'd kissed someone else. And after he'd kissed ... Well, Sara had kissed him, but that was irrelevant.

Wasn't it?

And why she should care seemed to be the greatest question. Why should she? Wasn't as if she was in love with him. Far be it for her to keep him from his masculine indulgences, or whatever men called those particular urges.

"Well, my lady, your *complication* awaits at the bottom of the stairs," said Lana. "It was all I could do to stop him from coming up here himself."

"I don't want to see him." Sara brushed past Lana, and into her room. "I'm going to bed. If we are to leave for Worcester in the morning, I shall need rest." Reaching back, she lifted the curls Lana had left from her coiffure. "Help me, please."

A few muffled words, and Lana began doing as she was told, unfastening the tiny row of pearl buttons at the back of Anna's green dress. "I am sorry things did not go the way you had wanted, my lady.

"I'll be fine." Sara smothered the emotion rising in her throat. "Just tired."

It was true enough; she *was* tired. Unfortunately, however, it wasn't as she'd hoped it would be. From dancing, from laughing, from telling everyone about herself, as they were all certainly eager to know her.

From dancing with *him*. Being in his arms as everyone watched in wonder, envious of how dashing, how elegant they looked together, what a marvelous dukedom they'd make.

No. Sara's female emotions were the sole culprit of her drained state tonight. Her feet weren't even tired. And she'd only talked to Anna. Oh, and said *hello* to a few guests here and there. Nothing spectacular. Not at all what she'd expected while anticipating her engagement party.

"I think I should like to write to my father," she said, and Lana stopped unbuttoning. "Just to let him know I am well."

Evidently satisfied, Lana continued with the buttons. "I shall fetch some of His Grace's house stationery for you, my lady."

"Thank you."

"And send for your bath as well. Miss Clearwater, the duchess's personal maid, purchased a fair lot of lemon scented soap this morning in London. Would you like to try it?"

As if lemon soap could take her mind off of him. "Yes, Lana. That would be lovely. Thank you." Indeed, it would be something if it could. At least she could bathe and attempt to get some sleep.

If sleep were even possible tonight.

Probably not.

No matter. She'd square her shoulders, walk tall, and smile as she'd been raised. Mistresses and gentlemen be damned, Sara Ballivar would not let a minor hit to her pride get the best of her. Tomorrow she'd be ensconced in a coach to Worcester with Anna, whom she was beginning to like very much, and together they'd spend the next two weeks listening to the boring gossip of old women.

Splendid.

And she didn't care that he would be there, too. If Anna could avoid Sebastian, Sara could easily steer clear of Justin. In fact, that was exactly what she was going to do. He deserved it. And as his intended, the penalty for his actions was hers to give. She'd avoid him and be all the better for it.

Stupid man. All men: *stupid, stupid, stupid*!

"I can finish myself," she bit off, not meaning to. "Sorry, Lana. I'd just like to be alone for a while, if you please."

"Yes, my lady. I'll return when your bath is ready." Lana quit the room.

Sara held her dress to her chest, shivering as the night air, wafting through the open window, hit her bare back. She wanted to cry. What a fool she was! For almost believing this could have worked, that perhaps he could love her, like she'd imagined when he'd told her they were to be a union.

Closeness, that is what he'd said, right after he'd made the comment about their living arrangements. Or, more plainly, their *sleeping* arrangements. If one could consider it sleeping, which in the way he'd explained, sleeping didn't seem to be a very big part of the picture.

Heat rose in her cheeks, and she shook her head. Thinking of him this way was not doing her any good, and thinking of him *that* way, when imagining what he'd meant by bedding her frequently, was most *definitely* not helping matters either.

The doorknob turned, clicked.

"That was quicker than I expected, Lana. I--" Sara started. Stopped. Her heart slammed into her ribs.

It couldn't be. He wouldn't have.

"Justin," she choked. "What are you ...?"

He shut the door, locked it. "I should ask you. After all, you're the one who ran away from our engagement party."

His cravat was undone, his coat unbuttoned. As if he'd spent the past half hour pacing a small room, or perhaps a courtyard. With *her*. The blond trollop.

That image in mind, gathering her wits came easy. "I had every right to excuse myself from Her Grace's festivities, I believe, my lord. Since you clearly decided to make a spectacle of yourself tonight, I saw no reason to make one of myself by staying."

"What you saw in the courtyard was not at all as it appeared."

"No?"

"No."

"Ah, so I assume you were just showing her out then? How kind of you to do it in such an affectionate manner. Truly, how lucky of me not to have caught you escorting one of Her Grace's male guests this evening." And then, because she couldn't help herself, the play of emotions on his face was far too amusing: "Kissing a man in the courtyard instead of a woman would have put quite a damper on the future of the Tethersal dukedom, would it have not? For the natural production of heirs, I mean."

That did it.

He closed the distance between them in three, maybe four, strides and grabbed her by the shoulders. "Deuce take it, woman, why must you insist upon being so difficult?"

Sara's body went rigid. Her fingers were still tightly wrapped round her gown, her only device in keeping the garment from falling to the floor, though he didn't appear to have noticed, thank goodness. He was too busy scowling down at her, anger brewing a storm in his dark eyes, chiseled features set, and his lips--why, God, *why* was she noticing his lips at a time like this?--drew a thin line.

Vexed with her, was he? Just from the kissing a man comment? Really, she could've done much worse. She waited for him to speak.

But then he didn't. So, she did.

"There is no need for this. I have moved on from what I witnessed downstairs. And while I regret to have left our party so abruptly, I fear I cannot return in this state."

"What state is that?"

Speaking to him like this, when his face was inches from hers, was interminable. "I am tired." He grumbled something beneath his breath. "So, unhand me, if you please. I should like to retire."

"She is my mistress."

An anchor sank, heavily, into her heart.

"Was my mistress," he amended.

"Was?"

He gave a short nod. A lock of dark hair fell over his forehead, and her fingers twitched, the sudden urge to brush it aside nearly causing her to let go of her dress.

She clutched harder.

"But not anymore." His hands tightened around her shoulders, but not unkindly. Comforting. Though why she should feel any kind of comfort with him, especially right now, was unnerving.

She was supposed to be penalizing him for his actions. Ignore him. Yes, that was the plan. But how could she? How could she possibly ignore a man like this?

Stupefied, she fluttered her lashes a few times.

"You do that," he said.

"Do what?"

"That thing with your lashes." His head tilted to the side. "You do that when you're trying to think of something to say."

"Oh." Indeed, she was trying to think of something to say. Some kind of response to the fact that, apparently, this ... *whoever* she was ... wasn't his mistress anymore.

But his thumbs were making tiny little circles on her upper arms. And the heat of his hands against her skin made her insides feel all warm and honey-coated.

"Do you?" he asked.

She blinked again. "Do I ... what?"

"Have something to say? I'd rather you tell me than allow those thoughts to be repressed, as I don't take well to women stewing on sentiments that involve me. Especially when they're disagreeable."

"I do not have disagreeable sentiments."

"Don't lie to me, Sara." His voice was surprisingly calm.

Fine. If he wanted to know what was on her mind: "You make a habit out of kissing your ex-mistresses, Lord Carrington?"

"No. I don't."

"She's the exception?"

"There are no other exceptions, my lady. Lady St. Clair was confused and upset."

"So, you kissed her."

"She kissed me."

Did he really think she was that dim-witted? "You seemed to be mightily involved in that kiss yourself, my lord. From what little I saw, that is. Shock sent my feet in the other direction before I could get a closer look."

"She kissed me," he reiterated, emphasis on every word. He paused, lifted an eyebrow. "Ah, Sara, Sara. Could it be that you are jealous?"

The accusation hit like a hammer to an anvil. "I most certainly am not!" And when he made no sign of backing down from his allegation: "In fact, I do not care who you kiss. Kiss whomever you wish, for all you seem most eager to do so anyway."

A soft rumble echoed in his throat. He brought her closer, if that was feasible. She was already pressed snugly against him. She imagined the whites of her knuckles were peeking through her skin, unyielding as her fingers gripped her dress.

His face moved closer to hers. "I think you do care who I kiss." His breath fanned over her cheeks, her nose, her mouth. "In fact, I think you want me all to yourself. That's what this is all about, is it not?"

Of all the-- "Arrogant!" She pushed as hard as she could against him, which did not help.

He didn't even flinch.

It did, however, cause the dress to slip from her fingers. The gauzy muslin fell off her shoulders, over his hands, which were still wrapped round her arms, and managed to stop just below the ruffled lace of her camisole. *All* of which managed (naturally) to garner his attention to her chest.

Now *he* was blinking. Good. Look at that, Lord Carrington. You do that thing with your lashes too. Only your little foible appears to happen when in fact you're at a *loss* for words.

Which he definitely appeared to be at quite an impairment of uttering a response, much less the plural of that.

Sara cleared her throat primly. "As you can see, I was preparing for bed when you took it upon yourself to walk into my chambers without knocking." My goodness, where on earth was this courage coming from? Her knees felt weaker than Lana's tea. "Now, if you will, unhand me, please."

But he didn't.

*** *** ***

He couldn't. A full week had passed since he'd touched her, since he'd kissed her, held her body against his in the rose garden. And he'd almost forgotten, almost let it slip his mind, how good this felt. How exquisite she felt in his arms.

Like she was meant to be here, and he was meant to hold her. As if this whole betrothal business hadn't been a load of unwarrantable nonsense. That their fathers somehow knew it would be as thus. That he would want her more than he'd ever wanted any other woman. More than Milly, anyone.

Strange, that. Yet, undeniable all the same.

Particularly since he was certain his eyes had given him away, and since he couldn't find the will to let go of her, even though she'd just asked him to. After all, that had been the bargain. He wouldn't touch her unless she instigated it. And he was sure--at least he *thought* he was sure--that wasn't the present case.

Still, he couldn't do it.

"Justin."

"I don't want her," he said. She stared up at him, brown eyes wide. "Do you understand?"

She shook her head, slowly, her bottom lip quivering. "You were kissing her."

If she cried, he'd lose it. There would be no stopping the inevitable. He'd sweep her into his arms, carry her to the bed, no more than a few feet from where they stood, and show her what he meant. Why he didn't want his mistress, nor could he fathom ever wanting another woman the way he wanted her, Sara.

"It was thoughtless of me," he said. "It meant nothing."

And I'm sorry hung in the air between them, but he didn't say it. That unrepentant part of him, a trait imbedded since birth, wouldn't allow passage to remorse or compunction.

He was bred a duke, not a poet.

"I don't expect you to understand completely," he said, "though I do expect you to trust me."

"Trust? I ... How can you ...?"

"I told you, Sara. I don't want her. That kiss you witnessed, it meant nothing. And it doesn't change our situation."

"Our situation," she repeated, blinking.

"That's right," he said, and he shouldn't have, but he did. He slid a hand to her back, held her body tight against his.

Her small hands curled into fists against his chest, but she wasn't pushing him away. If he didn't know better, he'd have thought she was aiding him, matching her small curves to his body in a deliberant attempt to prove how perfectly they would fit.

As if he hadn't thought of that already.

Knowing she might have thought it, too, was incredibly arousing.

He brought his other hand to the back of her neck. "Our situation," he murmured, "is quite simple." He lowered his head, repressed the urge to groan as her breasts heaved against his chest. They were perfect.

He dropped a kiss to the soft juncture between her neck and shoulder. "You're mine," he said, taken briefly aback by the breaking out of gooseflesh upon her skin. He'd never given Milly chills.

"And because you're mine …" He dropped another kiss to her shoulder, another to her neck. "I am at liberty to remind you that your trust in me is not up for negotiation. If I tell you it meant nothing …" A moan purred in her throat as he pressed a kiss to the hollow beneath her jaw. "It meant nothing."

He moved again to her neck. Her hands weren't fisted anymore; they were flattened, moving up, up his chest, sneaking into the collar of his shirt. Ah yes, he'd removed his cravat in the rose parlor while arbitrating between Sebastian and Anna. The damned thing had been too tight. Everything was too tight when dealing with those two. Cravats, coats, the room, the air.

But removing his cravat, unbuttoning his coat? Routine reactions to being an interceptor for what must have been the thousandth time between his sister and the man who aggravated her more than a woman who wore velvet in the summertime.

Now, he was glad for it. Because his duchess-to-be was explorative tonight. Her timid little hands were cool, soft against his naturally warm skin, and instantly he envisioned them elsewhere, smoothing the breadth of his chest, his arms, his stomach.

Lower.

"*Mo chuisle*," she whispered. "*Tá sé tapaidh.*"

He stopped, mouth lingering on the soft swan-like curve of her neck. "What did you say?"

"My pulse." Her sweet breath fanned past his ear. "It's so fast."

He kissed that pulse. "Indeed." He kissed it again, touched it with his tongue. She tasted luscious, savory. An appetizing mixture of salt and lavender and woman. "I can see that." Again, he shaped it with his mouth. "Taste it."

She made a tiny helpless sound. Chasteness, he acknowledged. Once more, he was reminded of her inexperience in these intimacies, these interludes that had become cravings on his part since he'd first touched her in Liverpool. He couldn't keep going on like this if he expected to keep her virtue intact until they were wed. Because at the moment, he was certain she was enjoying herself as much as he, and if she gave even the smallest notion of wanting more ...

He probably couldn't contain himself. They'd exchange marriage vows tomorrow instead of next month, or whenever the duchess planned on having the ceremony.

Yet, here he was, dropping kisses all over the line of her neck, debating whether he should just let her dress continue its path to the floor, so he could finally touch her. Without layers of gauzy green muslin impeding his hands, his mouth.

He had to stop.

"Sara?" He forced his lips from her skin. "We have to ... that is, I have to stop." Was he speaking to her or himself? Staring at her neck, slightly pink with his kisses, he wasn't at all certain.

He closed his eyes, swallowed. "You need to take hold of your dress, or I might ... that is, I might not be able to ..."

"Justin?" One of her hands slid to his cheek, and he opened his eyes, stared down into her flushed features. Those sincere eyes of hers blinked once, twice. "Don't you want to kiss me?"

He blinked, too. My God, but didn't she know? "Of course I do." He brushed the back of his fingertips down her cheek. "Don't you realize how hard it is to ...?"

"My lady?" The doorknob jiggled.

Sara drew her body closer to his.

"My lady!" her maid persisted from the other side of the door, jiggling the knob again. "The door, it is locked! Are you all right?"

They were in quite the predicament, he and his intended. Fiancé or no, he shouldn't have been in her room, and certainly not behind a locked door. His mother would have a mouthful of lessons on propriety should she ever find out.

Sara was shaking in his arms, her face buried against his chest. He tensed. Why had he thought this to be a good idea? He'd only wanted to explain himself, and by some miracle of which he cared not to question, she had forgiven him. Or so he hoped. But now he'd ushered himself back to square one, mindless fool that he was.

The shaking became more persistent, intermingled with what sounded like little puffs of air. Sobs, maybe. He looked down.

She wasn't crying.

Good Lord. Was she ... *laughing*?

"Lady Ballivar!" Mrs. Brennan rapped her knuckles to the door.

"Sara," he whispered, and she looked up at him, tears of laughter pooling in her eyes. Lud. Now he was fighting laughter. "I cannot be in here with you."

"Yes," she said, but she was smiling, "though you should have thought of that before you barged in."

"And locked the door," he said, looking over his shoulder. "Though I believe your Mrs. Brennan might break it down soon if you do not answer." He gazed down at her again, pressed a kiss to her forehead. Allowed his lips to linger. "Tell her you are all right."

She didn't hesitate. "I'm all right, Lana!"

The knocking ceased.

He kept his voice low. "That you're undressing."

"I'm only undressing!"

"That you'll be there in just a moment."

"I'll be there in just a moment!" She paused, upturned her face, her mouth mere inches from his. "What about you? You cannot very well go out the main door."

"I grew up here, Kitten." He nodded to her window. "I'll take the balcony."

"The balcony!"

"Shh," he said, and she caught her lip between her teeth. "You'll defeat the purpose if you make too much noise."

And then because he couldn't help himself, she was so lovely, so wide-eyed standing there, wrapped in his arms, he bent his head and kissed her, before she could answer.

Or make too much noise.

Or start swearing at him in Gaelic, though he did like the pulse racing sentiment she'd panted earlier.

Oh, yes. He vowed to make her say that one again.

"My lady, your bath will be cold!"

And he'd thought catching her in a loosened gown had been the discovery of the century. Finding her in a bath might have--scratch that, *would* have put them in a far worse predicament. A man could only take so much, could only hold out for so long.

A week. It had been a week.

Where were his senses?

He broke the kiss.

And bent his head again.

She received him easily. Her hands speared into his hair, her breasts crushed against his chest. Everything he'd imagined kissing to be was nothing compared to this.

"Pardon, my lady, but will you not hurry?" Mrs. Brennan persisted. "I do feel a bit ridiculous standing about like some sort of article."

Sara made in inarticulate murmur. "You should go," she whispered. "Though I do not know how you plan to cascade from my window, when Her Grace's guests are walking the grounds below."

"I'll manage." He took her face in his hands. She was young, his intended. Fair, small features, wondrous eyes framed in long, dark lashes. Looking at her nearly took his breath away every time.

He let her go, and she took hold of her dress. "I shall see you in the morning?"

He nodded, looked to the window, which was open, thank goodness. If he remembered correctly, this one did tend to stick, and, when opened, generally alarmed the entire house. Not such a good thing when one is attempting to leave a lady's chamber without drawing a magnanimous amount of attention to one's self.

Her hand touched his arm. "Do be careful, Justin."

He leaned forward, brushed a kiss to her lips. "Goodnight, Sara."

"Goodnight."

Quickly he slipped through the window, taking a moment to glance left, then right. Garden trellises, wound with tiny roses, framed four of the twelve windows at the front of the house, and Sara's room happened to be one of them. Sliding over the balcony with deft grace, he made quick work out of shimmying to the ground, taking care not to smash any of the duchess's roses. She'd be furious otherwise.

A few gasps elicited from the general area as he collected himself, brushed his hands down his front, pulled a pinprick thorn from his jacket sleeve.

"My lord?" A footman carrying a tray of champagne flutes blinked at him curiously. "Are you well?"

Justin grabbed a glass of champagne, downed it, winced at its bitterness--ah yes, this is why he didn't drink--and returned it to the tray. "Quite," he said. "Just found myself locked in from the inside, that's all."

The man looked up at the balcony from whence his master had just descended. "Forgive me, my lord, but isn't that--"

"That's all," Justin repeated, and the man nodded curtly. Loyalty among his family's servants would never require questioning. "You may go about your business."

"Very good, my lord." He turned to leave, paused. Glanced over his shoulder. "She is a beauty, my lord. If you don't mind my saying so."

Justin shifted his gaze to Sara's open window, lit by the amber glow of the candelabra on her nightstand. "Yes," he murmured. "Yes, she is."

TEN

Sara didn't see Justin until they were ready for departure, the morning was so hectic. She and Anna had made the decision to share a maid, to which Tippy gladly handed the honorable duties to the newcomer. That being Lana, who considered it just as well since she had taken it upon herself to shadow Sara's every move since last night.

Justin had evidently made it unscathed from her balcony. She had heard the commotion below within seconds of him exiting her room. After taking a few more fleeting moments to collect herself--the mirror revealed a tell-tale combination of flushed cheeks, swollen lips and glassy eyes--she opened the door to a fuming maid.

One who knew all too well that flushed cheeks and swollen lips didn't come from merely undressing.

Which, by the way, she had forgotten to do.

And so Mrs. Brennan had spent the entire evening and next morning ensuring her charge never left her sight. She helped Sara bathe, and stole glances at the door in between hair washing and toe scrubbing as if someone, particularly Sara's intended, would enter unannounced at any given moment.

Sara wrote to her father as Lana stood over her, braiding her hair. And when she had finished, post scripting that she hoped His Grace would come to visit her soon, Lana rang for a footman to fetch the letter instead of taking it downstairs herself.

She'd even followed Sara into the privy, upon which Sara insisted she leave at once. Steering her clear of her fiancé's kisses was one thing; watching her while she took care of her personal feminine needs was quite another.

Having a maid had never been this interminable.

"My lady, slow down please." Walking past the front door of Mayfair House and onto the stone terrace, Lana marched directly on top of Sara's heels. "Ooomph!"

"Lana, really! You must cease shadowing me like this. I cannot even turn around without you there underfoot."

She did it, just to prove a point. And, of course, nearly toppled into Lana.

"See!"

Lana's face turned red. "You know I only mean to look after you, my lady. Just as His Grace ordered."

Sara sighed, as Lana went on in a lowered voice.

"And I do not think he would be too happy knowing you've been allowing gentlemen into your room at late hours, and behind locked doors."

"He is my fiancé, Lana. Besides, you're the one who wanted me to talk to him."

"Not alone!" Lana sputtered. "Not half-dressed!"

"A minor mishap," Sara insisted. A delicious one, too. His hands had felt positively divine on her bare back. Those rough, workman's fingers searched restlessly along and underneath the straps of her chemise. Leaving trails of heat wherever they roamed.

"A mishap that will not happen again if I have anything to do with it," Lana announced.

Ignoring her, Sara proceeded down the stairs, and offered Justin a pleasant smile as he extended his hand.

"My lady." He raked a kiss across her knuckles. "Enchanting of you to join us. I trust you slept well? My sister didn't give you any trouble this morning, now, did she?"

"Prudence, Brother," Anna said, coming up to stand beside them. "Do you know the word? I daresay not." Her eyes flickered to Sebastian, who stood beside one of the two high polished, black-lacquered coaches, tapping a riding crop impatiently against his high leather boots.

He looked on at her for a moment, his brow puckered as though in deep thought, then averted his gaze.

"Yes," Sara said, deciding they were all in for a long two weeks where these two were concerned, the tension between them was so thick. "I did rest well. Thank you, my lord. And Lady Anna has been most kind and helpful."

Justin smiled. "She has her moments."

"I have many moments." Taking a footman's proffered hand, Anna climbed into the foremost coach, Lana climbing in after her. Then, poking her head out with a tight smile: "I'm just selective with their occurrences."

Sebastian shot Justin an exasperated look. "You coming?"

Justin dipped his head in a curt nod. "We'll stop in a couple hours for rest and luncheon," he said, his eyes flickering warmly down at Sara. "In the meantime, take my advice and fake sleep, else Anna bombard you with her tales of every ball she's ever attended."

"I heard that!"

As promised, they stopped about two hours or so after departing Mayfair. The coaches came to a halt alongside an open field, dotted with patches of wildflowers and several towering oaks. The sky was clear, painted a shade of pale blue inherent to this pleasant time of year. Lana unfolded a large blanket beneath one of the trees and laid out the sandwiches, fruit and teacakes Cook had prepared for their journey.

"Sara and I had a most fascinating conversation on the way here." Anna touched her napkin to the corner of her mouth. "With the exception of my dear brother, I've never heard someone speak with such an astute knowledge of horses."

"I must attribute my knowledge of the equine species to my father," said Sara. "He is quite the expert, you see. Attends most, if not all, of the races around Ireland, several of which he enters his own horses. Breeders are constantly asking his advice, and he faithfully attends the Dublin auction every month."

"Ah." Anna popped a grape in her mouth. "I think I should like to meet this duke. He does sound fascinating. Definitely more so than our own boorish English dukes and earls, viscounts." She cut a sly glance at Sebastian. "Marquises."

Sara couldn't help but notice Lord Beaufort's reaction to the rash statement. His handsome face pulled into a frown, his icy eyes regarding Anna with equal parts annoyance and longing. As though he wanted to shake her and, perhaps, kiss her at the same time.

"Vulgarity will not be tolerated, Anna," Justin said darkly.

Anna only cocked an eyebrow, as Justin went on.

"And I will not have you speak ill of our country's noblemen, however less learned they are on matters more suited to Ireland's noblemen, who are a tradition-oriented lot. It is true enough that the Irish have a knack for breeding horses. Our father's finest stallion was shipped from Dublin."

"This, I know," said Anna.

Justin set down his plate, regarded his sister with an almost paternal eye. "You are mistaken, however," he continued gently, "if you believe them to have any sort of uncanny ability which would render them superior over our lot."

"Not to mention," Sebastian said, "that titles would be non-existent in Ireland if not for the good graces of the King. *Our* King." He pointed a finger at Anna, his eyes lit with anger. "*Your* king."

Sara couldn't believe her ears. It was true, all of it. But the truth, that it was only from the King's desire to maintain order in Ireland that noble Irishmen, including her father, were given titles, didn't make it sound any less ugly. Especially coming from Lord Beaufort, who may as well have been the most offensive man she'd ever met.

Anna stood abruptly, her plate spilling from her lap to the ground. "I don't think I care to listen to this rubbish," she announced, as Lana worked quickly to pick up the discarded food. "A bit of fresh air seems to be in order."

"You *are* in fresh air," Justin ventured to point out, but she was already walking away.

Sebastian, exchanging a rather incensed glare with Justin, said, "I'm going for a walk. Care to join me?"

Justin shook his head. "Go ahead. But be quick about it, mind. We'll be leaving in a few minutes."

Sebastian hesitated, favored Sara with a smile that, if she didn't know better, appeared almost apologetic, then nodded and stalked away, cane in hand.

"My apologies on behalf of my friend," Justin said.

"You needn't apologize to me." Sara stood, as Lana, evident in her endeavor of pretending not to listen, began to pack the remaining food. "I know how Englishmen feel about the Irish having titles of nobility. I'm compelled to point out, however, our right to them."

Justin stood, brushed his hands down his front. "I do not deny that."

"Which part?"

"Both."

"Ah." Figures he would be among the English elite who regarded the Irish as nothing more than mud beneath their polished boots. The title he stood to inherit was one of the highest in England, so why should he have felt any different?

The elitist crouched beside Lana and, through her protests, helped her gather up the rest of the food.

Sara swallowed.

Muscled thighs strained against the light tan material of his snug breeches. Every inch of him bulged--arms, chest, thighs, all covertly hidden beneath layers of fine clothing. But even his clothing couldn't hide what Sara knew was there. She'd felt it, keened her own body against his. There was no denying the awareness she felt when he so much as glanced in her direction.

And then it hit her.

She could care for this man. Could see herself *loving* him.

Insane. She didn't even like Englishmen. Well, there was a time in the not-so-distant past she didn't.

Like last Monday, or thereabout.

Justin must have seen something in her eyes, for no sooner had she imagined herself capable of falling in love with him than she'd heard him bid Lana to accompany his sister and Sebastian in one carriage. That he and Sara would ride, alone, in the other.

Naturally, Lana argued like a Dubliner thrown out of a pub on St. Paddy's Day, but Justin was adamant. And in the end, she gave Sara a quick, assessing scowl, gathered the basket and blanket close to her chest and marched for the coaches, skirts rustling madly in the tall grass.

"She's a feisty one, your Mrs. Brennan," Justin said once he had settled into the seat facing away from the horses.

Sara was grateful. Riding backwards always made her queasy. "She can be," she acknowledged, eyeing him cautiously from her side. "But she means well."

"Of course."

"She only means to perform the duties requested of her by my father, which unfortunately consists of keeping me under a tight rein. Though really there's no need to--why do you not believe we have a right to title in our own homeland?"

His shoulders shook with laughter. "My goodness, Sara. All that in one breath? I'm impressed."

"Do not make light of it! I want to know why you believe such nonsense. Why you think English blood to be any better than mine."

He leaned back, mirth continuing to dance in his dark eyes. Stretched his arm over the back of the seat. "I don't think that. But I must admit, I wondered when this would be coming."

*** *** ***

The small space between Sara's dark brows puckered.

She was beautiful today. Not that she hadn't been beautiful every day, mind, but today she was absolutely riveting. Her purple traveling dress, though it covered every inch of her glorious body, all the way up to her neck where it was trimmed in a tiny frill, did nothing to halt the desire stirring in his loins.

Her eyes were the color of rich mahogany, flecked with shards of green. Her hair, a springing lock of which fell carelessly over her left breast, possessed the richness of the finest silk. His hands itched to touch it. To rub those satiny strands between his fingertips, press them against his cheek.

"What do you mean?" she asked.

He couldn't remember what they were talking about.

"You said you wondered when this would be coming," she clarified. "The sentiments of the English on the Irish having titles of nobility. Apparently you share Lord Beaufort's view on the matter."

"Sebastian doesn't share his own view on the matter. He was only reacting to my sister. And no, I don't believe that either. I think the Irish have every right to a title in their homeland. They fought for the same cause, on the same soil, shed as much blood as we did."

"Oh."

"However, I have just as much pride in my heritage as you do in yours, my lady," he said gently, and the corner of her mouth lifted a fraction. "And just as you will not stand for having your noblemen degraded, neither will I stand for the open degradation of mine. My father has been a tremendous asset to the Lords for years now, as was his father before him, and his father before him.

Though I believe I can accurately say none of them had the finesse of handling a horse the way your father can."

That last bit of flattery earned him a wide grin. "You know of my father's interest in horses?"

"Of course I do. He taught me."

Sara cocked her head to the side. "Truly? I had no idea that you knew my father. Previously, I mean."

"Before I met you? Yes, when I was much younger, eleven or so, and your father was commissioned with mine during the war, he spent a fair amount of time in Mayfair." He smiled reflectively. "Used to stay on me about keeping my heels down, gripping with my inner thigh."

"Not your knee," she put in. "Maintaining perfect rein hands at all times." She did a little gesture with her hands, one he recognized so well he found himself doing it too. "Small and ring--"

"--fore and thumb," he said, wiggling the same, and Sara burst into a fit of giggles.

Justin laughed as well, startled by how easily laughter came with this woman. His mother was like this, laughing about spur of the moment, ridiculous things such as puppies chasing their own tails, or the duke curling his lip when broccoli was on the menu--His Grace tended to scowl at her for making sport of that one--or an ordinary, offhand gesture such as the way one grips one's reins.

Truth be told, there hadn't been any room for humor over the past several months. Even his mother didn't laugh as much, which wasn't any wonder with the duke's illness.

Justin had been forced out of youth because of it. Tasks once performed by his father, he had taken on himself, slipping into a role he'd thought more fitting of an old man.

Once.

These days he wondered how some of the older noblemen did it. How they kept up with tenants and land and repairs and bills, maintained balance among them all, and still had time to take a seat in the Lords, where the peers hacked out laws, proposals for laws, issues on land and taxes ... It was enough to give anyone a headache. Add a wife and family to all those extensive obligations, and there you have it. A man at the brink of insanity.

So finding room for gaiety? Not likely.

But gaiety came as natural as breathing when he was with Sara. He couldn't remember the last time he'd felt such a spontaneous burst of joy.

"What an odd coincidence," she said, "that my father spent a great deal of time teaching another his most prized riding skills, just as he spent so many countless hours teaching me. And in an entirely different country no less." Her eyes rounded. "You, of all persons."

"I put very little stock in coincidence, Sara."

"Are you saying my father had a set agenda, then? That he knew your father might have made such an offer after the war?"

"I think your father, knowing you were his only child, wanted to make a good match for you. A duke's philosophies are rather straightforward. So, yes, I do believe he knew what he was doing."

"But I was only eight years old," she said, and in her eyes he saw what must have been years of hurt from this arrangement. From her life being decided for her, not being able to choose her own husband.

Though Justin couldn't very well see her married to anyone but himself now. Didn't want to.

"Eight years old," she enunciated.

"And I was twelve," he said tentatively. "Nearly thirteen. But it's not as if matches like these are uncommon. At first, I was rebellious to the idea. Even ran away the next day, though I didn't get very far."

"Where did you run to?"

"The confectioner's in London. Same day I met Sebastian. He was running for his life, as was I, or so I thought. Coincidence, I suppose."

Her mouth ticked a notch. "You don't believe in coincidence."

"Fate, then."

"That's the same thing."

"No," he said. "Fate is destiny, destiny is future. And my future, my lady, has been entwined with yours for as long as I can remember."

She swallowed, blinked a few times, which made him smile. He did find that little speechless quirk of hers quite endearing. But then everything about her was endearing.

She was charismatic and charming. Virtuously bewitching, as if that wasn't the oxymoron of the century.

She was a mesmerizing kind of attractive, a gem among a world full of dull, boorish aristocrats.

As for him?

Besotted. Smitten. By all of it: her beauty, her smile, her laughter, her wit. All the qualities he'd found subpar in every other woman, Sara possessed with salient passion.

"I almost find it hard to believe," she said, "a practical man such as yourself would believe in fate, you're so skeptical of coincidence. Even though, as you pointed out, they clearly aren't the same thing."

Deciding it was better not to lead her on under false pretenses, he said, "I don't believe in fate."

"You don't?"

"No."

She looked at him incredulously. "Then why did you say you did?"

"I didn't. I was merely offering an alternative to coincidence."

Her eyes narrowed. "I have no idea who you are, Lord Carrington. You say one thing, yet mean another. It is very irritating."

He grinned, thinking he'd never had as much fun. "Forgive me, then," he said, and her scowl faded a little. "I, by no means, meant to irritate you."

*** *** ***

Surprisingly, she wasn't *that* irritated. Fate wasn't a word men used in civilized conversation, unless attempting to woo an absentminded woman who knew nothing beyond making tedious comments about the weather.

Which was irritating in and of itself, a woman with no mind of her own.

Then again, that's what most men desired: a woman with no thought process but to please her husband and, of course, to give him heirs.

"I have been meaning, however," he said, sliding stealthily to her side of the coach, "to speak to you about what occurred at our little soiree last night."

Sara felt her throat tighten. "Haven't we already discussed the details of last night, my lord? Surely you don't wish to rehash it."

"I'm speaking of what happened afterward, my lady," he said with equal composure, "when we reentered the party inside."

The bet, Sara dolefully acknowledged. How silly of her to think he might have forgotten. "You speak of Lord Beaufort and Lady Anna, I presume?"

"Yes."

"Hmm. They didn't appear too terribly happy with one another, did they?"

"Not happy at all, no."

She tried not to dwell on how close they were. He reached for her hand and, stripping off her glove, threaded his fingers with hers. Sara's eyes slid shut.

"You're so warm." Her eyes shot open. Had she really just said something so tactless?

His free hand came to his face. "Am I?" He sounded surprised by the notion. "I hadn't noticed."

The tiny scrape he'd gotten from the thorn bush still marred his hand. It was healing, thank goodness.

He leaned in, cupped that same hand around her face. Palmed her cheek. "So are you." Wonder hung in his tone.

"I think," she said, "that is merely your own hand. I myself am rather cold natured."

"I don't think so. *Your* hands, however …" He took her hand, dwarfing it inside his. "Quite cool."

He pressed that cool appendage to his cheek, confined it between his shaven skin and his warm fingers.

Sara's heart pounded, the only explanation for the second thoughtless thing that suddenly exited her mouth. "Your hands." She caught her breath as he pressed a kiss to the inside of her wrist. "They're calloused."

"Riding spirited horses." His dark eyes met hers. "With the correct rein hands of course."

"Oh." Her attempts at speech were futile. All she could do was stare as his wide-set mouth, a feature she'd not taken too much notice of on a man until now, as it brushed yet another kiss to her wrist.

"You lost our bet, my lady." His breath fanned like licks of fire against her sensitive skin.

"Yes."

He was looking down now, seemingly intrigued with the lines in her hand. He pressed a kiss to her palm. "What do you suppose we should do about that?"

"Do?"

"About you losing our bet."

"Ah."

His eyes met hers. "I'm open for suggestions."

She hesitated. "I do believe we're spending time together now, my lord. That was part of our agreement."

"Indeed." Another kiss to her palm. "But that's not what I meant by spending a day and a night with you, Sara."

Good Lord, the way he said her name. For the rest of her days, she would never forget that sound, or the way it made her feel inside.

"When I'm ready to collect my winnings," he continued, matching his hand to hers, "we'll start early."

"It is early yet."

His mouth curved into that wicked grin of his. "Not nearly early enough."

Before Sara could question what he meant, Justin turned his attention to the window. "Look." He pointed to the scenery outside. "Worcester Hall."

Sara followed his gaze through the transparent glass and inhaled sharply. It was every bit as splendid as she had imagined. A lawn so perfect every blade of grass might have been hand-trimmed, meticulously cut yew hedges, and a grand stone fountain in the midst of it all.

And Worcester Hall itself? The French might have called it *magnifique*. The Italians, *magnifico*. But to an Irish girl like Sara Ballivar, who had never been one to openly *gape* over the stateliness in which noblemen build their homes (as if a massive house could make a noble man even nobler), it was indescribable. Because as the coach lurched up the driveway, approaching the grandest edifice she'd ever seen, Sara discovered she was, indeed, *gaping*.

"The hall sits upon forty acres," said Justin. "But that's just the house. The duke owns thousands of acres of forest, gardens and lakes, as well as several cottages, four churches and--well, to sum up, he's loaded."

The coach stopped. A footman opened the door and made haste in unfolding the steps, while another reached a hand in for Sara, aiding her from the vehicle. Justin stepped down behind her, settled a hand at the small of her back.

"Welcome to Worcester Hall, my lady."

Sara's eyes lifted, followed the scale of one tower to its heavenward aim. "Beautiful."

Justin murmured his agreement, his thumb making idle circles at the base of her spine. "I spent a great deal of time here as a child. Sebastian and I drove the duchess near mad running through the vestibules with our toy swords, *en guarding* her Roman statues."

Sara laughed. "Incorrigible, the both of you."

"Indeed."

"Mmm. Should I be worried?"

He raised an inquisitive brow. "Worried?"

She nodded toward the stately house. "The two of you running the halls with toy swords. I don't know that I can abide fearing for my safety through strange corridors, if my betrothed is running about with ..." Her words trailed, eyes locked on the set of wide, stone steps up which the footmen were carrying their luggage.

The smile fell from her face.

It couldn't be.

Her feet transformed into lead weights. Her thoughts raced, searched around every corner, sifted through every memory. Suddenly, time suspended, trapped her inside. Even the air and its accompanying sounds and smells came to a dramatic pause. She could hear nothing, smell nothing.

But she could see. Only what her eyes witnessed, standing there, clear as day, at the top of the stairs was, *had* to be, an illusion.

Somewhere from behind, she heard Lana whisper, "Dear God," in Gaelic, which wasn't good, Lana speaking of a member of the

Holy Trinity in the old language. It always meant one of two things. She was either angry or shocked close to fainting.

Sara suspected it was the latter.

Justin muttered something close to her ear, a hint of concern floating in his thick, honey drawl, but Sara couldn't respond. Couldn't move. Couldn't …

"*Dia duit ar maidin, bhean luí Ballivar*," the illusion spoke, and a smile as warm as Irish sunshine spread over his handsome face.

Sara could only murmur one word. "*Cav*."

ELEVEN

"Mr. Cavanaugh, I presume?" Sebastian stepped forward, and the man in question bowed. "Pleased to finally meet you. I'm sure my father has filled your ears with his plans for Middlesbrough, as he has spoken of little else for the past several weeks. My apologies on his behalf."

The gentleman, Mr. Cavanaugh, chuckled. "Indeed, he has, though I cannot very well put blame on him for it. My father's expressed quite an interest as well. In fact, it's been the general topic at every dinner party in Galway for the past two weeks."

Cavanaugh's eyes, greener than the surrounding lawn, flickered down to Sara, who was latched onto Justin's arm as if she were roped to it.

She knew this man. In what capacity, however, Justin couldn't place. Her body was ridged against his, her fingers dug into his upper arm, and he could have sworn he just heard her mutter some sort of plea underneath her breath.

"Are you all right?" he murmured, and she dipped her chin. "Are you certain?"

"Yes."

"You know him."

She hesitated. "Yes."

He didn't know why, but her reply caused the slightest pang in his chest. Maybe it was because of her reaction. The man had spoken in Gaelic; his voice, like hers, a musical mixture of English and Brogue. And she had responded with a gasp and a set of stiffened limbs.

Maybe it was because, instead of looking at him while he was addressing her, she stared at Cavanaugh, eyes full, lips parted. As if everyone else, including him--Justin, her intended, her fiancé, the man whose arm she was presently clinging to--had disappeared with the exception of this man.

This man who appeared more an intruder than one of Sebastian's business colleagues. His mere presence had stopped time, for goodness' sake.

The intruder began making his way down the steps, his gaze focused solely on Sara, and Justin, who would rather give a man the benefit of the doubt before passing judgment, felt an instant flash of dislike for him.

He was diabolically handsome, for one. And, at the same time, polished. Dark blond, closely shorn hair, crisp jacket and inexpressibles. The chain of his pocket watch winked in the full sunlight. He smiled, a mischievous thing, much like Sebastian's. Only Sebastian's was less irritating. Less directed at Sara.

Sara.

He looked down at her, surprised her features had softened by a margin. Her grip on his arm had also loosened considerably, regrettably. He shifted his gaze to Cavanaugh, who was coming to stand before them, and found the urge to scowl near impossible to suppress.

He'd never been so inordinately annoyed.

"My lady." The Irishman bowed with impeccable aplomb. "How good it is to see you again."

Sara loosened her clutch on Justin's arm even more, bobbed an equally flawless curtsy. "Mr. Cavanaugh. I trust your father is in good health, your mother as well?"

"Quite well, my lady, thank you."

"And your new sister? I hear she is the very image of her mother."

His teeth flashed white in the sun. "Aye, she is. A beautiful babe, indeed. Da is quite happy. And Mags just had her first litter, you know"--here, Sara let out a little gasp--"so the house is overrun with infantry. Ah, no pun intended, of course."

"Goodness!" Sara let go altogether, stepped forward.

Justin folded his arms. He wanted to reach for her, snatch her back. She was his, for God's sake. Appallingly, he didn't much like her giving attentions to another man.

"I can't believe Magaidh is old enough to have children," Sara said, her tone lit with cheer. "It seems as though she is still a child herself."

"Who are we talking about?" Anna said, before Cavanaugh could answer. "And shame on you, my dear soon-to-be-sister-in-law, for not introducing me to your friend."

Justin didn't miss the way the smile fell from Cavanaugh's face when his sister mentioned Sara's impending marital status.

"Ah, pardon me," said Sara. "Lady Anna, may I present Mr. Patrick Cavanaugh? Cav, Lady Anna, daughter of the Duke and Duchess of Tethersal."

Anna curtsied.

Cavanaugh bowed in a swoop-ish manor again, murmuring a well-rehearsed greeting.

It was all irritating. Sara, Anna, Cavanaugh. The whole lot of them.

"Magaidh is Cav's dog--"

"Mags, for short," Cavanaugh inserted.

"Yes, Mags," Sara said, and Anna smiled broadly. "She's a very beautiful *Madra rua*--that is Gaelic for *red dog*."

"A very ornery Madra rua," Cavanaugh obviously felt compelled to clarify. "In England, I believe they're referred to as Red Setters."

"We have those here, do we not, Justin?" Justin heard his sister ask, though he was surprised she'd felt the need to include him.

He was, after all, practically being ignored.

"We use them for hunting," he replied tersely.

"As do we," Cavanaugh murmured. "Though Mags is more of a family pet than a hunting dog. Ma spoiled her, you see."

"You mean, you spoiled her," Sara twittered.

Cavanaugh clapped a hand to his chest. "Me? Surely you jest."

"Surely, I don't," Sara countered with equal gaiety.

Justin winced. This teasing banter between them was sickening in the worst sense. He either wanted to punch the man in the face, or knee him where he was sure to be grounded for several minutes, perhaps impairing his ability to sire children.

"Justin." Sebastian had, at some point, joined him. "They know each other."

"Obviously," Justin said through his muddled thoughts.

"In what capacity, do you suppose?"

His fingertips, tucked snugly beneath his arms, dug into the palms of his hands. "I don't exactly want to think about that right now, if it is all the same to you, Sebastian."

"Oh for God's sake, Justin, you aren't jealous, are you? Truly, I had no idea they knew each other. Father's had a long distance work relationship with Sir Dunmore for months, but Dunmore himself wasn't able to make the trip to England. Tending to the wife, I suppose. So he sent his son instead, though I hear Cavanaugh is just as learned in steam engines as his father. Should be interesting to hear his take on the Middlesbrough project."

"Sebastian, stop talking," Justin said. He could feel the peaked signs of a headache coming on. "Please."

"Fine. But you need to buck up, and get out of this ridiculous mood. I can't deal with you like this for two solid weeks. I'm liable to send you packing right now."

Justin started to tell Sebastian where he could send himself packing, but his attention was stolen by the sound of his own name hitting his ears.

His gaze tangled with Sara's, and his chest tightened. She was undoing him, this woman, and given the present situation, he didn't like it.

"My lord?" She outstretched her hand to him. "May I introduce you?"

Maintaining composure, anger, whatever it was he was trying to do, he stepped forward. "By all means," he said. "Introduce us."

"Lord Carrington, this is Mr. Patrick Cavanaugh of Galway."

Cavanaugh bowed.

Again.

Nauseating, all these bows and curtsies.

Justin removed his hat and bowed too, because his mother would be horrified if she heard he hadn't. "Cav, may I present Justin, Marquess Carrington, heir to the Tethersal dukedom."

"And Lady Ballivar's intended since youth," Cavanaugh included as Justin came up from his bow. "Not that she still isn't very much young."

"Indeed." Justin tamped down the urge to haul Sara against him, tuck her hand back inside his arm. By force, if necessary. "A pleasure to meet you, Mr. Cavanaugh. I trust you'll enjoy your stay at Worcester Hall whilst discussing your mutual steam engine interests with the duke and Lord Beaufort."

He was a terrible liar. He knew it, and so did Sebastian.

So, it wasn't any surprise when Sebastian intruded tactfully with, "Why don't we all go inside, eh? Mother will want to see we've safely arrived. She's spoken of nothing but you, Lady Anna, and, of course, your betrothed since sending the invitation to Mayfair."

Justin inclined his head. "Then we must not detain the duchess."

"May I take your arm?" Anna cooed to Cavanaugh. "Thank you, kind sir. So, tell me all about Galway. I hear the cliffs are quite breathtaking."

"Indeed, madam," Cavanaugh returned. "The countryside as well. Truly, you must visit some time."

"Oh my, what a fantastic idea," Anna said, her words fading as she and Cavanaugh disappeared up the stairs and into the house.

Sebastian eyed them narrowly, turned to Justin. "Dinner tonight, followed by readings in the parlor. Mother wants a quiet party. The last one was much too riotous, or so she says."

Justin raised an eyebrow. "And whose fault was that?"

"Anna was screaming in the middle of the night," Sebastian said, "while running down the stairs. In her nightgown, I might add."

"Because you put a rat in her room."

"Only because she put basil in my soup!" He shoved a hand through his blond curls. "Damnable spice makes me swell up like a stuck pig."

Justin shook his head. "Dinner. Readings. Anything else?"

Sebastian turned his gaze toward Sara, who was undergoing what appeared to be chastisement from her maid. "You need to stay away from Cavanaugh." Keeping his voice low, he looked back at Justin. "At least for tonight."

"Why would I want to do a thing like that?"

"Because you need to calm yourself. And you need to talk to her." Sebastian nodded toward Sara, now standing cross-armed, staring past Mrs. Brennan, as if she were in a world of deep thought. "Find out how she knows him, I suppose. Not that it matters. He's only here for two weeks."

It did matter. It mattered because of the way he looked at her, the way the Irishman's features changed, softened when he gazed upon Sara. Justin knew that look as well as he knew his own name. He'd adopted it on enough occasions himself. Only Cavanaugh's expression hadn't appeared to be a put-on of artificial airs.

He looked genuinely overcome by the sight of her.

Justin flexed his hands. "Take Mrs. Brennan inside with you. I need to speak to Sara alone."

"I wish you would calm yourself first."

"I am calm, Sebastian. Now, go. Mrs. Brennan, God love her, will doubtless prove an imposition otherwise."

Sebastian sighed, gave a grand bow, and put on a charming grin. The man should have been an actor.

"Until tonight." Sebastian whisked himself away and to Mrs. Brennan, who (after a couple of initial refusals) tucked a hand inside his arm, and allowed him to escort her inside.

"Who is he?" Justin said after several seconds of silence.

Sara turned, started to respond. Closed her mouth again.

"It's not a difficult question."

"You're angry." Her eyes were round and bright as a harvest moon. She closed the distance to stand just before him. "I can see it in your eyes."

"I am not." Justin pinched the bridge of his nose, sighed. "I'm not angry. I just want to know who he is to you."

"He's Sir Dunmore's eldest son," she said, but that only vexed him more.

He could feel the veins surfacing in his forehead, a sure reaction when he was angered to the brink of yelling.

He would not yell. He had enough instilled discipline to maintain control. "Your acquaintance with him runs deeper than that, and you know it. I know it. So, please ..." He pinched his nose again. "Spare me these evasive answers and tell the truth."

"Do you have a headache?" she asked, apprehensive.

"A slight one."

"I can help, if you'll permit me. Here. Take your hat off." He did, and she reached up, touching the tips of her fingers to his temples. Gently, she began massaging in small circles.

He wanted--*needed* to pull away. But he couldn't. Her fingers were cool, and damned if what she was doing didn't feel heavenly. The pain was already beginning to dull.

His eyes slid shut.

"We've known each other since childhood," she said softly. "Well, since I was about four, I suppose, and he, sixteen. Our fathers are head of the C.P.I.A. in Ireland."

"C.P.I.A.?" He stifled a groan as her thumbs took the place of her fingers, and her fingers slid into his hair.

"Commission for the Preservation of Irish Architecture. It's an organization my father started to ensure our ancient castles don't become ruins like those in Rome."

"You've been to Rome?"

"No. Have you?"

"No. But I'd like to go someday." He opened one eye. "We should go together."

"Of course," she said. "Justin?"

He opened his other eye. Seriousness had settled into her small features, where merriment had been no more than an hour before. And as her slender fingers glided down the length of his face, heating through skin and bone, he had the strongest urge to envelop her in his arms. To make right whatever had contorted those delicate features.

If she needed comfort, he needed to be the one who gave it to her. Remarkable how his needs had increased tenfold since she'd entered his life.

She blinked a few times. Then: "Mr. Cavanaugh asked my father for my hand in marriage."

Astounding. The marrow in his bones had turned to ice in less than a second. "When?"

"Last year."

"And what did your father say?"

"No, of course."

Of course. He knew he had to ask the obvious, though he wasn't sure he wanted to hear it. And she might lie, though he hoped she wouldn't. Or maybe he hoped she would. He would be none the--who was he fooling? Of course he would be the wiser! Sara was a worse liar than he, for pity's sake.

"And if he would've asked you instead?"

"But he didn't ask me. He asked my--"

"If he would have asked you instead of your father." He paused because she was blinking again, and God help him, he really wasn't sure he wanted to proceed with this now. But he couldn't go back. "What would your answer have been?"

She blinked once, twice. Swallowed. "Yes." Her lips trembled, eyes welled. "I would have said yes."

Just like that, his headache returned.

And with a vengeance. He squeezed hard in between his eyes. Maybe if he broke the bridge of his nose, the headache would go away. Maybe he would even knock himself out. Anything to put his mind on something else besides this woman. This woman to whom he was betrothed but who had given her heart to another man.

And God only knows what else. Probably slept with Cavanaugh, for all he knew. The man sure looked at her as if they were acquainted past bows and curtsies.

"Justin, say something." Tears soaked her long lashes. "Please."

Giving up the breaking the nose notion (he did have a rather nice nose, not one of those oddly shaped, crooked things painstakingly characteristic of a great deal of noblemen), Justin raked a trembling hand through his hair, returned his hat to his head. Exhaled slowly.

"There's no way Cav and I could have ever been together," she said. "I was engaged."

"Engaged to me!" he barked, and she jumped back a step. "How could you have even entertained the idea of marrying another man, when you were promised to me?"

"Because I didn't know you! Did you think I spent my days pining over you? I had friends in Ireland, Justin! I had a life, a home." She swabbed a few stray tears with the backs of her fingers. "I can't believe we're arguing over this."

"Oh, can't you?" he retorted with all the ducal arrogance he could muster. "What did you expect? That I would just welcome the idea you'd rather have him over me? Come now, Sara, you're more intelligent than that."

She glared up at him. No tears, no sorrowful eyes. *Enmity*, he realized, and instantly wished he hadn't let it go this far. "I can't believe it," she said, gritting her teeth, "because *you're* the one who had the mistress."

Oh, he definitely shouldn't have let it go this far. The ducal expression fell.

Never had been very good at it, anyway.

"And yet here you stand, berating me over Cav, as if you've spent the past ten years of your life pining over me." A breathless laugh escaped her, though he could tell she wasn't very far from crying again. "You arrogant wretch. You didn't want this betrothal any more than I did, so what right have you to be angry over a marriage proposal I received almost a year ago? One that was doomed from the start, for how determined my father was to preserve me just for you."

"Did you give yourself to him?"

Her brown eyes raged anew. "What! How? Why?"

"I'll take that as a yes." But he knew, deep down, it wasn't true. No woman who had given herself to a man could manage to put on such innocent airs. And why he felt compelled to say what he said, well, he couldn't rightly say.

But her reaction was not what he'd expected.

She reared back her hand. Smacked him so hard his hand reactively flew to his face.

"Ow!" His cheek stung beneath his palm. "Why the hell did you do that?"

"For insulting me! For thinking so low of me you'd accuse me of ruining myself before I was properly married! For--no, do you want to know the truth, Lord Carrington?" She paused, asserted herself, tipped her chin. Proceeded to give him a slow once-over. "I did sleep with him."

Justin felt his limbs stiffen, his insides flame with anger. "If you are joking, madam, 'tis cruel," he murmured, but she was already talking over him.

"I slept with him and a dozen other men. Oh, I forget all their names." She laughed carelessly, a sound he didn't care for in the least. Particularly since it was at his expense. "You know how it is, don't you? But of course you do! You've had many a conquest yourself, isn't that right, Lord Carrington?"

"That's enough, Sara." Everything inside of him burned. He wanted to punch something or someone. Or, better yet, wanted to tear Cavanaugh from limb to limb. Then take pleasure in watching the pieces burn.

Good Lord, he'd never had so violent a thought. What was happening to him?

"You're right, my lord." She stepped back. "It is enough."

In a whirl of heavy purple skirts, she left, marching up the stairs, tripping up on a couple along the way, and into the grand hall.

Justin, sensible man that he was--and though what he really wanted to do was saddle a horse and ride until he was out of breath--followed her lead. She was already well into the foyer and moving onward at a fast pace, when he, stopping for a brief moment to compose himself at the doorway, finally stepped inside.

Laughter filled the air, accompanied by the sound of someone playing Mozart on a pianoforte. Sebastian's lively baritone boomed in the distance, most likely greeting the other guests, and for a second, Justin swore he heard Milly's playful soprano in the midst of it all. Impossible. The duchess would have never invited Lady St. Clair to a private house party. She might've secluded herself from the *ton*, but her morals were still well intact.

Remembering the duchess's and Sara's shared sentiment on the article being unbecoming of a gentleman, he removed his slouch hat and handed it to a footman.

He loved this place; it reminded him of the accounts of English history he'd read as a child. When homes were built to glorify the country and its leaders, and its leaders were as much warriors as they were noblemen. The smell of it was old, a welcoming combination of earth and wood with hints of the duchess's prized lilies, but the interior itself was new.

"Saints preserve us, Lord Carrington. I do believe you become more and more handsome every time I see you."

Ah, the duchess.

Justin turned his gaze upward. Caroline, the Duchess of Worcester, leaned over the railing of the staircase, and beamed down at him.

"Your Grace," he murmured, bowing. "Certainly your decorator deserves a raise. The house looks remarkable."

"Believe me when I tell you," she said, walking down the steps, "he is well compensated for his talents. How are your parents? Sebastian tells me your engagement party was splendid last evening."

Splendid was not the word that came to mind when recalling the chain of events at his and Sara's soiree. "Mother was satisfied with the turnout," he said. "She sends her love and condolences for being unable to attend this time."

"Dear Elizabeth." Caroline inclined her head. "I do miss her so. Oh, but I've just had the great pleasure of meeting your fiancée,

Justin. She and Anna have adjoining rooms." Her eyes, crystal blue as Sebastian's, grew wide. "She is very beautiful. Not at all what I expected, I must confess. Oh my, but what a dreadful thing to say! Do you see what happens when one secludes one's self from society?"

"Ah, my lady." Justin dropped a kiss to the back of her hand. "Truly, no one can compare to your beauty."

The duchess--Caroline, as she preferred to be called in close conversation--beamed. "You warm me to my very core, sweet boy. But I would venture to say that I do pale in comparison to your young bride-to-be. In fact, I don't believe I've seen a face quite so fair in at least twenty years, if not more. Kilkenny must have had his hands full, raising a daughter so beautiful." She popped her gloved hands over her mouth. "You see? There I go again!"

Justin laughed. "Caroline, my dear duchess." He crooked his arm, and she tucked her hand inside. "I like it much better when propriety's not getting the best of you. Indeed, it's why your parties are, have been, and always will be my favorite."

As they walked toward the sound of chattering guests, Caroline leaned in and whispered, "I do throw the best house parties, don't I? Even hired a group of Irish musicians for entertainment this time instead of the usual wind/string orchestra. A scandalous choice in all regards of decency, especially if one is apt to read that hosh-posh in the *Tattler*, but you know those gossip columns never did bother me." She waved a hand dismissively. "I haven't a care in the world for all that nonsense."

Justin almost laughed again. Caroline might not have cared for the gossip papers, but she did cause quite a stir when all the stories about Sebastian allegedly spurning Lady Alwin hit the columns. Kicked one editor in the shin so hard he was forced to use a cane for weeks and nearly broke the nose of another, both of whom retracted their stories the very next day.

No paper had printed anything scandalous about Sebastian, Lord Beaufort, since then.

And it was a good thing, too. Word spread within minutes of Caroline's display that she had the left hook of a professional boxer, and no one in their right mind wanted to deal with an ill-tempered duchess who had a knack for throwing good punches.

"Speaking of the Irish!" Caroline squeaked. Uncanny left hook or no, she was still as dainty as a field mouse. "You must tell me more about your fiancée, my dear. She truly is the most wonderful creature. Are you getting on well?"

Not at the moment, he wanted to say. "We are becoming acquainted."

"That is good. I suppose a bit of awkwardness is to be expected. Tell me, have you met Sebastian's guest yet? The one from Ireland who will be working with Sebastian and His Grace on the steam engine project?"

"We've met." *Unfortunately.*

"Excellent. A modest man, he is. About thirty or so, I presume, and one of the most likeable Irishmen I've met. Great knowledge on the industry as well, though I must confess, I do not have as great an interest as the duke and Sebastian."

"I don't think anyone has as great an interest as those two."

"True. Oh, Justin, I should tell you." She stopped in front of the doorway to the parlor, where everyone had gathered to await dinner. "I invited the Countess of Camden. She's been a delight in our Tuesday sewing circle, and I simply couldn't leave her off the guest list."

"The countess is a kind woman."

Caroline put on a rather sheepish grin. "She brought her daughter," she said between gritted teeth, and Justin felt his stomach turn. "Oh, and I can see you're not happy about that. I'm not either, but I couldn't turn them away. Mary said Millicent hasn't been out in a while and--"

"Well, that's a lie. She was at Mayfair just last night at my engagement party."

"Oh, good Lord! Elizabeth invited her to Mayfair?"

Justin risked a glance inside the parlor. He couldn't see Milly, but he could damn well hear her. Laughing and talking as if she hadn't a care in the world. When she knew he'd be here. And with Sara.

"I broke off the affair last night," he said.

Caroline sounded somewhat hopeful. "Just steer clear of her. The hall is big enough. Besides, you'll only see her at dinner and during the evening's events. Your days will be too busy for female company as it is. Sebastian's been dying to go fishing, and the duke's been too busy to accompany him. And Lord knows I can't fish to save my life."

"You've never fished with me."

"Have so! Don't you remember when the duke was away up North? And you and Sebastian begged me to go with you?"

Justin threw his head back and laughed. "How old were we then? Twelve?"

"Thirteen! And the two of you thought it would be funny to put handfuls of worms in the pockets of my pelisse."

His side hurt, he was laughing so hard. "You found them, though," he said in between breaths. "And gave us a good punishing too, if I remember correctly. Made us scrub every dish in the kitchen until our hands were raw. Even the ones which were already clean."

"The two of you deserved it. And I only found them because I stuck my hands--my *bare hands*!--in my pockets, and proceeded to smash into the ickiest substance I'd ne'er felt in my living life!" Her face twisted at the memory. "Oh, and the smell!" She did a full body shiver that made the curls atop her head bounce. "Disgusting."

"We're not much different now, you know, Sebastian and I. Only older. And a bit larger."

"And more mischievous," she added, and Justin smiled knowingly, unable to argue.

TWELVE

Sara paused at an arch in the hall, just before the next arch that led into the parlor where the duchess's guests had gathered.

She took a deep breath. Justin had just entered the room, the duchess, *Caroline,* tucked neatly on his arm, and they'd been laughing. House parties were supposed to be this way, she reminded herself. Happy, lighthearted gatherings in which one could let one's self cleverly slip across the boundaries of propriety, if only for several days at a time.

Only Sara wasn't feeling so lighthearted.

Happy wasn't what she'd call herself at present, either.

She'd changed into one of her newer dresses; a pale pink muslin trimmed in tiny bows, two of which gathered the material at her shoulders, another gathering the low-cut neckline, while the rest were smartly placed all around the skirt. Lana, who had been aberrantly silent since their arrival in Worcester, had aided in re-pinning her hair, leaving a few strands to frame her face and neckline, even suggesting she add a few drops of lavender oil to her wrists and in between her bosom.

All that remained was the simple task of intermingling with the rest of the party.

The room had fallen silent when he and the duchess walked inside. Mesmerized, all of them, Sara imagined. Justin had that time suspending effect when he entered a room, and Caroline, whom Sara immediately liked upon their introduction upstairs, undoubtedly possessed the same attribute. Sara wondered if they, she and Justin, would have the same spellbinding aura as husband and wife.

She suspected they would.

Then again, any woman would appear all the more breathtaking on his arm.

Yes, her betrothed was a beautiful man, and that made her grin a little in spite of herself. She took a step forward, then another, until finally she was at the door of the parlor, and Anna was waving for her to come inside.

Though she didn't move the room to total silence, as Justin and Caroline had, the guests quieted their chatter long enough to regard her presence. Cav stopped the slower rendition of the rondo he was playing on the pianoforte, favored her a wide grin, and proceeded to pick up on a familiar Irish jig.

Sara couldn't stop herself from smiling back at him.

A dream, it was, Cav being in England. And looking just the same as she remembered in his stylish ensemble of cream trousers and matching waistcoat, offset by a brilliant emerald green jacket. She'd missed him. Missed dancing with him, talking with him. Missed that feeling of a man expressing interest in what she had to say, no matter how great or small. No one had ever listened to her so attentively.

Well. Except for Justin. But that was neither here nor there considering he'd chosen to behave as a child and chide her for nearly accepting another man's marriage proposal.

Which, to Sara's mind, was utterly ridiculous.

Cav would have never made such an explosive display; hotheaded behavior wasn't in his blood. He was the epitome of class. Always well-dressed, always polite, always smiling, always willing to strike up an intelligent conversation. And he was always--*always*--surrounded by women.

At present, he was flanked by two elderly matrons, and Anna, who stood in front of him, and one other.

Sara tapered her gaze.

Lady St. Clair. Justin's mistress. No, *former* mistress, she acknowledged with a tiny sense of relief. She'd been invited, too? The insufferable trollop was smiling from ear to ear, positively marveling down at Cav, her white blond locks fastened tightly upon her head, a glass of lemonade in her gloved hand. But Cav didn't pay her any mind.

He smiled, winked at Sara.

Sara, ninny she was when attention focused solely on her, blushed and looked away.

All to find Justin staring boldly at her.

He was still angry. His stance was guarded: arms folded over his chest, legs spread shoulder-width apart, and those eyes ... His eyes appeared black as marble.

Caroline and Sebastian stood on either side of him, laughing and smiling as if in mid-recollection of some past memoir, but

Justin wasn't listening. Hadn't so much as flinched in the past several seconds.

The silent treatment would not do; she needed to speak to him. Needed to right this nonsense before they hated each other. Or worse, went into a marriage with nothing but enmity between them. She wouldn't have it. Her mother and father had been in love, and while she couldn't expect such a sentiment for herself, she could see to a cordial friendship with her husband.

Collecting thoughts, feelings and nerves in one fell swoop, Sara started for the other side of the room, and was more than a little surprised when Justin, murmuring an apology to his company, moved to meet her.

Only, before she could reach him, a familiar voice spoke her name, and her slippered feet came to an instinctive halt. She turned, Justin coming to stand directly before her. "Yes, Mr. Cavanaugh?"

Cav grinned. "Favor us with a song, my lady?"

All at once, Sara felt the blood rush into her cheeks. Anna, who was still standing in front of the piano, nodded gleefully. While Lady St. Clair's already thin lips formed an even thinner, disapproving line.

Sara swallowed convulsively. "I don't know any songs which would please our esteemed hostess."

"Nonsense. I am certain Her Grace's guests would welcome a fresh voice to the room. Especially one as lovely as yours."

Fiendish man. Sara did have an agreeable voice. Nothing so strong as to rival that of an opera singer, mind, but agreeable enough for close company. One could only find so much to do as an only child, and so she'd spent a fair amount of time learning traditional tunes, a few local pub songs (which Lana heatedly disapproved of), and a handful of Gaelic hymns.

Still.

A house party where she only knew a grand total of four people? Five, including her new friend Caroline, but not nearly enough.

"Indeed, Lady Ballivar!" Caroline brushed past an inert Justin, and touched Sara on the arm. "I wasn't told you could sing well. Furthermore, I wasn't aware that you and Mr. Cavanaugh were acquainted."

Sara didn't answer.

"Lady Ballivar and I are old friends," Cav replied.

"Splendid!" said Caroline. "Oh, but Lady Ballivar, please do favor us a song. And do not worry your head about my unfamiliarity of the tune. We shall all enjoy hearing a new melody as opposed to the old tunes played at every single party in England."

"Indeed, Lady Ballivar," someone else chimed. "Do sing for us."

"Yes, do," came a second.

Sara couldn't say no. She curtsied, and moved to stand beside Cav. "What shall we sing?"

His smile reached his eyes. "I'd rather you did the singing, love. I'll accompany you." He hit a perfect a-chord. "How about *Siúil a Rúin*? You remember that one?"

Of course she remembered. It was her mother's favorite. One of the songs she sang over and over while carrying Sara in the womb, or so her father had confided. But she never dreamt of singing it in England, at the private house party of a duchess, in the presence of her fiancé, who had not moved from his stance since Cav had said her name.

This day could not get much worse.

Sara wiped her clammy palms across the skirt of her dress a couple of times. Cleared her throat for good measure.

Cav hit the chord again. "*Siúil a Rúin*, my lords, ladies and gentlemen. One of our favorites from back home."

The room grew quiet as Sara began to sing--*I wish I were on yonder hill, 'tis there I'd sit and cry my fill*--and, thankfully, without cracking the first note.

*** *** ***

Justin had never heard a voice so beautiful, so angelic. In fact, he'd wager the angels themselves were watching from Heaven, their snow white faces gaped in envy. True, she wasn't an opera singer, but Justin had never cared for an intense vibrato. The opera was something he attended to keep up with society. To *save face*, as Sebastian liked to call it. But none of those prima donna songbirds held a candle to this one.

Father had been right to send for her. Oh, the old man had given his dying state as a reason for honoring the contract so quickly, but Justin knew better. His father had been dying for ages.

No, he'd used his wavering health as a rationale. Justification in sending for Sara earlier than was mentioned in the agreement. Because the old man knew Justin had gotten himself in too deep with Milly.

When he was a lad of twelve, sitting on the riverbank beside his father, watching as the sun settled into the western horizon, the duke had said, "A man needs to know what he wants out of life at an early age, Justin, or he'll never get there." And then he'd looked at his hands, twisted them about. Justin could still see the dirt gathered beneath his fingernails, beneath both their fingernails, a prideful mark of a full day's worth of fishing.

"Stay level headed," he'd gone on to say. "Speak the truth, even if it kills you. The language of truth is unadorned and always simple. Remember that." And Justin had nodded his understanding, though in truth, he didn't understand.

He understood now.

Now, at twenty-two, nearly twenty-three, years of age, Justin realized with sound assurance the meaning in those words his father had spoken that dusky evening in late June. Truth not only meant speaking the truth to others but speaking it to one's self. And he'd been lying to himself for months now.

He didn't want Milly.

He wanted Sara. This angelic creature who sang as if every note rose from her very soul. Who sat with him, laughing in a coach about how one holds their reins, her small hand encased in his as if ... As if she was already his wife. And he, her husband. This enchanting young woman who spoke a language he, in all his intelligent, well-educated, scholarly existence, had never come to understand, only to find he *wanted* to understand.

Because she spoke it.

When she finished the piece, a lovely, harmonious combination of English and Gaelic, and everyone began clapping enthusiastically, he became certain of one thing. Something he would have never openly admitted, even to himself. Until now.

He had fallen desperately in love with her.

He was ruined, smitten, besotted. Every adjective imaginable for a man whose heart had been stolen by a woman.

An age-old sentiment, that. But true nonetheless.

Sara curtsied and smiled, patted Cavanaugh on the shoulder, which Justin didn't care for, though he could see in her eyes, even as Cavanaugh looked up at her with that damnable infernal smile, that no passion lay there. The man may have asked for her hand, may have had it if she'd been free to give it, but she didn't want him. And Justin knew enough about female gazes to know when a woman wanted a man, and when she didn't.

Which meant Justin had been a complete and utter fool for chastising Sara over Cavanaugh. Which also meant he had to find some way to apologize. And apologies, while necessary at times, weren't exactly his forte.

Sara and Cavanaugh exchanged a few words over the sound of delightful murmurs and clapping hands, while Justin watched and waited. The friendship between these two would be difficult to bear, but for her sake, for his *own* sake, he'd bear it. He loved her enough to give her that.

Sara moved with easy grace around the pianoforte, smiling over her shoulder as Cavanaugh began playing another rondo. She was almost immediately bombarded by several of Caroline's guests, including Caroline herself.

Though his patience to speak to her, to be with her, wore thin, Justin smiled, and listened as they raved over her singing abilities. Some urged her to sing again, but in her innate modesty, she politely declined.

"I'll take it you liked the song."

Justin nodded toward the crowd surrounding Sara. "I believe everyone did, Sebastian. Your mother most of all. But, yes, I enjoyed the song."

"Every man's dream, that," Sebastian said. "Having a wife who is both beautiful and blessed with amiable vocal chords. A rare combination, indeed. Believe me, I've looked."

"You've made your way through every woman in the opera house?" Justin shook his head. "Yet, here you are, still unmarried."

Sebastian shrugged. "None of them interested me in that fashion. Well, not enough to carry one to the altar. Speaking of which, when do you suppose you'll be marrying our lovely Irish songbird?"

"That," Justin said emphatically, "is something we have yet to discuss. Father said the honoring of the contract was but two months premature, which means ..." He paused as Sara's gaze, heavy with exasperation, turned to him. The ongoing praise had become tedious, and she was looking to him for help.

"Which means you have a little over a month." Sebastian clapped a hand on Justin's shoulder. "Forgive me for being too forward, old chap, but I don't believe you'll be able to hold out that long. Correction, I don't believe *either* of you will be able to hold out that long."

Justin surveyed his betrothed. How lovely she was in her pastel pink gown. Every inch of her looked creamy, from the tips of her slippered feet to the coiffure of soft, dark curls piled atop her head. She reminded him of an exotic confection, all wrapped up in ribbons and bows. The very modicum of innocence.

Though from the way she kissed, and the way her hands had roamed inside his collar, as if she were just as eager to touch him, he was beginning to think she was anything but.

"Perhaps not," he finally said, and from the corner of his eye, he saw Sebastian smile elatedly. "And as much as I'd relish wiping that smug grin off your face, Lord Beaufort, I do believe my intended needs rescuing."

Unfortunately it was Sebastian who had to do the rescuing. The call came for dinner, and Caroline had already arranged for Sebastian to sit next to Sara, while Justin and Anna were assigned on the other side, directly across from them. Worse, Cavanaugh was seated to Sara's left, so if either he or Sebastian struck up a conversation they'd be forced to lean over her. Judging by the neckline of the dress she'd chosen, both men were in for quite a show.

Justin smothered a groan. He'd never understood the rules on seating arrangements; why shouldn't he have the right to sit next to his own fiancée? Granted, Caroline only had two formal dinners at her house parties--one at the beginning, the other at the end--so he couldn't justly complain. All other mealtimes were unceremoniously served sideboard-style, the general setup of the dining room consisting of several round tables where guests could serve and seat themselves.

This initial meal, and of course the last, were the only instances Caroline insisted on honoring decorum in her household. She was, after all, a reformed free spirit, and often referred to propriety as the dreaded *p*-word.

"Cavanaugh seems to be a fascinating person," Anna whispered over a spoonful of cress soup.

"Fascinating," Justin repeated, watching through hooded eyes as Cavanaugh made quiet conversation with Sara.

Sebastian, who--wonder of wonders--paid no attention to Cavanaugh and Sara, was speaking with the dowager to his right and had apparently just murmured some lewd comment. Her cheeks were turning redder by the second.

"He is thirty," Anna continued, "the oldest of six, and his father is not only involved in the development of the steam engines but also in the preservation of the ancient constructs in Ireland. Isn't that wonderful?"

"Spectacular."

"And although his father opposed the *Act of Union* or … what did Cav call it?"

"*Acht an Aontais 1800*." Justin sipped on a glass of watered-down wine, winced, and chased it quickly with a generous swill of milk.

"Yes!" Anna chirped, and then, leaning in to him, "Dear brother, why do you always drink the wine when we all know you've never liked it?"

"I *attempt* to drink," he said, "thinking I might eventually acquire a taste for it. You were saying?"

"It will not offend the duchess if you don't drink, Justin."

"You were saying?" he pressed, and Anna gave him a cynical half-smile.

"Only that Cavanaugh and his father, along with the Duke of Kilkenny, have been amiable supporters of the House since then."

"What is the point of this?"

Anna looked nonplussed. "I was only making conversation, which is more than I can say for you. Staring at Sara and Cav has been the highlight of dinner tonight, at least on this side of the table."

Justin peered down the row of guests lining their side. Sure enough, and with the only exception being the Dowager Duchess of Clitheroe, who was on the brink of falling asleep in her soup bowl, all eyes were pointed in the general direction of Sara and Cavanaugh.

"Of course, they could be looking at Sebastian," Anna suggested. "Shameless, that one."

"He's only being polite to an aging woman. You mustn't think so ill of Sebastian, Anna. He's not a bad man."

Anna's jaw tightened. "You know why I don't like him."

Justin set down his spoon and tilted his head toward his sister, keeping a covert eye on his intended. "It might interest you to know that upon Lady Alwin giving birth to Sebastian's alleged child, the native origin of its father was immediately thrown into question."

The small space between Anna's blond brows snapped together. "What do you mean, *native origin*?"

"Did you know," he continued, ignoring the icy glare he was receiving from Milly, who was seated on the other side and further down, "that prior to Sebastian asking for Lady Alwin's hand, she had spent the past several weeks traveling across Brazil with her family? Apparently the marquess has a fascination with other cultures, and has spent the better part of his life studying those of, shall we say, less-fortunate, uncivilized lands? Not that Brazil is uncivilized, mind. I hear the emperor has been quite the advocate since his taking over in '21."

Anna leaned closer. "Go on."

"In any case, the Alwin family stayed with one of the emperor's councilmen during their tenure in Rio de Janeiro. Rumor has it that of this councilman's ten children, our Lady Alwin was quite taken with his eldest son. So taken, in fact, that she begged her father to let her stay when it was time for her family to return to England."

Clearly unconvinced, Anna said, "I'd never known Lady Alwin to put on such a display. You must be mistaken."

"Perhaps," Justin allowed. "But after Sebastian discovered she was with child, and well, we all know what happened next. She attempted to return to Brazil. Only, her father denied her leave and swept her and her mother away from the Continent."

"Her reputation might have been saved had she stayed, and had Sebastian"--her blue eyes stole a quick glance at the source--"married her as he should have." Looking at Justin, she said, "I, too, never believed Sebastian would allow a woman's reputation to be ruined so contemptibly. Even if the child wasn't his. And I'm not saying that it wasn't. But even if it wasn't, the right choice would have been for him to accept the child as his own. The *ton* would have been none the wiser, and Lady Alwin's reputation would still be intact."

"You seem to have thought this over."

"I have!" She covered her mouth with her fingertips. "I have," she repeated. "Haven't you?"

"Sebastian's my best friend, Anna. What do you think?"

"Then if you have thought it over, as I have--many, *many* times--then do you not agree with me? That Sebastian should have accepted his fiancée, faults and all, and claimed the child?"

"The father of the child was half native Brazilian, Anna."

Anna's lips parted.

"Which was made perfectly clear when the child, a male child, was born with naturally bronzed skin and hair the color of black coal." He shifted his gaze to Sebastian, who was now contributing to Sara's and Cavanaugh's conversation. Thank goodness. "Seeing as Lady Alwin had red hair, and I can't imagine our Lord Beaufort fathering any offspring who isn't born with a mass of gold curls, I'd have to conclude that the child was, indeed, *not* Sebastian's."

When Anna did not respond, Justin added, "I do not believe Lady Alwin's reputation would have stayed any more intact had she remained in England and married Sebastian, than it is now. I hear she's made a fine home for herself, and her child, in France."

Anna did not say a word, only stared at Sebastian as if she were looking at him for the first time. Even as dinner ended, and Justin escorted her to the drawing room, she was speechless. The shock of it, of Sebastian actually having told the truth, had apparently taken her by surprise. In fact, Justin thought her to be close to fainting until Caroline, speaking over the guests as they were taking their seats, asked her to select the first reading.

"Oh," she said, snapping out of her hypnotic state. She stood, chose a random book from the shelf, and read the spine: *"The*

Sonnets by William Shakespeare." Satisfied, she announced confidently, "I'll be reading number one hundred and sixteen."

Justin took the empty seat next to Sara, as Anna began her reading. "*Let me not to the marriage of true minds admit impediments. Love is not love ...*"

"Grace be to God for Shakespeare," he whispered. "If that book had been anything but, Anna might have been in a bit of a predicament."

Sara leaned into him. "She doesn't read much, I gather."

"Gossip papers, mostly. Did you enjoy dinner? Caroline's cook always makes the finest lamb in mint cream."

"Yes, it was lovely."

*** *** ***

Sara closed her eyes. He smelled wonderful, the remnants of soap and aftershave and outdoors. His thigh brushed her knee, and Sara had the most peculiar urge to put her hand over his. She'd almost forgotten they'd argued.

"Lovely." He leaned closer. His sleeve nudged her bare arm, his breath tickled her cheek. "Lovely was the tune you sang for us before dinner."

Sara blinked, suddenly aware that her face was growing warmer. Her response came out a feeble whisper. "Thank you, my lord."

"*Love's not Time's fool, though rosy lips and cheeks within his bending sickle's compass come ...*"

"I would very much enjoy hearing you sing again," he murmured close to her ear.

The warmth in her cheeks spread down her neck, to her chest. "Her Grace asked that I sing once more before our stay has come to an end."

"*Love alters not with his brief hours and weeks,*" Anna read on, "*but bears it out even to the edge of doom ...*"

"I was thinking more of a private recital, my lady," he said, and Sara could almost hear him smiling. "Perhaps when we are alone."

"Oh." It was all she could think to say. He wanted to be alone with her. A simple request. She'd been alone with him several times now. But something in his tone promised the next time would be different. Only how, she did not know.

"Perhaps when you permit me our day together." His voice was so seductively smooth the tiny hairs at the base of her head prickled. "When I can have you all to myself."

"*If this be error and upon me proved*," Anna read, and Sara, turning her eyes to the other guests in effort to keep her blush at bay, swore her heart was on the verge of leaping from her chest.

Even Sebastian looked enraptured, his lips parted, eyes focused solely on Anna as she finished what was, in every circle of society, comparable to the *Holy Word*.

"*I never writ, nor no man ever loved.*"

Justin drew back and clapped with the other guests as Anna smiled and curtsied. All the while, Sara was paralyzed. Oh, she managed to clap--the sonnet was one of her favorites--but her hands shook so badly she had to fold them together and push them into her lap.

Justin wanted to be alone with her. She'd known this, hadn't she? This was one of the stakes of their bet, which had been a stupid thing to do now she thought about it. Proper young ladies didn't make bets with gentlemen. But she had, and he wanted a day with her. And a night, she reminded herself, a twinge of nervousness settling in her stomach.

"Tomorrow," he said, as Caroline chose one of the dowagers for the next reading.

"Tomorrow?"

"We're fishing tomorrow down by the river. You should join us. The duchess usually arranges for a picnic, *al fresco*. Granted, she won't be attending. She and the rest of the female guests usually stay inside, playing cards and gossiping over tea."

The nervousness in her belly began a slow rise to her throat. She blinked several times.

"You've made other plans." His brow furrowed. "You've decided to take tea and gossip with the ladies?"

Sara shook her head.

"Then what is it?"

She closed her eyes, opened them. "Cav invited me to go fishing tomorrow."

That did it. He frowned. His eyes, which had but a few minutes earlier been alight with warmth and mirth turned cold, the pupils receding from the irises.

She hadn't just disappointed him. Disappointment wasn't what she saw there, casting a shadow on his flawless face.

She'd hurt him.

"Justin," she whispered, barely. "I--"

"Don't." He held up a quieting hand. "Just ... don't."

"But I--" she began, but he was already standing.

His hands curled into fists, relaxed. For a moment, he stared ahead unseeingly, and she wondered what he might be thinking. If he was really that angry with her, if she'd genuinely hurt this steel-of-a-man by promising to attend an event with someone else. It was just fishing, after all. Couldn't rightly place it in the same category as an event, so to speak, much less consider it a grand occasion.

But Cav had invited her. She'd told Justin the truth about him, that he'd asked for her hand in marriage. What could she have rightfully expected his reaction to be? She would've been just as angry had he invited Lady St. Clair to something of equal import to her.

Blast. He'd sat next to her, talked with her, laughed with her, and she'd ruined it. She'd managed to be happy with him, fight with him, nearly make amends with him, and ultimately break his spirit all in one day.

This had to be some sort of record for feministic deficiencies.

He cleared his throat. "Enjoy the rest of your evening."

All Sara could do was stare up at him, and then *after* him as he, without so much as muttering another word, stalked from the room, resembling more of a raging lion than her pride-wounded fiancé.

THIRTEEN

The River Severn ran at the bottom of the hill, just below the gardens of Worcester Hall. Though the duchess, when hosting her annual house party, spent most of her time having tea and ladylike conversation with the other female guests, she always made certain her male guests were well taken care of, particularly when they fished. And as tradition would have it, the gentlemen spent the first full day of the house party doing just that.

From where she stood at the top of a steep incline, Sara could make out a sideboard filled with food and drink as well as a few small round tables, covered in white linen and nestled beneath the bows of a side-by-side pair of grand oak trees. The men were spread out along the bank of the river, their coats draped over the backs of their chairs. Anna joined her side, and together, she and Sara strolled down the hill.

"He'll recover," Anna told her. She bit off a piece of apple. "His pride is only wounded, and you know how men are about their beloved pride."

Sara shrugged. "I'm not so sure. You should have seen his face. If I'd been blessed with more than half a brain, I would've never mentioned Cav at all. He didn't ask that I accompany him, only that I join him at some point during the day."

"Which is what we're doing," said Anna. "And don't say you only have half a brain. You're quite the smartest young woman I know."

"Thank you. But I should have just kept it as so. You and I, having no interest in partaking in feminine conversation today, deciding to watch the men fish."

"Which, by the way, I'm very happy we chose to do. Especially since Lady St. Clair made an appearance. Heavens, I despise that woman. A menace, if ever there was one."

"I can't say I very much like her either," said Sara. "She stares as if I have the plague."

Anna nearly choked on her apple. "How morbid!" But then, with the faintest smile curling her lips, "Sounds like something I would say. Indeed, Lady St. Clair looks at everyone in that manner. Down the line of her pointy nose, though the rest of her is rather plump in comparison. I never understood what my brother saw in her."

"Experience perhaps?"

"Decisively overrated."

"Your brother doesn't seem to think so."

"My brother doesn't know what he thinks. Besides, I believe all this Milly business is a moot point." Her eyes glimmered as she glanced aside at Sara. "I believe he is quite taken with you. Hopelessly besotted, if you ask me."

Sara felt her cheeks flush. "How can you tell?"

"The way he looks at you, silly! How else?"

"Hmm." Sara felt her heart give a little flutter as she spotted the back of Justin's dark head. He and Sebastian sat side by side, heads bent in discussion over a lure.

"But I also believe this is a splendid idea," Anna went on, "you keeping your fishing date with Mr. Cavanaugh. Justin needs some incentive to realize just how enamored with you he really is. A little jealousy will do him good."

"I don't want to make him angry," Sara said. "Last night he was—"

"Last night was last night. Goodness, Sara, don't you know anything about men?"

"Apparently not."

"Well, I'll tell you. They get angry, they sleep on it, and they get over it. Today will be about you visiting with your handsome friend, Mr. Cavanaugh, whilst my brother learns a valuable lesson."

"And that is ...?"

"Never allow yourself to be at odds with your intended. He needs to apologize for being an arse about Cav."

"Anna!"

"What? Well, he was an arse, was he not?"

Sara paused. "Well, yes, but you needn't be so vulgar."

"Oh, all right." Anna tossed her apple core into the grass. "We shouldn't be so vulgar. Perhaps we should say something else. Some sort of code word for when someone is being ..."

Sara lowered her voice. "An arse?"

"Precisely. Oh!" Anna clapped her hands together. "I have it. We'll call them a toad."

"A *toad*?" Sara raised her eyebrows. "That's not exactly a nice word either. At least not when one is referring to a person rather than an amphibian."

"You'd rather we called them arses?"

Sara groaned. This must've been how Lana felt when Sara was spouting off curses in Gaelic. "Of course not. But we're comparing men to amphibians."

"Men *are* amphibians when they're being arses," Anna pointed out. "Mindless, slimy creatures."

True enough. "Toad it is," Sara conceded, and Anna smiled triumphantly.

"Just so you know," Anna whispered as they drew near the river, "even though my toad-of-a-brother and his toad-of-a-best-friend love it, I absolutely detest fishing."

Sara snickered. "Then I will regard this as an extreme favor. Look, there are tables and chairs under the tree. You can sit back and relax, away from the fish."

"They only catch and release. A novel concept to prove how manly they are, who can catch the bigger fish. But seeing as it is Mr. Cavanaugh who has invited you today--" here, she nodded toward Cav, who was standing, fishing pole in hand, on the riverbank "--and he has left his seat unattended, I believe I'll sit closer to the river."

Sara looked. The only empty seat was beside Sebastian. "But you'll have to sit next to Lord Beaufort. And there are plenty of chairs here beneath the tables. One of the attending footmen would gladly--"

But Anna was already marching gracefully down the hill. She favored her brother and Sebastian a wide smile as they stood and murmured their greetings. Clearly she and Sebastian had come to some sort of truce; she remained standing with him even after Justin had sat back down to rethread his lure. Within seconds, they were laughing and talking as if nothing disagreeable had ever transpired between them.

"May I offer you some lemonade, my lady?"

Sara turned to the footman and politely shook her head. "Not right now, thank you. Are there any extra fishing rods?"

"Of course, my lady," he replied, looking a bit surprised. "Shall I thread and bait it for you?"

"No, thank you," she said. "I can manage."

He looked even more surprised, but remained silent, picked one of the smaller poles resting against the sidebar, and handed it to her. "The gentlemen are in possession of all the lures, my lady. Shall I select one for you?"

"Thank you, kind sir," she responded, "but I can manage that too. You've been most helpful."

He bowed, and Sara descended the hill, not missing the glare of Justin's dark eyes when she failed to acknowledge him. Let him stew a bit. Anna said a little jealousy would be good for him, and judging by the way his eyes roamed from her to Cav as she approached the riverbank, it was working.

"Your fiancé's giving me the evil-eye," Cav muttered to her, but of course he was smiling.

She spared the smallest glance over her shoulder at Justin. He was visibly clenching his teeth, his eyes all but darting spears.

"I hope me getting killed isn't part of your little ploy." Cav cast his line. "I am here on business, you know. Da won't be happy if I end up dead before this deal is worked out with Worcester."

Sara attempted to look shocked. "Whatever do you mean? What ploy?"

He cocked his head to the side. "I wasn't born yesterday. You could've just declined my offer, you know, instead of using me to spark the devil in your fiancé."

"I agreed because I wanted to spend time with you, Cav. We haven't seen each other for quite a while."

"Months." His emerald eyes shifted to the rod in her hand. "Want me to bait that for you?" He glanced past her, toward Justin. "That should sting him a bit."

Sara bit back a smile. "Why I'd be delighted, Lord Cavanaugh." She handed him the pole.

Careful not to disturb the water, he set his own pole on the ground, holding it in place with his foot while he worked on Sara's.

"You always did tie the best lure," she murmured, watching as his fingers skillfully made a loop here and a knot there.

The side of his mouth twitched. "Don't play girlish games with me, Sara. I may be willing to lend aid to your little scheme, but I'm far from immune to female attention."

Her lips parted, and she nearly caught her breath when he gave her a flashing gaze beneath the sheath of long lashes.

She'd forgotten how handsome he was.

"I'll have you casting your line whilst that prim bottom of yours sits on my lap, if you don't behave," he murmured. "I'm certain that would get an ample rise out of Lord Carrington."

"Cav!" The outright impertinence! "Have you lost your senses?"

His shoulders shook with laughter. "I've lost plenty, sweet." He handed over her rod, perfectly baited with a spinning minnow lure. "My senses, however, are still intact. Now, cast your line. Or shall I do that for you too?"

She narrowed her eyes. "No, thank you."

He shrugged, picked up his own rod. Recast it with all the elegance of a skilled fisherman. "So, tell me. Are you enjoying England?"

"I like it just fine, thank you."

He snorted. "How convincing."

Toad.

"Pray tell, Lord Cavanaugh," she said, "what answer might I offer to make myself sound more convincing?"

"No need for that," he said gruffly. "In all the years I've known you, sarcasm has never been a prime feature in that unique personality of yours. I was merely seeking an honest answer to an honest question. We were able to make decent conversation at one time, were we not?"

He had her there. For as long as she could remember, Cav had been a part of her life. What with her father's close involvement with Cav's father, Sir Dunmore, and the hours upon hours the two stayed shut up in her father's study, she and Cav had created a close bond. He'd take her fishing, allow her to accompany him to town in his shiny curricle where they'd purchase apple tarts from Maggie's.

Sometimes they'd simply walk together. And talk. Oh, they'd talk of life, the land, and, later on, marriage. What he wanted from a marriage. What she *thought* she wanted from a marriage. She had only been fifteen, far from an expert on matters of the heart. From that moment, however, perhaps even earlier, something changed in the way she looked at Patrick Cavanaugh.

It was precisely when she fancied herself in love with him.

It was also when Cav began paying excessive amounts of attention to her. Calling upon her even when his father had no business in Dublin. Writing letters when they had gone days without seeing one other. From that day, the day they'd talked of marriage, Cav was always the first to sign her dance card. And though propriety limited him to only two per night, he found other ways to be near her.

One night in particular, after they'd finished a polonaise and were walking the perimeter of the room, he'd taken her outside into the garden. She could still see him, just as calm and collected as a nobleman ought to be, bright green eyes lit by the staked-torches lining the walkway, smile sparkling in his handsome face. He was everything she was not, confident in his wants, and he was as blunt then as he was now.

He'd come right out and confessed he wanted to kiss her.

That he'd wanted to kiss her for some time.

And kiss her, he did. Until she was weak in the knees from it, imagining they were the only two people on earth, and that she was meant to be with him, no matter what the contract in her father's desk drawer said.

The next day he asked her father for her hand in marriage.

He was refused.

Now here she was, standing with him--or sitting, rather, for a footman had just brought them a pair of chairs--on the bank of the Severn River, under the branches of a willow tree, at the house party of an English duchess. And instead of wanting his attention, of doing anything she possibly could to speak to him, to be near him, to have him hold her, touch her ... well, she was using him.

Or was she?

Yes, she was.

How had life become so complicated?

"Well?" His left brow arched so high his forehead wrinkled. "Are we to sit here in silence, or shall you answer my question?"

She'd forgotten the question.

"Is England to your liking? And spare me the triteness of 'I like it just fine.' No one likes this country just fine, they either like it, or they don't."

She bobbed her line a few times, resisted the urge to look over her shoulder at Justin. "I do like England. It's a lot like home, really. The land, the air."

"Mayfair agrees with you, then."

"The duke and duchess are very kind. And of course, there is Lady Anna. She has been wonderful."

"Ah, yes. A beautiful woman, that one. Surprising, she's not married."

"She is particular, I think. Unlike the majority, she does not seek a title."

"Sounds like someone I know." He gazed lazily at her from the side.

"I do not seek anyone, sir."

"Of course you don't." He shifted his gaze back to the water, breathed a long sigh. "No, you're betrothed to the tall, brawny one over there. If another man so much as looked at you, I daresay he'd pummel the poor fellow."

She didn't know why, but hearing Justin spoken of in a disdainful manner irritated her. "You judge him poorly," she said. "He is a gentleman."

"Naturally," he said grimly. "The firstborn of the Duke of Tethersal would be nothing less. Why else would your father have gone to so great an extent, betrothing his only child to a stranger? But"--he glanced past her, toward Justin--"I must say, at present, he does not appear so much the gentleman. I do believe he'd tear me to shreds if there weren't witnesses about."

"I told him you once asked for my hand."

Cav's eyes slid to hers. Glints of sunlight, tinkling through the branches of the willow tree, had cast ribbons of white-gold throughout his short, dark blond hair. He was thinking of something. What she'd said, perhaps? Did he regret asking for her hand? Regret ever meeting her at all?

"He wasn't entirely thrilled when I told him," she said.

"Why should he be concerned? You belong to him now, do you not? Always have, for that matter. Why should it bother him if another man once … still …" He looked away for a moment as if to collect his thoughts. Then, gazing at her again, "Why?"

Sara bit her lower lip. "Because he asked what I would have said had you asked me instead of my father."

Both brows rose expectantly.

"And I told him I would have said 'yes.'" She looked down at her hands, wishing she could seep through her chair, into the ground.

Until Justin, she'd not told a living soul; that she would have said yes had Cav asked her instead. Cav had done his duty as a gentleman, properly asking the father of the lady before the lady herself. How differently things might have been had he not given in to duty.

"Fancy that," he said, and turned back to the river.

"I'm sorry, Cav. I shouldn't have--"

"Do you remember," he said, keeping his gaze straightforward, "the first time we waltzed?"

"Yes," Sara replied quietly. "Lady O'Malley's summer ball."

"A fond memory, that. You were as nervous as a wee child, and I had to practically beg Lady O'Malley to let me waltz with you." He leaned forward, white linen stretching across broad, well-defined shoulders, and pulled his line in from the water. "But she finally agreed."

"The orchestra played *Lough Erin Shore*," she recalled, "and all I could think was how I was going to make it through an entire waltz without stepping on your toes."

He chuckled at that. "You only stepped on them twice."

"Thrice."

He shrugged, untied the minnow lure from his line. "I hardly noticed."

A brief silence ensued as he took up a wiggler lure with a set of sharp, tiny hooks attached to its belly, and began threading it carefully. Sara didn't know what to say. Hard enough, it was, controlling this speechless, eye-batting quirk of hers. The one Justin found so amusing.

"I kissed you that night." His brow pulled taut as the knot he'd just made loosened. He spared her an aside glance. "Do you remember?"

She nodded. Of course she remembered.

It was her first kiss.

And it was her last kiss.

That is, until Liverpool. When Justin had pressed her up against a book case, brought his body against hers, and kissed her with all the ravishing hunger of a man on the brink of starvation. Never had she been kissed so thoroughly, so passionately. As if he simply couldn't get enough of her. As if he'd devour her if she let him.

She'd kissed him twice since that day. On each of those memorable occasions, she'd surrendered to him without the slightest hesitation. Practically melted into his arms. And it had felt heavenly. It had felt ... *right*.

Heat infused her cheeks, and she looked over her shoulder, half-expecting to meet Justin's gaze. Sebastian and Anna were no longer there. Out for an afternoon stroll, perhaps, as they seemed to be getting on well all of a sudden.

Alas, Justin was preoccupied with changing his lure: dark head bent, equally dark eyes studying the knot he was making. The veins in his hands bulged, drawn by the balmy air to the surface of his tanned skin. His shirt sleeves were rolled up to his elbows, revealing a swell of sinewy forearms. To her chagrin, Sara couldn't repress the thought of being enveloped by them. Of having those steel-banded arms holding her body against his.

Funny, how she noticed the smallest details about him, when she'd never given a second thought to such features on any other man, including Cav.

"He's kissed you," said Cav. "Hasn't he?"

"Yes."

"Did you enjoy it?"

Affronted, Sara said, "I do not believe this is considered civilized conversation. You, asking me if I've kissed my own fiancé. Which, I might add, I have every right to do. It doesn't seem proper."

Cav shrugged, nonchalant. "Just a question. Mayn't the man who was the first to kiss a young lady inquire as to whether her experiences thereafter have been--oh, what shall we call it? Satisfying?"

"That is none of your business."

"Why can't you just answer the question?"

Sara wondered if his frustration stemmed from her refusal to answer his question, or the fact he still had not successfully tied his lure.

Maybe it was both.

"You should let me try," she offered. "My hands are smaller, and I may be able to tie the knot easier than--"

"Damnit!"

"--you."

In his rushed, irritated, attempt to thread the hooked lure, Cav had managed to hook his index finger instead. Strike that. His index *and* middle fingers.

"Ah, *rath dé ort*, Cav," she said, standing. Of course, he probably needed more than the grace of God to remedy this particular situation.

She kneeled beside him to get a better look at the damage. Blood seeped from the two spots in which the hook imbedded his fingertips. "We need to get the hook out."

He looked down at her, his face beading sweat. "I believe that's obvious," he ground out, as she reached for his hand.

"Let me see it, you silly man!" she chided, and he conceded, turning his palm up and displaying his fingers as reluctantly as one hands over a rare diamond. "I'll try not to hurt you. No, don't move."

"*Bí curamach.*" He sucked in a sharp breath through his teeth. "I said--"

"I'll be as careful as I can." She cut her eyes up at him. "But you're going to have to stop--" She broke off, her breath suddenly shallow.

A warm, strong hand had alighted on her shoulder. Her eyes shut, sealed. God, but she'd know his touch anywhere. She could be in a room full of people, brushing shoulders so casually one couldn't rightly tell who had touched them and who hadn't, and she'd know.

"Move aside, please," said Justin, and Sara turned her gaze upward to look at him. His dark eyebrows lifted. "If the hook isn't properly removed, the wound could deepen."

She nodded, allowed him to exchange places with her.

Justin kneeled before Cav, took the damaged hand with a surprising amount of care. His hand was a touch larger than Cav's, and much darker as well--two, three shades perhaps. She tried to remember if Cav's hands were calloused as Justin's were, and decided she needn't think on such things.

Cav was hurt, and she had the nerve to entertain ridiculous, unimportant thoughts.

But instead of concerning herself with Cav's dilemma, as she knew she should, Sara found herself unable to tear her gaze from Justin. Sweat soaked the slightly curled hair at the nape of his neck. His gleaming white shirt stuck to his back in several places. She frowned. The air was balmy, but not hot, and she wondered if he was merely hot natured, or if he'd really been that angry. So thoroughly riled from her façade with Cav he was literally sweating bullets.

She longed to put her hands on his back and soothe him, lean against him. *Kiss* him, if he'd allow her.

Sara took in a shuddering breath.

Kiss him, lean into him ... Goodness, what was wrong with her? Here she was, fantasizing about him. *Intimately*. Envisioning his beautiful, masculine arms, flexing with lean muscle as he tied a foot of line around the hook imbedded in Cav's fingers, wrapped around her. Holding her. Wanting her.

"Keep your hand steady," Justin murmured.

Cav swallowed, nodded his understanding. "*Go dtachta an diabhal thú*, ye damn lure." He winced as Justin applied a fair amount of pressure behind the wounds.

Sara bit her lip to smother a laugh.

Justin shot a disdainful glare at Cav. "What was that?"

"'May the devil choke you,'" Sara translated, and then she did laugh because it really did sound absurd. Who ever heard of the devil choking a fishing lure?

But Justin was not amused.

"Don't speak to me in Gaelic, please, Mr. Cavanaugh." He pushed the shank of the hook down to the skin of Cav's fingers. "If you …" He stopped, called for a footman to fetch him a towel, and focused on the hook again. Drew the line taut. "If you'd like to hold a conversation in Latin, or perhaps French, I'll be happy to oblige. Otherwise, I'll ask that you use proper English."

"English is fine." Cav inhaled sharply as Justin applied more pressure. "Just get this bloody thing out of me. Please."

"Lady Ballivar," Justin said, but he didn't look up at her. "Take the towel and be ready. The wounds will pour once the hooks are free, so a generous amount of pressure will need to be applied to stop the bleeding."

"All right." She obediently took the towel from the footman, who bowed and stepped back a few paces.

The sight of blood didn't bother her, but this particular sight did. Justin, crouched before Cav, the fate of one's fingers at the other's mercy. Doubtless Justin was beyond vexed. The veins in his forehead had surfaced. Wisps of his dark hair stuck to his face. She couldn't see his eyes, but she imagined they were just as angry, darkened to near blackness as they always seemed to be when his emotions were high.

"On the count of three," Justin said, and Cav curled his free hand into a tight fist. "One, two …"

But three didn't come. Justin had tugged the line so quickly, so firmly, Cav's face was still twisted in preparation when the hook pulled free.

Blood gushed from the two holes, and Sara rushed to cover his fingers with the towel. "Good gracious, Cav!" She pressed the material, hard as she could, to the wounds. "You nearly frightened the life out of me!"

Cav's eyes peeled open. "Ah, thank God." He sank into his chair. "Damned things hurt like the devil."

"What were you thinking?" She swatted his hand away when he tried to take the towel from her. "If you had been paying attention to your line, this wouldn't have happened!"

Cav didn't answer. Only grumbled something about stubborn Irish women beneath his breath, at which Sara did allow him to take the towel, even giving it a healthy shove that caused Cav's green eyes to flare with disapproval.

"I take it this isn't the first time," Justin murmured in a low tone, handing the damaged hook to an awaiting footman.

"Hasn't everyone been hooked once or twice?" Cav came to his feet. "One good time, at least." He gave Sara an assessing gaze, one she didn't particularly like considering he had always looked upon her with kindness.

Justin didn't seem to like it, either. His eyes, black as coal, shifted slowly from her to Cav and back again. Clearly dissatisfied with what he saw, he turned to the river, sank to his haunches, and began washing his hands in the cool water. A footman was quick to his side with a clean towel.

"I think I shall retire from fishing for today," Cav announced. "Have this looked at before infection sets in."

"Shall I come with you?" Sara lifted a shoulder. "I feel partly responsible."

"It's not your fault," he said. "And no, stay and enjoy the fresh air. You once were a good fisherman, or so I recall."

They exchanged farewells, and Cav turned and strode for the house.

"I certainly hope you enjoyed yourself."

Sara closed her eyes for a moment, taking in the hint of disdain in Justin's deep voice. She'd dealt with one headstrong man today, had managed to make him so irrefutably angry, he'd fish hooked his own fingers.

Which, privately, she felt he deserved.

But dealing with a man like Lord Carrington was an entirely different feat. Headstrongness was by far the lesser of his objectionable qualities.

He was drying his hands when Sara finally turned to look at him. "As Lord Cavanaugh said, the air is most fresh here by the river," she said, unable to stop her eyes from wandering over him.

He was completely untamed, linen shirt unbuttoned almost to mid-chest. Mud and water and grass smudged his light grey breeches; several drops of Cav's blood stained his right thigh.

By the time Sara refocused her gaze on his face her cheeks were burning.

One of his dark brows winged upward. "Seems as though you were taking in more than fresh air, my lady." He began a slow stroll toward her. "In fact, from where I sat, the two of you appeared quite cozy."

Sara stood her ground. Not because she was deliberately being defiant, but because she literally could not move. His progress toward her was too powerful, too knee-weakening, and the use of her feet was a task too difficult to achieve.

"What did you hope to accomplish?"

"Accomplish?"

He stopped a scarce two feet before her. "This little display of yours with Cavanaugh. What did you hope to accomplish?"

"My intention was to catch up with an old friend."

"You seemed to have an ample amount of topics on which to catch up. Neither one of you caught any fish, for all you seemed more interested in head-bent conversation and willy-nilly laughter."

"Did you catch any fish, Lord Carrington?" she retorted. "Because it seems to me you were more interested in watching me and Mr. Cavanaugh rather than managing your own rod."

"I can manage my rod just fine, thank you." Mockery danced in his eyes.

Sara blushed furiously.

He took another step forward, coming so close she could smell him; that male outdoorsy goodness that made her toes curl inside her slippers.

"And I caught plenty of fish today, though I will admit, my attention might have been more focused on fishing had my vision been unobstructed by you and Cavanaugh."

"Well, then, please accept my apologies for obstructing your view of the river," she snapped. "I shall remember that next time I agree to accompany someone else to a fishing excavation where you're sure to be in attendance."

His jaw set hard. "Let me assure you, my lady," he said emphatically, "that you will not be attending *any* excavation, event, ball, party, soiree, or any public outing for that matter unless I am the one who is escorting you. I will not tolerate the gossip hounds nipping at our heels because my intended has an urge to evoke the worst sort of emotion out of me."

"And what sort of emotion is that?" she challenged.

"Jealousy."

FOURTEEN

Justin was not accustomed to antagonism when it came to the wooing of a female. Truth be known, and although his attentions over the past several months had been centered solely on his mistress, he was esteemed wholly capable of sweeping virtually any woman off her feet. Granted, his charms weren't near as seductively eminent as those of Lord Beaufort, who needn't more than flash a smile to get a woman into his bed, but he could damn well hold his own. What Sebastian possessed in good looks, Justin rivaled in charm and charisma, and they both stood to inherit a dukedom.

Nothing could seduce a woman quicker than a man with a title.

Hell, even his father's prized mare preferred him over her own groomsman.

Why, then, was the seduction of his own fiancée becoming harder than driving a nail through a steel wall?

Justin stabbed a cut of ham with his fork and shoved it in his mouth, determined to quiet the hunger in his stomach. The sooner he ate, the sooner he could get out of the breakfast parlor, the sooner he could get out of this house. And, he thought broodingly, the sooner he could quit staring at Cavanaugh, who sat on the other side of the room, allowing Lady St. Clair to prattle in his ear.

Unknowing fool, Justin thought with some sense of pleasure, though the pain in his right temple wouldn't allow for too much self-satisfaction. He hadn't slept well last night. What with his argument with Sara, or whatever it was that had happened between them yesterday, and the splitting headache he'd acquired afterwards, it was a wonder he hadn't done the very thing he swore he'd never do.

But, no. He hadn't been that angry. Not enough to inebriate himself into a mediocre night's sleep, grumpy as hell though he was this morning. Drink would never do that to him again.

Pushing the thought from his mind, he bit off a piece of blueberry scone, and chased it down with hot chocolate. Cavanaugh and Milly were laughing and feeding each other grapes, with nary a care in the world for the other occupants of the parlor, who consisted of--Justin looked around--him and the footman by the sideboard. Enough to warrant their behavior inappropriate. Not enough for him to draw attention to himself by mentioning anything.

Milly was off his hands; that's all that mattered.

Justin forked a bite of eggs. Added a cut of fish in crème sauce.

How, he wondered, had Sara managed to gain the upper-hand? Moreover, why had he allowed her to take over his emotions? From the moment she'd passed him yesterday without so much as a glance over her slim shoulder, he knew what she was about.

And yet, he'd sat there like an ignorant schoolboy. Brewing with jealousy. Allowing her to carry on with Cavanaugh as if seeing her with another man, with the damned Irishman who wanted her for himself, wasn't the least bit bothersome.

Justin rubbed his temples between his thumb and middle finger, remembering fondly when Sara's cool fingers had done the same. Only her touch had felt much, *much* better.

Bothersome, she was. Outright maddening. He knew she didn't want her would-be Irish suitor. Determined that the night before last while watching them together at the pianoforte. Still. Seeing them together, talking, laughing, well, it … it rankled.

She doesn't want Cavanaugh. She doesn't. Does not.

"Morning." Sebastian slipped into the seat beside Justin, plate in hand. "May I join you?"

Justin regarded his friend moodily. "Seeing as you've already sat down, I'd say yes."

"Oh, come off it," Sebastian said as the footman, apparently well-accustomed to waiting on the resident marquess, added two sugar cubes and a generous amount of cream to Sebastian's coffee.

Sebastian took a sip, decided it was adequate, and waved the footman away. "So, what has you in such foul temper this morning? You're not still stewing over that incident at the riverbank yesterday, are you?"

Justin pretended he didn't hear. "You and Anna seem to be getting on well. You were gone for at least half an hour before rejoining us for lemonade."

"Hmm." Sebastian swallowed his coddled eggs. "She hasn't come right out and said so but I think she may have let this Helene nonsense go." He forked a piece of melon and added, "Finally," before slipping it in his mouth.

"Although," Justin said, "I would prefer you didn't take any more long, half hour, un-chaperoned walks with my sister. I do not want her reputation ruined before she finds a decent husband, and if someone sees her alone with a man like you ..." He paused, wondering how one puts something of this sort delicately.

Sebastian knew he was a labeled rakehell. To be sure, his only claims to salvation were his title, his business dealings with the locomotive industry, and, of course, his close ties to the Tethersal family.

But rakehell or no, he was still Justin's best friend.

"Then ..." Sebastian prompted, his fork hovering over his plate. His wintry eyes flashed with curiosity.

"We both know your reputation is lacking, Sebastian," said Justin. "We also know if someone were to see the two of you alone, even if it was the most innocent of situations ..."

"Like walking amongst the poppy field nestled by the river. Bird gazing," Sebastian supplied. "An activity both refreshing and educational." He sounded as convincing as any marquess. Sophisticated. Confident. Relaxed. "Is that what you mean by an 'innocent situation,' Lord Carrington?"

"Exactly. If a situation such as yesterday's bird-watching expedition should occur again, only someone ... say, one of your mother's gossip-hungry dowagers ... were to see you, then I think we both know what that would mean for Anna. And you."

"What that would mean for Anna." Sebastian hesitated. "You insinuate I would be forced to marry her?"

"For all your thoughtlessness on decorum, Lord Beaufort," Justin said, and allowed a footman to take his empty plate, "you do have an adequate understanding of the word." He blotted his mouth with a starched linen napkin. "Yes, that is exactly what I'm insinuating."

"Rubbish," Sebastian muttered.

"To anyone who might have seen, it is not rubbish."

"It was just a walk," Sebastian said after a few moments. "It's not like I took advantage. Besides ..." He stabbed a cut of honey-glazed pear and then twirled it about, watching as the syrupy liquid coated the delicate morsel on his fork. "Anna would never have me, compromised or no. Moreover," he added, a smile playing along one corner of his mouth, "it was just a walk."

"It was a walk with you," Justin said. "Reputation speaks louder than the rules we live by, Sebastian. You know that. If one of these batty old women were to see you, a renowned deflowerer of women, alone with my sister, word of it would spread like the pox."

Sebastian set his fork down. "I do not deflower women. These Holy Willy people do nothing but spout lies." He lowered his voice discreetly, though Justin could tell he was at the brink of an outburst. "I've never even bedded a virgin, for pity's sake."

"Too big a responsibility?"

"Yes!"

"Agreed."

Justin sipped his coffee, eyeing Cavanaugh and Milly over the rim of his cup. Milly was fussing over Cavanaugh's injured fingers, poking out her lower lip and fluttering her lashes as if she were naught but a girl in braids.

"I've never been with a virgin either," he murmured, though he didn't know why he felt the need to admit that bit of information. It could have been because his thoughts as of late had been curiously centered on when he'd bed his young, quite virginal bride for the first time.

He had no experience with virgins. Too clingy, the lot of them. Furthermore, he had no desire to take what he felt in his heart he did not deserve, what wasn't rightfully his. A woman's virginity was meant for her husband, and that was something Justin had never been willing to compromise. Not for any woman.

But Sara, he thought pensively. If Sara were free ... If they'd met under different circumstances, and she belonged to no man. If she, an innocent in the highest sense, had offered herself to him willfully, with no regard to propriety or the inevitable repercussions which would result from both their tactlessness ...

He would take her.

Without second thought, without care for the man she might marry. He'd lay her down, explore her body with his hands, his mouth. Cover her with kisses and erotic whispers until she was arching beneath him, begging for completion.

And he'd make love to her. Slowly. Passionately. Until they were both exhausted, lying in a heap of sweaty sheets and tangled limbs. Until she knew how much he desired her. How much he adored her. How much he …

Ah, but the thought of it, that he *loved* this woman, sent a flash of warmth through his body.

Uncomfortable, he shifted in his seat. He had to find a way to make things right again. This ignoring each other nonsense was driving him mad.

Sebastian was still recovering from nearly choking on his eggs. "What? You've never …?" He paused, swallowed. His gaze narrowed skeptically. "Well, Milly's obvious. But wasn't there Lady Ashford, Lady Wisley?" His eyes widened. "Oh, and that young beauty from Galena. What was her name?"

"Eva."

"Evangeline Hartford! God, but she was a lovely creature. Hair the color of red spun gold."

"Yes," Justin acknowledged. "But quite deflowered, I assure you. All of them were."

"Pity." Sebastian frowned. "I should think it would have been quite a triumph to deflower such a fiery young miss. No doubt she was an absolute ginger in bed."

"Don't be vulgar, Sebastian. Someone might have beaten her future husband to the finish line, but she was still a remarkably fine young woman."

"Yes, yes," Sebastian conceded. "Speaking of remarkable young women, Where is our lovely lot of female company this morning?"

"Shopping." Justin gestured to the footman for more hot chocolate. "Your mother wanted to show Sara and Anna the Cathedral, and I believe they are paying a visit to the dressmaker's."

"Ah, so you've spoken to your betrothed this morning, have you? No, no more coffee. Thank you." With a flick of his hand, Sebastian shooed the footman back to the sideboard.

"Your mother told me," Justin clarified. "No, Sara is not speaking to me. Walked right past me without so much as a glance in my direction."

And he'd watched her walk away.

That, he did not mention. She, a picture of infinite, young beauty, donned in a gown the color of wheat in early harvest, had strode past him as if he were a complete stranger. Just as she'd done the day before. And just like yesterday, he'd gazed after her with equal parts anger, possessiveness, and longing, until she'd disappeared into the coach with his sister and the duchess.

He curled his hands into fists on the table. He'd wanted to reach for her, snatch her back against him, and kiss her. Kiss her for all he wanted to punish her for being so damned haughty. Right there. In the hall. In front of everyone. He didn't care. It was Caroline's house party, and she hated propriety.

"Well, what happened?" Sebastian said. "The two of you were coming to good terms, or so I thought."

"Cavanaugh happened." Justin glanced across the room at the aforementioned.

"Cav? Oh, of course. By the way, you never told me to what extent he is acquainted with your Sara."

"He once asked the duke for her hand." Justin nodded toward Milly and Cavanaugh. "It appears as though Milly has found my replacement. Thank God."

"More fool Cavanaugh, then," Sebastian murmured. "And what did you say? Cavanaugh asked Kilkenny for Sara's hand? In marriage?"

"Of course in marriage, you fool. What other way is there?" Justin sighed and rubbed his brow. "They've known each other since she was very young, and I suppose she never told him about our betrothal. Needless to say, the duke turned him down."

"Naturally."

"Yes, naturally. And for what it's worth, I don't believe Sara wants him. But Cavanaugh on the other hand ..."

"You believe he still wants Sara?"

Justin nodded, watched with amusement as Cavanaugh whispered something into Milly's ear. She smiled and rose from the table; he, after her. Together, they left the room.

"Damn fool," Sebastian muttered. "Hope he remembers we're going to the archery field this morning."

"We have another half hour or so."

Sebastian adopted an unpleasant expression. "Do you think they can be finished in that short a time? Half an hour seems quite quick for ... Well. You know."

"Good God, Sebastian," said Justin, laughing. "Sometimes I believe you have no shame whatsoever."

"I have shame!" Sebastian objected. "Indeed, I think it is most shameful for a man to offer a lady he has just met only thirty minutes of his intimate time. She deserves at least an hour, if not three-quarters, do you not think?"

"An hour, is it?" Justin said, grateful for the lighthearted conversation. "Is that your general standard for bedding women to whom you've just been introduced?"

"Heavens, no!" Sebastian said, affronted. "Two hours at the least, and if she's easy to look at, three. Strikingly beautiful? No less than half a day."

"Poor woman. Half a day in bed, and she's surely complaining."

Sebastian smiled. "I've never had any complaints."

"Nor have I. So, what would you say to a morning ride before heading to the archery field?"

"I say ..." Sebastian downed the last bit of coffee in his cup. He rose from the table and made a short bow, at which Justin shook his head, chuckled, and stood himself. "I say, it's always a fine time for a morning ride."

As they walked together from the room, Justin retrieving his hat and gloves from the attendant, Sebastian leaned into him and added under his breath, "And apparently Lord Cavanaugh shares that particular sentiment."

At that, Justin laughed again. Heartily.

*** *** ***

Later that afternoon, on their way back to Worcester Hall, Sara found herself contemplating when *she* had laughed so heartily. Caroline turned out to be a delight. They'd visited the Cathedral, walked High Street, had a cup of tea at Periwinkle's and lemon-flavored madeleines at Décadence, a French pastry shop that specialized in cakes. Caroline had relayed everything she knew about the local area: its history, its people, both so colorful Sara couldn't help but think of Dublin.

They'd also visited Marigold's, the local dressmaker, and as the coach departed, the city fading quickly into stretches of untamed land, Caroline and Anna launched into a full discussion over colors and materials, which bonnet would match these slippers, and so on and so forth.

Sara, comfortable in her silence, stared out the window as city faded into countryside.

"I believe the cerulean silk will make a glorious ball gown," Caroline said to Anna. "But I cannot decide whether I want a full train in the back or the new corset style Mrs. Marigold mentioned."

"Why not both?" said Anna. "Although pearl buttons would look lovely beneath a full train. Particularly in contrast to the blue."

"Yes." Caroline tapped a gloved finger to her chin. "Perhaps you're right. Oh, and dearest, the red silk looked positively breathtaking on you! You must have a gown made of it. You simply must!"

"Absolutely not!" Anna said on a gasp.

Sara grinned to herself. Sitting amongst these two was like watching a comedy play from the front row.

"Red would make me look like a trollop," Anna continued to protest as Caroline giggled mercilessly. "A light-skirt. And you are laughing, Your Grace! Do you not agree with me?"

"Oh, Anna," Caroline said through her laughter. "You are trying to catch a husband, are you not?"

"Not!"

"A red dress," Caroline continued, "cut into a low, but not *too* low, neckline would land you a husband the very night you wore it. I can promise you that."

Anna was still not convinced. "A bright red dress would most certainly not land me a decent husband. At least not one who gives a fig about propriety."

"Lud!" Caroline exclaimed in an un-duchess-like manner. "The dreaded *p*-word? Firstly, the dress would not be bright red, you silly goose."

"Goose!" Anna nudged Sara's arm. "Did you hear that? The Duchess of Worcester called me a goose!"

Sara laughed, as Caroline continued.

"It would be a tasteful red. Like port wine, with an undertone of purple to compliment that young, milky skin of yours. A low, but not too low, neckline with only a small amount of lace. Off the shoulder, naturally."

"Naturally," Anna put in.

"You cannot very well wear a red ball gown in any other fashion."

"And secondly?" Anna prompted.

"Why on earth would you want a husband who limits himself by heeding all that *p*-word nonsense?" Caroline said. "I would think you of all women would want a husband with more wit about him than that."

"You can say the word, Your Grace," Anna teased. "I won't tell anyone."

"I am grateful," Caroline replied, placing a hand to her chest, "but no, I refuse to say it. In any case, it sounds to me as if you want an absolute prig for a husband. Why, the very idea that a man would not offer to marry a woman just because she wore a red dress to a ball is outright preposterous."

"Preposterous, Your Grace?" Anna giggled. "Really."

"Oh, do stop with the formalities, will you? That's almost worse than using the dreaded *p*-word."

"If you don't mind my saying so," said Anna, "you are every bit as capricious as Lord Beaufort. Always defiant of anything requiring the use of decorum."

"Sebastian is adherent to decorum more so than I ever was," Caroline murmured, fanning herself. "I blame that on his father. Speaking of the duke, however, he is due to return today. He'll be pleased to see you, Anna. And, of course, to meet the woman betrothed to our Justin."

Anna's elbow gave Sara yet another nudge. "She's speaking about you. *Silly goose.*"

But Sara had ceased listening two or three sentences prior. Peering out the window, watching the countryside glisten beneath the afternoon sun, she observed a group of gentleman in the distance. Justin was with them, bow and arrow in hand. He drew back, steadied, focused, and released. Retrieved another arrow and did it again, his shoulders, thick with muscle, bunching as he pulled the bow string taut.

"May we stop the coach, please?" Sara turned to Caroline. "Your Grace? Would you ask the coachman to stop?"

"Whatever for, dear?"

"I ..." She'd already come up with too many excuses today. "I think I'd like to walk the rest of the way. Get a bit of fresh air, if you don't mind."

"Well, of course I don't mind, child." Caroline reached a hand out her open window and tapped the side of the coach twice. "Stop! Stop, I say!"

"Sara," Anna whispered, "what are you doing? It's a long walk back to the hall."

The coach stopped, followed by the door opening and a footman poking his head inside. "Your Grace? Is everything all right?"

"Yes," Caroline said primly. Once again the duchess effect was in check, just like that. "Lady Ballivar would like to exit the carriage. Please assist her."

Without hesitation, the footman proffered his hand, and Sara took it, allowing him to help her down.

"Sara!" Anna whispered in earnest. "What are you doing?"

"Walking," Sara said from over her shoulder.

She gazed across the field, covered in a blanket of yellow poppies. They were target practicing: Justin, Sebastian, Cav and a tall man who couldn't have been anyone else but the Duke of Worcester, Sebastian's father. The duke and Sebastian were involved in conversation; Justin was selecting another arrow from a footman holding a quiver; and Cav was sitting down in a chair, a gorgeous black and white English setter sprawled at his feet, while a footman with an open parasol hovered idly beside him.

"I see," Anna murmured. "Well, I cannot abide standing about watching men shoot at wooden targets. So, I shall decline to come with you, and return with the duchess."

"Of course." Sara waved to the duchess. "My thanks for inviting me along, Caroline. Worcester is splendid, indeed. Particularly under your guidance."

"You are a dear, Lady Ballivar," Caroline returned. "Do have a delightful walk. Ah, and I see the gentlemen are practicing their archery. You'll have a delightful *and* entertaining afternoon, then. Justin is a marvelously accomplished archer."

"So I've heard." Sara set a hand over her brow, looked out again at Justin. He was in his shirtsleeves, breeches, and Hessians.

A marvelous combination, indeed, Sara mused, thinking how the man never seemed to be fully clothed.

"Well," said Caroline, "ta, darling." She tapped the door twice and the coach lurched forward, Anna waving a goodbye, while the duchess called from the window, "Do watch for snakes, won't you?"

"Oh!" Anna put in with a giggle. "And toads too!"

FIFTEEN

"My God." Bewildered and fascinated, Justin stared as Sara, walking through a field of wild yellow poppies, came into view. "What the devil is she doing here?"

"My lord?" The footman holding Justin's quiver stepped forward. "Did you say something?"

Bemused, Justin blinked a few times. Stared again. Yes, it was her. He wasn't losing his mind. The wind picked up, blew back her pelisse. Rippled her simple day dress, molded it to her body in all the right places. He could make out perfectly the line of her hips, the shape of her coltish thighs, the smallness of her waist.

He had to get a hold of himself. She was still angry with him, wasn't she?

Maybe she wasn't.

He certainly wasn't. Angry, that is. How could he be? Well, aside from the fact Cavanaugh had decided to join them, when Justin hoped Milly would occupy him for the rest of the morning, if not all day. But the man couldn't even work his fingers well enough to pull back a bow string.

A pity, that. Justin had the strongest desire to best the damned Irishman at *something*.

He definitely hadn't managed to best the man at garnering Sara's attention. Without so much as a glance in his direction, she walked straight for Cavanaugh.

Bloody perfect.

Cavanaugh grinned up at her. "Good afternoon." He closed the book he'd been reading, held his place with his forefinger. "You'll forgive me if I don't stand, won't you? My feet seem to be occupied at present."

"Not at all." Bending down, Sara gave the dog a good rub between his ears. "He's beautiful."

She was beautiful, Justin acknowledged, unable to pry his eyes from her. Springing ringlets of ebon hair hung from under her bonnet, cascaded delicately down her back. She wasn't wearing gloves either; he noticed a peak of a white fingertip in the outer pocket of her green pelisse.

"A bit lazy," Cavanaugh said. "But, yes, a beautiful breed of canine. Did you enjoy Worcester? I do hope you took the chance to see the Cathedral. A most magnificent structure, if I do say so myself."

So, the bloody idiot knew Sara had gone into town, did he? Wasn't it enough to keep up with one woman, let alone two?

"You've seen the Cathedral, have you?" Sara twiddled her fingers through the canine's thick coat. She was kneeling now, heedless to the possibility of grass stains on her gown.

The dog, *Phin*, didn't seem to mind. With every stroke of her fingers, he groaned deeply, eyes shut in pure bliss.

Lucky mongrel.

"But, of course," Cav said. "I've aided Father and the duke for some time now."

"Ah. I had forgotten." A trace of remorse, but for what? For not knowing Cavanaugh as much as she thought she had? "I do not think I ever paid much heed to your business affairs."

"We never discussed my business affairs," he said, and there was something in his eyes as he stared down at her that made Justin want to shake the life out of him.

He chose to make his presence known instead. "Good afternoon," he murmured. Sara's whisky eyes flashed up at him. "Come." He outstretched his hand. "Meet the Duke of Worcester."

Without hesitation, her cool hand slipped into his. "Thank you, my lord," she said, and rose to her feet.

Cavanaugh went back to his reading. The man had impeccable manners, for all he did a poor job of hiding his interest in Sara.

Sliding a hand to the small of her back, Justin leaned down, close to Sara's ear. "You look lovely." He squeezed her hand, gently. "I wanted to tell you so this morning, only …"

"Yes?" Her tongue darted out to moisten her lips.

Justin stifled a groan.

"I wanted. That is, I wanted to tell you, as well ..."

"Yes?"

"I apologize for behaving so foolishly."

"Shh." He loved the shallowness in her breath, the huskiness it lent to her tone. "No need for apologies."

"Oh, but there is," she insisted. A deep shade of crimson colored just the hills of her cheeks. "It was silly of me to ignore you as I did."

"So, you admit to intentionally ignoring me?"

"I wouldn't exactly say it was intentional."

"That is, in fact, what you just said." He tried not to smile, but it was useless. She was too delectable. "Did you not?"

She tipped her chin. "I was eager to be in female company. The duchess is quite the expert on local history, not to mention fashion."

"Have a nice visit at the dressmakers, then, did you?"

"It was perfectly amenable," she said after a moment. "Mrs. Marigold has an exceptional collection of fabrics."

"That, she does," Justin agreed.

"Furthermore." She attempted to pry her hand from his, but he wasn't about to let go. She tossed him a reproving scowl. "Furthermore ..."

"Yes, furthermore," he murmured. "I believe we're clear on that. Do go on."

"Perhaps I did ignore you purposely," she said, gaining momentum. "So what if I did? You deserved it."

"Two weeks in England and you're already punishing me? That seems a bit over reactive, don't you think?"

"Not when you behave in such ill-temper."

"I behave in ill-temper?" He jabbed a finger at his chest, just so they were clear on who she was accusing.

"Yes! For all the world as if you were a tot in diapers. I didn't come here to raise a child, Lord Carrington."

He drew her closer. "Then why did you?" he demanded, ignoring the fact that Cavanaugh was now glaring at them from over his book on England's wildlife.

"I thought that was made perfectly clear." As petite as she was compared to his broad stature, she sized herself up to him well enough. Chin thrust outward. Eyes round and incredulous. As if she expected *him* to back down from *her*. "My father sent me. I had no choice in the matter."

That stung. The moment he thought they were making headway, that the idea of being forced into marriage wasn't as disagreeable as they'd previously anticipated, back to the beginning they went.

Above all, a single, panging thought came to mind. She may not have wanted Cavanaugh, but she damn well didn't want him either. And that made him angrier than ever. Because, he realized, he *wanted* her to want him. Just as badly as he wanted her, as badly as he wished he *didn't* want her. Especially now it was clear she'd jump on the first ship back to Ireland if she could.

Cavanaugh stood, set his book in his chair. Cleared his throat. "Perhaps you would like to continue with your target practice, my lord? I would be more than obliged to introduce Lady Ballivar to His Grace, the Duke of Worcester. Truly, I do not mind."

Justin regarded him evenly. "I'm sure you wouldn't, Mr. Cavanaugh, but I'm well capable of handling the introductions between my fiancée and the duke."

Evidently the Irishman wasn't one to back down so easily. "I insist," he said. His gaze slipped to Sara. "Lady Ballivar appears to be a touch peaky. Perhaps a glass of lemonade and a short walk would help to restore her color? After being introduced to His Grace, of course."

Justin opened his mouth in retort.

"A walk does sound rather nice," said his bride-to-be. "The poppies are in full bloom, and I do think I would very much like to gather a bouquet for the duchess."

Cavanaugh needed no further invitation. He offered a poised, open palm to her, a banner of triumph on his face. "Shall we, then?"

"You have no chaperone," Justin pointed out, as Sara, once again, tried to pull her hand free of his.

He let her, albeit reluctantly.

"Forgive me, Lord Carrington," Cavanaugh replied, "but are you implying that I would attempt to take advantage of another man's fiancée?"

"I don't know you from Adam, Cavanaugh."

"Permit me to assure you, my lord, that Lady Ballivar and I have known each other since childhood."

"I don't give a hang how long you've known each other. You are not taking her anywhere without a chaperone."

"That won't be necessary." Sebastian stepped into the heated circle, along with his father, and without a care in the world for who was escorting who where, took Sara's ungloved hand and tucked it inside his arm. "Father, Lady Sara Ballivar, daughter of the Duke of Kilkenny, and Lord Carrington's esteemed fiancée. My lady, my father, The Duke of Worcester."

Sara bobbed an awkward curtsy from Sebastian's arm. "How do you do, Your Grace?"

Justin raised an eyebrow.

Cavanaugh's proffered hand balled into a fist and fell at his side.

"I do well, Lady Ballivar," Worcester said in his gruff tone. The duke was as tall, broad, and burly as a grizzly bear. One would have never placed him and the marquess as father and son. "Enjoying your stay thus far?"

All five of them -- even Phin, who was apparently in need of more feminine attention – blinked at Sara, as if they all half-expected her to confess to hating the place.

But she replied in kind. "England has been quite welcoming to me, Your Grace. I find it extraordinarily beautiful."

From the corner of his vision, Justin saw Cavanaugh roll his eyes. So, he didn't believe Sara either, and most likely with good reason. He'd known her longer, for one. Two, there was no knowing what she'd confided to him during their conversation by the river yesterday.

Justin cleared his throat, stepped forward. "Perhaps we should all go for a walk."

"I insist," Sebastian said as if making some grand announcement, "upon escorting the lady myself, without the rest of our company. Besides, you need to continue practicing your release. Don't assume I missed those last two arrows hitting the ground instead of the target."

The duke clapped Justin on the shoulder. "On that note, I believe I shall practice a few myself." He turned to Sara and bowed. "Lady Ballivar, your servant."

Sara bobbed another awkward curtsy. "Your Grace."

As the duke strode for the footman guarding the equipment, Justin turned to Sebastian. "Didn't we discuss this earlier,

Sebastian? Escorting young women about without a chaperone is inadvisable."

"We'll take Phin."

"You'll take--" Justin bit back an oath. "Fine. Go."

"Excellent." Sebastian clucked to Phin, and gestured to his other side. "We shan't be long."

"See that you are not," Justin said as Sebastian, walking tall, escorted Sara away, Phin trotting happily beside them.

"She's a sensitive girl," Cavanaugh murmured the moment they were out of earshot, "for all she does put on that impenetrable exterior."

Justin shot him a cautious glare. "She has spirit, yes, but I find that refreshing in a woman, don't you?"

"Aye." Cavanaugh nudged a clod of dirt this way and that with the toe of his boot. "She's an only child, you know. Motherless. And her father, while a good man, is heedless to her needs." He gazed ahead, squinted after Sara and Sebastian. "Her wants."

"You speak of the duke declining your proposal to marry her," Justin said rather than asked.

Cavanaugh's features hardened. "In a sense, perhaps. I was ... we were both ..."

"Disappointed?"

"Disappointed." A hesitation, then: "Yes. I suppose we were."

"Yet Lady Ballivar, Sara, knew she had been betrothed since childhood. She knew yet refrained from mentioning anything. Did that not anger you?"

"At first, yes, of course it did." Cavanaugh gave him a stern look, brow drawn, eyes tapered. "I may have been sick with emotion for her at the time, but no man in his right mind would ask for a lady's hand if he didn't know, to some extent, what the answer would be."

I would have said 'yes.'

Justin felt his insides turn cold. He could still see her trembling, tears threatening her eyes. Those perfect lips admitting she would have married Cavanaugh had she not been betrothed.

It was irrelevant, really. Cavanaugh couldn't have her. Never had the right to even look upon her, for pity's sake. Yet, here he stood, confessing he was once *sick with emotion* for her. Could still be, for all Justin knew. And who used that sort of talk, anyway? Sick with emotion, honestly.

Ah, but who was he kidding? Sickness, Justin mused, was precisely what he felt when he kissed Sara. When he held her, or so much as looked at her from across a room. Every part of him ached to bring her closer, to feel every inch of soft, pale skin beneath his hands.

Unable to restrain himself, Justin gazed across the field, and felt a sense of relief settle into his bones. Sara was still well in sight, hand tucked in Sebastian's arm, Phin trotting alongside her. They appeared to be engaged in conversation, Sebastian's head inclined toward hers, her face turned slightly upward as if listening intently.

"Her father had no reason to reject me," said Cavanaugh. "I stand to inherit a title, and while it's no dukedom, 'tis one of the finest in Ireland. Not to mention my investment in the new high-powered steam engines has made me a very rich man."

Justin almost laughed at that. Sara wasn't interested in money; he'd come to that conclusion from the moment he'd met her, standing by the dock in Liverpool. She was no more impressed with his title or his riches than an infant would be with a gold coin in hand.

Shiny, yet decidedly unimpressive.

So, he did allow a smile to linger on his face when he said, "Something tells me that riches hold very little bearing to Lady Ballivar. I suspect she'd be just as content living in a gardener's hut, eating stew off a wooden table."

One of Cavanaugh's brows rose in inquiry. "You suggest that riches mean nothing to a lady? Truly, Lord Carrington, I wouldn't suspect a man of your caliber as unaccustomed to the needs and wants of ladies in our society. Title and security mean everything to them."

"And Sara has both," Justin pointed out. "Without my illimitable assets. Or yours, for that matter."

"She needs a husband who can offer love and devotion." Cavanaugh's face glowed red. "I don't believe you, a man who knows nothing about her, nothing of her likes, dislikes--"

"I know enough to presume she wouldn't have gone through with a marriage to you," Justin bit off. "You, Mr. Cavanaugh, most certainly would not have made a woman of Sara's temperament happy."

"My God," Cavanaugh muttered. "That's it, isn't it?"

Justin blinked, confused. "Pardon?" He tilted his head a fraction. "What's *it*, exactly?"

"If Sara were given the right to choose between us, you're not certain it would be you." Cavanaugh mirrored Justin's gesture, inclined his head just enough for the sunlight to catch the satisfaction glinting in his eyes. "Are you? In fact, I'll wager that imperious conscience of yours knows she'd choose me."

The outright audacity of this man needled Justin's restraint. "And what, pray, makes you so sure? You haven't the slightest inclination as to what intimacies have transpired between us. For all you know, Sara could be a ruined woman."

"Don't insult my intelligence," Cavanaugh said tersely. "I'm not one of those impudent Irish lords Pitt whipped into submission. Sara's innocence is intact; else she wouldn't be walking with Lord Beaufort, she'd be with you."

"I have no intention of insulting your intelligence, or lack thereof, Mr. Cavanaugh."

Cavanaugh's expression contorted into a bona fide scowl.

"Be that as it may," said Justin, "permit me to ensure that *you* make no mistake. That you grasp my meaning, and are in full understanding."

Cavanaugh kept his silence, though by the flare of his nostrils, the raw anger in his eyes, Justin knew he had his attention.

"Sara belongs to me." Justin allowed a moment to pass, the air between them to thicken. "And you will cease to pursue her, or I'll make it my personal agenda to see that you never set foot on this island again. My family may have little dealings with your beloved steam engines, but we damn well have a magnanimous amount of pull with their English patrons. Are we clear?"

"Quite," Cavanaugh said through gritted teeth. "Anything else?"

Justin couldn't explain the sudden need he had to validate himself. Lord knew he didn't have to. But he also couldn't allow Cavanaugh to think he'd make Sara a bad husband.

Leashing his anger, because the good Lord also knew he had enough right now to commit murder, Justin said, "We lack history,

Sara and I. But I cannot validate driving a life, a marriage, and a dukedom into disaster just because we weren't able to choose one another. I'll be good to her," he added, looking Cavanaugh square in the eye. Not because he had to. Not even because he wanted to. But because, for reasons he could not explain, he felt it necessary.

"And I'll be faithful," he said. "I've always known that. Even before I met Sara."

Though minutely, Cavanaugh's frown softened.

Justin suspected that despite the attachment the Irishman had for Sara, her contentment meant more to him than his own wants.

Even if her contentment meant marriage to another man.

"She'll make a fine duchess," Cavanaugh murmured after some time.

"Yes," Justin respectfully agreed. "That, she will."

*** *** ***

Cav and Justin weren't the only people who felt Sara was on her way to becoming a Class-A duchess.

"You must cease baiting Justin with Mr. Cavanaugh," Sebastian said as they walked toward a meadow shaded by towering oaks. Moss, like streams of old ribbon, sheathed every limb, swayed back and forth in the breeze. "Courting games are entertaining to some extent, but not for a man who may soon inherit a dukedom, and one who needs a duchess who will prove both supportive and upstanding in society. Petty competitions between suitors are too time consuming, particularly when Justin feels he is one of them."

Sara twirled the yellow poppy Sebastian had picked for her between her fingertips. "I have no intention of baiting my fiancé with Mr. Cavanaugh, Lord Beaufort."

"Please do not call me by my title. Sebastian shall suffice." He cast an earnest, aside glance at her. "Enlighten me, will you? Did you truly believe that first encounter would go smoothly? Between Justin and Cavanaugh, I mean."

"I never really gave it much thought." She had, of course, and drawn the conclusion that thoughts of Cav and thoughts of Justin didn't intermingle so well.

In addition, these budding feelings and wanton fantasies she had for her fiancé were so much more intense than anything she'd ever felt for Cav. Traitorous, she felt, betraying the tender feelings she'd had for the man she'd once wanted above all others. And all to have them violently replaced with carnal thoughts of the man she truly wanted.

Her very handsome--very *English*--intended.

They walked for some time before Sebastian, scooping up a small hand of poppies and sliding them into the lapel of his light grey jacket, said, "Did Justin ever tell you about the day we met?"

"It must have been a day for the history books, I suspect. But, no. He didn't tell me."

Sebastian grinned, and Sara could honestly see why women found him so irresistible. Though the golden glint of a beard shadowed his face, his skin was smooth, flawless. Perfect teeth, too. Lips she imagined had kissed so many it was a wonder they were as full as they were, and not shriveled like a couple of prunes. Hair the color of wheat basking in those first rays of dawn. Eyes so brilliant, so icy blue, they were almost transparent, and as wicked as a pirate sailing the high seas.

"We were both eleven. Well," he said, "I was nearly twelve. He'd just turned eleven. But it was in London, and I was running from the blacksmith's son, scooting down Bond Street with all the fret of a criminal fleeing a Bow Runner. He wielded a hammer, you see, and I had naught but a handkerchief in my pocket."

"What on earth had you done? Stolen a horseshoe?"

"Oh good Lord no," he said, chuckling. "He caught me kissing his sister in a haystack."

"When you were eleven!"

"Almost twelve."

Sara shook her head, amazed. "Then what?"

Sebastian went on to tell her the entire story of his and Justin's implausible first meeting.

"Oh, my!" she said. "Did the young man come to?"

"We didn't stay around long enough."

"Tsk, tsk. That wasn't very kind of you. He might have been seriously injured."

"Oh, believe me. His nose was permanently crooked, but we couldn't linger. Not with our fathers' reputations at stake. Mischievous lads though we were."

Sara suspected they still were.

"We were, *are*, first and foremost, the sons of dukes," he said, adding ruefully, "I shouldn't have dallied with a commoner's daughter in the first place. But--" he shrugged, placed a hand over his heart "--I was in love."

"Fancy that," she murmured.

"Ludicrous, is it not? Needless to say, Justin and I have been inseparable ever since."

"A friendship made in heaven."

"I suppose one could call it that." Releasing her arm, Sebastian stopped, sank to his haunches. "Come Phin!"

The dog, trotting ahead for some time now, turned and rushed to his side. Nuzzled his nose against Sebastian's thigh, and Sebastian answered those silent pleas with scratches behind Phin's ears and beneath his chin.

"Justin is the best person I know," he said without looking up. "You'll not encounter a more honest, more devoted soul. He assesses what is expected, and does it. No second thoughts, no false pretenses. If he gives you his word, consider it golden."

"He is a good man."

"The finest. God knows I don't deserve such unconditional friendship." He stood, proffered his arm, and she slipped her hand inside. "Do you know what he told me the first time he saw you? The night we met you and your father at the docks in Liverpool?"

Sara blinked.

"Nothing," he said, smiling. "He was too stunned. Literally breathless. In fact, I was shaking with laughter because he was completely speechless."

"*That's* why you were laughing?" She searched her memory, recollecting every moment of that night. "I had no idea."

"Yes, well. He was nervous. When finally he mustered the courage to speak, I believe he said you were striking. Took him by surprise, you did."

"Well. I daresay I found him quite agreeable, as well."

"Agreeable? Trust me, my lady, there are plenty of young ladies who find him more than agreeable."

Speaking of which. "Tell me how he met Lady St. Clair."

Sebastian gave an arched look. "Not going there. If you must know about his past conquests, you'll have to ask him. I've never involved myself in his personal affairs or intimacies, and I'm not about to start."

"He is to be my husband," Sara protested.

"He is my best friend," Sebastian retorted, and Sara tightened her lips. "Do not be angry with me, Sara, I cannot bear female animosity. Now, shall I tell you another story from our childhood? This one happens to be about all the nights we sneaked out to go swimming in the river. My mother would faint if she knew the half of what we did during her annual house parties."

Sara nodded acquiescently, and proceeded to listen to tales of boyish mischief that very well might have made a good book if either devilish boy had the mind to write them down. When they arrived at the archery range, the duke was napping in a chair, his long legs sprawled out in front of him, hands folded atop his belly; Cav's nose was buried in his book; and Justin, quiver-wielding footman at his side, was steadily shooting arrow after arrow at a distant target.

"Ah, there now, you see?" Sebastian gestured toward Justin. "He's calm. Truly, my lady, I've never seen him behave so passionately toward another person." He inclined his head closer to hers. "What will you do to get his attention? He is completely focused on that target. Ah, and of course. A bull's eye."

"Bull's eye?" She'd never heard such a word. Sounded rather vulgar, actually.

"The center of the target," he said. "Really, Lady Ballivar, we must get you into London as soon as possible. The local language changes daily."

"So it seems." A sudden thought came to mind. "Sebastian?"

"Mmm?"

"You seem to be a bit of a good actor."

"A most improper comment to make to a marquess," he said, "but you have my attention."

"Play along, will you?"

"As long as my playing along does not include running about as if I were some sort of farm animal, I shall be happy to oblige."

Sara raised an eyebrow.

Sebastian mirrored it. "Don't ask."

"Wasn't thinking to," she replied, imagining another one of his tales of boyish devilry. "Just follow my lead. This should be short, and virtually painless."

His chin dipped in a single nod.

Sara cleared her throat a little. *God forgive me.* "Do you know, Lord Beaufort," she said, projecting her voice, "that I have never acquainted myself with the art of archery? It does appear rather fascinating."

Cav's book closed behind her.

The duke was still sleeping, thankfully.

Justin had paused for only a brief moment before setting his next arrow and turning it loose.

Sara gave Sebastian's arm a nudge.

"Is that so, Lady Ballivar?" His voice rang out like an announcer at the horse races. "It happens to be called the sport of kings, you know. A most excellent way of displaying one's strength and precision."

"Won't you demonstrate, Lord Beaufort?" She bit back a smile as Justin hesitated. And released.

"I dare not, my lady," Sebastian went on. "My experience at the sport is regrettably lacking."

"Mr. Cavanaugh, then?" Sara turned to Cav.

He held up his middle and forefinger, glared at her through hooded eyes. "I fear my source of pulling back a bow string is injured, my lady. But of course, you probably already knew that, now, didn't you?"

Sara was speechless.

Lucky for her, Sebastian was right on cue. "Forgive me, Lady Ballivar, for I am sure Mr. Cavanaugh, when he has full use of his fingers, is an extraordinary shot. However, if it is archery you would endeavor to learn, I daresay Lord Carrington would be the better instructor."

Sara knew if she ever expected to gain Justin's attention with this spur-of-the-moment, ridiculous charade, now would be the time.

And gain his attention, she had.

He was staring at her, all towering, six foot two--maybe three, he was so much taller than average--of strapping, powerful male. His hair was wild, rustling with every gust of wind.

He stretched out his hand, beckoned her closer.

The thought to refuse him didn't even cross her mind.

Sara left Sebastian's side and crossed the small distance on unsteady feet, wondering if it was humanly possible for a person to melt into the ground.

"I can demonstrate this to you," he said, "but you'll not be able to pull back the bow string on your own."

Sara nodded absently because his hand was resting at the small of her back, and every nerve surrounding that one, small area was dancing beneath her skin.

"The fistmele on my bow is too …" He broke off, likely because she was staring up at him, dumbfounded.

In truth, she did know a bit about archery. Her father was quite accomplished at it. But being this close to him conveniently caused everything she knew about the prestigious sport to slip her mind.

"Never mind." He pulled her round to his front, brought her body back against his. "Bow and arrow, please, Mr. Fox."

The footman handed him a longbow and feather-tipped arrow, and stepped back.

Sara's heart picked up a rapid rhythm as Justin's arms came around her, his hand covering hers as she gripped the bow shaft. Instinctively, she leaned into him, flattened her backside against the hard plane of his body.

Justin muttered an incoherent curse, and bent his head beside her ear. "No more moving, sweetheart. Now, put these two fingers here. This is your nocking point." He positioned the fore and middle fingers of her right hand on the bowstring, around the arrow, and wedged his fingers in between them. "I'll pull back. You feel the movement."

"All right." The motion caused their arms to brush, and his chest muscles to contract. Sara drew in a trembling breath.

"Do you feel it?"

She hoped he couldn't see the color burning in her cheeks. "Yes." Standing statuesque beneath him, he held her in perfect stance to release the arrow. He seemed to have stopped breathing; she could barely feel the rise and fall of his chest at her back.

"Justin?"

"Yes?"

It's now or never, Sara. "Perhaps we could spend our day together tomorrow." She shut her eyes, held her breath, wished with all she had that she could take it back.

But, "It would be my pleasure, my lady," he murmured. "Now. Release."

Sara let the arrow and her breath go in one, sharp movement, and felt her stomach quake with excitement as he whispered praises into her ear.

SIXTEEN

Insistent though Lana was that not only should proper young ladies refrain from accompanying their fiancés--alone--on expeditions in the out of doors (and apparently in the in-of-doors, by all that was moral) but they should also refrain from wearing enticing garments, Sara dressed very carefully the next morning for her outing with Justin.

She'd purchased the dress only a week prior to leaving Dublin for Liverpool, though at the time, she certainly hadn't planned on wearing it in England. It was for the upcoming soiree in Galway, hosted at the home of Sir Dunmore himself, where Sara had every intention of persuading Cav into eloping with her.

Shocking, how matters had changed so quickly.

Here she was, a mere month later, at a house party in Worcester, in a country she thought she'd loathe for all eternity, allowing Lana to fasten the small row of pearl buttons on the back of the dress meant to win her an Irish husband, and she was happy. Happy the dress wouldn't make its debut at a party she'd attended a dozen times over. Happy she wasn't trying to win an Irish husband because she was completely smitten with her English fiancé, and she wanted to look her best for him.

After all, he'd won the bet.

The least she could do was make his winnings worthwhile.

"You'd be mindful to watch your posture," Lana said, brushing several wrinkles from Sara's skirts. "You're liable to fall right out of that bodice if you so much as bend too far forward."

Standing straighter, Sara inclined her head and studied her appearance in the looking glass. The dress was of lilac muslin with a crisscross neckline, typical of the ancient Greeks, with a modern flair of capped sleeves and a lowered waist. A chemise was out of the question; the low bodice wouldn't allow for it.

"I won't need to reach for anything." Sara ran the tip of her finger along the delicate lace framing her neckline. "Lord Carrington will be there to assist me."

Lana had fixed her hair into a rather complicated coiffure, with curls here and sprigs of tiny lilac blooms there. She tugged a springing lock Lana had left to compliment her bosom (although

Sara suspected it was more to hide any visible trace of décolletage), and released, smiling as it curled again.

"Despite your insistence that my dress is inappropriate to be worn anywhere but inside the confines of my own room," Sara said, and her eyes met Lana's in the looking glass, "I must say you've done wonderfully."

"You do look beautiful," Lana admitted. "And it's not that I think you shouldn't wear the dress, my lady. It's just that, well, you'll be alone, and I don't--it's just that I ..." She shook her head, sighed.

"You don't trust Lord Carrington to behave himself."

Lana looked up. "He is a man, my lady. Not one of those lads in Dublin who doted over you with sugarplums and poetry on bended knee. A vast difference, there is, between lads and men."

"How well I know it," Sara said. "Lest you forget, Lana, I almost married Lord Cavanaugh."

"I haven't forgotten. Nor have I failed to notice the way he still looks upon you. He came to England expecting more than to discuss those blimmin' steam engines. Of that, you can be certain."

"Pish." Sara smoothed her hands down her front. "You only say such nonsense because you don't like Cav."

"On the contrary, my lady, I find Mr. Cavanaugh very agreeable. But he thinks himself to be as much as well. Thinks he's better suited for you than Lord Carrington."

Sara passed her a skeptic glance. "How do you know this?"

Lana's cheeks colored. "Overheard him speaking to his valet night before last."

"Go on."

"It was late, you see. I was on my way to bed when his valet caught me in the common area, just between the east and west wings, and asked if I could fetch his master some ointment for a puncture wound. So happened I still had a bit of drawing salve from when you cut your foot winter last, so I fetched it. Heard them talking between themselves just as I was approaching his room."

Sara remembered that cut. In fact, Cav and his father were visiting Dublin when it happened. To prove she was no typical debutante, she had removed her slippers while she and Cav strolled through a field near the manor. She began to skip and twirl about, singing a cheerful pub tune she'd heard the weekend previous in Dublin square. And Cav was laughing, encouraging her whimsicalness by clapping the beat for her.

Just as she whirled around to her favorite verse-- *'Down among the pigs I played some funny rigs, danced some hearty jigs'*--a ground thorn the size of a hairpin cut her foot, directly on the insole.

"Well," she said, "what did he say?"

"That he is better suited for you than Lord Carrington."

Sara tilted her head to the side.

"And if fate would have him alone with you for long enough, he could persuade you to leave England and return to Ireland. With him," she emphasized. "As his wife. He means to elope with you, my lady."

"What?" Sara turned around. "Of all the--that is ridiculous. He wouldn't."

"Ireland is your home, *a thaisce*," Lana said, and the tightly wound coil in Sara's heart, the place where home had lain dormant for the past two weeks, twitched responsively.

"Mr. Cavanaugh is well aware of the love you have for your country. Why, then, would you think him incapable of resorting to extreme measures?"

Sara watched in fascination as her maid's eyes danced with a conviction she'd not seen since she was fourteen and Lana told her she had to stop running about in her nightrail. *'You're bloomin', my lady,'* she'd said, followed by, *'Your father, God bless 'is Grace's heart, will have to fire the entire lot of the male staff for their wanderin' eyes, quickly as ye've developed. And won't no one be to blame but yourself.'*

"To use your love for Ireland as an advantage to induce you into eloping with him," Lana said. "He could give you back your home. He knows that, my lady. You know that."

Sara choked down the rising lump in her throat.

They would've lived in County Clare. Where the *Aillte an Mhothair*, the mighty Cliffs of Moher, stand no more than a few hundred yards from Cav's back terrace. Through a path nestled between two sloping, rocky hills, covered in a blanket of rich green grass, one could walk there with little effort. Barefoot even, if one was so inclined.

And there ...

Oh, there one could stand and listen to the sound of Atlantic waves crashing against ancient towering stone, breathe the salt-laden air, mingled with something indescribable. An aroma belonging solely to Ireland.

She closed her eyes, breathed deep.

Cav still wanted to marry her. It was almost unbelievable. And Lana was right: he could give her what she wanted more than anything in the world. Life and death in Ireland, the land she'd loved since she was old enough to run barefoot through emerald fields.

Her heart tightened again.

"Lana."

"Yes, my lady?"

Sara opened her eyes. "I think I should like to wear my lilac bonnet with the wide, satin ribbon." She couldn't think about Ireland. Too much more and she'd climb on the first horse she could find, gallop all the way to Liverpool, and board the next ship home. "It will compliment nicely, don't you think?"

"Indeed, it will, my lady. Indeed, it will."

Two minutes later, Sara was rounding the last curvature to the stairs in the outer hall, with Lana following close behind. Male voices, mingled with male laughter, echoed through the hall.

Justin, Sebastian, and Cav.

Her stomach quaked a little. The three of them had been virtually inseperable since Monday, but she wished they could've spared at least a single moment to part company. Dealing with one male was plenty demanding.

Sure enough, all three men turned around as Sara, exquisitely dressed yet ineffably nervous, reached the landing of the staircase. She gazed at Justin, and could not suppress her smile. Pure reverence, gathering as quickly as storm clouds in a clear sky, filled his dark eyes.

"Good morning, gentlemen," she said, and descended the staircase.

Like toy soldiers, they swept into a collective bow, murmured respective greetings.

"I hope you are all having a good morning."

Sebastian was first to speak. "Indeed, Lady Ballivar. We were just catching up a bit before your outing with--" he slapped Justin on the shoulder "--*Ugly* here."

Justin forced a grin. "I appreciate the support, Sebastian."

"Anytime."

Justin took Sara's hand in his, guided her down the last few steps. His eyes swept down. Then, up. For a moment, Sara swore she saw something there. Something other than appreciation. Perhaps even ... amusement?

Sara drew her brows together. "What is it?"

But Justin shook his head. "Nothing, nothing. You are ready, then?"

Sara brushed aside his peculiar behavior, nodded.

"Excellent." Justin bowed to Sebastian and Cav. "Have a splendid day, gentlemen. We won't be back for dinner."

"We won't?" Sara asked, surprised.

"No." His dark brows lifted. "That doesn't present an issue, does it?"

"I ..." Did it present an issue? Did it? And if so, did she care? "I don't foresee an issue, my lord."

"Good. We'll be on our way. I have a curricle parked just out front."

Lana made a sound of clear disapproval.

Cav apparently didn't care for the idea either. "Vastly improper. Taking a two person vehicle without even a footman to aid you should trouble arise. What if a wheel should become bogged down? Or what if a robber, seeing the crest of a nobleman emblazoned on the side, decides to attack?"

Justin was quick to retort. "As barbaric as you undoubtedly think me to be, Mr. Cavanaugh, I would never engage in any activity which would impose danger upon a lady. Especially the lady who is to be my wife."

Sara blushed.

Cav's face turned red, as well, though Sara suspected it wasn't from embarrassment.

"Furthermore," Justin said, "I am perfectly capable of freeing a carriage wheel from mud, and have even been known to repair one or two. As for robbers ..." A shadow of a smile tugged at his lips.

"They'd be foolish to even try. I hold the title at Gentleman Jackson's."

"It's true," Sebastian confirmed.

Jaw set, Cav fixed Sara with a gaze of equal parts concern, disapproval, and vexation. Heavens. He was just as bad as, if not worse than, Lana. Worrying about her as if she were some idiot who made a habit out of trotting off with random rakes. It was like having a couple of nipper dogs, biting at her heels.

"I'll be fine." She didn't bother trying to hide the impatience in her tone. "We're only going into the city, isn't that right, my lord?"

"Correct," said Justin. "Not that it would make any difference if we were traveling farther. We'd still take the curricle."

"Humph!" Lana picked up the skirts of her dress and stomped back up the stairs.

Sebastian let out a snort of laughter. "Now there's a dash of a woman, if ever I did see one. You'd think she had Swift blood running through those veins."

"Jonathan Swift, God rest his soul, was a great man," Cav bridled. "To make even the slightest funning comment about him is blasphemous to an Irishman."

"Oh for the love of--" Justin began, but was cut off by a highly composed Sebastian.

"For your information, Mr. Cavanaugh, I hold Mr. Swift in the highest esteem," he said. "So you needn't toss your Irish idealism at me as if I were an ill-educated nitwit. I stand to inherit a ducal seat in the House of Lords. Trust me, I know to whom I should reserve respect."

Sara bit her bottom lip to keep from laughing. She was really beginning to like Lord Beaufort, for all he was one of the most dramatic men she'd ever met.

But Cav wasn't amused in the least. Without sparing another glance in her direction, he turned on his heel and stormed down the hall, his boot heels clanking angrily on the tile floor.

"He has issues," Sebastian mused.

"All Irishmen of noble decent have issues," Sara said. "My father would have reacted just as defensively at the mention of Swift's name."

"How dreadfully boring," he said. "Life wasn't meant to be taken serious, else everyone would spend their days wasting away with worry instead of living." He turned to Justin. "Speaking of which, you two should be going. Much to see in our quaint little city."

"It is a lovely city," said Sara.

"The loveliest," Sebastian agreed. "You haven't, however, taken the tour with Lord Carrington. Knows it better than his own home. By the by, do feel free to stop by my apartments, though I cannot attest to its condition. I had to fire my last housekeeper."

"Whatever for?" Sara asked.

"Let's see." Sebastian rubbed his chin. "How shall I put this without coming across as vulgar?"

"She was engaging in sexual activities in Sebastian's bedroom," Justin supplied. "With his valet."

"Dear me!" Sara gasped. "I assume you fired your valet, too?"

Sebastian looked outright offended. "Good God, woman! Why would I go and do a thing like that? He's the only person who can deal with *this*." He pulled a lock of hair straight and then let go, narrowing his eyes as it sprung back into place. "Do you realize how difficult it would be to find a valet even remotely equivalent in skill?"

Before Sara could relay her feelings on maids being equally as important as hair connoisseur valets, she felt her hand being tucked into the crook of Justin's elbow.

"Fascinating as this conversation has proven," Justin said, "I fear all this talk about nothing has put us at a late start."

"Yes, yes." Sebastian waved a hand. "Good day to both of you."

Muttering a final comment about Irishmen and their flighty tempers, Sebastian bid them farewell, and Sara walked with Justin to the shiny black curricle waiting outside. Hitched with two stout geldings, the vehicle was detailed in red pinstripe, a highly fashionable new style of two-seated carriage, and bore the crest of Worcester.

"Beautiful," said Sara

"Yes." Justin pointed to the farthest horse. "That one there with the white blaze is Sebastian's horse, Armon. The other is Archibald."

"Yours?"

"Yes."

Sara scratched Archie's nose. "They're magnificent."

"Indeed." But he wasn't looking at the pair of chestnuts.

Warmth seeped down into her limbs, tickled the backs of her knees. Sara imagined kissing him again. Feeling those powerful lips moving over hers, plumbing the depths of her mouth. Chagrined, she pressed a hand to her cheek, looked away.

Justin drew nearer and tipped her chin, forced her eyes to meet his. "Are you certain you want to do this?"

"Of course."

"We may not return until late."

"I am certain, my lord."

"Good." He bent his head, hesitated for half a second before brushing a reverent kiss to her lips.

Sara had to stop herself from leaning into him. Too long since he'd last kissed her. Too long and too many days in between. One of his fingers traced a line down her cheek, left a trail of heat in its wake. She blinked up at him, surprised to see the space between his dark brows puckered.

"Justin?"

Quickly, he summoned composure. "We should leave. Much to see." He backed away just enough to offer his hand and help her onto the curricle.

Clean black leather sheathed the padded seat, and as Sara sat, it gave only slightly. She inhaled deeply, pulled the fresh air into her lungs. It was a glorious day.

Justin settled beside her, took up the reins and driving whip. His boots were polished to a high shine; tan breeches, in the new snug style, tucked neatly into them. She wanted to lay her hand on his thigh. Wanted to feel the strength of those horseman's muscles beneath her fingers.

Not trusting herself, she folded her hands in her lap. "Where are we going first?"

With a single snap of Justin's whip, the carriage launched forward. "Décadence."

Sara was immediately excited. "We went there yesterday! The madeleines are divine."

Justin chuckled. "Well, I suppose I can purchase some madeleines for you, kitten, but I hadn't planned on staying."

"Oh?" She tried not to sound too disappointed. After all, this day belonged to him. "More important places to go, I gather?"

"More important and interesting." He glanced at her askance.

"And after the cake shop?" Giddy, she was. When was the last time she'd felt this thrilled? She couldn't recall.

"I can't very well let you in on all my plans, now can I? Leave a little room for surprise and excitement, if you please." He paused. "Although ..." His gaze dipped down, lingered on her breasts, and Sara, sparks flickering everywhere inside her body, drew her pelisse tighter across her chest.

"Although?" she prompted.

"You're a bit overdressed for what I had in mind."

"Overdressed!" Why, she'd worn her best today. For him! "I am not overdressed, my lord. You are underdressed."

He laughed at that. "Touché. And to think, I even left my hat off today."

"I bet it's under the seat!"

His lips twitched. "Haven't you had enough betting? Your losses are what put us in this situation."

"Loss." She straightened. "I've only one loss to you, Lord Carrington."

"So far." He turned his gaze to the road ahead. They were nearing the city, its tightly nestled buildings becoming clearer in the distance. "I have yet to claim the other."

For all she wanted to reprimand him for the bold implication, she couldn't find the nerve.

Because she had thought about it. Hundreds of thousands of times. So much, in fact, mere musings had infiltrated into her dreams. And in dreams, why, one could imagine almost anything. Wasn't as if it could be helped, either; those fantasies infiltrated into the mind during the hours of peaceful slumber.

Only slumber wasn't so peaceful when Sara dreamed nightly that she was not alone in her bed. That he--that ... *Justin* was holding her. Close.

No. She couldn't reprimand his ungentlemanly comments. In fact, she admired his brazenness; that defiance she prided in her own person.

And so she sat in silence, hands tightly clamped together in her lap, and waited for him to help her down when they reached the French pastry shop on Friar Street.

"We'll only be a few minutes," he said, leading her inside, "but pick whatever you like. I assume you haven't had breakfast?"

Sara shook her head.

"I didn't think so. Ladies spend too much time dressing and not enough time eating."

"I didn't say I missed morning meal because I was busy dressing." She had, though now she suddenly wished she hadn't. It was all very peculiar, this want she had to look perfect for him. She'd never allowed Lana to spend this much time on her hair.

"You didn't have to." He leaned closer. His nose barely touched the rim of her ear. "And I didn't say I didn't like it, sweet. In fact, you've imposed a bit of a problem on me today."

"I'm sure I do not understand your meaning."

"I mean, my lady," he said, "I'm having a devil of a time keeping my hands to myself."

Luckily Sara didn't have to respond, which turned out perfect because he'd rendered her speechless. The baker, a portly Frenchman with red, pudgy cheeks and a tall baker's hat atop his balding head came to greet them. Upon seeing Justin, his entire face lit with glee.

"Marquis!" he exclaimed. "Bonjour! Bonjour! Comment allez-vous?"

"Je vais bien, merci," Justin said. "Ah, anglais, s'il vous plaît monsieur. My affianced does not speak French."

"Very little," Sara confessed, but the baker smiled.

"Excusez-moi, mademoiselle." He made an awkward bow. "I'm accustomed to the marquis paying his visits alone, you see. It has been some time, indeed! And your fiancée, you say?" He bowed again.

His girth, spilling over the ties of his baker's apron, reminded Sara of the political cartoons she'd seen of England's more generously proportioned noblemen.

"Monsieur Le Fontaine," Justin said, "Lady Sara Ballivar of Dublin, my intended."

The baker bent forward again, this time with a bit more aplomb. "A pleasure to meet you, *madame*. A favorite patron of mine is the marquis. Been stopping by since he was ... what? Eleven? Twelve?"

"Twelve, I believe, Monsieur." Justin rubbed the back of his neck, clearly uncomfortable with being remembered as anything but the towering man he was today.

"Well, I shan't detain you any longer." Monsieur clapped his hands, rubbed them together. "I know you have much to do. Much to do."

He waddled behind the counter and withdrew two rather large white boxes, both wrapped in blue ribbon. "I believe this is what you asked for, my lord. Shall I take it outside for you?"

"I can manage," Justin said. "I do, however, require an assortment of the madeleines for the lady."

"But of course!" And then he was waddling about again, filling a smaller box with a few of the cakes Sara had tasted the day before, and a few she'd wanted to but for the sake of her figure, decided against.

"I failed to ask." Monsieur wiped his sweaty brow. "How are the Graces?"

Sara laid her hand on Justin's arm. "The Graces?"

"My parents." To Monsieur, he said, "They do well, thank you."

"A fine man, the duke is." Balancing the boxes on his shoulder, Monsieur opened the door wide. The sun shone vividly around the polished curricle and surrounding old buildings. "Well," he said, slipping the boxes beneath the seat, "I am so pleased you came to visit. And you, my lady!" He turned to Sara, swept a bow, and upon standing straight again, began dabbing a kerchief to his forehead. "A pleasure to meet you, it was. The marquis has done himself well, choosing an Irish bride. In all my years, I've ne'er seen a woman to match the beauty of an Irish lady."

Sara dipped into a modest curtsy. "You are too kind, Monsieur. On behalf of all Irish ladies, we are most honored."

Monsieur took her hand, pressed it between his pudgy ones. "Lord Carrington should consider himself fortunate to have found you before I did, then, mademoiselle." Funning though he was, Sara had to give him credit for putting on so grave an expression. "I cannot imagine a finer life than one spent making madeleines for a lady such as you."

A throat cleared abruptly at Sara's shoulder. "All right, all right. We've tarried long enough." Justin retrieved Sara's hand from Monsieur's and slipped it firmly inside his elbow.

Sara bit her lip. He was protective of her. Maybe even a little jealous.

Her heart swelled at the thought.

"À tout à l'heure, my lord," Monsieur said as Justin helped Sara into the seat. "Do send my hellos to Miss Lucy. Tell her I added a little extra to the cakes this time."

"Miss Lucy?" Sara said as Justin sat beside her and took up the reins.

"You'll see."

*** *** ***

For the next several minutes, which could have been hours, excruciating as it was sitting next to Justin in silence, Sara watched the buildings go by. Watched the rays of sun shoot in and out among them like beams of pure gold. She toyed with the single curl hanging down over her shoulder, wove the soft strands between her fingers.

"You're quiet," Justin observed after some time. They'd passed the last building in the city at least ten minutes ago. "Is something the matter?"

"Where are we going?"

"Somewhere special."

Sara looked around. They were traveling a cobblestone road, grassy, stretching hills on either side, far as the eye could see. Oak trees, their enormous limbs in perfect proportion to their thick trunks, towered here and there, standing as regal gentlemen engaging in light conversation.

He pointed ahead. "There, just beyond that cluster of oak trees."

Through the old oaks, past a scattering of colorful, ornamental glass bulbs hanging like ancient pagan globes from the overlapping limbs, stood a white house. It wasn't until they drew closer, when the globes of blue and red, green, yellow and purple hung just above their heads, Sara heard the wind chimes, light and magical, like fairies dancing on dandelions.

Sara thought of all the fairytales her father had read to her as a child. Of fairies and dragons. Knights in shining armor. A prince boldly sweeping his princess off her feet.

Intrigued, Sara said, "It's beautiful, but ... what exactly is it?"

"This," he said, coming to halt under the Palladian-style portico extending from the front double doors, "is an orphanage."

Unsure she'd heard correctly, Sara asked what she felt was a perfectly valid question. "What on earth are we doing at an orphanage?" Then, "Not that there is anything wrong with orphanages, mind. Of course not. They are wonderful organizations, absolutely. Why, my father sees that the one in Dublin has all--"

Justin's husky chuckle interrupted her. "Sara, Sara," he said, allowing a young lad of no more than eight or so years to take hold of the horses. "You don't have to explain yourself. I'm well aware you find my choice in outing more than a little strange."

He paused and took both her hands, encased them inside his. "Especially when I'm certain you expected a day of under-exertion." Warmth, frivolity danced in his eyes. "Walks in the park. Tea."

She opened her mouth in reply, but couldn't find one. What could she say? She *had* expected all that. Of course she was surprised. More than surprised.

"M'lady?" a voice just on the verge of manhood said somewhere off to her right, breaking her chain of thought. "May I 'elp ye down?"

Sara took the proffered hand of a boy, whose Scots accent was so thick he might've fit right in with the pub owners in Dublin, and allowed him to help her down from the curricle. "My thanks," she said, and looked on to the house again.

One by one, children began trickling through the white painted doors.

Justin sank to his haunches. Laughing, they ran to him, looped their small arms around his neck; tugged at his coat, his hands. Played with the tassels on his boots.

He leaned into peppered kisses to his cheeks, mussed the smaller boys' hair. Chuckled when they hurried to put it back into place.

Sara blinked, mesmerized. Overjoyed, she was, they weren't having tea and conversation in Worcester. And they weren't walking through a park while she twirled a rose stem between her fingers.

His eyes met hers through the crowd of children, and Sara swore her heart stopped and started again.

God help her.

She was in love with him.

"Ladies, lads," he said, and Sara was fascinated by how quickly they all quieted to listen to him. "This is my fiancée, Lady Ballivar."

"Sara," she said, because suddenly she didn't feel like the daughter of a duke anymore. She removed her gloves, tucked them into the pocket of her pelisse. Stepped forward. "And what a pleasure it is to meet you all."

She was rewarded with the brilliant beam of a dozen smiles, and even a few curtsies and bows. They took her hands, greeted her with reverence, as if she were Queen Elizabeth reborn. And all the while, she found it nearly impossible not to look at Justin.

Because he was certainly looking at her.

A kind-faced woman with dark golden hair piled into messy bun atop her head appeared at the door. "Ah, Lord Carrington." She wiped her hands on the apron covering her worn day dress. Bobbed a quick curtsy. "So glad you came. Do come inside, won't you? The children were about to have ..." She paused. "Oh, but did you bring ...?"

"Of course," he murmured.

She clapped her hands elatedly. "Come along, children. Lord Carrington has brought us a treat."

Squealing with excitement, the children forgot all about Sara--and Justin, for that matter--and ran inside. The lady, who might have been no more than thirty if she was a day, fussed with a few straggling strands of hair around her face as she turned to Justin. Clearly she hadn't been expecting company.

But Justin didn't seem to mind. As though he spent every day doing charitable work, or having children assail him with hugs and kisses, he was decidedly tranquil.

"I have the quarterly reports ready for you," the lady told him, and he nodded curtly.

"Thank you, Lucy." He motioned to Sara. "My intended, Lady Ballivar of Dublin."

"A pleasure, my lady," said Lucy. "Won't you come inside? I'll send Tom out for the parcels. Under the seat, I presume?"

"Indeed," Justin said. "Monsieur says he added a little something extra this time."

"Splendid. The children will be most grateful. Come. Bella has a new pet she'd like to show you." She frowned a little, though her eyes remained cheerful. "A rat, my lord. Ugliest sight you've ne'er seen in your life, but she's got him trained, she has."

Turning on her heel and mumbling on about children who fancy rodents over normal animals, Lucy disappeared inside.

Justin took Sara by the hand and pressed a kiss to her knuckles. "Surprised?"

"Very." His skin against hers was sublime. Truly, she could swear off gloves and be forever content just to hold his hand.

"I hoped you would be." He brought her hand to his arm. "Shall we?"

"Justin," she said as he led her through the doors and into a well-lit foyer with wooden floors. "Why should Miss Lucy show you the reports for the orphanage? A patron does not usually bother himself with reports reflecting supplies and doctor visits and the like. His monetary generosities are normally the extent of his charitable involvement."

"Because I am no ordinary patron."

"No?"

"No."

"Why, then?"

He was still smiling. "Because I own the orphanage."

SEVENTEEN

"You... *own* the orphanage?"

Sara blinked. Blinked again. My, but she did have the prettiest lashes. An elegant sweep of dark, demure fringe. Noble women paid exorbitantly to have their eyelashes darkened, whereas Sara's were natural. Naturally that dark. Naturally that long.

Naturally that seductive.

Justin grinned.

Rendering his fiancée to near speechlessness had to be one of his new favorite pastimes. Although, he thought wickedly, it was certain to be replaced when he was finally able to ...

When *they* were finally able to ...

Deuce take it. With each passing day, his control wore thinner and thinner. But it was damn hard to take when she insisted upon wearing dresses such as this: yards of sheer light purple material, cut so low he had a wild suspicion she wasn't wearing a stitch of undergarments. All of which did a poor a job of hiding the goods underneath.

And that, the underneath, he had a fine portrait of in his mind. Call it two weeks straight of sleepless nights, envisioning what her young, undeniably soft, well-rounded body would feel like beneath his hands. Beneath his body.

"How did you come about that?" she said, untying her bonnet strings.

Had he said something?

"Justin?" She removed her bonnet, followed by her pelisse, and allowed one of the orphans to take them away.

"Pardon?" The ridiculousness of that complicated coiffure atop her head brought him back to his senses. He narrowed his eyes. Were those ... *lilac buds*? Why women felt the need to put their heads through such torment he would never know. Curls and pins and flowers, more pins. He much preferred it down.

"The orphanage." She pushed a wisp of dark curls away from her forehead. "How did you come to own it?"

"Ah." Yes, of course she would wonder how he came to be so charitable. Dukes, or elder sons who stood to inherit a dukedom as it were, were only expected to extend their charities in moderation.

They did have lives to lead, reputations to protect. Sullying one's hands, so to speak, wasn't precisely smiled upon.

Why should she expect him to be any different?

"It was once owned by Lord Vincent St. Clair," he finally said, "the late Earl of Middleton."

"Once," she echoed. "So, he sold it to you?"

"Not exactly. When St. Clair died, he had no heir. The earldom went to his cousin, a viscount of a small parish near Durham. Lord Byron Winthrop."

"I know him," she said perceptively. "He's visited my father on a few occasions."

"Regarding horse breeding, I'll wager."

She nodded.

"Yes, that is largely the extent of Winthrop's interest. He owns the largest stable of race horses in the country. When he inherited the Middleton earldom, however, he and the dowager countess went over St. Clair's assets, made cuts where needed, some good, some rather foolish."

"And this was one of them." She looked around, brow crinkled adorably. "St. Clair. Why do I know that name?"

"Because," he said, and winced a little when Sara's assessing gaze turned back to him. "St. Clair was Milly's husband." There was no need for formal names. She knew who he meant.

"Oh."

"It was her idea, actually," he said, "to tear it down. To be honest, most of the charitable funding St. Clair provided came to an end when he died. And Winthrop was more worried about his gelding winning the upcoming derby than the fate of a small orphanage."

She still didn't bristle. Not one bit.

"The orphanage meant a lot to the former earl, I gather?"

"Earl St. Clair was a very good man. He purchased the orphanage for the same reason I did. He couldn't bear to see it demolished."

"I see." She stopped to digest that information. "Seems as though St. Clair married below himself."

"Milly's the daughter of an earl, but she claims she was forced into the match with St. Clair. Although I cannot imagine a woman being forced into a better marriage than to the former Earl of

Middleton. He wanted nothing for himself and everything for everyone else. Including his wife."

"Who apparently despised him."

"Yes."

She tilted her head to the side. "She's not a very nice person, Justin, your dowager countess," she said tentatively. "Not a very nice person at all."

"No." And it was like realizing it for the first time. Milly wasn't nice. Wasn't even kind, for all she put on such benevolent airs. "No, she's not. And she's not *my* dowager countess," he added.

"What kind of a person would deliberately put a dozen children out of a home?"

"Milly doesn't care much for children."

"Why not?"

Justin shrugged. "She was an only child."

"I am an only child," said Sara. "And I think children are one of the most wonderful gifts God could give a person."

Inside his chest, his heart gave a profound thud. He took her hand. Pressed a kiss to her palm. Had to hold back a grin because she was blushing again. He did enjoy watching that wondrous shade of pinkish-crimson coloring her cheeks.

"A most marvelous trait in a woman." He brushed his lips across the heel of her hand, onto her wrist. "Nothing could please a man more than to know his wife will be a good mother to his children."

Her lips parted, only slightly. She was embarrassed, he realized, and how odd that was. That in so short a time, he'd come to know her this way. To know what emotion stemmed from a flutter of her lashes, the rise of a blush in her cheeks, or a falter in the normal, methodical lilt of her breathing.

He liked that, when her breath tapered. It made him feel as though this desire, this ... *longing*, wasn't one-sided.

"Justin." She pressed her lips together, only for a moment, to swallow, before whispering, "Don't. Someone will see."

She was right. He was a gentleman, after all. And although he did own the orphanage, could do whatever he liked with it, in it, around it, with whomever he chose, he could not forget himself.

Couldn't make an exhibition by mauling his fiancée in public places, speculating on all these inane ticks of hers that made him want to kiss her senseless, like a lovesick fool. Fool though he may have already been.

Probably was.

But fool that he was, apparently, or so he was beginning to think himself to be, being with her made him feel more alive than a boy stealing his father's best stallion and galloping through the front lawn. As if he could lose title, fortune, everything, if only to keep her and amuse himself with those adorable inane ticks until he was too old to see them properly. If that were possible. An heir to a dukedom willing to throw it all away for the sake of affection? Love?

Probably wasn't.

Possible, that is.

Good God. What an utterly female thing to do, pondering over feelings and emotions. Lord save him.

Asserting himself, because he wasn't a lovesick fool, and he most certainly was no female, Justin placed Sara's hand on his arm in the most unaffectionate fashion he could muster, and led her farther into the room.

"Tommy there," he said, pointing to the newest addition, "is from Limerick. His parents caught the fever on the way to Liverpool and passed away before the boat had even docked."

"How did he end up all the way here?" She watched closely as Tommy, palette of watercolors in hand, put the finishing touches on a pair of snow-capped mountains.

"Gypsies on their way eastward. They apparently intended on keeping him until he mentioned he'd once eaten owl when his family would have starved otherwise."

"Owl?" she repeated. "As in the avian?"

He nodded.

"Ew."

"You might be surprised what you'd eat if you were starving, kitten. Nonetheless, since gypsies believe owls to be bad luck, they dropped him off in town. Been here ever since."

"Poor dear."

"Not poor. He is well cared for, I assure you. They have a closeness here which cannot be obtained in the larger orphanages in, say, London or Bath. There are only twelve of them, you see."

"They're a family." She smiled as Bess, a small girl with a head short red curls, came trotting toward her, a string of what looked to be beads gripped tightly in her little fist.

Sara kneeled down, motioned for Bess to come closer. "What have you got there, young lady?"

Gnawing on the tip of her tiny index finger, her gaze shyly sheathed beneath long lashes, Bess said, "A present."

She handed Sara a white beaded bracelet, though it may not have been beads as he'd originally thought. Not rounded, but rather course and rough around the edges.

"'Tis made of seashells," Bess proudly told her.

That had been his second guess.

"From the coast in Suffolk."

Ah, yes. He remembered the seashells scattered about the beach of the North Sea like some sort of pirate treasure. Well. To an eleven year old boy with dreams of swashbuckling and pirating, they were treasure. His parents had taken him there while visiting the earl, Lord Howard, and he'd returned to Mayfair with a sack full of shells in all shapes and sizes, handpicked by him and his mother and Anna.

It was one of his best memories.

Sara was examining the little trinket, while Bess watched, waiting for a response, a word of praise. "It is lovely, just lovely," Sara said after she'd studied every shell carefully, ran her finger over it.

Bess smiled elatedly.

"Do you think you might, er …" Sara paused a moment. "Forgive me. I didn't catch your name."

"Bess, mum."

"Bess. Do you think perhaps you might tie it on me? I believe this ribbon matches my dress to perfection."

It didn't. The raggedy, crushed velvet ribbon stringing the seashells together was the color of a soldier's jacket, or perhaps the waistcoats of the Bow Street Horse Patrol: bright, *bright* red. And unless he was no longer in the know regarding women's fashions, which he seriously doubted as the brother of Lady Anna Carrington, red didn't blend so well with lilac.

But as Bess happily looped the bracelet around Sara's wrist, and tied the red velvet ribbon into a perfect bow, Justin imagined the most expensive bracelet couldn't have looked lovelier.

"Oh, I do believe this is my new favorite piece of jewelry." Sara didn't appear to care that Bess's dirty little hand, which Justin regrettably noticed also showed traces of yellow finger-paint, rested on her lilac muslin covered knee.

"The children and I are about to disperse to the back lawn, my lord," Miss Lucy said, having come to stand beside him. "Would you and Lady Ballivar care to join us?"

"Of course," he said. "My lady?"

"Yes, indeed." Sara stood, waved as Bess, skipping happily, followed all the other children from the room.

"Excellent!" Miss Lucy chimed. "The children have chosen rounders for our afternoon activity."

"Rounders!" Sara squealed as soon as Miss Lucy was well out of earshot. She squeezed his arm. "Oh, Justin. Do you think it would be terribly inappropriate if I played, too?"

He gazed down at her. How could he say no when her eyes were this bright? Not that he would have said, mind. He imagined *no* would prove to be a hard word to tell this woman in the long run.

"Not at all, sweet. Although ..." He allowed his gaze to slip from her face to the swell of her bosom.

She'd worn this dress for a reason. He'd already concluded that. And her reason was working quite well, as he was sure he'd envisioned sliding those delicate sleeves down her arms, revealing what he ached to cover in kisses, at least fifty times since seeing her walk down the stairs this morning. But it wasn't exactly what one would choose to wear had one known they would be engaging in sports with small children.

"The particular cut of your neckline," he said, "might prove a bit of a distraction when you're up to bat."

Sara looked down at herself. "It's a bit low, isn't it? I didn't think to bring a scarf."

Of course she hadn't. How else was he supposed to slip into the bouts of insanity today?

He did the only thing he could think to do. "Here." He untied his cravat. "You can use this."

"Oh, see here, my lord. I couldn't possibly. Why, what will you use for a neck covering?"

"My neck shall survive." He handed her the white silk strip of material. "Take it."

She looped it around her neck. And began tucking and stuffing.

Justin forced himself to turn around. What kind of man was he? Watching her as she dressed. And of all places, in the middle of an orphanage. Might as well have been a church.

How do you do, Reverend? No, no, just fine. My fiancée's merely covering her breasts. Can't have those things popping out unexpectedly, now, can we?

"Justin."

He turned. Grinned. He'd never look at that particular neck cloth the same way, maybe the entire lot of his neck cloths.

She waved a hand at her nape. "Could you?"

"Of course." He brushed her hands aside when she tried to help him. "Good girl."

He should've worked fast--how hard was it to tuck a scarf around the neckline of a woman's dress? But his hands moved slowly, deliberately, he realized, because he couldn't take his eyes off that smooth patch of peachy skin at her nape.

It was lovely.

It was soft.

He'd barely registered his breathing had picked up tempo until the small tendril curls hanging down her neck rustled slightly. And that lovely, soft skin prickled into gooseflesh.

He couldn't stop himself. He leaned down, tucked the last bit of his cravat into her neckline.

And kissed her.

And God help him, she moaned.

He slid his hands over her shoulders, opened his mouth. Tasted her. Lavender and salt and something altogether delectably pleasing. A flavor all her own, warm and feminine.

"We should go," he said, because if he didn't, they'd end up on the floor, against the wall or, preferably, in the nearest bed.

He backed up a step, proffered his arm. Kept his features taut as she took it. Without a word, on either of their parts, Justin led the way outside, wondering all the while if he'd ever, in all his life, practiced this much self-control. And then quickly concluded he hadn't.

Whoever said restraint was overrated deserved to be bound and flogged.

*** *** ***

As was expected given the general rules of time when one is having a splendid amount of fun, the remainder of the morning went by too quickly.

Sara played two games of rounders with the children, and only insisted upon pitching when it was Justin's turn to bat. Her accuracy took him by surprise; he completely missed the first pitch, his bat coming full circle in a swift, graceful arc. The second pitch was faster and had the slightest curve at the end, but it was well-executed, and he missed yet again.

Frustrated and determined, because he most assuredly could not miss a third time (especially with a female pitching), he gripped the bat, set his jaw. Narrowed his eyes in her direction.

This time, bat and ball connected.

Justin took off, ran to the sounds of whooping and hollering children and Sara's kind, yet commanding screams for someone, *anyone*, to strike him out.

"He's rounding to second post, he is!" Her normal rolling Brogue sounded like the thick drawl of a dairy maid. "Throw it to Tommy!"

From the corner of his eye, Justin saw Tommy drop the ball, a muffled curse spilling from his mouth as Justin ran past him. A slight pang of guilt hit his conscience: he was certain to make it all the way now. Tommy had retrieved the ball outside the Castle and was looking around, panicked, for someone to throw it to. And Justin, wanting the children to feel some sort of accomplishment, almost slowed his speed.

But he was also determined, twelve year old boy that he was, to get the tally.

Sending a silent apology to the goddess of children (Artemis, he vaguely remembered), Justin ran, fast as his long legs could carry him, fighting a chuckle because Sara had begun to scream frantically in Gaelic, toward Castle Rock.

"Throw it to me, Tommy!" The next second, she was in his eye line, running straight for him, one hand gripping the ball, the other hitching up her skirts.

Castle Rock might have been displaying the biggest slice of pie in the world, the both of them were pummeling so hungrily for it. The children were gape-mouthed. Miss Lucy was--well, he didn't know what she was doing. Probably slack jawed, too. Surely she'd never expected to see the owner of the orphanage, the sole provider of her and a dozen would-be deprived children, running like a madman across her back lawn.

He did not care.

From the look of sheer fortitude on Sara's red-splotched face, she didn't either. In fact, when she reared back her hand--the one gripping the ball--he was certain she meant to hit him with it. However, at the last moment, right before either of their foremost foot hit sanctuary, Sara lost the grip she had on her dress and stumbled forward, slamming full-length into him.

Staggering backward, Justin caught her in his arms just in time to keep the both of them from tumbling to the ground.

"He's out!" The sound of Tommy's voice was barely audible from the beat of Justin's own heart, thrumming madly in his ears.

"Is not!" Bess, bless her. At least someone was championing for him. "He's in!"

"Are you all right?" Justin looked down at the tangled mess that was his fiancée.

Slowly, slowly, her face upturned. If she'd hoped to keep that pile of complicated curls and twirls and pins and flowers atop her head, she would be sorely disappointed once she caught a glimpse of herself in a looking glass. Sprigs of curls were everywhere, stuck to her forehead, her cheeks and neck. One was caught in the corner of her mouth.

She blinked, presumably unable to answer for her state of shock. Or maybe it was because her breath was coming so hard Justin could feel her heartbeat pounding against his chest, which was remarkable considering his own heart was beating just as fast, if not faster.

"I'm fine." She pushed away, brushed her skirts off. Removed the lock of hair wedged in the corner of her mouth. Squared her shoulders. "Are you all right?"

"Never better."

Tommy and Bess were still arguing.

"He's in!" Bess reiterated, all three-foot-five of her dainty self marching across the lawn toward Tommy.

"Ah, Bess." Tommy threw his hands up in the air. "Ye'd 'ave to be bloody well blind to of seen 'im not as out. The lady's 'and touched 'im first. The ball 'it 'im square in the chest, it did. He's out," he added with all the firm conviction of a duke taking the podium in the Lords.

Sara looked down at the large, flattened rock beneath her right foot, Justin's left. "I believe," she said slowly, "that you were in."

He knew he was. He'd been playing this game since he was old enough to grip a bat properly. At Oxford, he and Sebastian, along with a handful of other gentlemen, spent almost every afternoon playing either cricket or rounders. Back then competition was everything, and winning was vital. They bet on every game, and whoever lost had to foot the bill at the local pub afterwards.

If the truth be told, when he hadn't been studying or engaging in bat-and-ball team sports, he spent most of his time either pickled in Scottish whisky or tupping the local girls. After class, before class, in between. Whatever it took to temporarily forget the one fixation that had weighed on his shoulders since boyhood.

Drowning oneself in Scotland's finest did wonders for unrelenting fixations.

Ironic how that single, unrelenting problem he'd been trying to forget then, he wanted more than anything now. As if that didn't add even more shame to the pile. He hated he had been that foolish. That he had allowed himself to stay that inebriated, around the clock, because of an inane piece of parchment.

But that inane piece of parchment, which, he'd been told, was signed by his father, the Duke of Kilkenny, and King George himself, had brought her--this remarkably beautiful creature standing before him in a dirt-smudged, yellow finger-paint splotched, lilac gown, with a rounders ball gripped firmly in her hand--to England.

It had brought her to him.

He shook his head, amazed he remembered through his reverie what they were talking about. He had made the tally. But: "You hit me with the ball before my foot hit the sanctuary," he announced coolly.

Somewhere from left field, he heard Tommy let out a gleeful, "Woo! Yes!"

Sara arched an eyebrow.

He loved it when she did that.

"So, that makes me out."

Her eyes narrowed slightly.

He loved that, too.

"Are you certain, my lord? I could have sworn ..."

"Please," he said, "do not swear on my account. Tommy is correct. The ball hit my chest before I reached sanctuary."

She stared at him skeptically, even as Tommy ran past her laughing, a giggling Bess chasing several feet behind, swearing she'd *sock him a good one* once she caught up with him. Soon all the children were chasing after Tommy. If Miss Lucy allowed it, which Justin suspected she certainly wouldn't (she was already bringing up the rear, yelling for Tommy to stop lest she give his cake to the dog, which was rather amusing as Justin was sure they didn't have a dog), they'd run after him all afternoon until the lawn was covered in collapsed children.

Justin leaned close to Sara's ear. "I pray our morning has proved amiable enough."

She didn't look at him, but continued to watch the small army of motherless children. "Amiable? Oh, it was more, my lord."

"I am pleased to hear it."

"I love to hear them laugh." She wrapped her arms around herself. "Makes me wish I'd had siblings."

Gently, he placed his hands on her shoulders. "Tell me what you're thinking," he whispered into her hair, and she shivered.

"Just that ... well, I think I might like to ..."

"Yes?"

*** *** ***

Speaking on matters of this nature was more difficult than Sara had anticipated. Especially with him.

She felt his hands first tighten around her shoulders, then begin a slow slide down her upper arms. "Tell me what you want," he murmured. "I'll give you anything within my power to give, Sara, you know that, don't you?"

She did know. Only, how he'd become so familiar, particularly when they'd only known each other for all of a fortnight, she wasn't at all sure.

Yet, she knew all the same.

"I think I might like to have more than one child," she said quietly. "Perhaps more than two. Several, even."

His hands stopped.

"That is, if time permits." If time permits? What was she thinking? "That is, I mean, if we have time to ... if you're not too busy with ..."

"You suggest, once married, we will not see each other often."

Partly, yes. Dukes were busy men. Marquesses were busy men. Men *in general* were, by nature, busy. In Dublin, she once heard the butcher's wife complain she hadn't seen her husband in a month because of a sudden influx in lamb chops. And Lana had once mentioned that up until her husband's demise, she might have seen him once, perhaps twice, a month for the increasing demand in gentlemen wanting their horses shod with lighter-weight shoes.

To this day, Lana despised horse racing.

So how much more would a man who held a seat in the House of Lords find himself absent, maybe months at a time, from home?

"Am I correct in thinking so?" he asked.

"You'll be busy, I am certain."

"That is true." Somehow his agreeing with her only made matters worse.

She wanted a husband who would be there, as her father had been there for her mother before she died. She wanted a family, one that included the man she married.

She wanted the impossible.

"When you want me, Sara, I shall never be too busy. That, I can promise you. However ..." He stepped to the side. "I have feeling we have matters to discuss." He kept his gaze straightforward, hands folded securely behind his back. "I've arranged for an afternoon ride, if that suits you."

"Of course."

He smiled, though he didn't look at her.

"On the curricle, you mean?" For perhaps the first time, she noticed the smooth yet distinct chiseled lines that made up his profile.

"No." Gentle humor danced in his dark eyes. "On horseback."

"Oh." She really had set the record for lame responses today. "Astride?"

Just as lame.

But he flashed a wicked half-smile, the one he'd apparently reserved for a situation such as this: conversing with quirky, green fiancée, who must have looked utterly ridiculous given she'd been running about with all the ardor of a five-year-old.

Thank goodness Lana was still tucked safely at Worcester Hall.

"Forgive me, my dear," he murmured, "but my ability to ride side-saddle is terribly lacking. So, yes, we--the both of us--shall sit astride. I hope you don't mind."

For fear of making yet another farcical comment, Sara kept silent and nodded her concurrence.

Five minutes later, after they'd said their goodbyes to the orphans and Miss Lucy, Sara and Justin mounted up.

"Ready?" Justin tossed a glance at her from under the brim of his Bushman's hat. As Sara suspected, it had been stowed neatly beneath the seat. "It's about half an hour's ride from here."

"Yes, but--*whoa*, Armon." Struggling to control Sebastian's massive gelding, Sara tightened her reins. "Where are we going?"

Justin grasped the brim of his hat in salute. "'*Where the bluebell and gowan lurk, lowly, unseen.*"

"Burns," she said automatically.

He dipped his chin in a short nod.

"That doesn't answer my question. *Where* are we going?"

There was that half-smile again. Persephone followed Hades straight into the Underworld with nothing less than that same devilish grin. "You'll just have to trust me."

EIGHTEEN

She did trust him, actually.

Even after they had ridden for a solid quarter hour before Justin so much as said one word (and then only to inform her they were turning into a particular path with low-lying beech limbs, and she should watch her head), she knew beyond a shadow of a doubt she was safe with him.

Sara relaxed to the methodic sway of Armon's elegant stride. She thought of Ireland. And of her father, praying he made it home to Dublin safely. She thought of Cav, what Lana had said about overhearing his conversation with his valet; his intentions to induce an elopement out of her. How absurd it was, if it were even true, that now--now, when her father had already shipped her to England--Cav wanted to elope.

Not that she believed he did, mind. But *if* he did--if he did, why now? Why when they had a dozen chances under the sanctity of Ireland, where elopement would have been easier, more feasible, than here, now, in England?

She should have never allowed matters to progress so far with Cav. Never should have allowed herself to think of him that way. And wasn't that an oddity in and of itself? That she once, in the not so distant past, wanted to be his wife? When virtually all her life she'd been reared to be the Duchess of Tethersal, known she was to marry an Englishmen on whom she'd never laid eyes? Yet, her sole want had been to marry Mr. Patrick Cavanaugh.

But that was then.

Now, today, her every thought put those innocent, naive daydreams she'd once had of Cav into the same dusty old box with all other childhood fantasies. What had been insignificant, sweetly cherished ponderings were now prodigious, vividly intimate musings.

Raw.

Wonderful.

It all dwindled down to this: She wanted her betrothed. Justin. The man she should have loathed for all eternity for the restraint his very existence had put on her life, she wanted him. Body, heart, mind and soul. She wanted to give him all; all she knew, all she was, would be. They belonged to him. She belonged to him.

And she loved him.

Desperately so.

Instinctively her gaze turned to the man on horseback in front of her, the Englishman who would be her husband. The more she looked at him, the more appealing he became. As if under her stare, he somehow became more masculine. Thicker, broader. Ridiculously impractical though it was, to her mind it was true. But she supposed that was to be expected when a woman falls in love with a man.

Which, she dimly acknowledged, was yet something else she should have never allowed herself to do given he almost certainly didn't feel the same. Oh, he wanted her. He couldn't look at her, kiss her, the way he did without feeling some sort of desire to take what was rightfully his in the first place. But love?

Not likely.

He was being practical, taking her on a day outing like this, regardless he'd won their silly bet. Duty meant everything to a man like Justin. And that's what she was to him. A duty. He was tending to what needed to be done, getting to know her as he'd been told to do (as she'd been told to do), and at the end of the day, he'd bow, kiss her hand, perhaps her lips (if she was lucky), and then he would go about his way. Perform ducal duties. Manly duties. Duties which didn't include his heart falling into the hands of his soon-to-be wife.

It didn't make him a bad person, certainly not, but it did mean he would never give her his whole self. She would be his wife. She would bear his children. She would be the duchess she'd been raised to be.

And she would love him in secret, regardless that he didn't share the sentiment.

At the end of the day, their fathers would clap each other on the back, declare the union a success, while she ... oh, she would privately wonder how it had all come to this.

Sara let out an idle sigh. A lifetime of loving a man who didn't love her. What would her mother have said?

Deciding that wasn't a question worth pondering over, she sighed again.

"We're almost there," Justin said in the suspicious tone that he was merely responding to something she'd said.

Which was ridiculous because neither one of them had said a word in the past three-quarters of an hour.

"I did not say a word, my lord."

"You sighed." He looked over his shoulder, held up two fingers. "Twice."

Intuitive man. So he had, however minutely, been paying attention.

Sara tipped her chin. "I was merely thinking."

He turned back around. "About?"

"Life, I suppose."

"Life, you suppose." He paused. "As in yours in particular?"

"I suppose, yes."

"Changed, has it?"

As if that wasn't the understatement of the century.

"In more ways than one," she answered honestly, because why lie? It wasn't as if he knew all the ways, the thousand different ways, her life had changed because of him. For all he knew, she was speaking of the betrothal and the move to a new country.

Or, even more inconsequential, the fact she had never played rounders with orphans nor worn a seashell bracelet threaded with old velvet ribbon.

"I know exactly what you mean." Confidence weighed heavy in his tone.

Did he? Truly? Of course he didn't. Not his fault, naturally, but still.

"I'm quite certain, my lord," she said carefully, for she did not want to insult him, "that our personal lives have been modified, each in their own respective fashions, over the course of the past two weeks. But that was to be expected, was it not? Certainly we realized prior to our first introductions that becoming acquainted with one another would bring about more changes than we might have anticipated. Do you not think so?"

Though he didn't answer immediately, his shoulders stiffened. Whether from her question, or because he was leading them into what looked to be another clearing, she couldn't say. But, as he stopped to move a low-lying branch, and allowed her to pass through the last bit of wood before the clearing, she caught a glimpse of something in his eyes when he looked at her. A dark, chilling passion that sent a delicious shudder racing down her spine.

There were no words for the way he was looking at her. Smoldering dark eyes paired with a rakish smile that spoke of naughty secrets. Secrets sure to put a permanent blush on her cheeks should she ever come to discover them.

"Certainly," he replied laconically, holding her gaze, as if he knew exactly what his eyes, the cynical upturn of his lips, were doing to her. He swept his hand gracefully toward the small field. "After you, my lady."

Giving Armon a gentle nudge, ignoring the strange little quake in her stomach, Sara moved past Justin and into the clearing.

And proceeded to forget why she'd felt so nervous.

Clusters of bell-shaped, bluish-purple flowers, hanging like maidens in full, frilly skirts, blanketed the entire clearing. Mesmerized, Sara dismounted, and continued to take in what couldn't be described as anything less than the atmosphere in a fairy story. The area was no bigger than a paddock one might use to train a colt, but every inch was covered, from the sun-warmed ground beneath Armon's feet to the shade beneath the canopy of surrounding beech trees.

"Bluebells." The ground crunched beneath Justin's booted feet as he came to stand beside her.

"They're lovely. You knew about this place beforehand, I gather?"

"For some time, yes. Sebastian and I took long rides when were children. Drove his mother to near madness because we wouldn't return until well after supper, sometimes later. But ..." He bent and plucked a stalk donning six of the dainty flowers. "We came upon this one day, and if the time of year is agreeable, the ground blooms as you see it."

"They only grow in April, then."

"And May."

"Ah." She gazed up at him. "'*Where the bluebell and gowan lurk, lowly, unseen.*'"

"I took a long shot on that one. At least I told you where we were going."

She gave him a gentle smack on the arm. "You most certainly did not! How could you possibly expect me to discern where you were taking me from a poem?"

"You're an intelligent woman. I expected you to figure it out."

"Well," she said, flattered by the compliment. "I suppose, given you've brought me to a place this breathtaking, I can forgive you for the vague choice in poetry."

He tipped his head in a short bow. "I would be much obliged. Poetry, I confess, is not my particular forte."

"And what, pray tell, *is* your forte, Lord Carrington?"

Anything she might have said to recant the ridiculous question vanished once his lips curved into that infernal grin of his. The one that made her feel all warm inside. The one that must have broken a hundred hearts when the ladies of the *ton* discovered he had been betrothed since youth.

He took her hand, raised it to his mouth, and her lips parted. "That, my dear lady, is something I intend on letting you discover for yourself. Once we are married, of course," he added silkily, just in case she had any idea of him ravishing her in the middle of a bluebell patch, or so she assumed.

Sara knew her cheeks had turned at least ten different shades of red. Every nerve, every millimeter of skin, every spot of air in, on, around her body seemed to ignite. There was nothing arrogant in his tone. Confidence and arrogance, she had learned, were two completely different entities, and Justin possessed the former with as much vitality as life itself. He was merely assured in his ability to satisfy her, though to what extent ... ah, but that was the question, was it not?

She was still contemplating the idea when he, letting go of her hand, unbuckled one of his saddle bags and retrieved a light coverlet in a blue brocade pattern.

"I thought we might have a picnic." He tossed the coverlet over his arm, opened another bag, and pulled out a small canvas satchel. "A nuncheon."

"That would be lovely." Armon gave her arm a gentle push with his nose. "But what will we do with the horses?"

"They'll graze in the clearing. Not to worry, my lady, they'll stay close. Here." He handed her the coverlet. "Spread this beneath a tree. Preferably one that isn't too knobby."

She nodded, and within minutes, they were comfortably seated beneath the closely twined bows of three beech trees. She with her legs tucked underneath her; he lying on his side, propped up on one elbow. They ate, exchanged light conversation. Watched the horses nibble amongst the bluebells. There were slices of fresh bread, smoked cheese, boiled pheasant and figs, and a flask of sweet lemonade that reminded Sara of hot summer days as a child in Ireland.

She took a sip from the glass they shared--Miss Lucy, for all her kindness and generosity had, quite artfully, packed only one--and handed it to Justin.

"So," she said as he was taking a drink, "I assume your absence from dinner and Shakespeare readings in the library last night were due to the planning of all this."

"Mmm." He set the glass down, used his thumb to swab away a droplet of lemonade from his mouth. "Only to ride into town and place the order with Monsieur. Miss Lucy hadn't the slightest idea I--*we* would be visiting the orphanage."

"You did not miss much," she confessed. "Dinner was delicious, of course. Anna, Sebastian, Cav and I sat together." She ignored the slight groan that came from his side of the blanket at the mention of Cav's name. "Discussed what each would choose for our readings in the library."

"And what did you choose?"

"The four of us did a small scene from *Much Ado About Nothing*."

He looked surprised. "You acted out a scene? In the midst of the gossipmongers?"

"Caroline was very pleased, actually. Besides, it was only a small scene."

"What scene?"

"An excerpt from Act II, Scene I--why do you seem upset? It was only a means of entertainment for Caroline's guests. You realize we are the youngest set in attendance?"

His brow crinkled, and he turned his gaze to a blade of stray grass by his elbow. He picked it up, studied it. "It's just that I would rather you saved your acting abilities, however encouraged by Caroline they are, for when I can be in attendance. Ladies in polite society do not tend to spontaneously act out scenes in plays.

Particularly when, if they are fortunate enough to be engaged, their fiancés are not present."

"Are you scolding me for my lack of propriety?" she said, and when he opened his mouth to answer: "Because it seems to me as if my acting out a scene in a Shakespeare comedy pales in comparison to you, taking me out for a full day of God-only-knows-what, while practically everyone in Worcester, or at least those in polite society, as you say, know we are, indeed, alone and un-chaperoned."

He gazed up at her through hooded eyes. "I don't require a chaperone to be with my own fiancée. Especially when everyone in polite society knows you've been mine for the entire span of a decade."

For a moment she couldn't find the will to answer. Her entire life she'd felt as if she wasn't her own person, owned by some mystery man who lived in a gothic castle on the outskirts of England. And that she should thank her lucky stars because of it. Because he was to be a duke, and not only a duke, but an *English* duke.

Only, now he wasn't a mystery man. He was every bit real. Here, in the flesh, lying precariously close beside her, twiddling a blade of grass between his fingers and looking ever the handsome cad one expected of a highwayman, not a marquess. And he still owned her.

But owned or no, she hadn't been born and raised in Ireland for nothing. She was, first and foremost, always would be, she decided right then and there, an Irishman.

"That is irrelevant," she finally said with all the Irish bristle she had inside her small body.

His retort was smooth and even. "It is quite relevant. Just because you didn't tell your Irish gentleman about your betrothal doesn't mean English society hasn't known of it for some time now."

Sara ground her teeth together. "He is not *my* Irish gentleman," she said, "and it is vastly impolite of you to say so."

That seemed to bring him down a peg. He may have been good at tossing witty retorts, her betrothed, but he'd been raised a gentleman. Politeness in the presence of a lady, no matter how angry one was with said lady, was an imperative rule in the gentlemen code.

"Forgive me." His eyes softened. "You've explained your ties with Mr. Cavanaugh, and I should accept that. I meant no offense."

"You do not offend me," she said, "but you must understand that Mr. Cavanaugh has been a part of my life for a long time. He is more a childhood friend now. Someone who was there for me when I had no one."

"Being raised without siblings must have been lonely at times."

"I suppose. But when one doesn't know what one is missing, how can they be certain?"

"You didn't have a mother," he pointed out, not unkindly. "That must have been difficult."

"Not so much. When I was born, my father hired Mrs. Brennan, and then it wasn't a week, two at the most, before he left again for England. So, I suppose you can say she's been something of a mother to me ever since."

"Hence her protectiveness." At her nod, he said, "I should consider hiring her on for when we have our own children."

"She's rather devoted to my father, but yes. I suppose we could."

A moment of silence ensued. The wind blew gently past them. The horses looked up at the sound of birds fluttering through the forest, then continued to graze. Sara took another sip of lemonade, and acknowledged this as the first time she'd shared a drink with another person.

It was oddly intimate.

Then again, so was this entire scene. Her pelisse lay folded beside her, his hat, her bonnet, his gloves, her gloves placed neatly atop it. His hair kept stirring in the wind, thick silken strands brushing carelessly across his forehead, over his ears. He flicked the blade of grass he'd been toying with for the past several minutes into the air, and narrowed his eyes as a breeze caught and carried it into the field.

She'd never forget this. Seeing him this relaxed, this at ease. It had to be a rare moment for a man with his responsibilities.

"You mentioned children earlier," he said.

"Yes."

He looked up at her, a hint of a smile lingering at one side of his mouth. "They require a lot of work, you know. But of course that is why people have wet nurses and children's maids."

"I intend to raise my own children."

His brows rose.

"In every way," she continued, "independent from the normal practice of handing them over to a wet nurse the moment they are born. I do not believe that parents, even in our society, should shirk the privilege of raising their own children."

She watched with apprehension as he considered this, hoped against hope she hadn't said too much or gone on like a blathering idiot. She did have a tendency of doing that every now and again.

But after blinking several times, and sifting through a number of facial expressions, the last of which left the faintest blush on the hills of his cheeks, he said, "Am I to understand that you intend on nursing the children yourself?"

Now she was blushing. Good gracious, how had they come about having such a conversation? She stiffened her spine.

"Yes," she asserted. "That is my intention."

"I see."

"You object?" Because if he did, she would carry out the plan she immediately made after spilling her mouthful of child-rearing expectancies.

And that was to dig a hole, and then crawl into it and die.

"No," he replied. "No, I do not object. I'm just ... surprised. Most women would find the very suggestion appalling."

"I am not most women," she said before she could stop herself.

"That was made very clear when first we met."

"I behaved rudely that night," she said. "Forgive me. Normally, I am not so cruel after first introductions."

"Ah, I see. So, the cruelty you save for after you've become acquainted?"

"Oh!" She swung at him, aiming for his chest. "You know that's not what I--"

His hand closed over hers.

"Meant." It was a mere whisper.

"Sara." He pressed a kiss to her palm.

"Yes?"

"If I were to call you my sweetheart." He kissed her palm, her wrist, her palm again. "How would I say that"--his eyes, dark with passion, met hers--"in Gaelic?"

She swallowed. "*A muirnín.*"

"*A muirnín,*" he repeated, and returned his attentions to her hand.

The old language had never sounded so enchantingly beautiful. He had said it perfectly, which, being he was at a disadvantage--his musical, well-bred drawl did have its limits--was rather impressive.

He kissed her again, this time on the inside of her elbow, and a rush of warmth claimed her entire arm, ending in a delicate trickle of tingles up her neck.

"My beautiful girl," he murmured, and Sara responded with a quiet, "*Mo chailín álainn.*"

He repeated it, his breath hot and ragged against her sensitive skin. Lazily his lips roamed up her arm, and with each covered inch, the last was left wanting.

"I feel," he whispered, gently, slowly sliding the sleeve of her gown off her shoulder, "deeply ..." He pressed a kiss there, and a new wave of warmth crawled up her neck, her ears, all the way to her scalp. "For you."

Dear God. He was seducing her.

"*Tá cion agam ort.*" His lips began a slow, seductive trail from her shoulder to her neck.

"Deeply." He kissed the delicate slope of her jaw.

She moaned. "*Domhain.*"

"Mmmm."

She felt his tongue slip beneath the hollow of her ear, and her skin prickled, chilled. Then, turned almost unbearably hot. Every part of her burned for this, for *him*. She wanted nothing more than to crawl inside him, to revel in his warmth, to keep this incredible, high sensation forever.

He traced the curve of her ear with the tip of his tongue, and she caught her lip between her teeth; he nipped at her earlobe, and she moaned.

She didn't know it could be this way. That love could feel so incredible. That her body could want what she couldn't understand; what she couldn't even begin to explain.

But she'd lost all thought, all care. And her body, it ached in places she'd never imagined could ache. Places that suddenly felt empty. Wanton. Desperate for fulfillment.

What was happening to her?

"Justin." His name passed through her lips as a plea. "Please, please," she begged, though what she was begging for, she hadn't a clue. Her insides felt twined and twisted. And though she wore no stays, no chemise, nothing but her possibly-ruined dress, drawers and stockings, the clothes on her body seemed more annoying than necessary.

As if to soothe whatever this was inside her, this foreign, wanton spirit, he murmured her name, kissed her throat, murmured her name again. He hooked a finger inside her other sleeve, and slid it slowly, down, down over her shoulder, the gauzy muslin barely resting below the gentle swell of her breasts. His body stilled, mouth lingering so close to her neck his lips brushed her pulse when he spoke.

"You're trembling." Gently, he squeezed her shoulder. "No need to be afraid, sweetheart, I promise. Nothing will happen you do not permit. Just relax."

I trust you. Her uneven breathing wouldn't allow the words passage.

One of his arms came around her, almost possessively, and before she knew it, he had lowered her to the ground. His shoulders loomed over her, blocking almost all sunlight save for the few rays illuminating his thick lashes. He caressed her cheek with the backs of his fingers, his eyes following the movement all the way down her neck to the slope of her shoulder.

The slow, appreciative drift of his gaze, the reverence of his touch, made her feel curvy, desirable, so utterly ... *female*. So very different from him. Where he was all hard mass, muscle and sinew, she was soft and pliable. Her body melted against his as if she had no choice in the matter.

She closed her eyes, and felt his hand mold over her shoulder, then slip lower. Lower still. His thumb hooked inside the neckline of her dress. He gave it one firm tug, and Sara gasped at the sensation of skin exposed to open, cool air.

A groan, more an animalistic growl, stirred from somewhere deep in his throat, and he muttered something. Perhaps it was a curse. She couldn't hear for the ocean pounding in her ears.

He caressed her then, and sweet heavens, it felt wonderful. The weight of his hand, the warmth of his palm, the light brush of his thumb, skating across her breast with a deftness that made her entire body shake, made her want to cry and laugh at the same time. He bent his head, kissed her throat, and she gripped his arms for purchase.

She loved him.

Loved him. More than she'd ever loved anyone or anything. She rolled her head back, loving the gentle, squeezing caress of his hand, the feel of his lips on her skin.

I love you. I love you.

"*Tá grá agam duit*," she said, breathing the words she longed to confess.

He raised his head; she opened her eyes.

His lips curved into a wobbly smile. "I seemed to have missed that one."

She slid her fingers to the back of his neck. "Nothing," she whispered, and pulled him down to her. "Just kiss me. Please, kiss me."

NINETEEN

Kissing her hadn't been part of the plan.
Well.
Maybe a small part.
But not like this. Not when they were in an inexcusably compromising position, lying down on a thin coverlet in the middle of a beech forest. On a bed of bluebells, he without his jacket or cravat; she without her pelisse.
Come to think, she might have even removed her slippers some time ago.
Never mind she was near bare to the waist, and, he admitted with a bit of primal male relish, had the most beautiful, well-rounded, supple breasts he'd ever had the pleasure of feeling beneath his hands.
A gentleman, he was, but even a gentleman only had so much self-control.
And hearing her, with that beautiful, melodic voice he'd come to adore, whisper for him to kiss her had been the final straw. Gentleman, marquess, heir of Tethersal, whomever he was, he'd reached his breaking point. None of those titles of grandeur mattered anymore.
He was a man.
And she was a woman.
He pressed his lips to hers with reckless abandon, and nearly swore in the process. He'd kissed her before--library, garden, bedchamber, for that's how they were imbedded in his mind--and each time was far more intoxicating than the last. More, on all three of those occasions, she'd kissed him back, even in Liverpool when she knew nothing about him.
But when she kissed him back this time, those previous kisses gained trivial status. As if those fleeting instances of their brief (very well, non-existent) courtship were mere practice sessions for this moment.
She wasn't timid anymore, his innocent Irish lass. Her tongue met his with a tenacious fervor that sent a jolt of pleasure through his entire body.

Hand shaking awkwardly, he held her face steady, and gave her mouth the full attention, the complete exploration it deserved. He captured her upper lip, and her lower, and allowed her to do the same, creating a primitive mating dance that made his blood boil and his groin tight. And then, bringing the dance to an exquisite climax, he swept his tongue inside, and was instantly gratified when she met him, stroke for stroke, pleasure for pleasure.

This is how it would be between them, he thought hazily as he moved his hand to cup her breast, surprised he still had the ability to produce a single, coherent thought for the elation coursing through his veins. They would learn, find what fit, and they'd be happy. Or, in the very least, content in their union.

And he would love her, and hope. Hope that someday she might return that love.

It might have been an epiphany, if he believed in such things, which he didn't. But it was a realization all the same, knowing he could never let her go.

Heart charged with renewed urgency, he allowed his lips a slow, antagonizing journey down her throat. She rose, arched against him. Tangled her fingers in his hair. Soft, indecipherable mewls drifted from her parted lips, and when he, finally arriving at his intended destination, took her into his mouth, she gasped.

"Oh!" And then, when he meant to raise his head, "No!"

"Shall I stop?" He flicked his tongue over her puckered nipple. It was dusky pink, lovely against her creamy skin.

He did it again, and this time she moaned.

"Sara?"

"N-no ..." Her throat worked into a spasmodic swallow. "Don't stop."

It was all he needed to hear.

Tentatively he took her breast again, closed his mouth around one tip while using his palm to caress and shape the other. All previous thought cleared from his mind, save for what he was doing. And what she did to him. Moaning her encouragement, whispering his name over and over as he made love to her with his mouth.

He had to make this good for her.

At some point in her life, she'd look back on this moment and wonder if he'd been gentle, affectionate, mindful of more than just his own needs. Which, he accepted, would go unfulfilled today.

But he could damn well satisfy her.

He moved his hand to her leg, stole beneath her dress to smooth over her calf. Up to her knee he cautiously slid, pausing for the most fleeting moment, waiting for that first sign of protest.

She didn't protest.

She arched into him like a cat, begging to be touched, stroked. He slid his fingers to the bare skin above her stocking. Squeezed gently, circled against her skin with his thumb.

"Justin," she breathed.

He moved his hand farther, farther still, to the soft, delicate skin of her inner thigh. She shifted and squirmed, but didn't object, so he inched up, found the lace trim of her drawers. Heat emanated from her core, and he pressed his forehead to her chest to gain composure.

He had to stay in control. Had to stay focused.

"Justin," she moaned, "please. Please, do something. I ache so."

Foreign though it must have been to a young woman with her lack of experience, Justin knew enough about the art of seduction to realize what was happening.

He bent his head, kissed her, and when he touched her--dear God, but she was so soft ... so silky, warm, wet--she practically leapt off the coverlet.

"Easy." He used the hand he had wedged beneath her back to keep her steady. Brushed a kiss to the corner of her mouth, another to her cheek. "I won't hurt you. Relax."

Little by little, he felt her body give way, and when he touched her again, her legs parted slowly, willingly.

"There, love." He slipped past the frilly seam of her dampened undergarment. "Let me touch you. Let me ..."

His finger slid inside with ease, and he caught her gasp with his mouth, kissing her and kissing her until, once again, her body fell limp beneath his. No one had ever told him how patient he'd have to be if ever this situation arose. Which, until recently, he'd never expected it to.

But he was glad now. Glad that it was him, Justin, pleasuring her, and not some other man who may or may not--ah, damnation, but he hated to even think it when he'd already admitted, albeit to himself, that he loved her.

Deftly he allowed his fingers to take on an ancient rhythm, a driving cadence he, even for his years, knew better than his own name. And when her body rose timidly to move against his hand, his mind went pitch with desire.

He needed her. Needed her to need him, and right then she did. She needed him for release, for purchase, he didn't care. Later, he could deal with the logical breakdown of this day.

But not now.

Now was not the time to analyze why, after several failed relationships, he had fallen in love with his own fiancée. Moreover, why he felt he couldn't breathe without her. And so he kissed her passionately, vowing with all he had that his very soul poured straight into her, into *this* kiss, *this* moment when he would bring her to that delicious pinnacle, and into euphoric bliss thereafter.

"Justin," she panted against his mouth.

He swore he'd never tire of hearing her say his name.

She bucked against his exhorting fingers. All at once, with an ardent cry that intensified his passion some hundred-fold, it happened. Her body shuddered, her legs shook. The tight, swollen flesh enveloping his fingers clenched and throbbed.

He stilled himself for several seconds, taking her in, how heart-wrenchingly lovely she looked, gasping for air. And then she bit her lower lip, aptly swollen from his kisses, and he couldn't refrain from dipping his head to kiss her again.

Pain, he thought dimly.

She was visibly enraptured, eyes glazed over, a wily little smile on her dewy face, and he was--he was in pain.

Good God. Whose idea was this?

He let his head fall into the crook of her neck, wondering if it was possible for a man to die from too much pleasure. Or, in his case, the lack thereof.

"That was ..." He heard her whisper, raised his head to see she was still smiling, lips wet as if she'd just licked them.

Acceptable, he hoped.

"Heavenly." Her eyes met his.

Better than acceptable.

"'Tis only the beginning."

Barely holding his emotions in check, for he wanted nothing more than to unbutton his breeches and finish this as it ought to be done, Justin pulled away. He pushed her dress back down, smoothed it with his hand.

She touched his arm. "But you didn't ..."

He raised his brows. Did she have any idea what she was asking? Certainly she didn't expect him to enter into a conversation like this when, indeed, he hadn't ... well.

"That is ..." The slim line of her neck worked in a swallow. "You didn't. You know."

Warmed by her concern, he pressed a kiss to her forehead. "Today was about you, sweetheart. My time will come soon enough."

He felt her brow crinkle beneath his lips. "But, shouldn't you ...?"

Intrigued, he propped himself up on his hand. "Shouldn't I ... what?"

She rose to her elbows. Boldly held his gaze. "I once heard the maids talking about--well, they said that when a man and a woman ... you know."

"Are we discussing intercourse now?"

Her mouth formed a tiny *o*, and then clamped shut.

"Because I'd rather we didn't right at the moment. Given my current state, you see." He cast a casual glance downward, and then, looking back at her, discovered she was no longer interested in his eyes, but in his breeches.

Or rather, he assumed, the evidence of desire straining beneath.

Instantly there was that urge, that burning want to take what would soon be his.

She was curious. He could see it in her eyes, which were, he noticed upon looking closer, near black for the irises dilated inside like full, twin moons.

His mind raced, dwindled into a few simple yet true realizations: She belonged to him, yes. She was unbearably beautiful--angels and saints above, yes, yes. She'd given him something neither of them would ever forget, yes, yes.

But she would never forgive him if he took her now, when they weren't properly wed.

Or would she?

No, she wouldn't.

"We should return," she said, drawing up her bodice. Righting her caplet-style sleeves. "People will begin to worry."

"By people, you mean Mrs. Brennan." He stood, and aided her to her feet.

"Naturally." She brushed her skirts. "Lana did not approve to start."

"As well she shouldn't have." He helped her into her pelisse, held her hair as she straightened her collar. "I imagine she'd have my head if she knew …" He stopped, swallowed.

Talking about it certainly did not help. But then how could he not? He'd touched her, kissed her, imagined kissing her in far more places than her upper body. This afternoon would haunt his every waking thought.

Bloody hell. How was he supposed to sleep at night?

"Justin."

"We need to go." His voice was thick, even to his ears. "Before it begins to rain and your dress becomes even more ruined."

"I think my dress is beyond repair, rain or no."

"Even so." He placed his hat atop his head, slipped into his jacket, picked a tiny lilac bud from his lapel--it was, relatively speaking, a bit ridiculous for her hair to have been decorated as if she were attending a ball instead of an afternoon in the country. "Shall we, then? We'll return to the orphanage, retrieve the curricle …"

"I do not regret it."

Caught off guard, and he was never caught off guard, Justin managed a feeble, "Wha--" before deciding he couldn't think of what to say.

"I don't," she said. "I won't."

"Well, which is it?"

"Don't."

"Ah."

"You do not regret it, do you?"

Was she kidding?

"Of course I have no regrets, Sara," he said, "but I cannot allow it to go any further until we are properly wed." Felt as if he were telling himself, for pity's sake, not her. Maybe he was telling both of them. Someone had to say it. God only knew what she might have allowed him to do if he hadn't stopped. But for good measure: "I just can't."

"Can't or won't?" She smiled playfully.

She would be the death of him. A smile like that, in a ballroom full of Britain's finest, he'd be staving off besotted fools left and right.

"Won't," he said firmly, and vowed he'd punch the first imbecile who dared so much as to slip a suggestive glance in her direction.

Her smile demure, for all the world as if she were a courtesan with years of womanly experience, Sara gave him an even, "Very well," before whirling about and marching toward the horses.

Justin clenched his hands into fists and followed, and he was still clenching, his whole body one big knot, after they'd retrieved the curricle and were on their way back to Worcester Hall.

Evening stirred, chilled the air. The symphonic sound of crickets and bullfrogs, turtle doves and a handful of other birds Justin recognized as native to this particular side of England, drifted all around them.

He tried to make polite conversation, asking her this and that in a meager attempt to suppress the thought of her naked and beneath him. But even the rolling, smooth sound of her elegant Brogue was more than palatable to his ears. It was hypnotic. Justin shifted uneasily, as Sara continued telling him about celebrating St. Michael's Day in Dublin Square.

"Granted, the holiday is more for the farm folk," she said. "Oh, but it is delightfully fun watching the locals dance in the square, the geese prepared using only the most delicious, traditional recipes, all of which are given to the poor for dinner that eve."

"Delicious, I'll wager."

"Oh, it is."

She touched his arm, leaned closer. They were close enough as it was. He could put his arm around her, and she'd fit perfectly snug up against his chest. But then he'd probably lose all conviction and stop the coach, ravish her right there on the seat. He'd have to turn around and head for Gretna Green, which was sounding more and more like the best idea he'd had all day.

A secret wedding, just over the border in Scotland at the old blacksmith's. No family, no friends, just the two of them.

"We really need to go some time."

"What?" Had he mentioned that out loud? Surely not.

"To Ireland," she said. "Attend the festivals."

"Oh," he muttered, relieved.

Only, he wasn't relieved. His body was still in knots, not to mention his heart felt as if it had swollen to melon size inside his chest. Saints above, if this is what love felt like, then how in the hell did people live without going mad?

Maybe he should mention it to her, eloping to Scotland. The deed would be done, just as planned since their childhood, and his mother would learn to live with it eventually--very well, maybe never. But she liked Sara, and that was saying something.

"You need to go some time," Sara said again. Her hand was still resting carelessly on his arm. "We need to. Together."

What he really needed was a bath and a good sleep. In the morning he'd write a letter to his mother, inform her that upon his return to Mayfair, he wished to be married straightaway. No extensive wedding planning. No sending out mountains of invitations. Just a small ceremony in close company. He supposed they'd have to write to Sara's father, but there was no law saying he couldn't do that himself, was there?

Yes, of course. He'd write his mother. He'd write Sara's father. And by the time the latter arrived in Mayfair, the former would have had ample time to do that motherly bit of planning a slightly-less-than-proper wedding.

It was the perfect plan.

"Yes," he finally said, and impossible though it seemed, when she responsively squeezed his arm, his heart swelled even more. He placed his hand over hers. "When we are married, I shall take you anywhere you wish. Anywhere in the world."

From the corner of his eye (he was, in all reality, trying to keep a steady watch on the road) he could see her beaming a smile that would've melted the heart of Hades himself.

"We did have a wonderful time today," she said. "Didn't we?"

Justin wondered if an adjective existed to describe what he felt in his heart, throughout his entire body, all the way down to the marrow in his bones.

Miraculous, it was. To have fallen this far, this unfathomably deep, into an emotion he'd accepted as something he'd never have the privilege of experiencing.

Love was, Justin realized, an indescribable feeling.

"Wonderful, indeed," he agreed.

Without another word, she laid her head on his shoulder.

And that's exactly how she remained for the rest of the journey to Worcester Hall, whereupon their arrival, a rather hysterical looking Sebastian--wasn't he supposed to be somewhere with Cavanaugh?--came running down the stone steps at a surprisingly frenetic speed.

"Justin! Good God, man, where have you been?"

Upon their reaching the curricle, Justin allowed the pair of footmen, running along behind Sebastian, to take the reins. Mind-boggling, it was, Sebastian's ability to ruin a perfect moment. Then again, he couldn't remember the last time his best friend had appeared so panicked.

Something was amiss.

Something, judging by Sebastian's disheveled appearance, was terribly wrong.

"Out," Justin murmured once he and Sara were on the ground, the footman having taken the curricle away. "Or did you forget? I told you we wouldn't be back until late, and yet, here we are. Early, by my calculations."

Sebastian raked a hand through his hair. "We received word," he said, "about two hours ago. From Mayfair."

Justin heart began that slow, sickening slide into his stomach. Some might have called it a sixth sense of sorts, but Justin, practical man that he was, knew it as pure instinct.

"My family," he said. "Are they …?"

But he was cut short by the sight of Anna bolting down the stairs, the skirts of her dress hiked high over her knees as she took the steps two at a time.

"Justin! Thank goodness you're back!"

"What the devil is going on?" he said, ignoring the fact that Cavanaugh was right behind her.

"We've been searching all over for you!" Her cheeks were inflamed, her blue eyes red around the irises. "Sebastian only just returned from searching all the way into town. Where have you been?"

This was really too much. He'd told them, all of them, that he and Sara would be returning late. "This is the last time I'm going to ask," he said. "What is amiss?"

"Your father." Fear blazed in Sebastian's eyes. "He's taken ill."

Anna immediately began to sob, and Sebastian was quick to offer his handkerchief, even going so far as to wrap his arm around her shoulders, allowing her to cry against his expensive jacket.

"Ill?" came Sara's soft reply, and Justin turned sharply, startled. She looked just as panicked as he felt, eyes rounded, face paled. "What do you mean?" she said. "He's been ill, has he not?"

"Yes." Sebastian's face was almost green against his snowy white cravat. "However, the duchess's message clearly stated that he ..." But he couldn't continue.

Justin didn't have to ask.

"Your father is dying, my lord." Cavanaugh's green eyes shifted to Sara. "And your father," he murmured, "is in Mayfair. Waiting for us. It seems he never left England."

TWENTY

Doubtless this had become one of the most frightening days of Sara's life. Frightening and unequivocally passionate, she allowed, since the day had actually been delightful up until the moment they learned the duke was possibly drawing his last breaths.

After that ... well. Everything started happening so fast, nothing, not even the single task of finding a clean dress to wear, seemed real. She settled on a cornflower blue, since Lana was so hell-bent on having everything packed posthaste, and her gray half boots as opposed to slippers, since (surprise, surprise) Lana had already packed all those too. No one was apt to pay attention to her footwear anyway, eager as they all were to leave for Mayfair.

Not that she wasn't eager; she was. She hadn't realized her father had never left England, hadn't given it much thought, really. After all, he'd wanted her to do this on her own, to get to know the stranger who was to be her husband.

Although, she mused, glancing one last time into the looking glass, Justin wasn't a stranger anymore, now, was he? Any man she'd allowed to touch her so intimately could not rightfully be considered a stranger. He'd laid her down on a bed of bluebells, exposed her to near nakedness, and kissed her body as if she were a pagan goddess.

It had been heavenly.

Beautiful.

Incredible.

He was more than just a name on a piece of parchment.

He was the man who would be her husband. And soon, she hoped, for she didn't know how much longer she could wait to have him. To be with him as a wife longs to be with her husband.

"Stop thinking about it, Sara," she murmured five minutes later as she entered one of Caroline's many side parlors. Bookshelves lined one wall, while Egyptian paintings and framed hieroglyphics on papyrus adorned the other three. The tables in the room-- one by the window, one beside each chair, and a large one in the center--were glass-top, given a modern flair with bases resembling pyramids.

Sara sat on a black velvet chaise that, with its feline stretch, intricate gold detailing and legs cleverly shaped as falcon wings, reminded her of a piece one might have found in Cleopatra's bedchamber.

And then, for the thirty-second time since they'd arrived at Worcester Hall, she thought about the kiss she and Justin had shared beneath the bows of ancient beech trees. On a blue brocade coverlet. Surrounded by a copse of softly fragrant bluebells.

Truly, the most prolific of poets couldn't have laid out a finer setting.

Of course it was more than just an ordinary kiss. Donne himself might have turned over in his grave had she lied and said it was. Though in retrospect, Sara believed that even Mr. Donne would've found Justin's kisses extraordinarily prose-worthy.

Some details simply could not be overlooked.

And yet, heart-stopping kisses aside ...

He'd touched her. Caressed her.

There.

All while his mouth had been doing wicked things, things she never dreamed possible, to her body.

An infinite wonder, it was, that she'd been able to function amply enough to undress, bathe, and redress. Seemed like an awful lot to do when all she wanted was to lie down for a while. And daydream about secret, hidden meadows and cool breezes, sweetly scented by flowers.

Justin touching and kissing her in forbidden places.

Determined to have at least one coherent thought past intimacies with Justin (the duke was supposedly on his death bed, for goodness' sake; she should be ashamed of herself), Sara straightened and peered through the doorway.

Outside everything was bustling. Sebastian's valet walked by, two bags in his gloved hands, nose stuck straight up in the air as if acting on such short notice was entirely too much to ask. Right behind him went Caroline and a fleet of footmen, Caroline giving precise orders in a high-pitched tone Sara was sure she only used when pushed to the point of hysterics.

Justin's valet, a lanky, dark haired man, strolled past the doorway, his lordship's famous hat in one hand, a garment bag in the other. And then, as if not expecting someone to be seated while everyone else was in motion, he backed up a step and looked in at her.

She stood because she didn't know what else to do. Was he addressing her? He hadn't said anything. Maybe they were preparing to leave?

Silently he looked in the direction from whence he came. Dipped his chin in a single nod.

Taking one last impassive glance at her, he left.

Confused, Sara opened her mouth to call after him, but found herself contrarily speechless when, in the very next instant, Justin's tall, male form swallowed the doorway. He was, as always when he wasn't in the out of doors, impeccably dressed. His breeches were dark, clean, his shirt gleaming white over a stunning brocade waistcoat of deep red.

He was dark, and he was large, and he was incredibly handsome.

Sara bobbed a curtsy.

"Good afternoon," he said, stepping inside.

"My lord," she murmured. "Are we leaving?"

"Soon." He was looking around the room, hands folded behind his back.

"It is a lovely parlor," she said because really, what did one say to a man whose father was dying? What words of comfort could she offer to improve the grave situation?

None, she decided, and she hated that.

She wanted to comfort him, wanted to make this all go away.

She wanted this man to need her.

"This was, *is*, my favorite room in Worcester Hall," he said. "When I was younger, I used to read here for hours. This"--he pointed to one of the many sheets of papyrus hanging on the wall--"is a blessing from Aten, the sun disc, to Queen Nefertiti upon the birth of her first child. She and the pharaoh, Akhenaten, worshipped only this god, and considered it blasphemous for anyone to do otherwise."

"Intriguing," she murmured, genuinely impressed.

"I should tell you," he said, still focusing on the papyrus, "that in the event my father passes, we may be forced to marry sooner than anticipated. That is, of course, after the family solicitor has read and interpreted our marriage contract."

"Why would it need to be interpreted?"

"Father said it would be necessary if this happened."

"If what happened, exactly?"

"If he were to die before the tenth year of the contract's signing."

"Oh."

Only once, when she'd been snooping around her father's office in search of stationery, had she caught a glimpse of the scrolled parchment. For fifteen minutes she'd stared at it, imagining what it said, amazed this single inanimate object held her life's fate.

And after, she'd dared to touch it.

But only after she'd made sure she was alone.

And then only with one finger, as if she'd half expected it to burst into flames right there inside the top drawer of her father's grand oak desk.

Which it didn't.

Obviously.

However, by the time she'd summoned the courage to pluck it from the drawer, the approaching sound of her father's footsteps caused her to lose all nerve.

She slammed the door shut, skirted from her father's office as fast as she could, and vowed never to let her curiosity get the best of her again.

As a result, she'd never read the contract. But apparently ..."You've read it," she said.

He turned around. "No. Have you?"

She shook her head. "I suppose we'll both be hearing it for the first time."

"Indeed."

The grimness in his voice made her want to crumple onto the floor or, in the very least, sulk in a corner somewhere. Somewhere she could think, contemplate the situation.

Not that it needed contemplating.

By the sound of his mother's letter, Justin was about to take over the dukedom. Which meant, in the eyes of upper society, he needed to marry. Just so happened he was already betrothed. Which meant, perhaps in a few days, Sara would become a duchess.

Put like that, it sounded ridiculously simple.

But it wasn't.

She loved him. She wanted to marry him. Wanted, more than anything in the world, to give him children, to watch them laugh and grow. To be there when their son fell and scraped his knee, only to feel her heart swell when his papa knelt down to comfort him. Or to see Justin's eyes light up at the very sight of their daughter, who, Sara knew, would look just like him.

But when he spoke of their marriage contract like *that* ... in that grave tone that made her throat work to fight back tears ... she just ... she just wanted to ...

No. She would not cry. Besides, the graveness might merely be grief for his father. Perhaps nervousness for the position he was sliding into. The Lord knew she would be nervous if she were him.

Because she couldn't very well go into the corner, curl into a ball and cry, she returned to the chaise and folded her hands in her lap.

"May I?" He motioned to the empty space beside her.

"Of course."

Apparently he'd bathed, as well. His hair was damp, and he smelled clean, masculine. Soap, sandalwood, and Justin. The most magnificent aromatic combination in the world.

"I apologize for the suddenness of all this," he said.

"Don't be," she replied softly. "It is not your fault."

"Yes, I know. But I should not have left Mayfair knowing he was sick." He rubbed his hands together, spanned the length of one with the other in a slow gesture.

"Then again," he went on, "he has always been sick. Long as I can remember."

"If you don't mind my asking," she said carefully, "what ails him? My father never spoke of it."

"Some form of wasting disease, or so the physicians tell us. Who knows? He appears fine, walks about, takes short strolls outside. But then he sleeps for days, and only after he has spent the past few writhing in bed with fever and night sweats.

"When finally he wakes, he coughs the worst substances imaginable. Sometimes there is blood; sometimes nothing at all."

He stopped, shook his head. Looked down.

Seeing him as thus was hard to bear. From the moment they'd met, he'd always appeared in control. Even when he kissed her, and by all that was logical, she had no idea how he was able to keep his emotions so in check, he maintained a certain balance. A level of equilibrium that spoke of years in constant restraint.

He was to be a duke. Naturally he was expected to curb any undisciplined tendencies. Crying (and he looked on the verge of doing just that) being one of them.

"Justin?" she whispered because it seemed right to say his name. "You can cry, if you want. I promise, I shan't tell anyone."

That made him chuckle. "I don't want to cry, Sara." His eyes found hers from the side. "Hit something, maybe. But not cry. Too late for that now."

"No." On sheer impulse, she laced her fingers with his. "It is never too late."

He gazed down at their adjoined hands. "That's something my father would say."

"He is a wise man."

"That, he is."

Looking down, she noticed for the first time the light dusting of hair on the back of his hands. She traced it with the tip of one finger, followed the line from wrist bone to the knuckle of his pinky.

Even this, a feature most would find too simple to spare a moment's thought, sent her pulse to racing.

"You have small hands, did you know that?"

"I hadn't given it much thought, actually." She flipped his hand over, pressed her palm to his palm. Aligned her fingers to his fingers. The tips barely reached his second set of knuckles. "You are right," she mused, tilting her head in observation.

An effortless bend and his fingers engulfed hers. "Very small," he said.

"I do not think my mother was very tall. In fact, Papa says she was no taller than a forest sprite, balancing atop another forest sprite's shoulders."

He laughed softly. Then, "Do you miss her?" he asked.

"Who?"

"Your mother."

"She died when I was born."

"Ah. I see."

"And," she continued with a shrug, "how can one miss someone whom they have never even met?"

He held her gaze for what felt like an eternity. His eyes were so dark, the lashes framing them so long and thick, she imagined there were many women in London green with envy. Why were men always blessed with long lashes? And dreamy eyes? And lopsided, heart-melting smiles?

Women needed those things too, thank you very much.

"Sara?" His thumb grazed her chin, slid slowly across her lower lip. "I am so glad you're here." His voice was husky. "Your presence has made this easier than it might have been otherwise."

"But we've not yet left for Mayfair." Because really, they had only known of the duke's potentially fatal state for an hour, maybe two.

"Even so." His fingers fell from her face, only to toy with one of the curls Lana had left loose from her coiffure. "I cannot accredit my calmness to anything but the fact that you are here, and before you were here, I wasn't ... that is, I wasn't nearly as ..."

"Calm?"

"I'm different now." His gaze slipped from hers to the spiral of hair he had twirled around two fingers.

If only he knew how that guileless confession made her long to throw everything she'd been taught out the window and kiss him. Right here. On Caroline's Egyptian chaise with the door wide open for anyone who cared to see.

"I'm different, too," she confessed, and just like that, his eyes met hers again.

Years from now, decades perhaps, she would look back on this moment and remember the way the air charged between them. Something *was* different.

And it was beautiful.

Real.

She would never be the same. Her love for this man had turned everything topsy-turvy. From her regard of Englishmen to the very rhythm of her heart, which sped up like a racehorse every time Justin entered a room – no, when he so much as entered her *thoughts*.

"I believe you are blushing, my lady."

She brought her fingertips to her cheek.

"I also believe," he murmured, "that I must kiss you right here, right now."

And so he did.

Tenderly his lips brushed hers, and Sara reasoned that this had to be the sweetest, most reverent kiss in the history of the world. That maybe if she thought hard enough, the world would simply vanish.

And maybe, just maybe, they could do this forever.

*** *** ***

Anna was snoring softly when Sara entered their shared coach, and she continued to snore throughout the entire journey to Mayfair. Sara didn't mind. If the roles were reversed, she reckoned a slice of solitude would be most welcome. Not to mention they were nearing the early morning hours of the next day, which explained the dull ache settling in her limbs.

Tired but unable to sleep, Sara leaned her head back. Watched the rain through the small window of what she'd determined by the exquisite painting on the ceiling as the same coach that originally brought her to Mayfair.

To Justin.

A fortnight ago this very coach was a prison, carrying her to be sold into a loveless marriage. Forcing her to live in a country she'd despised all her life, giving children to a man she would despise ten times more because it was his fault she was no longer in Ireland.

Ireland, where she knew the land, the people.

Ireland, where she felt safe, protected. Loved.

Only, this was her home now. England, whose people she'd come to love and respect. She even liked Sebastian, for pity's sake, and suspected a great many of Britain's most admirable would strongly disagree with her assessment that Sebastian, wonder of wonders, was actually a nice person. She'd even venture to guess that someday--granted, it would likely be in the distant, *distant* future--he'd make someone a fine husband.

And you are safe, she told herself, as they made the scenic drive through the immaculate lawn leading to the Tethersal residence.

You are protected. Loved. And if love isn't the sentiment Justin feels for you, why, it is most assuredly something close.

As their coach eased to a halt, the cries of the butler resounded from somewhere up ahead. Carried over the pit-pat-pit-pat footsteps of footmen running across the cobblestone driveway.

Horrid thoughts seeped somewhere into the vicinity of Sara's quaking stomach. Everyone--the butler, footmen, Justin's valet as he met the butler in the courtyard--looked dreadful. Faces blanched, eyes flared. As if they'd just witnessed a massacre, or perhaps (and a little less morbid) an exceptionally bad panoramic show.

"Are we already here?" Anna yawned, waking. She stretched her arms, blinked several times. "Sara, are you well?"

"Fine," she replied as the door swung open. "Only tired."

Anna yawned again. Her eyes, bloodshot and weary, were glazed over from hours up on hours of ceaseless crying.

"My lady." A footman offered his hand to Sara. "Please, if you will, make haste."

"What is the matter?" she asked, stepping down.

In the distance, Justin, Sebastian, and Cav were already speaking with the butler, Sebastian with his hand clapped over his mouth, Cav looking aghast. And Justin, well, she'd seen him expressionless, but this ...

This was something else entirely.

He looked stricken, yet chillingly pokerfaced.

The footman, who had just retrieved Anna from the coach, was in mid-sentence. "-been that way for days, and he just ... just could not bear the illness any longer."

Sara felt her entire body go numb. "What? What did you say?" The panic in her own voice surprised her.

His Adam's apple bobbled like a cork in shallow water. "The duke, my lady," he said, lips trembling. "He's dead."

TWENTY-ONE

For the hundredth time since arriving in England, Sara was at a loss for words. To crown the whole, it began to rain. Hard. What started as a minor downpour during their trip to Mayfair became, in the five seconds it took for a loud clasp of thunder to shake the ground with an accompaniment of several streaks of lightning to illuminate the night sky, a full blown thunderstorm.

"Let's get you inside, little one," someone said from behind.

Sebastian, Sara recognized.

Moments later, there he was, one arm wrapped firmly around Anna's shoulders, the other holding his own blue silk jacket above their heads. He turned briefly to Sara.

"Can you make it inside, my lady?" His voice amplified over the storm. "You shall catch death should you tarry."

Sara opened her mouth in response, but--

"I have her," came a male voice from somewhere above her head, followed by, "you two go on inside," which in turn was followed by the warmth of broadcloth enveloping her head and shoulders.

A firm hand came around her, gripped her shoulder. "You'll not die today, *a muirnín*."

Blinking back remnants of rain from her eyes, Sara glanced up and swore if her heart was previously in her feet, it now oozed out her toes.

Cav urged her forward. "You don't have to look so disappointed it is me and not him, you know. We've walked in the rain before. On two occasions, if memory serves."

"Three." Sara eyed Anna and Sebastian as they ran for the entrance.

"Ah, of course. After the debutante's ball in--watch your step there."

Sara lifted her soaked skirts above her ankles as they ascended the stairs. She needed to find Justin. Needed to comfort him, to be there no matter where he chose to go or what he chose to do: his father's bedside, a parlor where he could drown himself in whisky, it didn't matter.

"I should like to discuss something with you."

Sara felt her body go rigid.

"After having changed into something more befitting, naturally, as I wouldn't ask you to remain in wet clothes."

How kind, she almost replied, but cleared her throat instead.

"Would that be all right?"

"What do we have to discuss, Mr. Cavanaugh?"

"Ah, and we're back to formalities, are we?" He chuckled ruefully. "And I thought we had moved past that point, you and I."

"If you wish to speak to me," she said, patience thinning, "now is your chance."

He paused, nodded to the footman holding the door open, and handed his overcoat to another waiting across the threshold.

Darkness enveloped the entrance hall, save for a soft wash of orange light which bathed the tile floor and the Grecian statues, Hebe and Hercules. Sara looked up. Sconces lined the walls, and the orange light: candles flickering through amber glass. Funny, she hadn't noticed those before.

Then again, the last time she stood as thus, she was on Justin's arm.

Not Cav's.

And noticing anything other than the color of Justin's breeches, or perhaps the coat he'd chosen for that day, and over what color waistcoat, and in what pattern, and how it all looked on his gloriously muscled body, and how standing next to that gloriously muscled body made her feel all warm and fluttery inside was ... well, it was rather difficult. Impossible, really.

Sara let out a flustered sigh, made haste out of removing her bonnet and pelisse and handed--very well, *shoved*--them into the arms of an awaiting footman.

Where in heaven's name was Justin? He couldn't have gone far; Mayfair House was massive, but it didn't have wings in India like Worcester Hall. There were only a few parlors to which he could've retreated, unless he had retreated to his father's room. And if that was so, she'd have no choice but to wait.

She hated waiting.

Warm fingers slipped beneath her elbow. "I am not at liberty to discuss what I need to discuss with you in an entryway, Sara."

She wanted to slap him.

Instead, she jerked her arm from his grip. "Considering the circumstances, Mr. Cavanaugh, I find it more than appalling that you would wish to discuss anything. The Duke of Tethersal is dead, for pity's sake."

"No need for blasphemy. And cease the dramatics, if you please. I am well aware of the gravity of the situation. You do not have to remind me of why we are here."

"Why are you here, Cav? I know why *I* am here, but *you* ..." She stopped, bit her lip. She didn't want to discuss this. Didn't want to know why he was here, especially if it had nothing to do with steam engines.

"Never mind." She turned on her heel, determined to find Justin.

But Cav was quicker, and he had her by the elbow before she could take one step. "What? What were you about to say?"

"Nothing."

"Not true. Tell me."

"I am in no mood, Cav." And she wasn't. She wasn't in the mood for anything but locating Justin, and for the love of God, if Cav didn't let go of her, she swore she'd scream.

Or slap him.

Scream *and* slap him.

Maybe at the same time: The scream propelling the slap hard enough to leave a hand print on his face.

She quelled the impulse. Barely. And only because before she could open her mouth or rear back her hand to do either, a familiar voice, one she'd nearly forgotten over the course of being in a new country, in the midst of new people, said her name.

Wrenching her gaze from Cav's, Sara turned, looked.

Within reaching distance stood the Duke of Kilkenny. Her father, startling blue eyes mixed with equal parts happiness and despair, broad arms outstretched.

He smiled, whispered her name, and for Sara, it was like coming home.

"Papa?" At his nod, she ran to him. "Oh, Papa!"

His arms swept around her. He smelled of tobacco and cinnamon and horses, and Sara couldn't stop herself from burying her face in his shoulder. She felt like a little girl again.

"Oh, Papa." Emotion rose in her throat. "I am so glad you're here!"

"Ah, *a thaisce*." He patted her back. "I've missed you so. Elizabeth tells me you were at a house party in Worcester."

She nodded against his shoulder. "Justin, Anna, Sebastian, and I, but we've only been gone for a few days."

His hand stilled. "And you refer to Lord Carrington by his Christian name?" He pulled back, gazed down at her with tender amusement. "Already?"

"Quite a bit has changed since you left me in Liverpool, Papa."

"Indeed."

"Your Grace?"

Her father's eyes, so kind, so blue, narrowed over her shoulder. "Mr. Cavanaugh." His smile faded. "I was not aware of your plans to go to London. Dunmore said nothing."

Cav came up from his bow. "To Worcester, Your Grace." Nervousness twisted his features. "My father and I are in partnership with Worcester and his son, Marquess Beaufort."

"Steam engines, eh?"

Cav nodded.

"Fine way to fill one's pockets, I'll wager. Though I am surprised Dunmore sent you in his stead, busy as you've been with other matters."

"Other matters, Your Grace?"

"I believe you know my meaning, Mr. Cavanaugh."

Cav's cheeks colored.

Sara looked from one man to the other. Something transpired. Something hung there, unsaid, between her father and a paling Mr. Patrick Cavanaugh. Something apparently neither cared to discuss in her presence.

Unnerving, that.

Indignant, she curled her hands into fists at her sides. "If the two of you do not mind, I must go in search of Lord Carrington. Feel free to continue with ... whatever this is, which clearly cannot be discussed whilst I am present."

"We have nothing to discuss," her father said flatly.

"We have much to discuss," Cav retorted.

"No. We do not."

"With due respect, Your Grace. Yes. We do."

In the blink of an eye, her father had Cav by the lapels of his coat, and Cav, unaccustomed to the duke as anything but the very model of decorum, gasped, horrified.

"Listen to me, ye insolent mon." Father's Irish Brogue rang thick as molasses. "I know why ye've come. 'Tis a might low thing ye do, standin' 'ere in the home of my dearest friend as he lays without so much as a whiff of life in 'im. Ye do your father shame coming here on false pretenses, as they are."

Cav tried to speak, but his words exited as nothing more than a sputter. "I ... d-did ... n-no-"

"Do not insult me, lad. Had enough of ye as it is, I 'ave. I gave ye my answer, and when I gave it, I 'ad no intention of recanting the decision. I said no. I meant no."

Cav's face had turned from ripe tomato to brilliant, beet red. His eyes bulged, lips trembled. "Y-Your ... G-G-Grace ... p-please ..."

Muttering a curse, her father released him, and Cav staggered backward, coughing and tugging at his cravat.

"Of all the--what is the matter with you two?" Sara gazed first at her father, who, by the look of intense vexation streaked across his face, clearly felt no remorse for his actions.

She then looked at Cav.

And could not stand not to go to him. She may not have loved him, not the way she loved Justin, but he was still her friend. She would not deny him the same support he'd given her on countless occasions.

"Don't," Cav protested as Sara set a hand to his back and bent over him.

"You need to loosen your cravat," she said, keeping her voice low. She could see her father fuming from the corner of her eye. "Cav, please. Let me help--"

"I said *don't*." He all but spat the words.

"Fine, then," she said with equal loathing.

Men and their ridiculous pride.

"Gentleman?" she said. "Would you be so kind as to move this to another room? The situation at hand is of far greater importance."

"I have nothing left to say." Her father's educated tenor had returned. "I will, however, offer my apologies for my intolerable behavior." He nodded, curtly, to Cav.

Surprising though it was, Cav looked thoughtful. "Apology accepted, Your Grace. However, since you are unwilling to discuss the matter, I shall save what I have to say for your daughter alone."

The duke opened his mouth, doubtless to start another argument, but Sara was quicker.

"No!" Father's teeth hit in a solid clamp. "No more of this! A man's life has ended. And by God"--she shifted her gaze from her father to Cav and back again--"I will not tolerate arguing over trivial nonsense, when we should be lending our support to this family."

The duke's brows lifted. "I say, dear girl. Matters have, indeed, changed since your arrival in England. *You* have changed."

"Nonsensical as it may seem for the short length of time I have resided in this country," Sara said carefully, "I have grown attached to this family. They are good people, and they have lost their father. We should grieve with them, not arge over a matter which has nothing to do with anything now."

"It has everything to do with it," Cav countered, his gaze transfixed on Sara.

What the devil was he talking about? Sara drew her lips taut, trying with all her might to stay calm. "Even if that is true," she said, "which I do not see how it could be, now is not the time to discuss it. Don't." She put up a hand, as they both started to protest. "Please. I cannot abide the animosity between you." She raised her chin, smoothed her skirts. "Lord Carrington needs me, and I intend to find him."

"He is in the office of the duke," said Father.

"Then that is where I shall go."

"I understand your want to speak with him, my dear," her father said, "but there are times when a man needs to be left alone. I daresay the death of one's father merits as one of those occasions."

Tilting his head to the side, he extended his arm. "May I suggest we have a cup of tea, catch up a bit? I'd very much like to hear about your visit in Worcester."

Though hesitant, Sara acquiesced. Her father was right, of course, he was always right. But that didn't make it any less irritating, not being able to seek out Justin.

What if he was going mad with grief? What if he was throwing objects at the wall? Tearing curtains off the windows? She hadn't heard anything peculiar, but it was thundering rather loudly. Justin could've very well strangled the doctor by now, with no one the wiser.

"Come." Taking her hand, placing it on his arm, her father smiled. "I shall even permit Mr. Cavanaugh to accompany us." He stole a slit glance at the aforementioned. "If he can manage to hold his tongue."

"I would be honored, Your Grace." Cav's gaze slipped to Sara. "Lady Ballivar. I am certain you have knowledge of a room we can put to good use." Suggestiveness hung in his tone.

Sara ground her teeth. Cav was never suggestive. Straightforward, yes, and to a fault in most instances. Their conversation by the riverbank came to mind.

Sitting on his lap, indeed. She should've hit him for that, but the purpose of stirring Justin's jealousy would have been defeated. And heavens above, had she stirred it. Justin looked ready to commit murder that day.

Lucky for her, ducal composure had won out.

Cav might have been laid to rest at the bottom of the Severn otherwise.

"Won't you lead the way?" Cav's eyes danced with all the charisma of a snake charmer.

He was definitely up to something.

Mediator she was, however, Sara nodded her compliance. Besides, if Cav's intentions rang dishonorable, if Lana was right about his ambition to woo Sara away from England for an elopement, then she had every faith in Justin's prompt intervention.

He simply would not allow it.

*** *** ***

At this point, Justin wasn't sure of anything, let alone what he would and would not allow.

His father was dead.

And he was now the seventh Duke of Tethersal.

Two life-changing occurrences, each bound with the other, for without one, the other would not be, and Justin could not make heads or tails out of either.

Yet, he could think of nothing else.

None of it seemed real, for one. And second ...

Well. He didn't rightly know if there was a second. Second might have been finding this ridiculous book of global marriage customs on his father's desk an hour ago. When he'd needed somewhere, anywhere, to retreat from the chaos of his mother's and Anna's crying, combined.

It wasn't that he did not care; indeed, he did.

But some matters were better left to women, grieving in each other's arms being one of them, and Justin was in no mood to offer his comfort.

He needed to be alone. To think. Grieve his own way, he supposed, which was amusing considering he hadn't yet shed a tear. Did that make him heartless?

He took up the book on marriage customs and leaned back in the chair behind his father's desk. It was *his* desk now, *his* chair, *his* book, *his* library, *his* quill and parchment. Everything in this house, around it, down to the stables and the abandoned gamekeeper's house beyond, to the field of wildflowers and the small church beyond that ... It all belonged to *him*.

A castle in Scotland; one in Wicklow, just below Dublin; and another large estate home in Dover, the lawn of which extended to the white cliffs overlooking the Channel; all of them, his. If one squinted hard enough, one could see France from those cliffs.

Yes, even that view belonged to him now.

He should've been overjoyed. He was a very rich man with a substantial amount of power. He would take up his seat in the House of Lords, as he'd been raised to do. He would ensure Anna had a generous dowry to offer once she took it upon herself to cease her pickiness and choose a husband. He would put someone in charge of the orphanage in Worcester, as he himself was sure to be, at times, too busy to visit.

And he would marry Lady Sara Ballivar of Dublin.

That would be priority.

As Justin opened the book he'd found lying on his father's desk, atop his father's Tethersal-crested stationery, a single sheet of paper slipped from the inside cover, and onto his lap.

"What's here?" He set the book down, and took up the crisp sheet of fine vellum.

A letter. Written in his father's impeccable handwriting, and addressed to him. *My Dear Boy*, it said. His father had addressed him as so for years, especially when Justin was in for a lengthy bestowment of ducal wisdom.

He read the date aloud, acknowledged the letter had been written three days prior.

A sudden stitch of weariness crept into his shoulders.

Three days ago his father had been well enough to put pen and ink to parchment.

Three days ago Justin and Sara, Anna and Sebastian had left for Worcester, with naught a care in the world but two weeks of relaxation under Caroline's lackadaisical graces.

Three days ago his father was alive.

Shaking his head as if to ward off the panging guilt that if only he had stayed in Mayfair, if only he had been, *could* have been at his father's side, things may have been different, Justin began to read his father's letter.

My Dear Boy ... If you are reading this letter, then it is an accurate assumption that you, my dearest son, are now Tethersal, and that my very existence has at last come to an end. I left it inside this book in good faith that you, ever the curious lad of the strange and outré, would at some point find and read it. May I say, without straying from my intended focus, that the book in which you found my letter, which is now your letter, is an amiable read, despite its less than appealing title. The chapter on the Igbo people and their practice of polygamous courtships is most fascinating.

Justin chuckled. Indeed he and his father had shared an avid interest in books of bizarre subjects. Hence the shelves upon shelves--he looked around at all of them, towering grandly around the room--of books on Middle-Eastern literature, Egyptian mummification, the dialects of the Pygmy tribes, and how cows think, to name a few. Sure, one could find the complete collection of Mrs. Radcliffe's gothic novels, as well as Donne's poetry and Shakespeare's plays. Yet, sandwiched in between Radcliffe and Shakespeare were *Yodeling, A History* and *The Evolution of the Crane*, both written by Dr. Albert Regulus.

Justin often wondered how many libraries in London claimed those particularly inimitable pieces. And written in Dutch, at that.

A lingering smile curving his lips, he read on.

Firstly, and without knowledge of the state in which this letter will find you, it is my wish for you to know how extremely happy you, as my most beloved son, have made me, as your father. No man could have been better blessed than I. To have a son who is both intelligent and wise--yes, a vast amount of difference exists between the two--and who realizes the love of one's country, above all things, is the greatest love one shall ever know, has made me the proudest father and happiest man I could ever aspire to be.

Remember, Dear Boy, vigilance is crucial. Laws are not made without perseverance, and change will never be without constant determination.

In closing, I will leave you with this: "To love is to risk not being loved in return. To hope is to risk pain. To try is to risk failure. But risk must be taken because the greatest hazard in life is to risk nothing."

Find your way, Tethersal, and when your path should cross with opposition, and cross paths, you shall, stand firm. Fight for what you what you desire, what is in your heart and soul, what is rightfully yours. Remember, that which is worth fighting for, is worth dying for.

I love you, my son, my heir. By my troth, I leave you my legacy.
Yours in unadulterated devotion,
Phillip

Emotion pushed in Justin's chest. His vision blurred. The room stilled, shrunk around him, leaving only the sound of the persistent rain, pelting like warheads against the house, and the tick-tock of the rosewood grandfather clock in the far left corner.

He knew.

The duke, dying for years, in and out of sickness and health, knew this was the end. Obviously he'd prepared himself, as was to be expected. The duke never approached any task, great or small, unprepared. But then, how did one prepare oneself for death?

Justin read the letter again. And again, wondering if he should give up his obstinacy toward drinking. Brandy, a stout glass of it, would serve as a nice anesthetic to these blasted tears burning behind his eyes.

A knock boomed at the door, followed by, "Justin ... err, um ... Your Grace," followed by Sebastian raising his voice at someone.

"Deuce take it." Justin folded his father's letter, and slid it inside the pocket of his waistcoat.

"Your Grace? Are you in there?" Raised voices again, then, "Your Grace?"

Justin grumbled a curse. "For pity's sake, Sebastian. Come in."

The door opened, and through it came Sebastian and a man Justin hadn't seen in at least years. Simmons, the family solicitor.

"Your Grace," Simmons proclaimed, bowing. His waist had thickened, and it mushroomed from under his yellow brocade waistcoat, over his gleaming white jodhpurs. His whiskers, black with shots of silver, were surprisingly thick considering he was as bald as a coot.

"Simmons." Justin inclined his head. "Sebastian."

Sebastian bent stiffly at the waist. "Your Grace." His face was red, his eyes iced with anger. A patch of sweat beaded his forehead.

A rare state in which to see Lord Beaufort, indeed. Even when he fought with Anna, he remained oddly collected.

This was different.

"Something amiss?" asked Justin.

Sebastian said nothing but turned expectantly to Simmons.

Simmons blotted his forehead with his embroidered handkerchief and leaned forward, both pudgy hands planted firmly on the head of his cane. "Indeed, Your Grace. I have taken the liberty of reading your marriage contract to Lady Ballivar of Dublin."

Without me? Without Sara? Justin cleared his throat and stood, fingers fanned wide on the desk. "Be of sound mind, Simmons. I do not wish the reading of any document that includes my name or the name of my affianced to transpire without my presence. Is that clear?"

"Of course, Your Grace. My mistake. It won't happen again."

"See that it doesn't--for pity's sake, Beaufort. Sit down, won't you?"

Sebastian stopped pacing and shoved a hand through the shock of blond curls atop his head. "I prefer to stand."

"I prefer you to sit," Justin countered, and Sebastian did so, dropping into one of the velvet upholstered chairs positioned in front of Justin's desk. "Now, Simmons."

Simmons snapped to attention. "Your Grace?"

Justin leveled the solicitor his most daunting gaze. "What is this about my marriage contract? All should be in order for the two of us to be married directly. Of course, we will be in need of a special license, but I trust you to take care of that. And, naturally, all that I must do in order to claim my seat in the Lords, etcetera, etcetera."

"Yes, of course, Your Grace. But, you see, therein lies the issue at hand. You are now the Duke of Tethersal. According to your betrothal contract to Lady Ballivar, the succession has given you certain rights."

"I do not understand," Justin said skeptically. "What do you mean by 'certain rights'?"

"Perhaps freedom would be the better term." Simmons took a step forward.

"Freedom?"

Sebastian chose that moment to stand again, his words spilling so fast, Justin could hardly make heads or tails out of any of it. "Your Grace, I insist upon telling you this myself. Simmons may have misread the contract. These things do happen all the time, you know. The verbiage in old documents such as your marriage contract to Lady Ballivar is completely outdated. Perhaps we should hire someone for a second opinion, as I do not believe that--"

"You are in no need of a second opinion," said Simmons. "Forgive my bluntness, Lord Beaufort, but I am the solicitor for *this* family, not yours. I did not misread the contract. The words on that piece of parchment are as plain as day, signed by the Regent himself."

Sebastian's hands curled into fists at his sides. He looked to Justin for mediation.

"Please," said Justin. "Sit and rest awhile, my friend. There will be no need for a second opinion, as I am sure Simmons has read and interpreted the contract to the very best of his ability. My father trusted him, and so shall I."

Though his objection couldn't have been clearer, Sebastian sat and continued chewing his thumbnail.

"Simmons," Justin murmured. "Tell me what it says, and be quick about it. I have much to do."

The solicitor squared his shoulders. "Your betrothal contract is null and void, Your Grace."

Justin's heart sank. His hands clammed up. A wave of frigid panic swept through his chest, washed through his stomach and down into his legs. Sickness. Wretched aching.

This could not be happening.

Simmons wasn't finished. "So ..." He hesitated, apparently seeing the shock on his employer's face. Then carefully, yet clearly, "Congratulations, Your Grace. You are free to marry whomever you choose."

TWENTY-TWO

"I need a drink." Justin stalked past Simmons and yanked the bell pull. He needed his coat, needed to get out of this godforsaken house. White's wasn't far, about three blocks or so. Maybe the old droopy-eyed bartender could whip him up something along the lines of an amnesia draught.

Because he needed to forget Sara. To wipe his mind of her smile, her touch, her laughter. The way she felt in his arms. The way her body softened in quiet response beneath his hands. She didn't belong to him. Had never ... ah, God, but the thought of it made his stomach turn over as if he'd swallowed something disgustingly foul.

He yanked the bell pull again, harder this time.

"Damnation." He slammed his hand against the door jam. "Where is everyone?"

"More than likely attending to ..." Simmons cut himself short when Justin shot him a furious glare.

"I've heard enough for today," Justin snapped. He didn't want answers. He wanted silence.

And a drink.

Where the hell were all the servants?

A footman appeared. Bowed. "You rang, Your Grace?"

"My coat." Justin looked over his shoulder at Sebastian, who was leaning forward, elbows on knees. Head in his hands. "Lord Beaufort's as well."

"Very good, Your Grace." The servant whisked away.

Justin rubbed his brow, addressed his solicitor. "I have no need for anything further today. Do whatever it is you do and--I just have one question."

"Yes, of course. Anything, Your Grace."

"What exactly did the contract with Lady Ballivar entail?"

"Entail, Your Grace?"

"The stipulations which have now made it null and void." He hated that phrase, *null and void*. But it was exactly how he felt at the moment. *Empty*.

"Ah. Well, as it happens, Your Grace, the contract was of the common variety. It clearly states that in ten years' time, you are to wed Lady Sara Ballivar of Ireland, which according to the day the contract was signed, would have been approximately June 30 of this year, or there about. However, it also states that in the event you were to take over the dukedom within those ten years, the contract shall be null and void."

There it was again.

"That you, as the duke, should be of sound authority to choose your own bride at that time. I believe both your father and the Duke of Kilkenny wanted the contract to be fair to the both of you."

"Fair?" Justin snorted. "Fair would have been not creating the contract in the first place." How could they have done this? Prepare a contract, have it practically set in stone to the point of sending Sara all the way to England on an early arrival, and to what purpose? So they could become better acquainted? So they could ... what? Fall in love?

No one should have that much authority. Now he had no choice but to pay the price for allowing himself to fall in love with a woman who would doubtless book a passage on the first ship back to Dublin once she discovered herself free. She didn't have to marry him. She could marry any man she chose.

He, on the other hand, would learn to live alone. Because he didn't want anyone else.

If he couldn't have Sara, he'd never marry.

"Be that as it may, Your Grace," Simmons tentatively began, but Sebastian interrupted him with a loud, "That is quite enough, Mr. Simmons," which echoed throughout the room with so much authority, Simmons tottered back a few steps.

Justin met Sebastian's gaze from across the room, nodded. Sebastian would take over as he always did when Justin was all worded out. Or in this case, ready to throw the family solicitor out on the sidewalk, flat on his fat arse.

"Mr. Simmons," Sebastian said, all curtness now he had the stout man's undivided attention, "we find ourselves no longer in need of your services, at least not for today. I'll take it upon good authority that you can show yourself out? I'm afraid the servants of this household are preoccupied with other matters."

"Y-yes, of course," said Simmons, clearly unaccustomed to being wheedled by anyone other than his employer.

"You are too kind. We shall see you at the funeral."

"Which will be ...?"

"Whenever we send word." Sebastian coaxed Simmons to the door. "Now, be a good man, and leave His Grace to mourn the loss of his father, if you please. There you go. That way. Ah, you see? That kind footman is willing to escort you out. On your way. Shoo, now."

Justin heaved a watery chuckle.

Sebastian turned, brows raised. "What?"

"Did you just 'shoo' my solicitor?"

"That man tries my nerves."

"Mine as well," Justin admitted. "Thought it wasn't as if he was telling me anything I did not need to know." He just didn't *want* to know. That was the problem.

"By the by." Sebastian took his coat from the footman who appeared at the door. "Much as I am fond of drowning myself in a decanter of fine brandy at White's, Jus ... er, that is, Your Grace, I believe drinking at this point will do you more harm than good."

"At this point," Justin remarked, slipping into his own jacket, "I care not what you believe. And stop *Your Gracing* me. Makes me want to spill the contents in my stomach, for all the good it's doing me at present."

"Graphic," Sebastian commented wryly, as Justin strode from the room.

*** *** ***

"Was that ...?" Sara perked up on the sofa in the east tea room. Stared at the open doorway. *Justin?* She rose to her feet.

"What was that, my dear?" Her father set down his chintz teacup. "Did you say something?"

"Lord Carrington." She peered outside the doorway, looked left and right. Left again. She could've sworn she just saw Justin and Sebastian walking toward one way or the other. But they were nowhere in sight.

She stepped out into the hallway.

"He is probably going out," Anna replied distractedly. She'd joined them--Sara, Sara's father, and Cav--in the tea room some twenty minutes ago. The duchess still remained to be seen. "Sebastian was no doubt at his heels."

Sara nodded. "I believe so."

"As I said," Anna murmured into her tea cup. "Inseparable, those two. I should've expected no less than Sebastian's gluing himself to Justin's side once we reached Mayfair. He was practically a son to my father."

"You seem to be in amiable spirits, considering the circumstances, Lady Anna." Cav was seated across from Anna and Sara's father, thumbing through a pressed copy of today's paper. He'd behaved himself for the most part, the only exception being his attempt to seat himself beside Sara, at which he was quickly rebuked by the duke and ordered to sit elsewhere. "Truly," he said, "you seem rather ... refreshed."

Anna smiled congenially. "I thank you, Mr. Cavanaugh. It pleases me to know my father no longer suffers. Perhaps that is the refreshment you see."

"Indeed."

Sara stole another glance down the hallway. No maids. No footmen. No Sebastian. And, most unfortunately, no Justin. Certainly they wouldn't have gone out in these conditions? They could be hurt, killed.

"Come away from the doorway, my dear," her father said. "You do no good to yourself, pining after Lord Carrington's whereabouts as so. I am certain he shall return shortly."

"I should go to him." She didn't want him to be alone, or maybe it was she who didn't want to be without him.

"You will do no such thing." She'd heard that particular tone in her father's voice before. "Now, sit down, Sara." And when she blinked at him in surprise: "Please."

Lifting her chin, Sara walked stiffly to the sitting area and seated herself beside Anna, who offered her a weak smile of consolation.

"I do adore that color on you, Sara." Anna brushed her hand lightly over the skirt of Sara's pale blue muslin.

"Thank you," Sara said feebly. "Likewise. This pink is lovely."

"Do you think? I wasn't sure."

They had changed out of their soggy, rain-soaked gowns--Sara to her pale blue with tiny white flowers, and Anna to a gorgeous gown of solid, pale pink muslin--before joining Cav and the duke for tea. Naturally Lana threw a small tantrum, complained that Sara had managed to ruin not one, but two gowns that day, each of which had cost her father *enough to feed a family of six for a blimmin' year.*

But Sara couldn't find the will to counter Lana's chastisement. She was tired; she was hungry. More than anything, she longed for Justin. It was as if a part of her was missing.

"Pink is not a color I would normally choose for myself," Anna went on to say. "With my light hair and complexion, it tends to make me appear washed out."

Washed Out. Exactly how Sara felt at present.

She folded her hand around Anna's. "Perhaps we should take a turn about the room?" Because sitting on this uncomfortable sofa any longer, thinking of nothing but Justin, was liable to kill her.

"A most agreeable idea, Lady Ballivar." Anna stood and linked her arm with Sara's. Cav and the duke stood as well. "My limbs need loosening. The rain put quite a chill in my bones. Please, do sit, gentlemen."

Cav and the duke murmured their acknowledgments and returned to their seats, Cav sticking his nose in his newspaper, the duke staring off into the space, slowly sipping his tea.

"Your father seems distant," Anna said quietly as they passed a statue of the goddess Helene. "Is he all right?"

Sara looked over her shoulder. "He grieves for your father. After all these years, he still considered the Duke of Tethersal to be his dearest friend."

"My father spoke of your father often. He would tell us, Justin and myself, that is, stories of when they were on campaign together in Brussels, and all the nights they spent waiting for Emperor Bonaparte's armies. Spook tales, I always thought. I was never able to sleep afterward."

"My father never spoke of it." Why not? Sara suddenly wondered. "Perhaps the memories were too horrific."

"Perhaps."

They promenaded past Cav and Sara's father, the latter giving no sign he'd even noticed them.

Cav looked over his paper, dipped his chin. "Lady Ballivar. Lady Anna."

"Mr. Cavanaugh," they said in unison, and continued around the room.

"I kissed Sebastian," Anna whispered once they were out of earshot.

"What!"

"Shh!"

Sara peeked over her shoulder to see that Cav was gazing peculiarly at the two of them.

"Everything all right?" he asked.

"Fine," Sara said at once. "Just lost my footing."

This seemed to satisfy him, and he went back to his paper.

Anna let out a little giggle.

"You kissed Sebastian?" Sara asked, discreetly now.

"Well, actually," Anna said, "I do believe he kissed me."

"What happened?"

"Well ... I went into my father's room with my mother, Justin and Sebastian. The family solicitor was there, too."

Sara felt her brow pucker. Why would the solicitor be here so early on?

"Mother almost collapsed, but Justin caught her in time," Anna said. "And I ... well, I had been crying for some time, you see. And yet, when I saw him, my father that is, I ..." She paused, as if trying to find the right words. "I could not cry."

"Oh," Sara said softly. "Shock, perhaps?"

"Even so, I was rather angry with myself. Why could I not cry? So I left the room, and Sebastian, well, he followed." She stopped, glanced over at Cav and the duke, who paid them no mind, and continued in a whisper. "He told me I was too lovely to be so angry all the time."

Sara held back a smile. So, it hadn't been merely her imagination when, after Justin had chided Anna in the foyer of this very house, Sebastian had seemed distressed. Sebastian had gazed upon Anna with longing, and now it was clear why.

He was in love with her.

Well. Maybe love was a bit too strong of a word. Fond of her, perhaps. Yes. Didn't Papa always say boys teased the girls they liked the most? And wasn't Sebastian always fighting with Anna over the most childish matters?

Enlightened by her discovery, Sara said, "Then what happened?"

"Well," Anna said conspiratorially, "he told me that he was sorry for my loss, that he loved my father too. And then, well ..." Her cheeks turned brilliant pink, lips curved into a smile. "It just happened."

"And? How was it?"

"Sara!" Anna gasped, and then, lowering her voice back to a whisper, "What a thing to ask!"

"Well?"

"It was wonderful. Oh, but he does kiss finely, Sara. Very finely. Although ..."

"Although?"

"Nothing could ever come of it."

"Why ever not?"

"Because," Anna said, "he is a rake. A scoundrel. He could never be faithful, and I refuse to marry a man who cannot devote himself to me fully."

Sara didn't want to either, but she'd already decided she'd live with Justin's infidelities. Even though it would more than likely kill her.

They walked past Cav and the duke again, and this time, just as Cav murmured his polite acknowledgment, the duke rose to his feet.

Sara and Anna came to a halt.

"Pardon." He raked a trembling hand through his hair. "I believe I shall go out for a while. Clear my head."

"Are you all right, Papa?"

"Yes, of course," he said, too quickly for Sara to believe he was, actually, all right. But she didn't question it. "I shall return shortly."

"Shall I accompany you, Your Grace?" asked Cav.

The duke regarded him evenly, hesitated, and said, "Yes. I believe you may."

It couldn't have been any clearer that Cav really had no desire to leave; he exchanged a look with Sara that, to her mind, might have been a silent plea for her to insist he stay in the room.

Sara raised a brow. "Do take good care of my father," she said, and nearly laughed as Cav gave her a scowl becoming a four year old.

His lips thinned, eyes turned a shade of dark, murky emerald; the sea, blackening under a night sky. "As you wish, my lady. His comfort is priority."

As the duke left the room, Cav stalking irritably behind him, Sara let out a laugh.

"You are so bad!" Anna chided, but she, too, was laughing. "Poor Mr. Cavanaugh. He wants you all to himself, you know."

"Well, he cannot have me."

Anna was still laughing. "You have grown attached to my brother."

"I ..." How did she put this without sounding like a lovesick halfwit? "I find him agreeable, now we have become better acquainted."

"You needn't sound as if you are still forced to marry him." Anna gave Sara's arm an affectionate squeeze, and it was almost as though they were sisters, gliding about the room as if they'd done so a thousand times. "I know you want to marry him. I see it there, in your eyes. You love him, no?"

Sara felt her cheeks inflame. Was she so obvious? She'd tried to be discreet with the admiring glances in Justin's direction, the stares of unadulterated longing.

"Well?" Anna persisted.

"I suppose I do, yes."

"Oh!" Anna squeezed Sara's arm. "I knew it! I am so happy for the two of you. Really, I am. No one could have been a better match for my brother."

"I am pleased you think so."

"I *know* so. Have you told him?"

"No!" Sara said, stopping altogether. "Why should I have done? It matters not, does it?"

"Not matter?" Anna gripped Sara's shoulders in her hands. "Of course it matters!"

"Why?"

"Is it not obvious? He loves you too, and if you do not tell him--"

"What?" Sara whispered, aghast. Could it be true? Had Anna witnessed in Justin's eyes the same affection she'd seen in Sara's? "How?"

"I. Just. Know." Anna punctuated every word with a tap of her forefinger to Sara's nose. "He is besotted. Cannot think of anything else. He even told Lady St. Clair to leave the house party, lest he throw her out on her arse himself."

"He said that!"

"More or less. He might have been more discreet."

"Indeed," Sara murmured, still trying to come to grips with the fact that Justin might love her. The only question was ... would it be enough?

"So you see," Anna continued, "you must tell him. It would make matters so much more pleasant. If he realizes you love him in return, he'll have the strength to move forward, all the more for us all to move forward. To get past what we knew was inevitable."

"What about you and Sebastian?"

Anna jerked her head back in surprise. "What about me and Sebastian?"

"He kissed you," Sara reminded her. "I do not believe Sebastian would kiss you unless he truly wanted to."

"Pish." Anna waived her hand, and sauntered back to the sitting area. "There is no me and Sebastian," she said, sipping her tea. "It was only a kiss. That is all it was to me, and most definitely all it was to him. A comforting gesture for the loss of my father. Nothing more."

Not only did Sara refuse to believe Sebastian, rakehell though he was, would kiss Anna unless he truly wanted to, but she also didn't believe he'd do it for comfort's sake. Anna was his best friend's sister. Rakehell or no, Sebastian would never do anything to impair his relationship with Justin.

Unless, of course, it was worth it. And Sara was about to tell Anna just that when Cav entered the room looking rather vexed.

"Mr. Cavanaugh. I thought you were accompanying my father to ... er, wherever he was going."

"Change of plans."

There was a bang, sounding like a vase or perhaps a small statue hitting the floor, followed by a growling curse, and a higher-pitched voice saying, "So sorry, Your Grace. I'll have that cleaned up right away."

"Just get rid of it," came the low reply.

Justin. He hadn't left. He was still here. Oh, but he didn't sound happy.

And then there were footsteps, several of them.

"Who do you suppose ...?" Anna began, but was cut short by Cav, who had apparently anticipated the question.

"His Grace, the Duke of Kilkenny, His Grace, the Duke of Tethersal, and His Lordship, the Marquess of Beaufort."

"Justin," Sara said without thought or care to the glare of disapproval Cav shot in her direction.

"I thought for sure they were going out," Anna murmured, and when Justin entered the room, followed close by Sebastian and a befuddled looking Duke of Kilkenny: "We thought you were going out. Is something amiss?"

Though impeccably dressed in a pair of fresh and, more importantly, *dry* black breeches, a crisp shirt and cravat with a marvelous brocade waistcoat of azure blue, Justin seemed strained, his features taut. As if at any moment he might spew up the pheasant they'd shared earlier.

"Yes," he said, and shoved a hand through his hair, adding *disheveled* to his constricted appearance. "Yes, something is amiss."

"What's happened?" asked Anna.

"Apparently," Sara's father said hesitantly, "something that requires all our presence." At Justin's nod, he added, "I assume Phillip's funeral arrangements are being carried out?"

"Yes, of course," Justin replied. "But that is not what I--" He stopped, turned to the footman standing just inside the doorway. "My mother. Fetch her, please."

The man bowed, murmured, "Your Grace," and exited the room.

Right, Sara thought absently. *He's the duke now*. Should she have curtsied? But then he hadn't even acknowledged her presence; hadn't so much as glanced in her direction. A little irritating when hours earlier they had been locked in the most scandalous of positions in the middle of a beech forest.

In awkward silence, they waited, the only sound being the abrupt clearing of Sebastian's throat when, after a fleeting moment of his eyes locking with Anna's, she blushed and turned to take a seat on the sofa. Giving up on Justin's acknowledgment--he was presently studying a painting of couples dancing at a ball--Sara sighed and sat beside Anna.

"What do you suppose is going on?" she whispered.

"I have no idea, but"--Anna gave a short nod in Justin's direction--"never have I seen him like this."

The duchess entered the room, dressed in black bombazine from head to toe, her eyes bloodshot, face pale and tear-streaked. The men bowed, murmured their greetings. Sara and Anna stood and bobbed curtsies.

"Your Grace," the duchess murmured as Sara's father took her hand and brushed a kiss to her knuckles. She turned to Justin, eyes brimming. "Your Grace." And then she promptly burst into tears.

"My lady." Sara's father wrapped his arm around the duchess's waist, and ushered her to the sitting area. "'Tis all right," he whispered into her ear. "He is with God now. My lady, please. Please, do not cry."

They sat down together, and the duchess buried her face into the duke's shoulder. "Oh ... oh, Bradley," she sobbed, her entire body shaking. "Why?"

"Shh." He folded an arm around her trembling shoulders. "There, there, Lizzy. Do not cry, I beg you."

Sara blinked. Never had she seen her father comfort another human being this way. It was strange, yet decidedly endearing.

"Right, then," Justin said, garnering everyone's attention. "Since we are all here, I have an announcement to make. Simmons and I have discussed several important factors over the past hour, all of which affect nearly every person in this room."

"Simmons?" asked Sara.

Finally, *finally* Justin looked at her. But his gaze was so even, so impassive, she wished he hadn't done. "The family solicitor," he said, and just like that, his eyes left hers again.

Inconsiderate man. Didn't she deserve more attention than this? Sure, she wasn't the only one in the room, and his mother probably needed more attention than any of them, but shouldn't he have at least said 'hello' or 'how are you' or ... or something?

"It appears as though my marriage contract to Lady Ballivar is hereby null and void."

"What!"

Sara looked around, and suddenly realized it was she who had gasped the outburst. Her hands went clammy. A dull ache accumulated in her belly. It couldn't be. It just ... *no*. It was impossible. How?

"How?" Sara sought out her father's eyes. "How?"

Kilkenny, who still had the duchess cradled beneath his arm, did not answer. His face was grim, drawn as though he'd eaten a bad piece of fruit.

"By all means." Justin moved closer to where they were seated. "Explain to us how this change of events has come about, Your Grace."

Sara gazed from her father to Justin, who still wouldn't look at her, and back again. "Father?"

"Lord Carrington," he said, "has taken over the dukedom before the tenure of your betrothal contract has been met."

"Meaning?" Justin prompted him. His stance was powerful: feet shoulder width apart, arms folded over his chest, head inclined.

Sara couldn't decide if he seemed more upset or relieved, expressionless as he was, peering down at her father.

"Meaning," the duke continued, "that Phillip and I arranged the contract to be null and void in the event that you took over the dukedom at any time before the ten years were met." He shrugged and added, "Your father and I felt that a duke should be able to choose his own bride, regardless of our own feelings on the matter."

"Which were ...?"

"That the two of you would make a good match, naturally," he said, as if shocked Justin would venture to think otherwise.

"Naturally," Justin drawled, and his dark eyes slid to Sara. "Without thought or care to who we would be, or how we would feel once we were of age to actually honor the contract. You simply ... made the choice for us."

Sara was shocked. Beyond shocked, she was mortified. He might as well have said he hated her, for all he'd practically just announced to the room that he didn't think they were a good match.

How could he?

Well. She would not sit idly; allow it to go any further. Rising, Sara smoothed her skirts, tipped her chin, and even though she was dying inside, somehow managed a, "Please excuse me," before brushing past Justin for the door.

"Sara," she heard him whisper, but she couldn't find the will to heed.

She left without another word, without giving anyone an inch to add a retort or comment.

Even when, as she crossed the threshold into the hallway, he called her name, louder, for a second time.

TWENTY-THREE

Seconds passed as Justin stared at the doorway through which Sara had virtually run.

He'd hurt her.

Days ago he'd made an oath to inflict physical pain on anyone who would dare cause her harm, and he'd gone and done the unthinkable. Watched her beautiful face, the color in her eyes, transform from an expanse of lucent shock into a veil of anguish.

All because of him.

His heart clenched, head pounded. Going after her was useless. Especially since he, being a member of the male species, would find some covert way to make matters worse.

"What," Kilkenny said as Justin, relinquishing the notion that he should find Sara and set matters straight, finally turned around, "did you hope to accomplish by saying *that*?"

Justin ground his teeth. He'd been in a foul mood before entering this room, and now he was damn well ready to kill someone. "She needed to know the truth."

"The truth!" Kilkenny snapped. "Since she was but a wee child, she's shaped her life around a marriage to the Marquess of Carrington."

"Ah, but therein lies the crux of the matter, does it not? The contract says nothing about her marrying a duke. As you said, a duke should have the right to marry whomever he deems worthy."

"My daughter is worthy!"

"I never said she wasn't. But the facts are simple, Your Grace. She was to marry a marquess, not a duke."

"Your father made the contract." Kilkenny opened his hands in a defenseless gesture. "We added the clause about your taking over the dukedom any time during the span of the decade after the fact because it seemed like the right thing to do."

"My father's idea, no doubt." Justin thought of all the lectures his father had given on making sound decisions, stepping up, being not only a man but a duke. Bloody brilliant considering now he had the authority to make those ducal decisions, this one was out of his control.

"Actually no," said Kilkenny. "That was my idea."

"Forgive me," Sebastian said before Justin could ask the duke why, if he wanted a good match for his daughter, he would see fit to insert such a stipulation. "But I always thought the marriage contract between my friend here and Lady Ballivar had something to do with the Regent producing an heir ... not producing an heir ... or ...?" He sank into the empty space beside Anna, stretched his legs out in front of him. Laid an arm along the back of the velvet upholstered settee.

Anna straightened, hands clasped firmly in her lap. She exchanged a glance with Sebastian, who regarded her with a gentle smirk and a raised brow. Her cheeks colored, and she quickly looked away.

"Or something to that effect," Sebastian finished, continuing to gaze at Anna, now fidgeting with a piece of lint on the arm of the sofa.

What the deuce was that all about?

Justin shook his head. "How do you know anything about the terms of my betrothal contract?"

"People talk," said Sebastian. "You, of all people, should know that."

"Indeed."

"Originally," Kilkenny said, "when Phillip and I spoke of making the contract, it was to be under the assumption that if the Regent failed to produce an heir within the ten year tenure of the contract, then upon its expiration, it would be honored."

"But ..." Sebastian paused thoughtfully. "That is to say ... and do forgive me, Your Grace, for being so direct. But weren't you and Tethersal a trifle, ah, how shall we put it? Foxed at the time?"

"Sebastian," the duchess quietly chided. It was the first time she had spoken without crying since entering the room. "There is no need for vulgarity."

"He is right, my lady," Kilkenny admitted. "But the war had just ended. Those particular provisions were never meant to be the real merit behind the contract." He smiled ruefully. "No. I discovered that after we were both sober, and he produced the real contract, drawn by his solicitor."

"So, really," Sebastian said, "the contract was a normal writ of betrothal. Yes?"

"Yes." Kilkenny gazed up at Justin through tapered eyes. "But I did not mean for my only daughter to come all this way, to leave the only life she's ever known, only to have her spirit crushed like she was naught but a piece of rubble 'neath a horse's hoof.

"Mark my words, Tethersal." He pointed a thick finger at Justin. "You will understand when you have a daughter of your own. When all you want for her is security and happiness and someone ... *someone* who will be good and faithful to her. A man who will love and respect your daughter as you have. And yet *you*," he emphasized with a jab of his finger, "have treated mine as if she were no more than a chamber maid."

"She has been well cared for," Justin said, peeved by the duke's insinuation that he, Justin, would purposely do anything to hurt Sara. The woman he loved. The woman for whom he'd rather die than allow anyone to cause her pain.

Even though he had, indeed, done just that. Served it up royally, too, causing her to nearly stumble over her words as she fought to control the tears swimming in her eyes.

Oh, yes, he'd noticed the tears.

"And I have only," he fought to continue, "*ever* treated her with respect and dignity. She is a fine young woman, deserving of nothing less. Including a husband who will love and cherish her, and I ..." He stopped himself. He needn't reveal this well of emotion rising inside. The agony of knowing Sara no longer belonged to him.

She would leave England, go back to her home in Ireland.

She would be free to marry whomever she chose.

Surreptitiously, he shifted his gaze to Cavanaugh, who was standing off to the side, eyes averted, hands folded in front of him.

She would marry him. Patrick Cavanaugh. He was the right choice, and really, nothing else made more sense. The man could give her what she wanted. Love, cherishment, security.

Children.

Justin cringed inwardly. The thought of Cavanaugh with his infernal good looks, covering Sara's petite, naked body with his, made Justin's blood boil. Cavanaugh kissing her, touching her, making love to her in a marital bed. Where time after time she became impregnated with child after child after child. Cavanaugh's children.

Daughters. Sons.

Plural.

Because Sara said she wanted several. And Justin had no reason to doubt her. Children flocked to her as if she were the pied piper incarnate, so why wouldn't she have enough sons and daughters to pack an entire town?

"Well," murmured Kilkenny, "what's done is done."

Indeed.

Justin regarded the Duke of Kilkenny with, what he was certain was, a shamed expression. He shouldn't have spoken to her so harshly; he hadn't meant it. Wanting Sara came as naturally as breathing, and contract or no contract, he still wanted her.

However, did she want him? Were a handful of stolen kisses and a few fleeting moments of passion enough to keep her? She'd known Cavanaugh since childhood, had spent a chunk of her life talking with him, dancing with him, getting to know him. How could Justin possibly compete with that?

He couldn't.

It was that simple.

If he didn't get out of this room, with these people, namely Sara's father, then he was liable to start smashing objects against the walls. That ugly vase from Spain, the one with the dancing pigs his mother so prized, would be the first to go.

"Sebastian?"

Sebastian stood, straightened his jacket. "Your Grace?"

"White's." Justin turned to the footman stationed beside the door. "Have my coach brought 'round."

"Very good, Your Grace."

His mother, now the dowager duchess, stood, Kilkenny rising quickly after her. "I hardly think now is the time for you and Sebastian to flit away to your club, Your Grace."

"Don't." Justin put up a hand, turned his head, bit back an oath. A sharp inhale through his nostrils and he attended his mother evenly. "I shall not permit you to address me as *Your Grace*, Mother. I am still your son."

"Yes, you are still my son!" Her hands fisted. In one was a silk kerchief bearing an intricately stitched "T"; his father's. "But you are also a duke, and as such, you should remain with your family. Mourn the loss of your father."

Justin's chest tightened. He hated seeing his mother like this, worn and stressed. He knew he needed to stay, but he just couldn't. Sara was here, probably packing as they spoke, and he couldn't bear to remain knowing in a few days she would be gone.

Out of his life.

Forever.

"I cannot," he said. His mother went rigid with disapproval. "Sebastian, you coming?"

"Of course."

Anna closed her eyes and sighed. Whether from Sebastian vacating her side or the animosity hanging in the air like a breadth of dense fog, Justin couldn't say.

He hoped it was the latter; else he'd have to strangle his best friend.

And really, he didn't much care for drinking alone. If, that is, he was so inclined to drink, which he hadn't been for longer than he could remember. But nothing else would dull the pain as effectively. Not after he'd lost Sara, then gone and made an ass out of himself afterward.

"Have you nothing else to say, then?" Kilkenny said as the dowager drifted to one of the Venetian windows overlooking the east garden.

Through the rain-streaked glass she stared, blindly, her back ramrod straight, chin lifted. As though she could weather the most ferocious storm, if only to maintain what small ounce of dignity she had left.

"No," Justin murmured hoarsely. "Nothing."

Kilkenny shook his head at the same time Cavanaugh shot Justin a glare of raw censure. The gates of hell may've very well opened right there in the depths of the Irishman's green eyes, inflamed as they were. He was well beyond angry; only a fool would've said otherwise.

But Justin, tired of everyone in this damned room, especially the Irishman who stood to be Sara's husband, couldn't stop himself: "Something to say Mr. Cavanaugh?" Because if the bloke did have something to say, now would be the time. That wretched vase of Mother's could easily be smashed against a head instead of a wall.

"Only that you're making a grave mistake," he replied brusquely. "I warned you of her sensitivity, her spirit, and what have you done? Broken it."

"This is out of my control," Justin said, frustration barely held in check, "and this conversation is over." He glanced at Sebastian, who nodded his understanding, and turned for the door.

"You stood here and spoke offensively to her as if she were nothing to you," Cavanaugh said hastily, and Justin, feeling every muscle in his body tense in response, paused at the door.

This was not happening. Cavanaugh, who may as well be shouting his victory from the rooftop for all the ways this entire situation had gone to his benefit, was choosing now to slap Justin on the wrist for speaking to Sara in an unpleasant manner.

Justin swore under his breath. Turned around.

"You hurt her," Cavanaugh continued, clearly struggling to tamp down his anger. "Deliberately. In front of everyone, I might add, and to what purpose? To prove to all of us"--he motioned to the others, who were so quiet they appeared statuesque--"your outright defiance of having been betrothed all these years?"

"I have nothing to prove," Justin said petulantly, because he didn't. He couldn't prove his love to Sara when he'd behaved like a selfish bastard.

"Don't you?" Cavanaugh challenged, and took another step forward.

"We're finished, Cavanaugh." Justin flourished his hand with finality. "You've won, and I do not possess the fortitude to endure any more of this ... this ..." There were no words for what *this* was.

Defeated and irritated beyond all reason, Justin stepped back, fearing if he didn't, he'd have Cavanaugh by the scruff of the neck and strangled before the next clap of thunder.

The Irishman swallowed his retort and steeled his jaw. Apparently he didn't find a great deal of appeal in the idea of a tearoom brawl either. Too much the model of perfection, Justin suspected resentfully. At least Sara would never have to worry about her life being anything less than ideal.

Ideal husband. Ideal life.

He had to get out of here.

"Pardon," he managed to mutter, and then, "I believe my father will be buried the day after tomorrow." He stopped, swallowed, ran a hand through his hair. Blinked a few times, just as he always did when he was fighting for words.

As Sara did when she had something to say.

"Although I am certain you are eager to return to Ireland," he said "I would regard it as a mark of profound favor if all of you would stay for the service."

Anna murmured a soft, scarcely audible, "As would I," and managed to smile when Kilkenny offered a reassuring, fatherly gaze.

His mother, however, did not turn from her inert stance at the window, but Justin could see her throat working. Hopefully she wouldn't start crying again. At this point, he didn't think he could stand to stay and offer her comfort.

"We would be honored," Kilkenny said, though Justin sensed the anger lingering in his tone. What close relationship their families once had would never be the same, if it even existed at all. Justin suspected once the duke and Cavanaugh and Sara left, all ties would be broken.

They would have to be. He couldn't very well have them over for Christmas holidays, while Sara and Cavanaugh's children toddled around the house, reminding him constantly that Sara wasn't his.

"No," he muttered.

"No?" Kilkenny echoed.

Cavanaugh's brows rose in inquiry.

"That is, I thank you for your loyalty to my family," Justin amended. And before the duke could respond--and, more importantly, before Justin lost his well-practiced composure--he quit the room, Sebastian-- his unfailing, devoted friend Sebastian-- close on his heels.

*** *** ***

Two days later the duke was laid to rest. Though the continuous rain would not permit a lengthy service, the rites were reverently performed, and there wasn't a soul present who left the cemetery without knowing just how much the late Duke of Tethersal had meant to the kingdom. Loved by all who knew him, he was. And without pretense of the illness he suffered for over a decade.

Even the servants couldn't walk past his portrait, positioned in the honored spot at the top of the stairs, without bursting into tears.

Sara decided it was all relevant to the entire situation. The duke was dead. Her betrothal contract was non-existent. It still hadn't stopped raining. The dowager's flower beds were in standing water. Ironic considering Sara felt as if she, too, were drowning. What little piece of a heart she had left ached constantly.

She imagined, on some level, it always would.

Because nothing would ever be the same. She would never be the same.

She'd fallen in love, given her heart freely, and to what end? All to have her original preconception of English nobility reiterated a thousand times over when Justin, peering down at her in his god-like, ducal manner, practically admitted he didn't want her.

Even as they gathered at the gravesite, he couldn't look at her without narrowing his eyes. As if the very sight of her was outright painful. And all the while, as they stood huddled in pairs beneath a canopy of black parasols, shoes muddy, backs soaked, Sara repeated Justin's words over and over in her head.

Without thought or care to who we would be, or how we would feel once we were of age ...

God, but she was a fool to have believed he loved her.

Sara sat at her vanity, staring into the oval mirror as she drew the pins, one by one, from the coiffure Lana had arranged that morning before the funeral. After peeling off the black bombazine gown she'd borrowed from Anna, for the entire garment was soaked and sticking to her skin, she'd slipped into a nightgown and sent Lana for some tea, hoping the hot liquid would aid in restoring warmth to her body.

But this chill she couldn't seem to shake; the crawling thought that in two more days, she, her father and Lana would leave Mayfair for good.

She'd never see Justin again.

Sara swallowed and blinked back an errant tear, her eyes hazing. Eventually he would marry. He would have children, heirs. Sons and daughters who looked just like him with a few contributing features from their mother, whomever she stood to be. Someone beautiful, Sara imagined, for Justin could have any woman he wanted. Once word got round of his new bachelor status, an incursion of hopeful mamas would arrive, shoving their young daughters at him at every turn. With that amount of attention, he would be married within a month.

Because every mama's dream was for their daughter to marry a duke. Wealthy, impoverished, handsome, unattractive. Money and looks made no difference. A duke was a duke, and Justin was primed for the taking. A duke--a *man*--for whom a woman would give up every penny to her name if only to have him as her husband.

Sara's only regret was that he was never hers.

As she placed the last of her hair pins on the mahogany table, Sara let out a shuddering sigh. The clock on the wall read seven-thirty; any minute now a maid would appear at the door to summon her for dinner, and just like yesterday and the day before, she would politely refuse. Sharing a meal with the man she loved, who didn't love her, was too much. She could not bear to look at him, knowing he wanted her gone, knowing she'd never forgive herself if she broke down and cried in his presence.

Tears filled her eyes again. She braced herself, clutched the edge of the table, and fought for composure.

"My lady?"

Sara drew a long breath. She had to find strength. Someway, somehow, she had to be strong. "Yes, Lana?"

"The duke wishes to see you."

"Tell my father I have a headache."

"Not ... that duke." Lana came to stand behind Sara, and their gazes met in the mirror. "The other duke."

Sara saw the space between her brows pinch. Her eyes were red, her cheeks splotchy. "I couldn't possibly."

"He insists, my lady." Lana rested her hands on Sara's shoulders, squeezed gently, and, picking up a silver-handled brush from the vanity, began running it through Sara's waist-length tresses. "He seemed ... desperate. He paces the library with all the ruthlessness of a madman."

"A madman?"

"Not that I am familiar with his moods, mind. But he appeared quite put out."

"Doubtless because he wishes for us to leave sooner. His eagerness to be rid of me now our contract is dissolved could not be more apparent. When he looks at me," she added, swallowing convulsively, "it's as if he ..."

"As if he longs for you?" Once more, their eyes caught in the glass. Lana tilted her head to the side, continued smoothing Sara's hair.

"But ... you don't even like him."

"My regard for the duke has nothing to do with how he looks at you, my lady. Besides ..." She wound a lock of hair around two fingers and let it slip free, slowly, until it rested in a soft curl over Sara's shoulder. "He has grown on me. Responsible, he is. Intelligent, a gentleman. And he cares for you. Deeply, I would venture to suggest."

Sara's eyes squeezed shut as the memory of Justin, sliding her sleeve over her shoulder, dropping kisses all over her skin, assailed her.

'I feel deeply for you,' he'd said, as her body burned.

"All your life I have observed from a distance," Lana continued. "Watched as you've caught the eye of man after man, some of whom were not of the genteel breed." A soft roll of laughter chirred in her throat. "I believe the milliner's son has been in love with you since you were naught but a wee lass."

Lana rested the brush on the table, met Sara's gaze in the reflection of the mirror. "But not one of those men, gentleman or no, ever looked on you the way he does," she said, tucking a lock of hair behind Sara's ear. "When his gaze falls upon you, it's as if the entire room vanishes."

"He stared at me during the duke's funeral service as if he loathed the very ground on which I stood."

"Tsk, tsk, sweet one," said Lana. "Those were not eyes of loathing you witnessed on the opposite side of His Grace's grave. Although it is a true wonder you weren't as boggled as I by the sensuous glances tossed from that precarious Lady St. Clair toward Mr. Cavanaugh."

Sara had noticed, but it was of no consequence. Sensuous, provocative gazes or no, Cav would see right through a woman of Lady St. Clair's breeding. He had no tolerance for a woman who did nothing but tease him.

"Cav can take care of himself," she murmured.

"Of that," Lana replied, and began plaiting Sara's hair for bed, "I am certain. But be of sound mind, my lady. The duke's eyes, grim though they were for the loss of his beloved father, did not look upon you with loathing. On the contrary, those were the eyes of a man aggrieved because he believes he has lost the woman he loves."

"Then why hasn't he tried to talk to me before now? He's had every opportunity."

"Every opportunity?" Lana snorted. "Locked yourself in your room for the past two days, you have. And seeing as the duke is a gentleman, he would never breach the threshold of your bedchamber, no matter the reason."

"He did before," Sara pointed out, but Lana ignored her.

"You need to do as he asks." She carefully tied the end of Sara's long braid with a white satin ribbon. "Go talk to him."

Sara closed her eyes, tightly. "But what if all he wants to do is hurt me? Men do that, you know. They say words, harsh words, with the sole intent to wound."

Lana's warm hands folded around her cheeks. She bent down, pressed a kiss to Sara's forehead. "If that is what you think of him, *a thaisce*," she said, lolling Sara's head back against her chest, "then perhaps it is best we return to Dublin. Because although I do not believe his intention is to add to your distress, you are the one who must make the decision."

Three days ago, she had inwardly admitted to loving him. Did she not love him still? But of course she did. Love wasn't a fickle emotion, she knew. It would take a great deal more than his arrogance to remove him from her heart. And if he wanted to speak to her, didn't she at least owe it to him? Didn't she owe it to herself?

Numb, Sara opened her eyes. "All right. I will go and speak with him. But I am hardly dressed to--"

"A dressing gown, my lady," Lana said excitedly.

Sara could not believe her ears. Justin *had* grown on Lana. The man was capable of anything if he could win Lana, determined as she was to despise anyone who would take to Sara romantically. Just like a mother hen, she was.

"Lana." Sara stood, and obediently outstretched her arms as Lana helped her into the light blue robe made to match the ribbons fastening the front of her gown.

"Yes, my lady?"

Clasping Lana's hands between her own, she said, "You have been like a mother to me all these years, and I want you to know how grateful I am. It was you who helped me up after my first fall from a horse. And it was you who taught me to sit properly, to be a lady even as I resisted." She smiled, softened her voice. "Even when my father thought I was a lost cause."

"Your father never thought of you as a lost cause," said Lana. Her lips quivered, tears filled her eyes. "You are his world, always have been. He never remarried because he thought no one was good enough to be a mother to you. And he wouldn't have some young debutante infecting your rearing with less than acceptable behavior."

Small droplets of tears fell from her eyes, rolled down her cheeks. "Throughout everything he has ever done, in every decision he has ever made, he has always, always, thought of you. No father's love could be greater than Brad--" She hesitated. "Than the duke's love for you."

"You love him," Sara said rather than asked.

She knew it was true; had known for some time now. If the way in which Lana described Justin's rapt gaze upon Sara was any indication, then Lana had been in love with the Duke of Kilkenny for years. Because when their gazes tangled, even in the fleeting moment of crossing paths in a hallway, there was no denying the desire charging the air between them.

And it wasn't any wonder. Together they'd raised a child, brought her up to be the lady who would be the Duchess of Tethersal. Should there have ever been any doubt, from working together in such close proximity, with such an intimate task at hand, that the two of them would develop feelings, one for the other?

"Yes," Lana said after seconds had passed. She turned around, ran her hands several times over her muted grey skirts. "Yes, I love him." And then, facing Sara again, her eyes swimming with tears, "Most ardently."

"Oh, Lana." Sara pulled Lana into a tight embrace. "You should tell him so. You should."

"No, *a thaisce*." She thrust Sara at arm's length, grasped her shoulders. "You mustn't worry about me. Or your father. We will find our own way, he and I. Now is about you, making a decision for what you want. And if that is Justin, then he awaits in the library, downstairs."

"I may not possess the strength to speak."

"You'll find courage, sweet girl," Lana said reassuringly. "You always do. Now, go." She ushered Sara to the door. "And mind that you are not seen. Frolicking about the home of a duke in the evening hours whilst dressed in your nightgown is not exactly smiled upon."

"Thank you, Lana." Sara stepped out into the hall, took a quick look around, confirmed no one was there save for a lone footman standing at the base of the stairs (he could be dealt with easily enough), and turned back to Lana. "Clear."

"Go," Lana urged quietly. "Before it is too late."

She hoped it wasn't.

Sara tiptoed through the hallway and down the stairs, stopping only to tell the footman she was headed to the library for a book.

"Be quick about it, my lady," he murmured, perusing her nighttime attire with a sharply raised brow.

Nodding her compliance, Sara continued along the hall into a second hall that, if she remembered correctly, led directly to the library where Justin waited. Where she would risk her heart being broken forever if he should reject her.

Goodness. How terribly frightening this was.

She eased around one corner, looked both ways, and rounded the next. A whispering draft skimmed across the floor, and the candled sconces lining the walls flickered. Chills crawled up her legs. It wasn't far now; just a few more paces.

Taking a deep breath--she could do this, *she could*--Sara lifted her bare foot to take another step, and froze.

Footsteps, boot-clad and swift, drew near.

She gasped, started to bolt for the library, but decided against it. Looking a fright in front of Justin was not an option. She braced herself against the wall under a huge gilt painting of a meadow in spring, and waited, eyes clamped shut.

"Sara?"

Sara's eyes shot open as a male figure stepped out of the shadows.

Oh, no.

It couldn't be.

"Is that you?" Cav stepped forward, closed the distance from his side of the hall to hers. "Good God. What are you doing out of your room, dressed like this?"

"I ... I was going to the library. For a book."

"I see." His eyes, glistening in the candlelight like green glass, swept over her. "I'd advise you not to romp around dressed so--"

"Did you need something, Mr. Cavanaugh?"

"Actually, I do," he said, looking amused. "I need to speak with you."

"But I--"

"No more delays, Sara." His warm fingers closed around her upper arm, and she shivered. "Now."

Reluctance in every step she took, Sara allowed Cav to lead her away, wondering all the while if her almost-fiancé was still pacing like a madman.

*** *** ***

Although he would never aspire to indulge in the volatile behavior becoming a madman, Justin was, indeed, pacing. He had paced and paced, trudged the wide span of the library--back and forth, back and forth--so many times it was a miracle he hadn't made a sizeable trench in the wooden floor.

Where the hell was she?

Had he not made himself clear to Mrs. Brennan? Had he not said it was urgent, imperative, and that his heart might very well crumble into a million pieces if she should refuse to see him? That he might find himself deduced to standing outside her window, begging like some drunken, overzealous, blubbering idiot for her to come down?

All right.

Maybe he hadn't gone that far.

But he had mentioned it was urgent. And though he knew Mrs. Brennan didn't particularly care for him, would likely rather see him staked and on display in Dublin square, even she wouldn't deny him this. This one chance to speak to Sara, to lay his heart on the line, to tell her that, with all of his being, he loved her. And if given the chance, he would spend the rest of his life doing whatever it took to make her happy.

Bloody hell. It was murder waiting like this.

Justin looked to the open door of the library for the hundredth time since he'd watched Mrs. Brennan leave to carry out his request. He looked at the clock. A quarter until eight. Fifteen minutes. It had only been fifteen minutes, and he was ready to tear out of the library, take the stairs three at a time, barrel into Sara's room, and demand she hear him out.

He shoved a hand through his hair, curled his hands into fists at his sides, and continued pacing. He knew he ought to be patient, but *hell*. Patience meant little to nothing right now. In two days she would be gone, and patience would have gotten him nowhere. Within seconds of her feet hitting the Irish soil, Sara would be swept away and married to Cavanaugh.

Justin couldn't allow that to happen without her first knowing the truth.

That she belonged with him, not Cavanaugh.

Deuce take it, where was she?

The clock ticked again. Seven forty-six. Outside the rain strengthened, whereas Justin had momentarily thought they may have been in for clearer skies. Not a chance. Another week of this and England was bound to be the next Atlantis. He couldn't wait another week. He had less than two days.

That did it.

Justin stormed from the library, tore down the hall at an accelerated pace. He'd gone into her bedchamber once without permission; he'd do it again. Propriety be damned, he was finished keeping everything bottled up inside like an iron kettle on a hot stove, waiting to spew its lid.

Lengthening his steps, Justin turned the corner leading into the hall where his mother kept her favorite paintings. Turner, Lawrence, and Constable. They were all there, portraits and landscapes alike, hanging as crown jewels in all their artistic glory. Normally he stopped to admire them, but not tonight. Matters far more pressing than the artwork of romantic artists lay ahead, and he wasn't about to let one more night pass without saying what needed to be said.

What he should have said while they were in Worcester, before everything had gone to hell.

Shaking the thought from his mind, for there was no wisdom in dredging up what was already said and done, Justin pressed on. Up ahead the glow of candlelight, flickering amber across the tile floor, caught his eye. He slowed his steps, tapered his gaze. The servants closed all doors to all rooms in the evening, and though it was early yet, he couldn't remember having seen anyone meandering through the house.

Yet someone was in the music room. Who?

His mother had gone to bed; Anna, too. Kilkenny was in Justin's office, writing correspondence and nursing a stout glass of brandy. Sebastian was undoubtedly doing the same, minus the correspondence. And, big surprise, Sara was upstairs being stubborn.

So who could it possibly be? The door stood ajar, and voices, hushed yet distinct, carried from inside.

Voices. Not one, but two.

Justin ambled forward. This was his house, and he had every right to know who among his guests found it pertinent to carry on secret conversations during the late hours. Gathering composure, he laid a hand to the door. Pushed it further open.

And what he saw, what he beheld in that moment made him wish he hadn't been born with even an ounce of curiosity in his mind. It took all he had not to fall to his knees and weep. Because his heart had surely stopped beating, and his eyes, frozen though they were at present, were certain to emit tears once he found the ability to blink.

Cavanaugh, bent on one knee in front of Sara. Her small hand clutched inside his as if his very life depended on it. As if he was in the middle of--

Lord save him.

Cavanaugh was proposing.

Sara looked up, her gold-flecked brown eyes round, lips parted in shock. Obviously she hadn't expected an interruption. Meaning she had anticipated Cavanaugh's proposal. And apparently, Justin observed broodingly, while dressed in her nightgown. The same angelic garment she'd worn the night he'd visited her room at the inn in Liverpool. Seeing her then had started a fire in his belly which never stood to be quenched. Now was no different.

Because he wanted her as much now, no *more,* than he did then.

But he was too late.

Justin felt his jaw set, his chest constrict. Somewhere in the dark recesses of his mind, he thought he heard her whisper his name, but she appeared blurry through the haze that should have been his eyes.

He had to get out of here.

"Pardon," he managed to mutter and then, as an afterthought, "My mistake."

And then he did the only thing he could do.

He executed a stiff bow and left the room.

Leaving his deteriorated heart behind as the door clicked shut.

TWENTY-FOUR

"Oh, no," Sara muttered, and then, rising to her feet, "What have I done?"

"He could have said something." Cav stood and straightened his black silk jacket. "Instead of standing there, gaping as though one or the both of us had sprouted two heads."

"He thinks you were proposing to me."

"I *was* proposing to you," he reminded her. "You, however, turned me down."

"Cav," she said wearily. "You do not want to marry me."

"No?"

"I would make you terribly unhappy."

"You could," he said, tilting his head and looking down upon her, "let me be the judge of that. You said yourself that had I asked you instead of your father, you would have agreed. And there are many ways in which we can learn to make each other happy, to have an agreeable marriage."

"I don't love you in that way, and you know it. Why put ourselves through a lifetime of simply being comfortable with one another?"

"People do it every day."

"We are not most people, Cav."

He paused contemplatively. Let out a shallow breath. "No. I suppose we are not."

"I know when you marry," she said, and placed a hand on his arm, "you'll wish it to be for love. And that is commendable, Cav, don't you see? Think of all the happiness we shall miss should we marry and attempt to make a life without that kind of love. The kind that burns so deep inside--" she laid her hand upon his chest, directly over his heart "--it is all-consuming."

Cav took her hand in his, brought it to his lips. "You love him, then," he murmured and at her slow, yet sure nod, "Then you should know that he loves you."

"He told you this?"

"He did not have to. A man simply knows these things. Trust me."

Silence ensued as they stood inert, both, perhaps, searching for the right words to say. Sara, looking up to Cav with all the admiration of a sister peering up at her big brother; Cav, studying Sara's hand, as if it was the last time he'd ever see the delicacy of a woman's fingers.

"Cav?" she finally said, breaking the silence.

"Hmm?" he murmured absently, rubbing the pad of his thumb in slow circles over her cuticles.

"I must go to him." His gaze met hers. "I have to tell him. He needs to know how I feel."

Reluctance swam in his intense green eyes. Sara knew he still wasn't convinced, yet she couldn't fault him for it. For years, it had been the two of them, and it only seemed natural that, had she been able to shirk her marriage contract, she would marry Cav.

"You are my dearest friend, Cav, do you realize that?"

"Yes, I do." He pressed a kiss to her knuckles, tapped a fingertip to her nose. "No one else could tolerate your brazenness as I have for all these years unless they were, as you say, a dear friend."

Sara rolled her eyes upward, as if to weigh the suggestion. "Hmm ..." She set a finger to the corner of her mouth. "So this is why I've very few friends."

Cav chuckled at that, and she, with him.

"Where do you think he went to?" he asked after a few moments. "Hopefully not out." He turned his gaze to the window, upon which the rain pelted angrily. "'Tis death out there, for certain."

"I do not know," she replied honestly, feeling nervous all over again. The hurt she'd witnessed brewing in Justin's deep brown eyes was devastating.

"Where would *you* go, Cav?"

"Me?"

"Yes, of course. You are a man."

"Last I checked," he affirmed, smiling crookedly.

Sara cocked her head to the side. "You know what I mean. What would a man do in this situation? Where would he go?"

Cav dragged a slow hand through his hair. "Out. I couldn't stay in this house knowing you were here. Knowing I just witnessed another man proposing to you," he added, gazing down at her, eyebrow arched.

"Out," she repeated. "As in ..." She looked to the rain-streaked window.

"When a man's heart is broken, my dear," he said gently, "neither rain nor sleet nor snow can keep him from breaking free of whatever has caused him pain. I suspect, given his obvious skills in horsemanship, he is heading for the stables." He shrugged and muttered, "That is what I would do."

Sara thought about that for a moment. Releasing a quick, determined breath, she said, "Very well, then. To the stables, it is." She marched for the door.

"Sara, you cannot be serious." Desperation hung in Cav's tone, his steps, as he strode after her. "You cannot possibly think it prudent to go out there, in the pouring rain. You'll be ill. You'll--"

"I do not care!" she said, whirling on him. "Rain, sleet, snow. I cannot let him go like this."

Slowly, slowly, Cav nodded his understanding. "At least allow me to escort you to the door." He proffered his arm, and Sara slipped her hand inside. "That way I can send a servant for my great coat. You should try to preserve something of your dignity, dressed as you are."

"Thank you, Cav." They advanced down the path of hallways leading to the main entrance. "Truly, I hadn't meant to venture out tonight, but--"

"He sent for you."

She looked up at him, even as he kept his gaze straight ahead. "How did you ...?"

"A man knows these things, love. I may have proposed to you ..." He stopped in the foyer and beseeched a footman to fetch his great coat. "But I also knew Carrington, ah, Tethersal, pardon, was desperate to do the same. It was only a matter of time before he summoned you. I am only surprised he had the patience to wait it out while you were hiding out in your room."

"I was not hiding."

Cav took his heavy, woolen cloak from the footman, nodded his thanks, and draped the material around Sara's body. The soothing combination of spice and fresh-cut green grass enveloped her.

"You needn't lie about it." He settled the hood over her head. "Give some credit to the man who watched you, as a lass of fourteen, hide because the cook was serving Brussels sprouts with lamb chops."

Sara made a face at the memory. "It's unnatural for cabbages to be that small."

Cav only chuckled and motioned for a footman to open the door. A rush of wind and rain swept through, stealing Sara's breath. It was dark, cold. Even through the layers of cloth covering her body, the chill in the air cut to the bone. Her heartbeat accelerated.

Justin was out in this.

She had to find him.

"Be careful, Sara." Cav pressed her hand, brought it to his lips, and placed a firm kiss to her knuckles. "If something were to happen to you ..."

"I know." She laid a hand upon his cheek, feeling her own cheeks flush when he turned his head to press a kiss to her palm.

He would have been good to her, Cav would've. But this urgent love she had for Justin was so strong, so powerful, that whatever life she may have tried to make with Cav--and try, she would have; for the sake of her children; for the sake of the value she put on honoring one's husband--would have suffered.

"Go," he urged, applying gentle pressure to the small of her back as he coaxed her across the threshold. "Before the rain worsens. Before I change my mind about standing aside while you do this."

Blinking back the dampness from her eyelashes Sara stepped out onto the stone terrace. A clasp of thunder quaked the surrounding earth. Lightning, reaching as thin, hoary fingers, crackled across the night sky. In the midst of the front lawn, the trees and shrubbery smarted against the continuous pelting of the rain.

Sara drew the hood of Cav's cloak tighter around her face and tread forward, wishing she'd thought to wear shoes. Her feet were freezing. The walk to the stables would be difficult, not to mention she wasn't certain Justin had gone in that direction. But then again, it was as good a start as any. She could saddle a horse easily enough, could ride bareback if she had to, as Father had taught her as a child. Only where she would go once she had a horse, she did not know.

She looked over her shoulder, to the safety of the house where Cav still stood in the open doorway, wondering if she should turn back. If she should let this go and pray Justin returned in time to--

Sara froze. The unmistakable sound of hooves, tearing and sloshing across saturated earth, stole through her thoughts. A whip cracked, and she gasped. The low drumming drew nearer, faster. Sara rushed to the stone rail of the steps and leaned over, peered into the distance.

In seconds the figure of a man on horseback came thundering out of the darkness. Sara's breath caught hard in her throat. Her heart slammed reactively against her ribs. *Justin. Justin.*

Without thought, she leaned further over the railing, the stone digging painfully into her abdomen. "Justin!" she screamed, but he galloped past without one glance in her direction.

Sara barreled down the steps, shivering against the frigid rain as Cav's heavy cloak flew off her shoulders. She would not go back. Even when her teeth began to chatter, and her skin, practically bare to the unyielding elements, prickled with gooseflesh, she refused.

She had to stop him.

"Justin, please!" she shouted, though she was almost positive he could not hear her. The rain was coming in heavy sheets now, soaking her clothes, her hair. "Please! Stop! Stop!"

By some miracle of God, because in all reality it couldn't have been anything but, Justin's mount skidded to a halt.

Sara blinked several times, watched through glazed eyes as Justin's entire upper body went rigid. His shoulders squared; his back stiffened. When his head turned, giving her a blurred view of his sharp features, Sara swore her heart was on the brink of ripping in two.

He had to turn around. He just *had* to.

"Justin." Sara trembled as, stepping from the last stone step, her bare feet sank into the ground. "Please turn around." The words passed as little more than a whisper. "Please look back at me."

The mount spun then, rear hooves pivoting with a grace commanded by only the most skilled of horsemen, and cantered toward her.

Sara remained static, stunned with equal parts fear and relief. Fear for the anger visible in the hooded set of his dark eyes as he brought his mount to an abrupt stop before her. Relief for the knowledge that evidently he wasn't too far gone; that her pleas had not been in vain.

That maybe she wasn't too late.

For a moment he simply stared down at her, his features hard, his dark hair plastered to his head. His cambric shirt, the only article of clothing he wore save for his dark breeches and riding boots, was soaked. He was as vulnerable as a man of his station could be, yet unequivocally terrifying.

Sara wrapped her arms around herself. As if that would protect her from this ominous male who, at present, appeared more a ruthless highwayman than a duke. Shuddering, she tried to step back, but her feet were immobile, frozen.

She looked down. Maybe she could will them to--

A large hand, bronzed by the sun, soaked by the plaguing rain, appeared before her eyes. Sara looked up into Justin's hard features questionably, but he said nothing. Only held out his hand, palm facing up, in blatant invitation.

She could still turn back. Cav would send for dry clothing, have a fire stoked, a pot of tea made. In three days she'd be back in Ireland, her home, the land she loved, where she could spend the remainder of her life in quiet spinsterhood. Comfortable. Unhappy, maybe. But only for a little while. Until she found some way to cut Justin from her heart. From her soul.

Who was she fooling?

Fingers trembling so violently they appeared as foreign objects, Sara slipped her hand inside Justin's, and gasped as his fingers closed, vice-like, around hers. Before she could think to ask how this was going to work (for she assumed he meant to give her aid in settling to the space behind him), Sara felt herself being hauled upward and planted between the horse's neck and Justin's hard body. His arm came around her, protectively.

"Hold steady," he murmured into her ear, and Sara felt an instant rush of warmth consume her shaking limbs.

Wrapping her arms around his waist, she turned into him, pressed her cheek against his chest. There, she clung, not knowing where they were going or if she even wanted to know. Justin hadn't abandoned her. Hope remained, and Sara intended to hold onto it with all she had.

And so she tightened her arms around him, buried her face into the saturated folds of his gleaming white shirt, where underneath his skin laid hot and smooth. He smelled wonderful. She felt his heart, beating rapidly against her own skin. The arresting male power that was his arm, fastened solidly around her waist.

Unable to stop herself, Sara brushed her lips to his chest, and allowed herself a wicked little smile when he inhaled sharply. Another tentative kiss to his chest, another to the hollow beneath his Adam's apple. Deep, rumbling groans stirred in his upper body, vibrated against her lips like the predatory purrs of a jungle cat.

"Don't," she heard him growl. His hand fanned, clamped down onto her hip.

"Don't ... what?" She touched the tip of her tongue to his burning skin, remembering fondly when those very words had been asked of her. By him. When he was the seducer, and she, the dumbfounded innocent.

But that was the old Sara. This ... *wanton* version of herself wanted to touch, kiss, and feel. To experience what she'd only overheard in the hush-hush conversations among married women and the female servants in her father's household.

Daringly she licked the fascinating curvature that was his neck sloping into his collar bone, tasting salt and earth and--

"Confound it, woman!" His hands clasped onto her shoulders, wrenched her from his body.

Sara's lips parted in shock, her hands flying reactively to push against his chest. They'd stopped--she hadn't even noticed a change in the horse's gait. Over Justin's shoulder stood the hallowed structure of a thatched roof cottage with stone walls. If not for the well-trimmed shrubbery surrounding the place, she might have thought it abandoned, ancient as it appeared.

"Where are we?"

"Gamekeeper's cottage." He slid to the ground, his boots sinking into the sopping mud. "Abandoned."

"It does not appear abandoned." She brought a hand to her brow, shading her eyes from the rain.

"I keep up the place. Here." He reached for her, and she complied, taking a firm hold on his shoulders as, hooking an arm beneath her knees, he pulled her down and cradled her against his chest.

"I can walk," she said, even as her arms looped themselves around his neck. She felt inexplicably tiny, swathed in his embrace as if she were no more than a small child.

"Your bare feet say different," he murmured, and trudged toward the cottage. "I cannot believe you ran out in the rain. What were you thinking?"

"I wasn't."

"Clearly. Can you reach the knob?" he asked as they approached the front door. Made of aged wood with a small, iron-latticed window and lion's head knocker, it made Sara think of castles rather than solitary cottages.

"I think so." Leaving one arm curled around his neck, she reached down and turned the cold iron knob until it clicked.

Justin kicked the door open and stepped inside, pausing long enough for Sara to shut the door behind them before he deposited her on a wooden stool.

"I have to tend to the gelding."

Sara gaped up at him, dazed.

"Can you start a fire?"

"I ..."

"Never mind." He turned for the door. "I'll do it when I return. There are blankets in the chest at the foot of the bed." He flicked a wrist toward the small four-poster on the other side of the room. "I'd advise you find one and get yourself warm."

"When will you be back?"

"Shortly." He walked out, slamming the door behind him.

"Shortly," she echoed softly, looking around. At least he wasn't going to leave her here, stranded and freezing. Actually she *could* start a fire. If he'd given her the chance to answer, he might've learned that about her. Then again he was angry, and waiting while she stuttered over straightforward questions was likely too much to ask.

With an exasperated sigh, Sara got up and took a quick assessment of the cottage. It was reasonably large, though it consisted of only the one room with naught but a few meager furnishings. There was the bed, clean and inviting considering the frigid state of her limbs. An old roll-top desk with pen, ink and parchment against one wall; a rustic oak armoire against another; a woven floor covering with archaic foliage and frayed edges in the center; and of course the three-legged stool, next to the fireplace, on which Justin had plopped her mere moments ago.

Perhaps she'd better start with the fireplace.

Locating a neat pile of dry wood resting beside the hearth, Sara heaved a couple of the smaller logs into her arms and threw them into the grate. Thankfully the gamekeeper--or former gamekeeper, as it were--saw fit to leave behind his matches and a few tallow candles. Sara grabbed one of each and set to work igniting a flame.

She forced herself not to turn around when the door creaked open and shut, this time with a bit more ease.

"You started a fire."

Sara wanted to laugh. "You sound surprised."

"A little." The echo of his slow stroll as he moved toward her was both chilling and exciting, and Sara felt a tiny shiver of joy race up her spine at the thought of having impressed him. "Where did you learn to do that?" he asked, sinking to his knees beside her.

"My father taught me." She stoked the fire carefully, watching with satisfaction as, little by little, the flames grew into vibrant peaks of orange and yellow.

"It appears as though your father taught you a great deal uncharacteristic in the upbringing of a young lady."

It was the most he had said since yanking her up into the saddle with him.

"I suppose you could say that. We Irish weren't built to be all frills and lace, you know. Our intelligence means too much to degrade ourselves by not using it."

"I would think no less of you." The warm glow of the fire bathed his handsome features in shades of amber and orange, adding to his dark eyes a fervor she could not explain. He smiled at her, only the faintest curve of his lips, but it put a stutter in her reply all the same.

"I-I ... that is ..." She tore her gaze from his and focused on her hands, folded neatly in her lap. Making sense of anything was impossible when he looked at her that way. "Thank you."

He said nothing, but rose to settle onto the hearth, where he began tugging off his muddy boots, followed by his woolen stockings.

Sara sat in silence, and stared from the corner of her eye. His breeches were soaked, dirty, ripped in one place directly above his knee. His shirt was ruined. Not that it mattered. He could buy a hundred more to replace it.

But what fascinated her more than the disheveled state of his clothing was the length of skin from his knee to the very tips of his toes. Bronzed and covered in soft dark hair, his calves were lean yet muscular. His feet were smooth and chiseled and so much larger than her own. On each of his toes, the nails of which were clean and well-groomed, was the lightest dusting of hair. It suddenly occurred to Sara that she'd never seen the toes of a man, had never even thought to wonder about such things. But there it was.

"You should get out of those clothes."

The bold statement shook her from reverie.

"You're trembling," he pointed out, just as he was stripping off his shirt. "That wet gown needs to come off, if you are to warm yourself properly."

Now she was *really* trembling. Slack-jawed and all. And not because of his suggestion; she knew the cold, wet gown clinging to her body was liable to give her a chill, resulting in what would most likely be a cough and sniffles. Or worse.

No, the swarthy mass of muscle and sinew, gleaming raw as sin itself in the firelight, had arrested her full attention.

Sweet merciful heavens. Who knew through all those layers of clothing, that *that* lay beneath?

He began unbuttoning his breeches, and Sara shot up, stumbled back a couple of steps before, anchoring herself on the stool, she finally found her feet.

"What are you doing?"

One dark eyebrow winged upward. "Only what you should be doing." Leaving his breeches unfastened, he strode for the oak chest at the foot of the bed and retrieved two quilted blankets. He threw one to her, and it fell in a soft heap at her feet.

Sara gazed at it for a moment, debating. Should she? Shouldn't she? Was it proper? Did properness really matter at this point?

"I'm turned around," he called over his shoulder, and she looked up, smothering the moan rising in her throat at the sight of his uncovered torso.

Swallowing her pride, and whatever else it was making her this nervous about being naked in a room with him, Sara untied her robe and nightgown, working as fast as possible with her shaking hands. Heaven only knew when he would turn around, and she couldn't possibly face him bare and vulnerable. It was humiliating enough having to divest her clothing while he stood, albeit with his back turned, on the other side of the room.

Sara peeled off what was left of her soaked clothing, and let it drop to her feet. Stepping out of the wet pile, she picked up the blanket, and wrapped herself up, tight as she could without cutting off her circulation.

"All right," she said, and he turned around, not sparing a glance in her direction as he sauntered back for the warmth of the fire.

Slowly she padded to the space beside him, and together they stood in silence, side by side, with only the sound of their breaths and the crackling of the fire to abet the quiet.

"Cavanaugh asked you to marry him."

It took Sara a moment to answer. "Yes. Yes, he did."

"I suspected as much. It was the only natural thing to do, enamored as he is of you."

"But Justin, I--"

"And of course he is the right choice. He will be a good husband. A good father."

"Yes, I know. But--"

"And you'll be able to live in Ireland." His profile was as stone, Sara noticed, gazing up at him. Cut and hard, with a tiny muscle in his cheek pulsing sporadically. "Where you long to be."

She hesitated. "Yes, that is true. But you do not understand. I--"

"Yes, I do understand." His eyes flashed down at her, and Sara felt the agony behind them. He wasn't saying this for her; he was saying it for himself. Announcing it, perhaps, as if by speaking it aloud, so it would be.

"No," she said. "No, you don't."

"How could I not? What is there *not* to understand? You are marrying Cavanaugh. It could not be any plainer."

"Justin, I--"

"You don't have to explain." He turned to stare at the fire. "There is no need to explain when--"

"You don't understand."

"--Cavanaugh's who you would have chosen from the start--"

"Justin, please listen. I--"

"--and who am I to stand between the two of you now that you--"

"Justin, stop." Lord, but her patience was wearing thin.

"--can be together as you wanted to before--"

"I said no!" she shrieked. His gaze shot down at her, his heavy brown eyes laden with disbelief. Bristled, she added, "And you whittle my patience by interrupting me over and over as if you hadn't a care in the world for what I may have to say in response to these accusations!"

"Accusations?" he echoed, once the initial shock had worn off.

"Yes! Accusations! Cav did ask me to marry him, but I refused."

"Why?"

She stared up at him impatiently. "Don't you know?" Shaking her head, fighting back tears, she whispered, "Haven't you known for some time now?"

Later, when she thought about standing in the old cottage, gazing up at Justin with all her emotions splayed there before him like an open wound, Sara wondered how she had mustered the courage to do it. Although she was quite brave when she wanted to be, could hold her own against a man who fancied himself witty, confessing her feelings was one of the hardest things she'd ever had to do.

Sinking into the wooden floor might've been easier. Not to mention Justin had become eerily silent, and that made her wish she'd never said anything at all. That she'd kept her heart-wrenching secret to the grave.

But when his arms came around her, and her body was brought against his, Sara knew.

He loved her. The words may never leave his mouth, but it mattered not. She would say it enough for both of them.

She pressed her cheek to his chest, relishing in the warmth of his skin as he held her close.

Justin. She belonged to him. This beautiful, warm, intelligent man who might've been her enemy had they met under different circumstances. He owned every bit of her. Heart, body and soul. And oh, how every one of those fragile pieces longed for him.

Even as close as they were now, with only a fragment of soft fabric between them, it wasn't enough.

She needed him. Wanted him.

"Justin," she whispered, and he buried his lips in her hair. His breath, warm and inviting, fanned the tiny curls framing her face, tickled her sensitive skin.

"You don't want Cavanaugh."

The words sounded almost ridiculous now, the point moot. "No," she whispered, and when his fingers touched her chin, tipping her face their gazes met, "I only want you."

Relief. Liberation. Amazing how words, so few, so minute, could change his expression from uncertainty to ... *freedom*. He pressed his lips to her forehead, and Sara flattened her palms to his chest, waiting.

"Good." His lips brushed her temple, her cheek, burning every inch of skin lazily traveled, and when his mouth paused over hers, Sara felt every nerve in her body ignite.

His lips touched hers in the softest caress. "Good."

And before Sara could ask if that's all he had to say, if her rejection to Cav's proposal was merely plain, ordinary *good*, his arms tightened around her and with a fierce growl, he said, "Because he cannot have you."

The whimper had barely left Sara's throat before her mouth was covered with his. Desire swept through her, claimed every inch of her body. This is what love felt like, to love and be loved. How could she have even entertained the thought of marrying someone else? She needed this man. As sure as life itself, she needed him. Reaching up, she splayed her hands over the back of his neck, and brought him closer.

Their tongues met, tangled. Justin whispered her name over and over, his breath hot against her cheeks. In the inner depths of her mind, Sara wondered if it would always be this way. If kissing him, feeling his hands spread like irons at the small of her back, would always cause her legs to grow *this* weak, her insides to burn *this* hot.

It felt like nothing and everything, all at once.

"Sara." His lips drifted from her mouth to her cheek to her ear. He nipped gently at the lobe. "I need you."

"Oh." Her breath caught in her throat as his mouth meandered down the line of her neck. Gooseflesh covered her delicate skin, soothed only by the gentle strokes of his hands, which had, at some point, stolen underneath her blanket.

"You're so soft." His hand glided down her back, and up her side to cup her breast. "So smooth." His head bent, and Sara gasped as his mouth closed over her hardened nipple.

The sensation sent darts of pleasure to her core, shot warmth down into her belly and in between her thighs. He'd done this before, only a few days ago to be exact, but this time... this time it was different. She was naked, the quilted coverlet having fallen to her feet, and his hands were everywhere, stroking her, caressing her.

"*Mo mhúirnín bán.*" The words scorched her skin as he kissed a trail along the underside of her breast.

"*My fair darling,*" she translated, breath bated, dimly wondering when he'd learned Gaelic.

"Mmm." His hands curved over her bottom. In a gentle motion, he brought her body flush against his. The hard jut of his erection burned hot against her belly.

Sara swallowed anxiously as he dipped his head and brushed another kiss to her lips. "*Ba bhreá liom suirí a dhéanamh leat, Sara,*" he murmured, and oh, his voice sounded so alluring, so deliciously male Sara's body arched into him of its own accord.

"I want ..." Her pulse throbbed madly beneath the weight of his mouth. "I want to ..." Fingers digging into his upper arms, she struggled to maintain equilibrium. His hands were kneading her bottom, rocking her rhythmically, deliberately against his hardness. And it felt wonderful. Sweet. Erotic.

She didn't think she could bear this much longer, this yearning to be taken by him. To be loved in the most intimate way imaginable. Wildly she scrambled to grip his shoulders, praying he would do something ... *anything* to end her torment.

"I want," he repeated, breathlessly as she had. "Tell me, Sara. Tell me what you want."

She couldn't. She just couldn't. Even in her wanton condition, it was too scandalous.

"Shall I say it?" He sucked the tender skin beneath the slant of her jaw, ran his tongue in hot path to her ear. "I want to make love to you, Sara."

Before she could protest or concede or whatever it was she should've said in response to his lascivious admission, he swept her into his arms and carried her across the room. She planted kisses on his neck, nibbled playfully beneath his jaw, where the faintest hint of an evening beard roughened the surface. The scent of him, spicy and virile, danced through her nostrils. She wanted him, and as he laid her down on the feather mattress, his eyes meeting hers with the intensity of a prowling lion, she was certain he knew it.

Because his eyes glowed with the same countenance screaming through every vein in her body.

"Justin?" Her cheeks burned; the hairs at the back of her neck prickled. He looked so confident, and yet she was so-- "I don't ..." *Nervous.*

"What is it, sweet?" He stretched his long body beside hers, and Sara swallowed convulsively, her gaze wandering from his chest to his taut stomach to...

"I fear I do not know ..." There was no way this was going to work. He was much larger than she, and-- "That is, I know very little about these matters."

"Did Mrs. Brennan never speak to you about the intimacies between a man and his wife?"

"Of course," she said at once, and his brows lifted. "That is, she told me a little." Her eyes drifted down the striated lines of his body once more. *I seemed to have missed the part about proportions...*

"Ah," he said after a moment. "You are worried we won't suit. Is that it?"

Absently, she nodded. But Justin was laughing, a deep masculine sound that made her belly feel warm and her limbs, tingly.

He reached for her, cradled her against his body. Pressed a tender kiss to her forehead. "Trust me, kitten." His hand roamed over her hip, followed the sleek, creamy path to her thigh. "We'll suit."

And then he was kissing her, his lips firm and demanding, and Sara lost all coherent thought but for the sensuous spell he masterfully wove. The hand he had resting on her thigh grew restless, exploring her knees, her calves, and up again to the gentle lee between her legs. And all the while his lips moved down, down, worshipping her neck, her breasts, her belly and--

"Justin!" She rose to her elbows.

He lifted his head. His eyes, nearly black with passion, met hers. "My lady?"

"What are you doing?" Her stomach, beaded with tiny droplets of sweat, rose and fell with every labored breath.

A languid smile curved his mouth. He bent his head and brushed a kiss to the inside of her thigh. "Making love to you, my lady." His tongue traced a small circle where his lips had been a moment ago.

"But you can't ... you can't do that. Not *there*."

"No?" Another kiss, another sweep of his tongue.

Sara shook her head frantically.

One last brush of his lips, and he conceded. "Another time, then."

She opened her mouth to question the reference, but he was moving up her body, dropping kisses to her belly and through the delicate vale between her breasts. Lolling her head back against the pillows, Sara moaned incoherently, reveling in the warmth of his hands as he massaged her breasts, the erotic sensation of his mouth as he kissed her neck. And when Justin settled his body in the feminine cradle between her thighs, her body arched in submissive response.

She was ready.

She had to be.

He slipped a hand between their bodies, and in the next moment, Sara felt the hard pressure of him at her entrance. Uncertain what to do, she held still.

"I've been told," he murmured close to her ear, "this may be uncomfortable for you the first time."

"I don't care." And she didn't, she realized. This ache had to be satisfied, and if the only way to do it was to bear through a bit of pain, well, she would soldier through.

She wrapped her arms around his neck, arched against him in silent invitation. "Please, Justin," she breathed. "Love me. Please."

A cry, followed by a sobbing moan, peeled from Sara's throat as Justin took her mouth in a hard kiss and thrust forward.

Sara froze, her fingers digging into Justin's shoulders. Pain ensued. Stinging, pinching. Then liquid warmth. Dutifully she braced herself, feeling her body work and stretch to accommodate his persuasive intrusion.

She couldn't help it. Tears pricked her eyes. Even as Justin lay perfectly still, whispering tender words against her lips.

"Ah, God, Sara. I am sorry. So sorry." His lips brushed hers slowly, softly, while the tight place where they were joined clenched and throbbed. "It is only after the first time. I promise it will not hurt like this again."

"It's ... it's not that bad. In fact--" She wriggled a little, adjusted herself beneath him. "Perhaps if you were to move."

He did. A slow withdraw, followed by an easy, painless thrust. Pleasure, hot and consuming, spread through her, raced into all her extremities. His hands slid under her bottom, closed every last inch of space between them, and Sara moaned.

Instinctively she moved with him, rising to meet his slow, thrusting rhythm. The pain had long since subsided, replaced by an aching need that kept building with every calculated push. Surely no one could make it through this and live. Her insides were on fire, stoked by the weight of his body and the sweet brushes of nuzzling kisses to her neck.

And then all at once, her muscles tightened, and he must've sensed it because his rhythm quickened. Waves of pleasure crashed through her body, lapped at her thighs, sent tingles into the oddest places: her toes, her fingertips, her breasts. He pushed forward again, and with a primal groan, his body shuddered and his muscles contracted.

For several seconds they merely lay there, limbs tangled, breaths coming in shallow pants. Sara ran her fingers down his back. Traced tiny circles over the strands of sinewy muscle. She loved the feel of him, adored every curve, every crevice, and when he raised his head, gazing down upon her with passion-dark eyes, she couldn't help but smile.

"*Tá grá agam duit, Sara,*" he murmured, and laid a gentle kiss on her lips.

Heart swelling inside her chest, Sara reached up and brushed a lock of silky hair away from his eyes. "And I love you," she whispered, her added sentiment of *always* dwindling into an unintelligible moan as his mouth took hers yet again.

TWENTY-FIVE

The irony of it, Justin realized some time later, as he was holding his soon-to-be wife in his arms, was he and Sara had wasted so many years of their lives simply not knowing.

But then, how could they have?

She had been in Ireland, and he had been here, living the debauched life of a man with healthy appetites. They would've gotten on well as children, he allowed, as both held affection for sports and horses. But then what? The marriage contract would have eventually imposed a problem when Justin went off to university, where lascivious behavior among gentleman was accepted as standard practice.

So, perhaps the timing really had been right.

Justin raked the back of his knuckles down Sara's arm, over the creamy curve of her hip. She slept soundly, his lovely lady, her long black lashes resting across the crescents of her cheekbones, her delectably swollen pout parted just enough to make his groin stir. A fan of black silken tresses lay draped over his arm where her head rested, and Justin had to tamp down the urge to plunge his hands through it. To toss her head back and devour her neck as he buried himself inside her again and again.

The thought of it almost made him chuckle.

Almost. Sara would be hard-pressed to keep him at bay once they were married. Even now the burgeoning desire to awaken and take her was damn well killing him.

They had made love twice more, the last exertive union leaving their bodies humming and sweaty in the blissful aftermath. Lovemaking had never felt this good, this *complete*. Side by side they'd laid, breath heaving in and out of their chests. Even then, Justin couldn't stop himself from touching her, from running his index finger in soft sweeps up and down her thigh. She was perfect, Sara was. And she was made for him. Of that, he was convinced.

Slowly her labored breaths had steadied. And as sleep overtook her tired body, Justin brought her against his chest and closed his eyes, hoping he, too, could finally rest. Sleep had been impossible for the past couple of days, worried as he was over losing Sara. But surely now, after she'd given up everything to be with him, after she'd confessed her love and he had nothing more to worry over ...

But no, he couldn't bring himself to do it; she was too beautiful in slumber to miss a single moment. Sleep, for him at least, would have to wait.

And so as he lay quietly, listening to the soothing rain, the periodic crackle of the fire dying in the grate, and the steady waft of Sara's breathing, Justin reflected on his last thought before he'd concluded sleep was no good.

Sara had said she loved him.

Of course, he'd said it first, and the Lord knew he'd have to remind her of *that* from time to time.

He could picture them in an argument. After a few years, naturally, as he was sure she'd have no complaints until at least their fifth anniversary. Maybe later. But eventually she would find something to complain about, she being Irish and he being the arse he knew he could be.

"You're late again," she would snap, her lip curling in that way she had. The one that made him want to kiss her senseless.

"I'm afraid Parliament does not regard time the way you do, sweet," he would respond, lifting a brow for a good measure. "And mine is in high demand at present." Because it would be, and he could only hope she would understand once the summons were sent for him to take his seat.

But of course, this was Sara. Defiant, Irish, Sara. She would fight him nail and teeth just because she could. Hell, she'd probably march her petite self into chambers and demand her husband be *released this instant*.

After she'd spouted a few Gaelic curses, naturally.

"I'm needed in London, Sara." He'd step closer to her, narrow the distance between them. "You know this."

"I care not what *they* need," she'd say, those beautiful brown eyes ablaze. "*I* need you here."

"Is that so?"

"Yes!" Her hands would go to her hips. "That is so!"

"And what, pray, do you plan to do about it?" He'd reach out then, skim his knuckles down the side of her breast, just because *he* could.

And of course she'd smack his hand because they were arguing, and how dare he touch her when she was trying to make a point. And by then he'd have lost the point because he was an idiot who couldn't keep his hands to himself. At least not where Sara was concerned.

"What am *I* going to do about it?" she'd demand. "*I* run this entire household, Your Grace! While you ... *you* toddle off to London every day! I think the real question is what are *you* going to do about it?" The challenge in her eyes would be too irresistible not to touch her.

And so he would. "This," he'd growl, snatching her into his arms and crushing her mouth beneath his. Somewhere in the midst of all the mind-blowing passion, which would be smack-dab in the middle of the foyer, he would remind her, "Don't ever forget, Sara. I said *I love you* first."

Then he'd carry her upstairs and make love to her until she screamed his name. Until she was gripping the sheets for purchase, her head flailing about his pillows, breasts pert and rosy from his kisses.

Justin swallowed. Oh, yes. That would be--

"Mmm."

Exactly.

"Good morning." She squirmed in his arms, stretched her slender legs and, drawing up again, wedged one of her smooth calves between his. Then she made the little *mmm* sound again, sighed it, her warm breath teasing the underside of his bicep.

She was right. Even in his ridiculous fantasy, she was right. He'd never make it to London. Hell, he'd be lucky if he ever made it past the threshold of their bedchamber.

"Justin." She tucked her face beneath his chin, nipped at his throat.

He tightened his arms around her. Did she have any idea how mad she drove him? Since the moment they'd met at the docks in Liverpool no less. Even then he'd wanted to climb in after her, into the carriage where she'd practically forbidden him to look, God forbid touch.

And oh, how he'd wanted to.

Now here she was, wrapped in his arms, snuggled up against him. And he was hard as a rock, ready to take her. Ah God, to be inside her. It was, quite easily, his new favorite place to be.

"You've been awake," she softly accused. She touched her tongue to the pulse pounding in his throat. Her hand began a slow meander over his pectoral muscles, the skim of her fingers so light he couldn't stop himself from groaning in response. She had the touch of an angel.

"For a while, yes," he admitted, running his fingers down the small of her back, over the swell of her bottom, and back up again. "I couldn't sleep."

"Bad dreams?" Her hand moved further down to graze over his abdomen, and Justin felt the muscles there tighten reactively. She caught the cleft of his unshaven chin between her lips and sucked, even as her hand prowled onward. Down, down.

"I hope not." Her fingertips trickled through the tuft of curls at the base of his stomach.

Justin managed a strangled, "No," before her fingers wrapped themselves around his length and he lost all ability of coherent speech.

She laughed; a warm, husky sound that made his veins dilate and the blood inside unbearably hot. "I think," she murmured, dragging the tip of her tongue across his lower lip, "I shall have a difficult time keeping up with you, Your Grace."

Justin groaned, and with deft urgency, took possession of her mouth. He wasted no time with courtship. No coaxing, no soft brushes until she opened with a sigh. No. He plunged in, tasted her with the rapaciousness of a wild beast. He wanted her.

Again and again, he wanted her.

Sara responded eagerly, meeting the ravenous plunder of his tongue with her own, and all the while, she kept her hand, too small to wrap around him fully, in a slow, albeit awkward, stroke.

She had no experience, but he was glad of it. Glad he'd be the only man ever to touch her, teach her, watch her unravel in his arms as her body reached climax.

"Sara." He cupped her face in his hands. "I know you must be sore. Yes?"

"I suppose." Her eyes were smoldering, a deep black-brown reminding him of the wood he'd seen from Lebanon. "A little."

"Then we should wait." God only knew how hard it was for him to make such a suggestion. But he'd heard from various gentlemen, most of whom were in Sebastian's coterie of corrupted acquaintances, that the loss of a woman's virginity left her tender for at least a few days afterward.

Hence the reason most men, especially *those* men, preferred women of experience. And though Justin no longer shared that particular sentiment, would gladly confess to any man how pleasing it was to bed a woman for whom one carries a deep affection (virgin or no), he still found it a little difficult to put her feelings before his.

"But what about you?" she asked quietly.

Especially when she was more worried for his comfort than her own, God bless her.

"What about me, love?"

She slid her hand all the way up his length, eliciting from him a grunt of pleasure when her thumb grazed over the tip. "You are … well."

This was too much. Even in her brazenness, her want to touch him as he'd touched her, she radiated innocence.

Justin pressed a kiss to her forehead. "Mornings," he began, attempting to quickly calculate how he should explain. This was as new to him as it was to her. "Mornings are always like this for a man, my dear."

"Oh?" She pulled back, gazed up at him. "I wonder how you are able to arise from bed in such a state."

"Good God, sweetheart. It is not *that* bad." Reaching down, he gently pried away her hand, brought it to his lips. "You do realize marriage is inevitable for you and I, yes?"

"Of course."

"That said, I should also inform you that when my mother finds out, she will immediately burst into action for the planning of a huge affair. Even in her grief, a wedding is too irresistible."

The small space between Sara's dark, softly winged brows knit. "A huge wedding."

"You disapprove?"

She inhaled deeply. "Huge weddings," she said, "take a great deal of planning. There are so many arrangements to be made. Invitations, flowers, dresses, announcement parties."

"And all of that, as we well know, takes a vast amount of time."

"Precisely." The anxiousness in her reply was so evident, so desperate, an instant spark of cheer flashed in his heart.

She didn't want to wait either.

How in the name of God had he gotten so lucky?

Choosing his words carefully, he said, "We could elope."

Her eyes widened. "Your Grace?"

"Have I told you how utterly arousing that sounds coming from these beautiful lips?" He kissed her again, thoroughly this time.

And for a moment, as their tongues were, once more, entangling, and his body was, once more, becoming fully aroused, Sara seemed to forget the suggestion altogether.

But: "Did you mean it?" she said, tearing her lips from his.

"Sara," he said, and settled for a kiss to her cheek. "I want to marry you." He tipped her chin, setting her round-eyed gaze to his. "And if you'll have me, I'll gladly marry you as soon as tomorrow. Tonight, if it pleases you."

"Tonight! How could we possibly be married so soon? The license--"

"Unnecessary. If we elope, that is."

"To Scotland?"

"That would be the plan, yes."

Sara paused, blinked. "How long will it take to get there?"

"Several hours by coach, but then"--he flashed his most charming smile--"my team of horses is infallible. Only a couple of stops in between, if that, and we'll be across the border well before dawn."

A hint of a smile tipped the corner of her mouth. "My father will be furious."

"My mother will call the authorities," he murmured, nuzzling the feminine hollow of her neck.

"Lana will attempt to strangle you," Sara put in with a husky giggle. "Or wag a finger in your face until you become cross-eyed."

"Mmm." He dropped kisses all over her neck, her shoulders. His hand adhered to her breast, and she moaned, pushing herself more fully into his palm. "What on earth," he murmured, circling her nipple with the pad of his thumb, "am I going to do with a finger-wagging maid?"

"What on earth am I going to do with a cross-eyed husband?"

"You'll wish you had married Cavanaugh when I can't even see straight enough to kiss you."

Abruptly Sara's hands came to his face, forcing their gazes to catch. "Never," she vowed. Her eyes appeared to pulse, they were so wide. "I could never want him. Nor anyone else, for that matter. No." She swiped her thumbs across his cheekbones and pressed a hard kiss to his lips.

"No one but you," she whispered. And Justin, certain as he once was that an emotion as strong as love would never find its way into his heart, into his very soul, found himself, in those fleeting seconds, almost overwhelmed to tears.

He kissed her. And he kissed her. Reached to her, through her, with all he had. Everything he felt for her--every emotion, every ounce of passion--poured from his body to hers in that moment. In *that* kiss.

And when he'd taken her again, against what he knew was right for the delicate state of her body, but in submission to her sobs and pleas for completion, Justin realized his heart belonged solely to this woman. With sanguine conviction, he knew. And oh, what a glorious epiphany that was.

"Marry me, Sara," he murmured against her lips, as they laid there, bodies joined, hearts pounding.

"All right, Justin," she whispered, and softer, as he was bending his head to kiss her again: "I shall marry you."

*** *** ***

Within the hour they were dressed and attempting to tread as quietly as possible through the entryway of Mayfair House. Beseeching a footman to locate his valet, and to *do it quietly or consider himself terminated*, Justin led Sara to the bottom of the stairs and proceeded to lay out the plan for their elopement.

"Have Mrs. Brennan pack your carryall--"

"You've already told a footman!" she protested. "Lana will alert the entire household just by her cry of shock when I tell her we mean to elope."

Justin rolled his eyes. "Fine. Ready yourself, then, and meet me downstairs in an hour." His gaze roamed from side to side as he added, "No one will wake for at least another two hours or so."

"My father is an early riser," Sara whispered urgently.

"Half an hour, then," he amended. "A coach will be waiting out front."

Nodding compliantly, Sara stood tiptoe as Justin's head bent over hers. Swift and hard their lips met, molded. Her body swayed into his embrace, and he responded greedily, splaying his hand under the curve of her bottom and bringing her up firmly against him.

Blearily, through the deep, delving kisses and the tell-tale signs of her body's own arousal, Sara's mind registered the need to stop. They had little time.

"Justin." She fisted the collar of his soiled shirt, and he replied with a grating, "I know. I know."

"If we do not stop--"

"I know," he said, even as he took her earlobe between his teeth and worried it gently.

Finally she felt his arms slacken, and with a muffled curse, he pushed her forward, using the hand he had spread across her bottom to urge her up the first two steps.

Knees still weak, Sara reached for the railing to steady her traitorous legs, while behind her, Justin fought to steady his labored breath. Heaven help the both of them once they were enclosed in a coach. The northbound road was too long to sit quietly on opposite sides, while carnal longings stirred between them.

"Walk softly, kitten," he whispered as she crept slowly up the stairs, the white-grey marble cool beneath her feet, "else we'll be waiting months to marry."

Unable to resist, she gathered what little strength she had, tossed a wry grin over her shoulder. "And you'll be waiting months to have me."

Tamping down the urge to laugh at the unmistakable groan of displeasure she received in response to her teasing statement, Sara continued up and around the curvature of the stairs, smiling as Justin's booted footsteps faded into the distance.

The encompassing halls of the upper rooms were dark, quiet; the palladium sconces had long since extinguished. If she hurried, there would be time to stuff a couple of dresses, stockings, shoes, gloves and undergarments into her carryall with a few minutes to spare for a quick bath. The water would be cold, as the maids would have filled the tub hours ago, but she would simply have to make do. Her feet were stinging, her legs sloshed with mud from the ride back to the house, and the tender, intimate place between her thighs was terribly sore. Perhaps a brief soaking, cool though it may be, would help restore some portion of her normal self.

Just as Sara reached for the brass doorknob to her bedchamber, she heard a click, followed by a light shuffling of feet. Instant fear breached her sequential thoughts: carryall, bath, dress, downstairs, coach ... *Justin*.

A gasp pierced through the darkness.

Turning around slowly, for God only knew who it could be slipping from their room for a midnight snack or perhaps a discreet visit to the privy, Sara took a deep breath and held it prayerfully.

And hoped against hope it wasn't her father's eyes she'd encounter there in the shadows. Or worse--

"Lana?" Narrowing her eyes because surely her luck couldn't be *this* bad, Sara whispered, "Is that you?"

Hesitation. Then, a barely audible, "Yes."

"What are you doing?" Sara teetered forward, careful to step only on the pads of her feet.

Lana looked from side to side, eyes round, her springing chestnut curls falling in long tendrils over one bare shoulder.

Sara tapered her gaze, taking in the odd scene with careful scrutiny. Lana, hair down, cheeks flushed, lips parted and bee-stung, dress practically falling off, eyes darting in all directions. Sara looked closer, peered past Lana's pale shoulder (which she was desperately trying to keep covered), and scanned the closed door behind her.

Nothing appeared out of the ordinary.

Except.

Sara shifted her gaze downward, and discovered something quite ordinary. So ordinary in fact that had she not known for sure they were in England, she might've thought they'd never left Ireland.

A silver coffee service with French rocaille detailing, every piece of which reflected the signs of recent use.

Only one person she knew drank coffee in the evening.

"Lana," Sara whispered, staring at the shallow pool of brown liquid in the bowls of the silver spoons. "This is my father's room."

"No."

She peered at Lana curiously. "No?"

"That is ..." Lana closed her eyes, sighed, and in the faintest whisper said, "Yes. Yes it is." She brushed past Sara, her steps light but quick, and headed across the hall for Sara's room.

Bursting into motion, Sara hurried after Lana, nearly tripping over her own feet in the process. She didn't have time for--oh, but she had to know. She just had to. Why was Lana in the duke's bedchamber? Well. She knew *why*, but why did Lana seem so upset? Sara entered her room and carefully eased the door shut.

Lana was sitting before the vanity, face in hands, shoulders trembling. Incoherent mutterings filtered through the spaces between her fingers, where her hands were too small to cover her face. A petite woman, Lana was, though blessed with the curves of one of the pinup models Sara had seen in one of Dublin's smuttier gossip papers. Which in high society wasn't exactly the most fashionable body type. And while she couldn't be described as beautiful, for beauty these days meant thin *everything*, she was amply pretty and in possession of all her teeth.

And apparently she had captured the Duke of Dublin's eye. Maybe even his heart. The thought, even in her presently rushed circumstances, made Sara smile.

"Lana?" She stepped tentatively forward.

Intending to halt Sara's advancement, Lana put up a shaking hand and continued to sob into her other. But Sara wouldn't have it. She grasped Lana's hand in her own and knelt down beside her.

"Lana, listen to me. I am not upset."

"I am s-s-sorry."

"Why?"

"I sh-sh-shouldn't have b-been ..." Hard sobs overtook her.

Sara looked around and found a linen handkerchief lying on the vanity beside a jar of lavender hand cream. "Here." She handed the slip of cloth to Lana. "Dry your eyes. Please, Lana. I am not angry.

Or upset." She shook her head, trying to gather the right words, finding there really were none. "Or whatever it is you believe should have been my reaction to finding you ... well ..."

"Leaving your father's bedchamber?" At Sara's slow nod, Lana said, "I should not have stayed, but ..." She closed her eyes, balled her hands into fists on her lap. "I have no self-control when it comes to him."

Sara placed her hands over Lana's. "Because you love him," she insisted knowingly. Because she *did* know. She knew now what it meant to have no self-control. To have no resolve when wrapped in the arms of the man you love. When his words and his kisses and the very touch of his fingers on your skin cause all sense of propriety, dignity and inhibition to vanish into nothingness.

"Lana, I need you to help me."

Lana's brow pulled. "At this hour? But you just ..." Her eyes widened. "You spoke to him, you--where have you been?"

"There is no time. I need you to pack my carryall and my reticule and"--she glanced down at her thin, ruined night rail--"help me get cleaned up."

"What happened?" Lana took one of the blue satin ribbons tying the front of Sara's gown and studied it. "This was your favorite night rail."

Sara lifted one shoulder insouciantly. "A small sacrifice," she said, rising to her feet. "But I have less than half an hour to bathe, pack and meet Justin downstairs, and if we work together--"

"What!"

Sara pushed a finger to her lips. "For pity's sake!" She undressed quickly, tossed the pile of gown and thin undergarments into a corner, and headed for the bathtub. "I cannot very well elope--ooh!" Shivers crawled all over her body, her skin instantly dappling into gooseflesh, as she eased herself into the cold water. "If you alert the whole of England."

"Elope!" Lana squeaked. "Oh, no! No, no, no! Oh, my lady, why you ..."

Lana's sentence muffled into unintelligible murmurs as Sara allowed her entire head to slump back into the frigid water. Her long hair sloshed around her, and for a moment she wished she could stay there. At least for a few solid minutes. Enough to convince herself that she and Justin weren't losing their minds by curtailing the expectations of their parents in running away together.

Sara let out a slow exhale through her nose, quivering as the bubbles tickled her face and ruffled her eyelashes. Yes, they had made the right choice. She was in love with him. And he, with her.

A real love match, she thought, and came up for air, finally, slicked her hair back, wiped her eyes

Ah, but she loved the sound of that.

TWENTY-SIX

Justin stepped into the hallway beyond his office and checked his pocket watch. "Ten minutes," he muttered, and privately wondered when ten minutes had become equivalent to an eternity.

He'd bathed, shaved, and dressed. Packed a bag befitting an overnight trip, though he didn't know how long they'd be gone. Much time had passed since he'd last visited Scotland. A tour, maybe even a brief holiday, might be in order. There were several medieval castles with amiable lodgings, all of which boasted bedchambers so lavishly adorned one might find little to no reason to venture outside.

Justin could think of several reasons to keep his new wife occupied well enough to forgo leaving the bedroom.

He breathed deeply and ambled forward, forcing licentious thoughts of Sara, naked and beckoning to him from a bed of rich red satin, to the back of his mind. For now. They had to get out of this house first. Unnoticed. Easier said than done when the estate commanded a small army of servants, sworn to silence on the instructions of his valet.

Though refusing to apologize for the impending elopement, he'd written his mother a brief letter of explanation and left it, too, with his valet along with a letter patent to Parliament, establishing his legitimacy. Everything was in order save for making Sara his wife, and that would be remedied soon enough. Stopping just outside the music room, Justin checked his watch again.

Eight and a half minutes.

What on earth was he supposed to do for eight and half minutes?

Turning his gaze to the open door of the music room, Justin returned the watch to his pocket and walked inside. The smell of fresh polish, mingled with hints of lemon and starch, filled the air.

He scanned the room, taking in the gleam of the highly polished grand piano, the majestic sweep of the starched blue curtains, the bundle of fresh flowers, plunked in a glass vase full of lemons, perched happily on a side table, and Sebastian.

Sebastian?

Clear on the other side of the room, at the end of the blue baroque settee the dowager had purchased specifically to compliment her arrangement of stringed instruments, sat his best friend.

Or, rather, *sank* his best friend--his posture left a lot to be desired.

"Sebastian?" Justin walked over to the cluster of matched furniture, which consisted of the settee, two complimenting chairs, and an Italian cello displayed on a wooden stand.

Sebastian's head was turned, resting in the palm of one hand. Held precariously between the fingertips of the other and, Justin noted warily, dangling over the intricately detailed rug that matched the blue baroque sofa that matched the entire corner of this room his mother had shrewdly commissioned, was a full glass of amber liquid.

Swallowing anxiously, Justin moved to take the glass from Sebastian's hand, but Sebastian shifted, and Justin immediately withdrew. Better to catch the glass should it slip rather than wrestle it from a man who appeared three sheets in the wind.

Then again, the glass was full.

Perplexed, Justin settled into one of the chairs opposite Sebastian and leaned forward, forearms on knees. "What is the matter?"

Slowly, Sebastian peeled his palm from his forehead and ran his fingers through his thick hair. "Complicated," he murmured. "When did you get here?"

"Just now. What do you mean, complicated?"

Sebastian massaged his forehead. "You do not want to know."

"Try me."

Again, Sebastian shifted uneasily. "I do not think it--"

"Hand that over, will you?" Justin reached for the glass of liquor, and just in time before it sloshed onto the rug. "Appears as though you've not touched it, anyway." Placing the glass on a side table, Justin licked a droplet of the liquid from his thumb. *Ugh. Brandy.* How anyone managed to down that stuff was a mystery to him.

"Poured it," Sebastian said. "Couldn't drink it."

"I see." Reflexively, Justin consulted his pocket watch. *Six minutes*. "Look, Sebastian. I'm in a bit of a rush, and you are clearly implacable--"

"There's been talk."

"Talk?"

Sebastian nodded, leaned forward, hands clasped. "I am surprised you haven't heard by now, fast as news travels in this town. Then again, you've been reclusive for the past few days."

"With good reason," Justin murmured, and Sebastian nodded obsequiously. "So, then, inform me."

Raking both hands through his hair, Sebastian closed his eyes and blew a heavy sigh. He looked exhausted.

Justin resisted the urge to check his watch again. "Sebastian?"

"I was caught in a questionable position with a young woman."

Justin had to tamp down the laugh rising in his throat.

This was nothing new.

"This is what has you so upset?" Then, realizing how incredulous that sounded: "I mean to say, you've had that particular tattle stirred amongst the gossipmongers before, Sebastian."

"She is a lady." And the way he said it, accompanied by that piercing stare for which Sebastian was so ineffably famous, made Justin's skin crawl.

He couldn't remember ever seeing Sebastian this serious.

"A lady," Justin repeated slowly.

"Yes." Sebastian rested his forearms on his knees, head in his hands. "And I care about her." A brief pause, then, "About her reputation, that is. She'll be ruined if I don't ... if I don't--"

"Marry her?" Justin tried to wrap his brain around Sebastian getting himself into any sort of trouble with a respectable lady. Oftentimes, more than often, Sebastian stayed away from the marriage market misses, preferring experienced women over the innocent.

This lady, whoever she was, must have been a sight to behold if she'd managed to garner Sebastian's attention. And then to coax him into a compromising position, witnessed by tongue-wagging matrons? Sebastian? Never. For all his rakish history, he wasn't *that* thick.

Threading his fingers together, Sebastian gazed unseeingly past Justin's shoulder and gave a short, awkward nod. "It appears so."

"And ... you do not want to marry her?"

Sebastian looked at Justin then, his brow drawing taut. "I would make a terrible husband, Justin, you know this."

"I've always known if the right woman came along, you would step up, do right by her. Honor your marriage vows. Do not act as though it isn't true," Justin added at Sebastian's snort of disbelief. "You would. I know you would."

Sebastian seemed to think about this for a moment. "Yes. Yes, I suppose I would." He shook his head, rubbed his eyes. "I'm in a pickle."

"Have you spoken to her family?"

Sebastian's shoulders stiffened; his jaw set. "I am working on it," he answered after a few seconds of hesitation. "A long time, it's been, since I've had to speak to a lady's family regarding ... well."

"Asking for her hand." Thumbing open his watch, Justin heaved a regretful sigh. There was no way to discuss a matter of this caliber in three minutes. And if he tarried any longer--Justin looked to the door, the distant sound of servants' conversations garnering his attention.

No. He couldn't.

"Sebastian, I--" He felt like an arse. In any other circumstance, he would stay. Try to aid Sebastian any way he could, make suggestions, offer to go with him to speak to the girl's family. Whoever they were. "I cannot stay and discuss this with you right now, Sebastian. Forgive me, but I ... well, I've made a commitment I cannot forgo."

Justin rose to his feet, as did Sebastian. "We shall speak when I return, all right?" He clapped a firm hand on Sebastian's shoulder, and squeezed. "I promise. We'll put our heads together and figure this out."

"I fear it may be too late by then."

Consumed with the need to check his pocket watch once more, Justin missed Sebastian's worried expression as well as the anxious swallow that gripped his throat. "It is never too late, Sebastian."

*** *** ***

Patience, Sara thought as she sat waiting in Justin's black lacquered coach, could sometimes be maddening. She'd made it downstairs in record time, she imagined, for a lady on the way to her own wedding. With five minutes to spare, she had halfway expected Justin to already be out front waiting for her. But he was nowhere in sight, and so Sara reckoned he was wrapping up a few last ducal details before their departure to Scotland.

Handing over her bag and parasol, she'd allowed a footman to help her into the enclosing shell of the coach. Darkness surrounded her, the lanterns having been left unlit. In the distance, the nascent dawn grayed the black sky, granting visibility to the encompassing grounds. Birds flew like small shadows across the haze. The towering oaks revealed themselves one by one, standing as silhouetted portraits against an achromatic sky. A slow smile spread across Sara's face.

This was her home now.

She drew a ragged breath, raised her chin a little. The warmth of fresh tears pressed behind her eyes. Oh, how she'd longed for Ireland since she'd arrived. To some extent, she still did.

But now England lay just as dear to her heart. Hope emanated from this land, from *this* country. Hope entwined with a love she never dreamed possible. It surrounded her like summer, warm and impossibly vibrant; sweet and cheerfully fragrant.

The door opened, and Sara breathed deeply, continuing to stare into the expanse of lawn with her head leaned back and a smile upon her face. Absently, she traced the tip of her finger over the row of jagged seashells encircling her wrist, drawing from memory all the precious children from the orphanage in Worcester.

Her children would play here someday. Here, on this vast expanse of green lawn, with sticks in their hands and frogs in their pockets, while laughter--theirs, hers, Justin's--consumed the air.

"Your thoughts are distant, my love."

Sara rolled her head to the side and favored him a contented smile. "My thoughts are always distant."

"Not too distant, I hope." Justin shut the door and eased his large body onto the empty space beside her. A sensuous waft of sandalwood and clean male skin stirred the air. "Or if so, I do hope I can be there with you."

She reached up, touched her ungloved fingers to his shaven cheek. "You are always with me."

Smiling lopsidedly, he tilted his head and lowered his lips to hers. Sara sighed with pleasure, leaning into him as he urged her lips to part, then tenderly swept his tongue inside.

Thus for the next few minutes this arduous interlude went on. The coach lurched forward, jolting their bodies closer, but Justin didn't stop. His arms came around her, firmly, his mouth crushing hers with feverish urgency.

Sara wrapped her arms around his neck and without forethought, gave into him completely. She kissed him harder. And when his fingers began fumbling with the row of cloth-covered buttons at the back of her dress, she did not protest. Only twined her slim fingers through his hair and surrendered fully to the pleasure he gave.

Pleasure she now realized would never cease.

Yes, it *would* always be this way. And with that intense realization, she began pulling at his cravat, eager to touch his warm skin. To feel him.

"*Justin. Justin,*" she moaned as his lips trailed her throat, his hands tugging her bodice down over her shoulders.

A groan rumbled deep in his throat. "No chemise," he murmured as his hand closed over her bared breast. His breath burned against her neck. "Am I to have no relief?"

Sara smiled wryly. "I think that is a question you shall have to answer for yourself, Your Grace. Are you willing to take me in a carriage?"

His head rose, his eyes flashing in their dark ardor. "*God*, yes." He captured her mouth in a heated kiss.

Before Sara knew it, she was in his lap, her bent knees clamped on either side of his lean waist, straddling him. His dark head sank down, and Sara gasped, cried out, as his mouth closed hotly over the top of her breast.

"Oh, Justin. I love you," she breathed as his mouth moved lower, leaving no inch of skin un-kissed, until, taking her fully into his mouth, she cried out yet again.

"And I love you, Sara."

The words poured like sugar water into her heart.

Desperately she clung to him, one hand gripping his shoulder, the other clasping the back of his neck. While his hands skimmed her thighs, hiking her skirts up to her hips. He cupped her bottom, brought her forward as he slid further off the seat.

Sara moaned, the intimate contact shooting through her body like a jolt of electricity. She urged her hips forward, pressed herself against his hardness, wantonly. It didn't matter anymore. Duchess though she stood to be, she couldn't deny the inflaming desire that was Justin's hands on her skin.

His fingers traced the seam of her drawers then tugged, pulled, until the soft fabric gave with a decisive rip. He raised his head. Gazed at her through dilated eyes as one finger slid through slick folds.

Sara gasped.

"Does it hurt?" His voice was thick, masculine. "I don't want to hurt you. Tell me."

Sara chewed at her lower lip. "A little."

"Here." Lifting her from his lap, he settled her onto the cushioned seat, and went to his knees on the carriage floor. "Sit still."

"What are you doing?"

His lips curled wickedly. "Loving you." He pushed her skirts up to her waist, hooked his hands under her knees, and brought her forward with a hard tug. "Is that not what you want?"

"Yes, but I--"

"Shh." His dark head bent. "No protests, kitten." He kissed her inner thigh. "No telling me 'no.'" Higher his lips roamed, his hands setting along her thighs, parting them. "Or 'don't.'"

At this she felt a drift of hot breath at her center, then the draw of the tip of his tongue, and if there was ever a time she blushed harder, Sara couldn't name it. The intimacy was almost unbearable. Shocking. Yet to deny him seemed completely irrational.

Pointless, really.

Especially since he was now so into it, his tongue flicking and teasing, then delving and stroking, that Sara felt to stop him would be downright criminal. She arched into him, thread her fingers through his hair, wanting more. *Needing* more.

Desperate for breath, she moaned his name.

He groaned, and the sensation permeated through her. Created an inexplicable sensation as infernal as it was heavenly. The interior bubble of the coach appeared to darken, then brighten into a plethora of dazzling colors. She fisted his hair, rising almost completely off the plush, green velvet seat, as waves of euphoric bliss claimed every fiber of her being.

It was almost too much.

Shudder after shudder wracked her body, and when finally the thralls of ecstasy subsided, Sara opened her eyes to see Justin braced over her, his hands resting on either side of the seat. He was smiling, too, his head inclined slightly to the left as if contemplating her reaction.

Sara opened her mouth to speak, decided there were no possible words, and promptly pressed her lips back together.

"You disapprove?" His head lowered, bringing his lips in the barest brush over hers. "Or have I merely managed to render my Irish bride speechless?"

The sheer huskiness in his voice made Sara's blood boiled anew, and she squirmed a little beneath him. "I do not disapprove," she admitted, though her cheeks burned at the confession.

An airless chuckle huffed from his chest. "My innocent darling. We have much to embark upon, you and I."

He kissed her then. Deeply. So deeply, in fact, Sara was still fisting the lapels of his coat when he eased himself onto the seat beside her.

"Come here, sweetheart." Propping one leg up on the seat, he leaned back against the wall and brought her body up hard against his. "There, now. Better?"

"Very much." She pressed her cheek to his chest. Tiny sparks of sensation continued to ripple beneath the surface of her skin.

"Are you tired?"

"Not at all." And she was surprised to discover she really wasn't. Too much anticipation. "You?"

"Mmm. No." His lips brushed the top of her head. "But I'm content."

"Very content," she agreed, and his embrace tightened. "You didn't tell me why you were late."

"Didn't I? I was detained by Sebastian."

"Sebastian?" Sara turned her head, her eyes meeting the square line of his strong chin. "I am surprised he is awake at this hour."

"We are not the only people who had little sleep last night."

"Oh? What happened?"

With a sigh that caused Sara's body to rise up, then down atop his, Justin began to relay the conversation he'd had with Sebastian less than an hour ago in the music room.

"Did he tell you her name?"

"Honestly, I did not give him the time," he murmured, toying absently with a piece of the lace ruching on Sara's sleeve. "I was too eager to meet you, and the servants were already stirring about the house. I could not risk divulging in lengthy conversation. But he did seem quite upset. Even poured himself a drink but couldn't touch it."

"It is early morning," Sara pointed out.

Justin gave a short laugh. "You don't know Sebastian. If he pours himself a drink, he damn well finishes it. No, he was too worked up. Never have I seen him act like this over a woman. If I didn't know better, I'd say he's smitten."

"In love?" she asked hopefully.

"Let's not go too far. It would take quite a woman to ensnare Sebastian into marriage, much less genuine affection."

"Hmm." Sara could say no more.

She knew. If she had to swear by the grave of St. Patrick himself, Sara would gladly march up to County Down and place her hand on the ancient headstone, daring anyone to contradict what she knew was fact.

Sebastian had compromised Anna. Or if not compromised, gotten the both of them into a situation deemed worthy of either asking for her hand or leaving her eternally ruined. Just being seen with Sebastian would likely ruin anyone, lady or no.

The most mind-boggling ignorance of it all was Justin's. And Sara couldn't very well tell him, could she? He'd probably order the coach to turn around so he could wring Sebastian's neck. Then he'd lock Anna in her room until she was too old to remember who had put her there and why.

Gracious, no. She couldn't tell him. He'd find out soon enough, and then they'd all have hell to pay.

"So," he continued, "I told him we would discuss it when I returned."

"I think that is best," Sara agreed. "Although, privately, I do hope he figures this out on his own. Or, at least, with the lady he intends to marry. It is, after all, between them and them alone. No one else's opinion matters."

"Her parents might disagree."

Sara hesitated. "I think in time they may grow accustomed to the idea. Sebastian is a good man, for all he puts on that devil-may-care façade. He has a good heart, and he is honest."

"This coming from the woman who, upon our first meeting, thought us all incorrigible, untamable brutes?"

Raising her head, Sara looked dreamily into his dark eyes and gave him an impish grin. "I've discovered you corrigible, Your Grace. In fact, I find you almost charming."

"Is that right?" His mouth kicked up in a sensuous smile, as she nodded and grazed her lips across his. "Tell me, my lady, do you believe you'll find me tamable?"

At this, Sara couldn't hide the rapturous emotion budding up in her heart.

Nudging her nose playfully against his, she said, "That remains to be seen, Your Grace. But I hope not."

And after he'd kissed her again, so thoroughly the words exited through swollen lips and by bated breath: "I *certainly* hope not."

EPILOGUE

The End of the London Season

"I pray they are not terribly upset with us."

"Everything will be fine, kitten. Just relax."

Coming to an abrupt halt on the last stone step, just before the landing, Sara gripped Justin's arm and peered up at him. "Did you remember all the gifts?"

His lips parted in hesitation. "What gifts?"

One swift intake of breath sent Sara's hand to her mouth and her heart to a rapid pounding. "You forgot the gifts! Those were our peace offerings, Justin! How--"

"Calm down, Sara. Calm down." He was chuckling, the fiendish man.

Sara narrowed her eyes, waiting for his explanation.

When at last his laughter subsided, his beautiful dark eyes shimmering with tears, he said, "I did not forget the gifts." He gestured to the carriage below, where a handful of footmen hurried about with luggage and gift boxes piled in their arms. "They are all accounted for, I assure you."

She swiped a gloved hand across his upper arm. "A devil of a man, you are. Making me worry like that."

His mouth quirked. Devilishly. "Yes, I know, Duchess," he murmured, eyes twinkling so she felt a breadth of sensual heat coil inside her belly. "I'm a devil, and you're a witch, if ever I did see one. But you're my little witch," he silkily added at her gasp of shock. "And I wouldn't have you any other way."

He tilted her chin with two gloved fingers, dipped his head, and set his lips to hers. She curled her hands into his lapels, and the kiss deepened. Time suspended. Right there, on the outer steps of Mayfair House. Footmen rushed past with murmurs of, "Your Grace, Your Grace," and arms stacked clear to their chins with presents for family and friends alike.

Presents Sara hoped would soften the blow of their elopement.

"Bless my soul."

Jolted back into reality, half-heartedly though she wanted to be there at present, Sara pulled her lips from Justin's.

"You've been gone for nearly two months," Lana chided, hands on hips.

Her very well-dressed hips, Sara noted, taking in Lana's muslin gown. Blue and white striped with a low, scalloped neckline and ruffled ruching around the hem. Highly fashionable. *Very* expensive.

"And you haven't yet had enough kissing?"

It took a moment to register that Lana was still talking. Sara fumbled her response.

"What the duchess means to say, Mrs. Brennan," Justin said on a gentlemanly bow, and Lana bobbed a curtsy, "is that kissing, I daresay, has become quite the memorable pastime for the two of us. If you'd like, we could take another couple of months to ourselves. Although I cannot promise the scene shall be any different upon our return."

"You shall not!" The chestnut ringlets, spilling cleverly from Lana's perfect coiffure, jounced with her objection. Tiny pearls glistened from her earlobes.

Sara had never seen the woman looking so ... well, radiant.

"There is too much going on in this house to merit yet another honeymoon. Come." She motioned for them to follow. "Before the dowager tears down more wallpaper."

"My mother is tearing down wallpaper?" Justin tucked Sara's arm inside his elbow and followed Lana. "Why?"

"Nothing matches, she says," Lana said, throwing her hands up in the air as she crossed the threshold. "Too dark, all of it. Too busy. Too this, too that."

Sara lifted the skirts of her buttery-yellow day dress and stepped aside just before her feet got tangled in a pile of gauzy white material, piled in a heap by the door.

"Oh, mind those curtains," Lana threw over her shoulder. "They're to be returned to the draper's."

"Why?" Ah, now she could speak. Brilliant. Sara handed her bonnet and gloves to an awaiting footman.

"Wrong shade of white, the dowager says." Lana waved down a young man carrying a pile of folded lace tablecloths. "Those are for the banquet room, lad. And they had better be ironed, mind. We cannot have wrinkles ridging up under the plates."

Justin and Sara exchanged anxious glances.

"Madam." The young man scurried off, nearly toppling into a large, black-coated figure as he rounded the nearest corner.

Lana breathed a deep sigh and smoothed her hands down her skirts as the Duke of Kilkenny approached.

Sara instinctively moved closer to Justin, her limbs relaxing as she felt his hand press against the small of her back.

"Let me," he murmured, and she nodded.

The duke did not appear too upset, though his hands lay clenched at his sides. He came to a halt beside Lana, who cleared her throat and passed an uneasy glance to Sara.

Sara started, but her husband--ah, but he was an elegant man--stepped forward and swept a graceful bow. "Your Grace," he said, as Sara's father returned the polite gesture. "How fortunate we are to find you here upon our return. I hope you did not find our absence too upsetting."

"Indeed."

Sara gulped, audibly. "We only did what we thought best for--"

Her father raised a hand. "I am not angry about your elopement. Although I daresay giving my daughter away in the midst of my peers would have been a grand gesture on my part, it unfortunately does not signify now the deed is done."

Silence ensued for decades until Lana, closing her hand over the duke's balled fist, spoke into the thickened air. "What your father means to say is that we are overjoyed for the both of you." At his short, yet compliant nod, she added, "And we wish you a life full of happiness as husband and wife."

Justin bowed again. "We thank you for your well-wishes."

"Your absence, however, has put this house in uproar," Sara's father went on to say. "The dowager is on the brink of madness."

Justin frowned. "My father's death--"

"--has nothing to do with it," her father finished, and Justin's expression went from grim to puzzled.

"What do you mean? Has something happened?"

"You could say that," Lana supplied.

Just then, the dowager came rushing down the corridor, her heels clip-clopping furiously across the gleaming marble tile. Face red, lips thinned, she tossed orders over her shoulder to the man marching after her, who from this angle looked to be--

"Cav?" Sara peeked around her father and Lana and the dowager, who was nearing at ferocious speed.

Sure enough, Cav's green gaze met Sara's from over the dowager's slim shoulder. Thrilled he had apparently stayed for the Season, Sara smiled and gave him a small wave, but Cav didn't seem equally enthused.

He held up the pad of paper on which he had evidently been scribbling the dowager's snippy requests, and drew his finger across his throat.

Sara slapped a hand over her mouth, stifling laughter, and Cav grinned. Apparently Lana wasn't the only one who had been sucked into whatever had the dowager up in arms and tearing down wallpaper. And the Lord only knew what else. Sara looked around, searching for anything out of the ordinary.

"Mother. Please, for the love of God, tell me you have not bullied my guests into servant status during my absence." Justin folded his arms over his chest, his stance set wide.

"Language, Tethersal." She came to a stop in a furl of heavy black silk. "Mr. Cavanaugh offered to do this for me. Which is more than I can say for you, trotting off to God-only-knows where while this house--*this* house--" here, she threw her hands up in a grand gesture, nearly smacking Cav, who dodged at the last second "--lives in utter chaos."

One of Justin's dark brows shot up. "A bit of a dramatic term for redecorating."

The dowager sucked in a deep breath. "*Redecorating?*"

Cav's cheeks puffed out with a quiet whistle, and he moved closer, oddly enough, to Sara's father, who had the bridge of his nose pinched between thumb and forefinger.

Lana made an incoherent noise. Something of a gasp, or perhaps, more characteristically, a Gaelic curse.

"We are *not* redecorating!" the dowager gritted, and Sara shoved a hand to her throat. "We are having a wedding!"

"What?" Justin's hands fell to his sides. "A wedding? What the--" He paused, clenched and unclenched his hands, and then, his tone a trifle more calm, said, "I don't understand. The duchess and I eloped to Scotland, Mother. I left you a note. A wedding is not necessary."

With a flit of her hand, the dowager brushed aside his explanation. "Not your wedding. Anna's." She turned to Cav. "Is that everything, Mr. Cavanaugh?"

Sara's hand slid from her neck to her open mouth. It couldn't be ... could it?

Cav was checking his list. "Six gowns, one white, five ... damask ginger." He shook his head, sighed. "With bonnets, gloves and ribbons to match. Oh, and slippers."

"Mmm hmm, yes." The dowager clasped her hands together. "Make certain one pair of those slippers is large enough to fit an elephant. That distant cousin of Phillip's, God bless her, has the feet of an Amazon."

Cav scribbled the additional information.

"Wait a minute, wait a minute," Justin said, his face wrought with confusion. "Anna is getting married?"

The dowager blinked at him as though he'd gone mad. "Did I not just say so? Now, hurry up and get changed. Surely there is something I can find for the two of you to do."

With that, she waltzed off, snapping her fingers to at least five servants, who immediately fell in step behind her.

Moving to Justin's side, Sara gazed up into his perplexed features and laid a gentle hand to his arm. "Justin? Shall we go upstairs? You're tired, and perhaps if we change and have a spot of tea before …"

"My sister is getting married," he said. "My sister is--" In the blink of an eye, his expression altered from confusion to realization. His jaw slackened, eyes widened.

A chill chased down Sara's spine. "Justin?"

"Where is he?" The anger stirring in his eyes was incalculable.

Lana took a cautious step forward. "Your Grace. Perhaps we should first--"

"Where is he!" he demanded, nostrils flaring. "I'll tear this house down, Mrs. Brennan."

Lana gasped.

"With respect to your understandable anger," Sara's father intoned, pushing Lana behind him, "I do not believe killing the groom, at this point, will solve anything."

"He's in the conservatory," Cav supplied, and received a prompt glare of disapproval Lana. "What? He would have found him anyway. It's his house," he added with a flick of his wrist.

Squaring his shoulders, Justin took a few steps forward, turned to their present company, and swept a deceivingly humble bow. "Pardon," he said. "It appears as though I have a meeting with the groom in the conservatory. Do enjoy your afternoon, everyone. Your Grace, Mrs. Brennan, Mr. Cavanaugh."

A wily smile curled his lips as his dark eyes met Sara's. "Duchess."

"My lord," Sara muttered, followed by, "Heaven help us," as her husband disappeared down the corridor, his strapping form swallowing the doorways and frightening the staff as he strode past.

Sending a silent prayer to the man waiting unawares in the conservatory, Sara turned about, clasped her hands together, and with a smile becoming a duchess said, "So, who wants to open their gifts first?"

Made in the USA
Columbia, SC
01 June 2018